THE TROJAN HORSE

THE TROJAN HEARSE

by

J BRIAN HEYWOOD

TSS
MARKETING

British Library Cataloguing in Publication Data
A catalogue record for this book is available from the British Library

ISBN 0-9544615-0-9

Typeset by Amolibros, Milverton, Somerset
This book production has been managed by Amolibros
Printed and bound by T J International Ltd, Padstow, Cornwall, UK

J Brian Heywood has had a long career in commerce and has held chief executive positions in international companies both in the UK and USA. He has had a number of books published on business matters including two in 2001. One of these has already been translated into four of the world's major languages including traditional Chinese. This is his first novel and he believes that to date it is the most important statement he has ever made. The book is based on disturbing incidents that he has seen or obtained information on over a period of almost forty years.

CHAPTER ONE

Ironic cheers greeted the British seaman as he opened the ferry gates and allowed the travellers to begin their journey. With a wry smile, he responded to the collective sarcasm with his party piece.

'Sorry for the delay, folks, but soon you'll be in sight of the White Cliffs and from there it's only a short step to the Promised Land.'

A few of the passengers, British I assumed, laughed at this comment, but the rest remained politely silent. The Belgian port of Ostend on a cold and cloudy day in early December 1954 was neither the place nor the time for this type of banter. As I passed the seaman, our eyes met for a moment or two and my guilty conscience caused me to wonder what his reaction would be if he had been blessed with the ability to read my mind. Had he been gifted in that way, he would have discovered that my colleague Elaine and I were about to enter Britain for the first time to join a group dedicated to destroying the country's economy and changing both its political and cultural identity.

My mind-reading worries were due to the fear of being apprehended during the crossing. This fear was very real because at the time we assumed that our arrest would result in a lifetime behind bars. Interestingly though, many years later it was made clear to me that the most likely result of our being arrested at this moment would have been two days' interrogation, after which we would have been released to begin our assignments. The reason given for this surprising statement was that as we were providing information rather than acting as spies and stealing it, the security forces would not have known what to do with us. A fascinating thought when you consider that our group eventually caused more damage to Britain than it suffered during the two world wars.

Despite my security fears, as soon as the boat cast off I looked for my co-conspirator among the other passengers and eventually saw her standing by a rail staring north in the general direction of England. Even from a distance I could see that her jaw was set and that her face shone with determination. As I turned to look away I noticed that a young man was casting admiring glances in her direction. I had witnessed similar admiration for Elaine during our journey through Europe in the last few days and it worried me because I was never completely sure how deep her feelings for me went. However, as always when this doubt arose I reassured myself that I had a major advantage over any potential competitor for her affections because we were expected to work together very soon now as a husband-and-wife team.

'How are you feeling, Martin?' The voice belonged to Mark Pembridge, the organisation's supervisor in the north of England and consequently the man Elaine and I were to report to during the foreseeable future. His question had a comical edge to it as it was delivered on the move, from the corner of his mouth and into a strong wind. I was beginning to associate Mr Pembridge with silly situations. It was obvious that he had asked the question on the run to avoid anyone thinking we knew each other but that did not explain why he had to ask the question. When he turned and looked back at me I nodded and he moved on. This man was becoming a pain in the neck with his strange concern for our well-being. It was true that Elaine and I had received far more training than anyone else in the organisation and therefore the loss would be substantial if we were apprehended on entering Britain, but I could not understand why he was treating us as if we were children.

We had arrived in Brussels four days ago and had expected to fly directly to London the next day. We had not anticipated any problems going through passport control and customs because we had genuine British documents created in our names in the relevant British offices. My passport indicated that I had been on a two-month business trip around Europe and my luggage was made up of two large suitcases containing dirty washing and various bric-a-brac to justify this illusion.

Nevertheless, Pembridge turned up shortly before we were due to leave for the airport in Brussels stating that he was troubled by what he described as unusually heavy security measures at the British airports. He had chosen to avoid the risk this presented by travelling to meet us by ferry and train. There was seemingly no doubt about Pembridge's identity because the couriers who had escorted us through western Europe knew him and had received confirmation from London of his imminent arrival when we got to Brussels. This communication from London also informed us that Pembridge's travelling companion, a fat scruffy man called Sid Jones, was British and that consequently we should not discuss our origins with him. Elaine and I were both worried by the unexpected appearance of these two men and at the earliest opportunity we sought out the senior courier and I lost no time in raising our concern.

'Are you absolutely sure that Pembridge is completely kosher?'

She smiled back, 'He's certainly genuine, if that's what you mean. I've known him for a long time. He's a Russian patriot and a hero through and through—do you know, he once led a cavalry charge on horseback against German tanks.'

As she walked away, Elaine muttered, 'Now why doesn't that give me confidence in our new boss?'

Alternative travel routes were discussed frequently over our first two days in Belgium. At one point Sid Jones announced that he had made arrangements for us to fly from Ostend to a small airport in Kent, but then some problem with this arrangement came up and we were finally given tickets for the ferry.

I got as close to the front of the boat as I could and then looked back. From this position I could see that Pembridge was keeping me under observation and Jones was taking a similar interest in Elaine. This constant nannying was getting on my nerves but I

3

told myself it could last only until we got through the customs and passport checks at Dover. To pass the time away I concentrated my attention on the view ahead. After a few minutes Pembridge came alongside:

'Fantastic view isn't it?'

'Yes, it is—I was just trying to imagine what it must have been like to lead a Viking raid on England.'

'Oh, well, if you're fit enough to be thinking of raping and pillaging I'll go and get a drink.'

I turned and watched him in amazement as he walked away. From his last comment it seemed that he really had been expecting me to feel ill. I was confused and the thought occurred to me that perhaps he was expecting me to be seasick. Then, slowly but surely, as if preordained, I began to feel very sick.

I was acutely embarrassed, because although I had never travelled for any length of time on the sea before, I had always assumed that seasickness was associated with fear. In the circumstances I held the rail tight and told myself to concentrate until the discomfort went away. By concentrating hard I maintained an outward appearance of normality for some time. However, my problems increased when I discovered that I had great difficulty moving my arms and legs in the direction I wanted them to go. Then I had difficulty in focussing and I heard, or thought I heard, voices relating to another time and another place. As I held on to the rail my grip on reality was declining fast.

Eventually, I must have passed out because the next thing I remember is Pembridge and Jones dragging me along the deck and putting me in a sitting position. At one point I heard Jones say to Pembridge, 'You and your fear of flying.'

I was not able to stand up or concentrate properly until we landed in Dover. But then with Pembridge's help I managed to stagger through passport control and customs.

Pembridge explained my condition to all and sundry with the same words: 'He's always suffered from seasickness but stupidly took the advice of a friend, who recommended two stiff whiskies.'

Throughout this period I was conscious of my surroundings and I could hear snippets of conversation, but most of my brain was dealing with other subjects at other long-ago points in time. The combined effect was extreme tiredness.

✍

I had previously been instructed to avoid contact with Elaine until we were brought together at our destination in Chorley, Lancashire, towards the end of the following day.

Once we had got through customs Pembridge sat me down: 'Your friend Elaine has been slightly seasick but she's well enough to keep to her schedule so Sid's taking her to the railway station. Listen. We may have blown our cover by having to nursemaid you, so we have to get her away from here as quickly as possible. Do you understand what I'm saying? No! For Christ's sake you don't! Let's see if we can walk it off.'

At some point he must have decided that I was not going to be able to walk it off and he left me on a bench on the Dover seafront while he tried to find a room at a local hotel. He eventually found a hotel with a vacancy in the nearby town of Folkestone and returned with this information just after a local policeman had approached me.

'Are all these suitcases yours, sir?'

After this question was repeated several times, I answered truthfully, 'I have two suitcases.'

I was vaguely aware of another voice: 'The other one is mine, officer. My friend and I have just travelled over on the ferry from Belgium. He became very seasick and is taking some time to recover, so I've just booked him into a hotel in Folkestone and have sent for a taxi.'

The policeman left saying, 'I'd get him to a doctor if I was you, he appears to be in another world—and I've never heard of seasickness still affecting people once they're on dry land.'

I vaguely remember travelling by taxi to the hotel but I must have gone to sleep as soon as I lay on the bed. I woke up in what must have been the early hours of the morning to see and hear

Pembridge arguing in a whisper with a large young man. Surprising though this was it did not stop me going back to sleep almost immediately. When I woke up again I found that there were now two large young men in the room and one of them was shaking me. At first I thought that Pembridge had left but then I saw his body on the floor wrapped in carpets. Almost immediately a hand was placed over my mouth to prevent me crying out. Then the two men set about convincing me that we were all on the same side by referring to circumstances that an outsider would not have known about. I was still very woozy and found it hard to concentrate. My first visitor poured water over my face and shook me.

'Listen, for God's sake listen to me. Pembridge called the boss from here several hours ago. The boss couldn't understand why he'd repeatedly disobeyed his orders, and sent me over to find out what was going on. A fight started and Pembridge broke his neck falling. My friend brought these carpets and a van so we can get rid of the body, but we need you to make sure no one's around when we put it in the van.'

They pulled me out of bed and dragged me over to the sink, which they had filled with cold water. After plunging my face in it several times I began to realise that my brain was operating as a single unit again. Further realisation came thick and fast and I blurted out, 'Someone must have drugged me.'

The second man intervened: 'We have no time to discuss that now. It's four o'clock in the morning, and if we delay much longer people will start to arrive for work.'

The van was brought to the front of the hotel and then after I had gone through the routine of checking that the night porter was out of the way and that there were no other prying eyes around, I watched as they bundled the body in the van.

Pembridge's killer then said, 'Look, we can't just dump him anywhere, so it's going to be four hours at the minimum before I can get back to pick you up. In the circumstances I suggest you use the time to think up a good excuse for your antics yesterday.'

I had been thinking about what had happened on the ferry and said, 'I think Pembridge must have drugged me.'

He grinned at me. 'No, that won't do as an excuse. Pembridge needed to bring you over in good shape.'

I went back to my room and lay on the bed but now I was too hungry to sleep. It occurred to me that my visitors could be with British Intelligence, but I pushed the thought to the back of my mind. I had no alternative but to trust them, because they probably represented the only chance I had of ever seeing Elaine again.

As I lay there, I tried to think of anything in my past life that would explain both my sickness and my behaviour on the ferry.

CHAPTER TWO

I'm told that few adults retain more than the briefest memories of the their early lives and that any such early memories are likely to be those that had the most effect on the child at the time they occurred. If that is true then my early life must have been very boring because my earliest memories begin when I was between seven and nine years of age and lived in an orphanage with Elaine and a number of other children. One of these was a boy of about eleven or twelve who took Elaine and me under his wing and protected us from the rats and other children. He bossed us about but he was a basically kind person and we accepted his leadership.

One day some adults came and gave us what was later described as an intelligence test. How they did it I am not sure because none of us could read or write at that time. All three of us were then taken on a long journey to a special school, where we were given our new names. Our young leader was eventually given the name Stephen.

I remember that we were all very happy with our new situation because we were now warm and well fed. We joined a class of nine other children with ages ranging from eight to about eleven or twelve. The only other class in the school contained children in their mid to late teens but we never got to know them.

During the first two years we were taught rudimentary skills including Russian grammar and received an introduction to one foreign language—English. Halfway through the third year we were told just to speak in English and officially from that point on English was the only language we were allowed to converse in during school hours. We were told that we'd been chosen for a special career, working in an English-speaking country. If my memory serves me right, none of us was worried about this development. In fact we were all conceited enough to glory in how special everyone thought we were.

We qualified in the various subjects not by taking examinations but when the teachers and instructors thought we knew the subject in depth. If anyone was slow in a subject it was expected that the others would help him or her to get up to scratch. By and large this worked, but inevitably over twelve years not everyone was able to stand the pace and only five students were still going at the end of the course and only Elaine and I remained from our group in the orphanage. Sadly, Stephen only got as far as the third year. We noticed he'd been feeling irritable for some time and we were not very surprised to hear that he had dropped out of the course to take up something less arduous.

Over the full training period we studied and qualified in English language, mathematics and all the basic sciences. In addition we studied medicine in some depth and we became adept in Anglo-Saxon financial systems, to such an extent that we were encouraged to play games based on the New York and London stock exchanges. However, our rewards came in biscuits rather than dollars or sterling. When we got into our teens we received extensive training in unarmed combat, gunnery, bomb-making and bomb disposal. Later we endured some difficult courses in advanced physics and chemistry. We were trained to run and swim over long distances and finally to drive cars and tanks and fly fighter planes and helicopters.

One way the long working day was made endurable was by the use of films and audio recordings. Typically we had a sixty- to ninety-minute film before the evening meal and a thirty-minute film after it. The longer films came from a great many different countries but we could always understand what was taking place because of the use of subtitles. These films usually had the same theme—some king or despotic ruler was cruel to the people he ruled. At the end of each such film a lecturer would interpret the real meaning of what we had seen. Over time, their conclusions became confined to the statement—power corrupts and absolute power corrupts absolutely.

We were told that greed and the lust for power had existed since time began and that even leaders who originally intended to help their people often finished up by being the most cruel and doing the most harm. So we learned that for the majority, the normal human state had always been slavery. We were told that as the various tribes and countries got larger through conquest, layers of control or management were created by which the smaller chieftains or kings had the right of life and death over their own slaves. But in turn, they then swore an oath of allegiance to the overall king of the country.

Then over the last 150 years or so the Industrial Revolution began. We were shown how the development of industrial science could have benefited all of mankind but instead it was used to create wage slavery in the first countries to industrialise and the subjugation of native peoples all over the world. From film archives, books and lectures we saw how the British and other European countries created colonies all over the world.

The Americans, Japanese and almost every other large nation that was prepared to ignore the moral factors in their pursuit of wealth and glory then joined in. We saw how this insane grabbing of wealth had led to the horror of millions of deaths during World War I.

Halfway through our fourth year we received a series of lectures on our own glorious revolution of 1918, in which the seeds were finally sown by which freedom would ultimately result for all the world's people. We all agreed that government by all the people and free from the greed inspired by capitalism was the only way forward from now on.

To bring an end to our introduction to communism the senior lecturer summed up by saying, 'You have heard over the last few days how the workers of the world have finally established their right to be treated fairly. I agree with your collective opinion that capitalism has no place in the world we are about to create. But be warned, the capitalists will not give up their power without a fight. Your training has been carried out with the single aim of preparing you to be the instruments by which freedom will be introduced across the world and you must be prepared for the capitalists to fight you in any way they can.'

We were then shown a series of films regarding the rise, in both Europe and Japan, of fascism, which was clearly the very opposite of communism. Fascists, we were told, believed that they would prosper only by taking other people's land and murdering the indigenous population. We looked in horror as a number of short films showed the fascists successfully marching through western Europe.

The next day started in the normal way with light exercise followed by breakfast, but we were all then introduced to a new lecturer—a kindly middle-aged woman. She surprised us by saying that the information we had all been given yesterday happened just four years ago. We were all disturbed by this news and began to realise with some trepidation that a great deal of death and destruction had occurred over the four years and we were now about to hear of it. Prior to that moment we had no knowledge that the world was at war.

She paused after giving us this information and then said, 'Yesterday, we left the evil Germans trying to get at the almost equally evil British. The Germans made preparations for a landing but eventually decided not to attempt one because they could not risk trying to get an army across the sea.'

She then closed some of the curtains to dim the room.

✍🏻

For a moment she stood with her back to us and then said, 'Children, I want you to be brave.' I can remember looking at Elaine when this was said and I think we all dreaded what was coming next. Looking very sad, the lecturer continued: 'After lacking the courage to attack the British, the Germans decided to attack a country where the people were interested only in their work and making the world a better place.' She waited for her words to obtain maximum effect and then said, 'Yes—they attacked us, the Soviet people.'

The room was quiet for a moment and then the curtains were drawn completely and a series of newsreel films followed. Some of these films were of Russian manufacture but others were clearly American, British and German in origin. Whatever their origin the message was the same—thousands upon thousands of our people had been brutally killed by the Germans. I felt sick and angry at the sight of the atrocities shown and I could see that all my fellow-students reacted in the same way.

The film show finally stopped and the curtains were opened just enough to let some light in. Our new lecturer then said, 'Will you all now get down off your stools and sit or lie on the floor.' When we had done so she continued: 'Children, as you know, you came here from a number of orphanages. I now have to tell you that you were originally sent to those places because you were found alive near your homes after the Germans moved on—you were victims of the carnage shown in the films you have just seen.'

At this point the lecture was brought to a halt because steady whimpering had been replaced by widespread grief.

It was some time before she was able to continue. Clearly, we were all extremely upset and were all intent on asking questions about our own situation. The lecturer was very upset herself, but agreed to answer our questions. She acknowledged that when we had previously asked about our origins we had all been given the same answer—that our origins were unknown.

Then she said, 'Nothing was kept back from you apart from the German involvement—we simply don't know where you came from. Some orphaned children were found alive close to their dead parents or were identified by the few adults who survived. I am afraid that none of you could be identified in any way and as some of the adult survivors were taken to work in slave camps by the Germans we can not be absolutely sure that your parents are dead.'

Almost as soon as these last words relating to our parents were out of her mouth she appeared to regret saying them.

After a further emotional delay she insisted that the authorities had been right not to tell us the complete story earlier. 'You were all too young to understand what had happened when you arrived here. By the time you were old enough to be told the doctors began to realise that each of your brains had already taken steps to remove most of these horrific memories. How many of you can remember anything about the horror I have been describing?'

Five members of our group could remember some incidents that indicated that they had been involved in all-out war, but the others, including Elaine and me, had no such memories.

The lady looked at each of us in turn. 'I have found my task this day very difficult. In a way your little group has suffered more than anyone else in the conflict, because your past life has been taken away from you. But please accept that your country has tried to compensate for this by providing you with a unique level of care and education—all while it is fighting for its life in the most brutal war of all time.'

Naturally, we all wanted to know how the war was going and she smiled for the first time in the day and said, 'The magnificent Soviet army has smashed the German advance and destroyed much of their army. Hitler, like Napoleon before him, is in retreat. I am sure you'll be able to contribute to the cause of universal socialism in due course, but this war will be over well before you finish your studies.'

About three months later the news reached us that our soldiers were on the outskirts of Berlin and soon after we heard that the war was over. In due course we saw various films depicting the final events of the war. These films included close-ups of the various allied leaders, political and military. We all thought that these foreign leaders looked untrustworthy. Within weeks of the war ending we were becoming aware of the increasing imperialist aims of our capitalist allies, particularly the Americans. These short-term allies were clearly very much against the fact that we were successful in bringing freedom to other countries in eastern Europe and elsewhere. It rapidly became apparent that our training had not been in vain because the leaders of capitalism were intent on curtailing the Soviet Union's legitimate aims wherever they could.

Elaine and I had always been close friends and this developed as we got older. Our other school friends and the lecturers laughed and joked at our expense when we started to hold hands. However, when a lecturer caught us hugging and kissing we were hauled in front of the administrative head of the school.

Much to our embarrassment, this lady started her lecture by saying, 'If you continue this practice, Elaine will soon be pregnant and the cause of world freedom will suffer a major setback because she will not be able to pursue the career she has been trained for.'

Inevitably, we were forced to promise that all forms of physical contact between us would cease for the foreseeable future.

However, my spirits were lifted considerably by her final comments: 'It's just a question of waiting really, because it's virtually certain you'll be sent to the same destination as a twosome, and that should result in your being married at some appropriate time.'

As we left the office I said, 'That wasn't too bad, was it, and it's good that people like her assume we'll work as a twosome.?'

Elaine glared at me: 'Let me assure you there was no chance of my becoming pregnant. I bloody well resent that bitch's comments and the way you meekly accepted them.'

At the start of our final two years we received the first of two visits from a man who was to dictate the course of our lives from that point on. Several days before his first visit we had been warned that this man was very important and would expect our total attention at all times. There were six of us still on the course at this time and I remember we were all marched over to a large building we had not been in before.

Then an assistant in a strange uniform came over to us and said, 'Please stand to attention, three abreast, while I check to see if the general is ready to see you.' She knocked on the door and a deep voice said, 'Send the bastards in.'

14

When we came to a halt in front of the general's desk we saw an amazing sight. On the wall behind the desk were the American flag and a number of recognisable American icons. On the desk was a nameplate reading—General Dwight D Eisenhower. Most surprising of all General Eisenhower was sitting behind the desk smoking a huge cigar.

The reaction of our group members varied enormously. Some appeared shocked and some laughed nervously. There was silence for about twenty seconds and then Eisenhower said:

'Well, I think you probably all failed that test but we won't know to what extent until the film is processed.'

He then got up from the desk, took off his American military tunic, turned the nameplate over and proceeded to shake hands with all of us. We could then see that he did not look anything like Eisenhower—the build-up and surroundings had to varying degrees fooled us.

After putting on another jacket he said, 'My name is Winston.'

As this was the Christian name of the British leader Winston Churchill we anticipated further trickery and our general reaction made this clear to him.

He smiled again: 'Friends, Winston is my name, and it's the only name you'll ever know me by.'

This first meeting turned out to be a getting-to-know-each-other session. He surprised us by knowing each of our names and how we had been rated on each subject matter. He spent the rest of the morning stressing how important the next few years would be if the Soviet system were ever to become universally adopted.

He completed his review of world affairs by saying, 'The entire capitalist world now sees the Soviet Union as a major enemy and one that they have to destroy.'

He then asked all six of us to join him for lunch. Since starting on the course we had always eaten well but this lunch was luxury beyond our wildest dreams. It was obvious that he was both trying to impress us and was also making a statement about our importance to the future freedom of the world's working people.

15

He left the school in mid-afternoon but before leaving he gave us the results from the film he had referred to. 'None of you was adequately in control of your emotions on meeting General Eisenhower. Your body language will need to be under complete control once you begin your assignments.'

Of more importance to me, he told us that Elaine and I would start our first assignment as a twosome. This time Elaine seemed quite pleased to hear this news. Two other teams were to be formed; another male-female partnership and a team of two men.

After Winston left, one of the lecturers told us it would be twelve months, that is, the start of our final year, before he returned. We began our penultimate year with gusto because it was the year when we first got to play with the big military hardware. Sadly three months into the year our colleague Elizabeth was killed, through no fault of her own, while learning to fly helicopters. Months later Elaine and I were still worrying that we might be split up as a result of this. Eventually, however, the other three men, David, Peter and Paul, were grouped into one team. Then the lecturers decided to impart some added competition into the proceedings by saying that the top performing team would probably go to the top target country and the second to a lesser target country. As we took it for granted that America was the top target and America was where we all wanted to go, a real competitive spirit developed in all of us.

Over the last few years of the course, the end-of-year break was extended from three to four weeks. We were taken to different places in Russia as a group with one or more of the lecturers always present. Away from the school we were relaxed and the places we saw were interesting and exciting. They included nuclear power stations and massive underground arsenals. However, I much preferred the week we spent doing nothing at a Black Sea resort. Elaine suggested that this proved that I was basically lazy.

When we returned to school from the holiday we were surprised to find that Winston was already on the premises. We knew that our final year would concentrate on the country we would be sent to and that Winston would very likely inform us of our fate as soon as we saw him. Consequently, all five of us were in a high state of tension as we waited outside Winston's office. Suddenly, the door opened and the great man came out beaming and full of congratulations on our results over the year.

Then his mood changed. 'I can't tell you how sorry I was to hear of Elizabeth's death but you should know that I don't hold any of you responsible for it.'

As none of us was present when Elizabeth was killed we did not anticipate any share of the blame but we were all intent on displaying the correct body language and so no one made a comment.

Winston then led us into his office and the first thing we saw was a large map of the British Isles on the wall. He looked at each of us in turn and then said, 'Congratulations, Martin and Elaine will join our team in the north of England and the other three will be based in Northern Ireland.'

We were clearly all still trying to send out the right body language and so tried to control our disappointment, but eventually Paul smiled and said, 'I look forward to my time in Ireland but I presume teams from another school got the USA.'

Winston again looked at each of us in turn and then burst out laughing. He pressed a buzzer and trays of alcoholic drinks were pushed into the room.

He invited us to imbibe but added, 'Be careful with the alcohol though because the next hour or so is likely to be the most important time of the entire course.'

Over the next few hours Winston talked at length with obvious enthusiasm and passion. After he finished we were all totally convinced that we were going to the right place and we were about to embark on the most exciting and rewarding period of our lives.

He started by asking us to turn our chairs round and look at the map of the world on the back wall. The map was of British manufacture and had the so-called British Empire and possessions marked in red. However, his first comments covered the world in general.

'My friends, wherever you look on this map there are people who are conveniently described as spies because their real job is very different from what is written on their calling cards. These people owe allegiance to a different country from the one they live in and as a consequence they strive to find information that will be beneficial to their friends. Our spies risk their lives to find information that enables us to pursue the struggle to free the world's workers. In cities and towns all over America, Britain, France and the rest of the capitalist world we have people involved in espionage—people who are looking for secret information. In turn we know that most of these countries have their own spies in various parts of the Soviet Union.'

Warming to his task, Winston followed up by saying, 'Now you are in a very different business. Our entire organisation and your long training period is dedicated to making people unhappy with their capitalist society and as a result take steps to embrace communism. Therefore, it is not in any way accurate to describe us as spies.'

He then walked over to the map and stuck his finger in the middle of the USA.

'Do you really want to try to convince these people that their country is on the wrong track? Before you answer, I freely accept that many Americans were out of work and living on charity between the wars. But the last war was of enormous benefit to the USA. The country is blessed with an abundance of almost all the natural resources that are used in the modern world and they were able to use them to the full from 1942 onwards while their own country was safe from danger and therefore the cost of war damage. Remember that ideally they and all true capitalists want to fight economic not military wars. Before 1942 their strength in natural resources, particularly the space to accommodate an ever-increasing population, ensured that they would eventually become the capitalist giant of the world, but the war meant that they achieved that pre-eminent position that much quicker. During the war they cleverly managed to sell their desperate British ally a group of rusting warships in exchange for much of that country's ownership of the leading American corporations and so prevented the British from benefiting further from growth in the American economy.

'Other opportunities like the warships-for-shares venture meant that the American economy was in fine shape during and after the war, but we, and the rest of the Europeans, suffered badly economically and are all still suffering. We are still paying for the war and will do so for many years yet.

'However, two or three years after the war ended it actually seemed that the American economy might finally go off the boil. To counteract this they introduced Marshall Aid—a stroke of genius that effectively exported their own unemployment by giving goods, which could not always be described as essentials, to their allies. Marshall Aid provided an added benefit to the American government and business communities in that as full employment resulted, they alone of the participants in the war did not have to go to the considerable expense of setting up a welfare system. Therefore, what might seem a generous gesture to some people effectively kept American industry going. It made their capitalist leaders even wealthier and held back the recovery of their allies. But the American people see Marshall Aid as one of the most generous international actions ever taken.

'Remember too that most Americans are first or second-generation citizens. These people will be very much aware that they or their parents all left poverty somewhere else in the world to enter the USA. Even though they are almost entirely wage slaves, they are well housed and well fed. In addition, when the economy is prospering in a capitalist society, there is always the chance of starting a business that creates its own wage slaves. Finally, you should realise that almost everything that appears in print and in films in the USA glorifies the country and the authorities are continually rewriting history to make the glory even greater. If I was an American, I would follow the American dream—I certainly would not listen to you.'

Winston then stared at the ceiling for a while before saying, 'However, even if it was easy to convince Americans of the value of communism, our main target at this moment in time would still be Britain.'

At this point we were aware that Winston was studying our reactions to his last statement.

Then he continued, 'You may remember Churchill's radio broadcast when he announced to the British people in 1940 that France had surrendered to the Germans. He told his people that the full might of Germany, which now included the economic power of most of western Europe, would soon be directed at Britain. Finally, he indicated that the fate of the entire world depended on Britain's ability to defend itself. When this final statement was made it caused some amusement in different parts of the world, just as it did to several of you when you received a lecture on this subject earlier this year.'

It was obvious that our body language was under pressure at this juncture because we had all laughed at Churchill's claim when we first heard about it and now it was obvious that Winston had been informed of our reaction.

Winston then pointed to Britain on the map and said, 'Let's examine Churchill's statement. The war lasted a further five years from the time he made it and involved almost the entire world before the Germans were defeated. The British put up an amazing military and economic performance during this time but it was certainly matched by the Germans. True, the Germans had many allies in Europe and controlled the industry of a great many other countries, but no one could deny that the fight put up by the Germans was extraordinary.'

He could see we all felt uncomfortable by his last statement, but he waved his hands in the air and shouted out, 'Why should we deny it? Our own enormous effort during this last war is all the more remarkable because we faced German soldiers who knew that the only alternative to fighting and winning was fighting and dying.'

He then looked around the room with an air of disappointment on his face. 'I can see you are all misinterpreting what you have been taught. Your minds are all convinced that as we beat the Germans we must be better fighters and better people. You are falling into the same trap that allowed Hitler to prosper—he told the Germans that they were the master race and their destiny was to rule the world. It worked, of course, that little piece of propaganda—just as it has worked for all the tyrants throughout history.'

Winston took several long puffs from his cigar and studied all our faces in turn. It was clear that he was disturbed by our apparent lack of enthusiasm for his words but he was also enjoying his presentation. He started again with a smile on his face:

'I'm sure you were all impressed with the speed that the Germans conquered all before them in western Europe during 1940. It was particularly impressive to conquer a much larger French army in just a few short weeks. Does that make the Germans better fighters than the French? Well, does it?'

Peter was the first to react by saying, 'I would say that the war demonstrates that the Germans are better fighters but the French are better people.'

Winston reacted quickly, 'That's interesting because just a century and a half ago the French army under Napoleon had little difficulty in walking through the German states and destroying their armies. Does that mean the French were intrinsically better fighters then but it all changed around in 150 years or so?'

Before anyone could comment further he added, 'The British had little difficulty in beating off the Italians during this last war but 2,000 years ago the Italians had little difficulty defeating the British tribes. Can the difference be explained by 2,000 years of improvement in fighting prowess by the British and an equivalent decline by the Italians?'

Seeing that no one was going to answer this last question Winston waved his cigar in the air and said, 'The truth is that virtually all the world's races have had their period of power and conquest. It all depends on how well the people and armies are organised and the believability of the quest they are offered. To a large extent the quest depends on how successful the country or race of people has been in living memory and the myths that have been created on the back of that success.'

He stood silently for a while with his back to us, then he continued, 'Look at all the countries marked in red on the map—

just look at the British Empire and remember that the British Isles contains just over one and a half per cent of the world's population.'

He turned towards us again and added, 'All that territory controlled by a country with just one and a half per cent of the world's population. Should we accept that the British are a nation of supermen or did they just benefit from the fact that they started the Industrial Revolution and on the back of that success and some organisational skills they part accidentally and part deliberately created myths? Myths that caused friend and foe alike to believe that they were special?'

He waited for us to comment and one by one we mouthed, 'Organisation and myth.'

He took a great deal of satisfaction from our reaction and told us in some detail that we had just learned an important lesson.

'Look,' he said, 'it's perhaps necessary for our military personnel to believe they were born superior to their potential enemies but it is absolutely necessary that you understand what makes a country successful in military and other matters. It is after all fundamental to why we are all here. Your task for the foreseeable future is to remove the myth that the British are special and replace it with another myth that they are inferior.'

He paused, saw that we were all confused, and allowed himself a little smile before continuing. 'The fact that the British held out in 1940 and finished on the winning side owed a great deal to the myths that their ancestors created over the previous century or so. At the end of the conflict, however, the British nation was tired out and a period of retrenchment and rest was always on the cards. The war had seriously damaged the economy but the average Briton had every reason to believe that things would get much better very quickly. However, over the last few years their lot has actually got much worse and I'm glad to say this is mainly because my existing teams have been busy replacing one set of myths with another. Nevertheless, the British still represent the biggest threat to the future of world communism. Take a ten-minute break now and then I'll explain why.'

When we reconvened we were all in thoughtful mood. Winston

started the session by saying, 'Now let's get back to Churchill's statement. It took five more years to defeat the Germans and the allied armies included the large American contingent. If the British had collapsed the Americans would never have got involved—that surely means the Germans would have won the war—doesn't it?'

Before we could answer he added, 'Forget the Americans. If the British had been defeated, or worse still the British fascists had taken over in 1939 instead of Churchill, then the Germans would have beaten us and eventually conquered the world—wouldn't they?'

Seeing our discomfort at his statements Winston stared at each of us in turn and said, 'Come on, think for yourselves. If the British, their navy and their empire had joined in with the Germans it must surely have meant our defeat by 1942 at the latest—yes?'

At this point Winston had got his argument across. We did not like what was being said but we all reluctantly accepted the logic. Seeing that he had convinced us, Winston then quietly concluded, 'Churchill was indeed right and so I suppose we must all be grateful that the British resisted. However, the point I am getting at and the entire reason for my organisation's existence, is that it could all have been very different. What you have to understand is that in just over thirty years two world wars have been fought. Wars that would not have started if the Germans had not looked for territory and empires and the British particularly had not opposed them. This could have been very different because these two countries are not natural enemies. Britain is made up of two basic tribes—the Anglo-Saxons who as you know are Germans, and the northern Celts, who were Germanic peoples who just happened to move into northern Europe before the Anglo-Saxons. Just imagine if Britain and Germany had created a one-race joint economic and foreign policy concept before World War I. In those circumstances the rest of the world would have been in real economic and military danger from a political and military union with around five per cent of the world's population.'

He paused for another drink and appeared deep in thought. Then he smiled and said, 'If you're following my argument you will surmise that as these two countries did not join up in order to dominate the world before World War I started, then the bitterness caused by that war largely took the opportunity away. That would appear logical, I'm sure you'll agree. It follows, then, I suppose, that now after World War II the opportunity has receded to such an extent that it's almost non-existent—would you agree?'

Not knowing what was coming next we were all naturally reluctant to comment. Winston understood our caution, smiled broadly and continued: 'There are two basic reasons why this Germanic empire has not been created. The first is that the British could not see a reason to share their wealth and glory with anyone else and the second is that all the other western European powers, such as the French, Italians and the Dutch, had different agendas. So, forty years ago the British did not want to join up with the Germans and the Germans would probably not have wanted it either. Of equal importance, however, the French, Belgians and Dutch are located in between Britain and Germany and would have been more than upset to see such an alliance being formed.

'Now, my friends, the situation is very different. The war has devastated both countries. The Germans cannot contemplate foreign wars or any form of external adventure on their own in the foreseeable future and the British are losing their empire and with it their power in the world. The British are clearly the Americans' main partner and are essential to the Americans' continued presence and influence in Europe, but the Americans desperately want to keep the British in their place. Given such circumstances the British and Germans may come to see great benefits in an alliance. There is no other logical partner for either country.'

After a further pause Winston continued, 'The second obstacle to such an alliance is also rapidly disappearing. For a number of reasons we now believe an economic and political alliance of 300,000,000 western Europeans is a certainty within the next few years.'

Up to that point we had made few responses to the great man's words, but now the threat of a united western Europe became a major fear for all of us and we all started talking at the same time.

Winston raised his hands for silence and said, 'Why do you fear a united western Europe?' Individually and collectively we let it be known that we mainly feared the threat of a massive combined army facing us from the west.

Winston looked annoyed and very disappointed but finally he said, 'You keep falling into the trap of thinking about future conflict from a purely military perspective. Tell me, do you think the Europeans or the Americans would ever launch a non-nuclear attack on the Soviet Union if they believed that we had nuclear weapons?'

One by one we had to agree that it would not make sense because our generals would definitely retaliate with nuclear weapons if they were available.

At this point Winston started to struggle for words but eventually he regained his composure and said forcibly, 'Yes, you're correct, there's no chance of a major conflict between communism and capitalism that does not involve nuclear weapons. Therefore, I doubt if a major conflict between the two groups will happen and if it does there is nothing we can do about it—it is not our problem and it is not something that should concern us. I keep telling you that capitalists are not interested in military wars and there is a very good reason for that. Capitalism bears with it the profit or greed motive that is deliberately absent in communism so that all the people can benefit from combined efforts made. Sadly, profit and greed work far quicker than communism in creating wealth because of the wage-slave element. Consequently, it will take us longer to obtain the same level of prosperity for our people than would occur under capitalism.'

Sensing our general unease at this statement, he stared at each of us in turn before continuing: 'I can see that my last comment surprised you, but I have to prepare you for your time in Britain and I want you all to understand exactly what the situation is. It is sad that communism is taking longer to create what most people see as prosperity but that's how it is. One reason why it will take longer is that we don't have the financial, physical and trading infrastructure that most western countries have developed over several hundred years. If we want the best and fairest system to live under, we don't want it to fail because people in countries like Poland see that citizens in the west have cars and washing machines and therefore imagine that life is better in the capitalist world.

'Would you now all forget military confrontation—we don't want it and I can promise you that the Europeans don't want it either.'

Peter interrupted Winston's verbal flow by asking, 'Why then would the Europeans want to create a political union?'

'That,' said our future leader, 'is the nub of the matter. People in Europe are constantly being informed by their newspapers that the key to economic success is efficient mass production of goods. They are also told that the Americans have a tremendous advantage in that they have a home market of over 150,000,000 people and consequently are able to produce goods more efficiently. Naturally, some Europeans imagine the advantages that they might obtain with a home market of more than 300,000,000. It is inevitable that this market will be created over the next few years, but we can live with such a trading bloc on our western borders if it happens slowly, and no one provides it with dynamic leadership.

'At this moment, the various European countries are growing their economies at a combined rate of about two to three per cent a year. We can live with that and we can live with a European growth of up to five per cent when the European Union is formed. However, we could not expect communism to be attractive to other countries if their growth rate was much higher than five per cent and we could also expect trouble within Russia if that happens.

'Unfortunately, economic recovery from World War II is not necessarily going to remain at a low level for the capitalists. We can see a situation where growth could explode at more than ten per cent a year. To make that possible one of the larger European countries would see the need to approach another similar sized country and suggest a total removal of all tariff barriers between them and a joining together of certain key industries. To make it attractive one of the countries would need to have one of the two main financial centres in the world, an international trading infrastructure, and possess an empire so that raw materials, cheap additional labour and other markets were available.'

Now we could all see what he was getting at and were keen to register our support.

Winston, however, was obviously keen to finish his presentation and he continued by saying, 'Friends, as you now realise, only Britain meets these requirements. I know its empire is disintegrating but such a scheme would enable it to create long-term relationships with all those red-marked countries on the map and perhaps bring some of the early defaulters back into the fold. For reasons that are obvious to us but are too complicated to explain at this session, they will approach the Germans first and the Germans will readily agree. But Britain will have the credibility to make this move only if it's quick to regain its economic drive and past glory and its people rekindle the myth that they are special. If they do, they will give the Germans, the other northern Europeans and eventually the rest of western Europe a smooth path to embark on fast economic expansion. An expansion based upon a racial view of Europe and Europeans. We must, at all costs, stop the British leading the drive to European unity and to do so we have to give them a new and different understanding of who they really are.'

He finished his drink and then said in a loud voice, 'Now you know why we're all working in Britain. One of our team there recently coined the name the Trojan Hearse for our operation. This name is very apt as on the one hand it uses ancient Greek legends to remind us that it's easier to destroy an enemy from within its borders. In addition, it also demonstrates our determination to carry the British desire for fast economic expansion to an early grave. I look forward to seeing you all next year,' and with that final comment he left the room.

CHAPTER THREE

The commotion outside my hotel room had been continuous for several minutes before I managed to open the door. When I did, I was just in time to see Pembridge's killer make a crude gesture to a pompous-looking man in exotic pyjamas. He pushed past me into the room.

'Are you bloody well deaf as well as dumb? I've been knocking on this door for ages!'

Even in my half-conscious state I realised that I had to avoid a confrontation at this time. For one thing, the brief glimpse I had of Pembridge rolled up inside the carpet told me that his head injuries were far more extensive than could have happened from a single fall. It was obvious, therefore, that this man either had an uncontrollable temper or the killing was intentional. But more important still, he was my only link with Elaine.

I tried to placate him. 'Okay, you had a lousy night but it's over now—let's have breakfast and relax.'

'Breakfast and relax—not on your bloody life, we're leaving right now—I have to get you to some godforsaken place up north and be back to meet the boss in fourteen hours' time. By my reckoning I'll need to break the world record to do it.'

I stared at him hard, I needed to take the heat out of the situation, but I was very hungry and I had not changed my clothes since entering the country.

'In that case the answer is simple, I'll have a quick wash and a quick bite to eat and we'll be off.'

With that I started to wash my hands and face. When I completed the task I discovered that I was alone and my unopened suitcases had gone. I looked out of the hotel window, intending to give chase and saw that he had placed the suitcases in the car and was returning to the hotel.

He re-entered the room looking less aggressive and said, 'Look, I'd already paid the hotel bill before I came to the room, why don't we compromise by buying food at the first shop we come to and eat and drink while we're travelling?'

'Okay, let's go.' My desire to complete the journey as quickly as possible was almost as strong as his.

Once we got underway I tried to be friendly. 'I have a valid driving licence on me so I could do some of the out-of-town driving, if that will help?'

'No thanks, for all I know you might have a problem with carsickness as well as seasickness.'

All I could think of saying in response was, 'Suit yourself, I was only trying to help.'

I was not pleased to be reminded of my problems on the ferry, but his snide remark gave me every excuse to relax and the opportunity to study the country and the people in some detail. The route took us through London, an experience I found both daunting and exciting as I tried to pick out the places of interest that I had stored in my memory. Later, I was surprised by the beauty of some of the countryside and even more surprised that in the towns we drove through the people appeared happier and better fed and dressed than I had expected.

Once we had got through London and onto the less busy roads I tried to engage my companion in conversation, but he was not going to co-operate. About the only thing I learned from him during the entire journey was that he and the other man who had come to collect Pembridge's body were Winston's bodyguards. He refused to divulge his own or anyone else's name and insisted I should only refer to Winston as the boss.

When I was convinced that I would not get any further information out of him, I transferred to the back seat at the earliest opportunity and tried to take stock of my situation. Throughout the day my mind had been leaping back to my collapse on the ferry and now the subject filled my thoughts. It was obvious that at the very least I had caused problems for Elaine and had seriously damaged my own career prospects.

The most disturbing feature was that when the attack of seasickness first started, I began to feel like a young child and reacted to my discomfort without any of the self-control and self-discipline that we all develop gradually in our pre-teenage years. It was disturbing because there was rarely any adults around to seek comfort from when I was in the orphanage and I felt that the hardships of my early years and subsequent training made the experience all the more surprising.

I was dozing when we reached our destination, the bus station in Chorley.

My companion quickly removed my cases from the car and then said, 'Come on, get out, I haven't got all day. Wait by the side of the refreshment cabin in the centre of the station and one of the locals will pick you up.'

As he drove away he wound down his window and gave me his final thoughts. 'This is a good meeting place because it could be an hour or so before someone comes for you. They don't move very quickly in these parts—that should suit you. But don't worry— you can buy a snack from the cabin and the loo can't be far away.'

In my conversations with the bodyguards I had tended to back away from confrontation, partly out of embarrassment regarding my performance on the ferry and partly because I needed help to regain contact with Elaine. Now as I waited in the cold and damp atmosphere of the late afternoon I began to get very angry about the way I was being treated. I'd taken various insults on the chin so far but once I had made contact with Elaine these people would see a different side to my character.

After waiting for an hour in these conditions I also began to feel hungry and so I gathered together some of the money I had been provided with and approached the cabin. The young man in front of me had just placed an order and as it seemed a good idea to be guided by local knowledge, I repeated that order.

The sandwich tasted very good and I was just finishing it when a voice behind me said, 'Martin, it's good to see you again.'

On turning, I was confronted by Mr Sidney Jones.

Before I could respond he added, 'I see you've discovered one of Lancashire's great delicacies—salad sandwiches from Chorley bus station. I'll have two, thank you very much.'

From his gestures it was obvious that he expected me to pay for his food and the girl serving giggled and started putting the delicacy together. I passed the money over and anticipated that he would take the sandwiches to eat on the final part of the journey or later in the evening. Much to my annoyance, however, he started eating the first one while he began what was obviously a well practised chatting-up routine with the sandwich lady. This went on while he ate the two sandwiches and despite various interruptions I made suggesting I was tired and would like to be on my way.

His version of sweet talk got more and more aggressive, and finally the embarrassed girl told him she had no intention of going out with him. Her admirer then shrugged his shoulders and walked off without another word. By the time I had picked up my suitcases he had a twenty-yard start on me and it took a minute or two to catch him up.

As I caught up with him he turned, smiled at me and said, 'She's really a nice girl—not like the bitch you came over with.'

I was so surprised that he again got a yard or two ahead of me. By this time we were on the busy main road and I felt it necessary to control my growing anger. Eventually, we came alongside a car, which he indicated I should get in. I threw my luggage in the back of the car, got in the passenger seat and slammed the door shut. He got in at the driver's seat and put his hand out to shake hands again.

I ignored his hand. 'Mr Jones, I will kick your head in if you ever insult Elaine again and go even further if you try pestering her. Your lack of professionalism astounds me.'

My companion did not seem to be unduly concerned by my outburst. He said, 'You use big words for a bloody socialist. Obviously, you had a good education. Me, I'm just Sid Jones, a poor old working-class man from Yorkshire.'

He then broke off the conversation, started the car and drove off at speed. Then he chuckled out loud and said, 'Imagine you calling me unprofessional and yesterday I almost disposed of you on more than one occasion because you were so bloody incompetent and dangerous.'

His words enraged me but there was no point in responding to them. Quite clearly, I would have to work hard in the near future to balance out my mistakes of the previous day, but I saw no benefit in trying to justify myself to this clown.

Then he dropped a bombshell that really depressed me. 'Although I'm just a working-class boy, Winston promoted me today—I'm your boss.'

After the first shock of hearing that I would report to this man, I began to feel that it was such a stupid situation that it could not be true. However, if it wasn't true then Sid must be an impostor, which suggested an equally unpleasant scenario. While dwelling on this possibility I became aware that we were coming to a halt beside a largish farmhouse and another car was following close behind.

Sid quickly got out of the car and snarled, 'Don't make any trouble.'

I had already deduced that if I was in trouble then Elaine must also be in trouble and consequently I would have to let the situation develop a lot more before taking any aggressive steps. In addition, of course, I was not armed and I could not imagine my tormentor being so improperly dressed.

For the second time in two days it crossed my mind that I might be under the control of British Intelligence. However, I could not believe they would employ anyone remotely like Sid and so I quickly dismissed the idea. I followed him to the farmhouse door conscious that just one person had got out of the other car and was closing in on us.

Sid eventually turned and directing his words at this man said, 'James, meet Martin—Martin, this is James.' Then to no one in particular he said, 'Martin is having difficulty adjusting.'

James Cameron turned out to be a tall man in his late twenties or early thirties. He wore a reasonably smart suit, had longish black hair and wore glasses. He looked like a well educated professional man, which in a way he was. More important to me at this point he was friendly and pleasant.

He stuck out his hand and said, 'Nice to meet you, Martin, but I hear you had a bad crossing.'

Sid interjected, 'It was a good crossing. I had five pints on the boat and didn't feel a bit queasy, but our two new recruits are delicate souls.'

Again I ignored the jibe and addressed the newcomer. 'Where is Elaine?'

Sid reacted aggressively: 'We have more important things to talk about than your bloody girlfriend.'

I finally lost my temper and grabbed him by the throat but James had anticipated my reaction and quickly stepped in to force us apart.

He then said, 'Sid, let's all calm down, it's perfectly reasonable for Martin to be worried about Elaine.' Then he turned to me and said, 'Look, Martin, I promise you that Elaine is happy and well and that you'll meet up again in the next few days—but please, let's sit down because we need to talk.'

At that moment the telephone rang with an apparently important message for Sid. I got the impression he wanted to stay and insult me but after some firm pressure by James he left the premises in a hurry, and looking flustered.

A relieved-looking James then said in a whisper, 'Martin, I engineered that call to Sid to get him out of the farmhouse so that we could talk freely.' Then when he was certain that Sid was well away from the premises, he added, 'Over the next few days we'll need to talk at length, to be sure we can trust each other.'

I was about to say that one way he could gain my trust was to provide information on Elaine's whereabouts. However, he anticipated my question as easily as he had anticipated my attack on Sid.

'I made a brief call on Elaine shortly before setting off to meet you. She's in good spirits and she has friends—she's living on a temporary basis in a house with two other Russian girls.'

After a few more details were passed over, I believed him and relaxed considerably.

He saw that I felt a little happier and carried on briefing me. 'As you might expect, Winston normally likes new recruits to visit him as soon as they set foot in the country. But he is incredibly busy at the moment and as he anticipated a problem developing between you and Sid, he asked me to hurry north to make sure there was no violence. Look, Martin, you must understand that your strange behaviour yesterday threw us all into a panic. By chance, I was with Winston when Sid called from Charing Cross Station asking for permission to liquidate you and I can promise you that the atmosphere was electric. Eventually, Winston refused to sanction your demise but he insisted that you be put somewhere safe for a few days so that we could evaluate your suitability for the tasks ahead.'

I had to accept that their concern was reasonable and because I wanted to clear the deck and start again I resolved not to make too many excuses. Therefore when he said, 'Do you have an explanation for what happened to you yesterday?' I simply replied, 'James, I have racked my brains about this ever since I recovered and if my problem was self-inflicted then I can only assume it was caused by a mixture of excitement and seasickness. I can only add that it never happened before and I genuinely believe it will not happen again.'

After considering my statement for a minute or so, James seemed satisfied and made a call direct to Winston. When he completed his conversation he said, 'We have to stay in the farmhouse for three or four days—during this time various people including a psychiatrist will visit you. If you pass these tests your career will continue as if nothing had happened. After all, it's of vital importance to our cause that your training isn't wasted unless it's absolutely essential.'

I was disturbed by the thinly veiled threat in these words but I felt I had no alternative but to go along with their decision.

I then began to think again of the problems I had created for Elaine. 'Presumably Elaine will not be subjected to three or four days of tests?'

The response demoralised me: 'No, she did not collapse on the boat deck crying like a baby and screaming in a mixture of Russian and English.'

I looked at him in disbelief. 'I'm sure that cannot be true.'

'Oh yes it is, just an hour or so ago Elaine confirmed the story. Fortunately, Jones assumed the Russian words were just gibberish and Elaine swears that if any Russian-speaking member of British Intelligence had been present they would not have read anything into the situation other than that you were a drunk who knew how to swear in several languages.'

'What did Pembridge say about my actions on the boat?'

He hesitated before answering: 'The bodyguard did ask him what you had said but he reported that he only heard you crying.'

'Then if Pembridge and Jones didn't mention Russian words being spoken why did Elaine refer to them?'

James smiled: 'I guessed that the gibberish that Jones referred to might just be Russian and so I told Elaine that both Pembridge and Jones had told me you had been speaking Russian.'

He saw that I was surprised by his comments. 'Martin, if you are ever given a similar task to the one I have today you will realise that for your own personal security it is essential to establish exactly what happened. Apart from that I also wanted to see how far Elaine would go to protect you.'

I felt very uncomfortable with his words but decided I should go on the offensive. 'All right, James, now you know, what are you going to do about it?'

He looked at me and said, 'You will find that we all need friends we can trust. I like you both and I promise I will never use that information against either of you. But if I thought you were a danger to us it would be very different.'

I was not completely sure what to make of his last comment but decided that some form of conciliatory statement was necessary. 'I'm finally beginning to understand the treatment I've been getting since I arrived in this damned country. In fact in view of what you have just told me, I'm surprised that I was left on my own for an hour at the bus station.'

'Oh, don't worry, Martin—you were always under observation, and it was always our intention to let you stew for an hour to see what you would do—now let's go and eat.'

We drove off in his car for a short distance and ate at a local pub. Conversation was naturally limited while in the pub but I did discover that James had been a member of the earlier class at my training school. I would not have recognised him from the limited contact we had previously enjoyed and he claimed not to have recognised me.

However, while undergoing training he had met up with Stephen, my friend from the orphanage, and two girl members of my class. Apparently, as these three were a few years older than the rest of us in our year they had at one stage been involved in physical training with the older group. James described Stephen as a 'tough little so and so who eventually lost his nerve'. When I asked for a more detailed explanation he admitted that he didn't have one and was only quoting words he had heard at the time.

We returned to the farmhouse and James showed me the bedroom that had been allocated to me. I noted that the only way I could leave the building was to go past his room. He ushered me into a comfortable living room with two easy chairs and produced two glasses and a large bottle of Scotch.

Having poured out ample drinks he made himself comfortable and said, 'This explanation could take a very long time. You see, I have to explain the actions and achievements of a genius. A man who has the ability to both see and understand things that pass others by—a man who can communicate his ideas and enthusiasm in such a way that he will have people believing anything he wants them to.'

Almost involuntarily I said, 'Like the idea of a world dominated by a British and German alliance.'

'Yes,' he said, 'exactly that.'

Seeing that I was looking for a more detailed response, he went on, 'I admit in 1954 that the concept looks somewhat ridiculous but we all thought it was a distinct possibility a few years back, and Winston still thinks there is a chance it could happen. Let's face it, most of the British aristocracy expressed their admiration for Hitler in the years leading up to1939, and clearly preferred his version of socialism to the one that was being practised here. Winston was convinced they would seize the opportunity, before the end of the 1940s, to offer salvation to a defeated foe. But he also thought they would make this move only when they realised that they didn't have the population or resources in Britain to maintain the country's previous dominant position in the world. So, in a funny sort of way, by holding back the British economy in the immediate post-war years we were for a while at least increasing the risk of the union taking place.'

I was confused. 'Can you tell me what has happened in the last year or so to remove the threat?'

'Last year or so? No, you've got it wrong. Winston had probably gone a long way towards preventing a British-German partnership as early as 1946, and in the process he gained enormous credibility in Moscow. He came up with a simple ruse to ensure that the Germans developed a real ongoing hatred of the British. He created stories that RAF Bomber Command destroyed German residential areas out of blood-lust and revenge and deliberately killed far more people than was necessary to win the war.'

James then looked at the ceiling and smiled: 'Winston claims that our entire team put in no more than ten weeks' work creating this situation. He honed his special techniques during this exercise and the story was spread by various means throughout the heavily bombed areas of Germany.'

I raised my hand to interrupt. 'James, only last year Winston told all my classmates that our most important task was to prevent this northern European alliance and now you're telling me that the problem disappeared in 1946.'

He rolled his glass in his hands for a moment or two before

answering: 'Martin, I did tell you that Winston was not totally convinced that the danger had gone away. In any case he needed to continue to stress the danger of this alliance to ensure that Moscow agreed to release you into his care. If at any point he acknowledged that the danger was over then Moscow might have removed our funding completely and tried to transfer you to other work.'

Then with a beaming smile forming over his face, he added, 'You should understand though that the event that has most likely prevented the British and Germans from creating an alliance is the formation of the welfare state in Britain. I believe that by 1952 the damage to the British economy caused by the welfare state had convinced Moscow that the threat had gone completely. Fortunately for us they also believe that Winston and his team played a major part in bringing it about. We think they kept our funding going because they realised that the effect we were having on the British economy might just result in Britain adopting communism quickly and then the rest of Europe would follow even more quickly.'

I shook my head. 'James, I don't understand how the welfare state could have been so important and I don't see how Winston could have brought it about.'

There was a brief lull before I got a reply. 'I won't tell you how we did it until you've passed the tests we will put you through over the next couple of days, and in any case it would take too much of the time we have this evening. But the effect it had is easily explained. In 1948 the British created a welfare state and immediately reduced the country's ability to recover from the war. The creation of this—let's-sit-back-and-share-everything-out policy—effectively stopped both them and the Germans taking on a world role for the foreseeable future. Perversely, they also made it easier for their European neighbours to kick-start their own economies with more realistic and affordable welfare schemes. So, there you have it, my friend—at the worst possible moment for them the British created a welfare state in which each person got more or less the same weekly wage whether they worked or not. If this was not crazy enough they took up to ninety per cent of some workers' income in tax to pay for the services being provided. In the circumstances the entrepreneurs either went overseas or went on the dole. Anyway, the net result is that the British, who were on the winning side in the war, are still being subjected to rationing of all manner of goods, when their European neighbours are beginning to prosper. Effectively the British have now got nothing to offer the Germans.'

James had paused at this point but as I could not think of anything to say he continued, 'Anyway, as I said before, Moscow kept us going in the hope that we represented the best chance of converting Britain to communism quickly. But they refused to fund any other training courses after yours. Not only that, they increased your direct military training so that they could use you in other ways if the opportunity arose. Winston was horrified when he met your group last year—he said you were being trained as soldiers.'

Realising that I was having difficulty taking in all this news, James decided that some background information was necessary. 'Martin, you should understand that until recently we have enjoyed a good relationship with Moscow. Okay, they cut the training courses but they had very good reasons for doing that. We have had some incredible bad luck—only five of you got through from your course and I'm the only one left from my course.'

'Good God, what happened to the others from your year?'

'One was killed in a car accident but others have just disappeared. I'm not in a position to elaborate on that this evening.'

'Well, can you tell me what happened to change our relationship with Moscow?'

At first, James appeared startled by my question but answered readily enough: 'After his visit to your training school last year, Winston got an audience with Comrade Stalin as a reward for his efforts over the years to further the cause of communism. This went well apparently and Winston was presented with an historic carpet. It's a strange-looking thing but he's very proud of it.'

After a lengthy pause, he continued: 'Then almost four weeks ago we got a shock, Winston received a communication from his main contact in Moscow stating that the presentation had been a mistake and that Winston should have received something different. Winston was asked to return the carpet, which they now described as a wall covering. We did some research on wall coverings and as a result Winston has decided not to return the item. He has not yet signified his refusal but Moscow have cancelled our funding until it's in their safe keeping. As a result we will have to be wary of Russians in the future and we will all have to get jobs and pass over twenty per cent of our earnings to boost the organisation's coffers.'

My mind was in a total whirl at this stage, as it became obvious that Winston's group was now at odds with my country. However, it was equally obvious that I had to be careful with my comments particularly as it was apparent that James was not going to say another word until I had reacted to his last incredible statement. In the end I took the easy way out:

'Why has Winston refused to return the thing?'

In response I got another beaming smile, but then he became more serious:

'Have you heard of the Amber Palace?'

'No, I have no knowledge of the place.'

'No problem. The Amber Palace may or may not be involved in the situation anyway. When the Nazis marched east in 1940 they looted everything of note along the way. It has always been assumed that they stripped the Amber Palace clean because none of its contents has been discovered since. The alternative of course is that entrepreneurial locals liberated the various treasures before the Nazis got there, but if that was the case you'd have expected some of the pieces to have appeared on the market by now. Winston now believes that his wall covering, which he still uses as a carpet, may be the key item from the amber collection and the only one that's surfaced. In the circumstances it will not only be extremely valuable but could have enormous political significance. On balance, Winston thinks that he ought to hold on to it for a while until its value becomes clearer. He does not intend to hold on to it indefinitely, but by keeping it for a while he can demonstrate his power and look for an opportune moment to negotiate its return.'

'Why is he taking a risk like that?'

James interrupted me: 'Don't read too much into this situation, Martin. If Moscow is not going to train any more people for us then we don't need them because we can acquire the funding by other means. Therefore why should we kowtow to them if they're doing nothing for us? They believe that we're likely to be a major factor in turning this country into a communist state, so they aren't going to do anything to reduce our effectiveness, are they?'

It seemed to me that it was a dangerous game that Winston was playing but perhaps not quite as disastrous as I had first thought. After thinking about the situation for a moment or two I realised that I had to say something that would not alienate me completely.

Eventually I said, 'Well, all this has come as a hell of a surprise but I suppose that as long as Winston knows what he's doing then the Trojan Hearse team will be okay.'

James was clearly pleased with my reaction and quickly threw in the comment, 'Good. The situation has been explained to Elaine and she has adopted the same positive view. I promise that both of you have made the correct decision because any alternative is unthinkable.'

I was not aware that I had made a decision but in view of what he had told me about Elaine's view, I was happy to go along with him.

I got the feeling that I was being accepted and took the opportunity to ask a question on a subject that had been puzzling me.

'What was the problem with Pembridge?'

The response surprised me:

'Pembridge was always the one die-hard Moscow man in our group and after Winston decided to delay returning their treasure we wondered if they'd try to get to him. About a week ago he approached Winston with this crazy story that he ought to travel to Brussels in order to escort you to this country. Winston decided to play along with this request but insisted that Jones accompany him. Mark was always terrified of flying and without telling Winston he sailed across. Jones reported back when they got to Brussels and informed Winston that they had crossed by ferry. Winston went almost berserk and he instructed Mark to fly back immediately. But Pembridge's fear of flying must have got the better of him. He ignored Winston's instructions and decided on the ferry crossing.'

I started to feel uncomfortable because some of the comments being made did not add up.

James saw my concern. 'Do you have a problem with any of that?'

'Yes, I'm afraid I do. Within a matter of minutes you've told me that Moscow is upset that you've lost so many of the people they've trained for you. Then you tell me I was nearly eliminated yesterday and I saw for myself that the presumably valuable Mark Pembridge was killed simply because of problems with the crossing. None of that makes sense to me.'

He appeared deep in thought and so I took a risk and carried on: 'Why kill Pembridge because he wanted to remain loyal to his country? Surely, all Winston needed to have done was to say to Pembridge that he knew Moscow had been in touch with him. It would have scared the life out of him and he would have been forced to ignore the instruction that Moscow had given him. In that way Pembridge would have closed ranks around Winston and you would not be a further man short.'

He did not react immediately and I was just wondering if I had said too much, but when he spoke again his manner was conciliatory: 'Martin, I am going to tell you something that I don't have the authority to tell you. But I'm going to trust you to keep our secret because otherwise this conversation is going to go round in circles. First of all, you were in no danger from Sid's threats. However, there was at one stage yesterday the chance that Winston might decide to get rid of both you and Elaine.'

He ignored my attempts to interrupt and continued: 'It's all to do with timing. Winston got the demand for the return of the carpet

42

after the other team from your class had arrived in Ireland, and for a variety of reasons we knew that Moscow did not have the time or the opportunity to contact them. The same could not be said of you and the lovely Elaine. For all we knew you could have been briefed to spy on us, and if there had been any proof of that then it would have made sense to eliminate you. We could not afford the time and effort to keep you under observation. So when Pembridge came up with the request to visit Belgium to aid your return Winston gladly accepted the idea on the grounds that he would soon find out who the intended mole was.'

'How could he do that?'

'Quite easily really. Pembridge would have to contact the Russian group in Brussels and Winston has a man in that group. Just before your ferry docked in Dover, Winston got a call from his contact and discovered that Pembridge had been promised the leadership of our merry band and in turn had given away information that is damaging to us. Winston is under pressure at the moment because he has to change location. We had no alternative but to eliminate Pembridge, but the news got Elaine and yourself off the hook.'

'That convinces me Pembridge must have drugged me prior to getting on the boat.'

James shook his head: 'I promise you that does not make sense. He delivered you back to the UK and called Winston to say you'd been seasick. Your being ill on the boat therefore increased the pressure on him because he'd avoided flying—no, it doesn't make sense. As I told you, Pembridge admitted to the bodyguard that you were whimpering on the boat. The bodyguard reported that he was about to add something else but then stopped. I think he was going to say that you started speaking Russian but then stopped because that would put him under more pressure. Remember, he had to keep close to Winston for a while if he was to deliver his promise.'

'James, you appear bloody determined to think the worst of me. But during the first fifteen minutes on the boat Pembridge asked me at least three times if I was feeling okay. I think he'd drugged me and was surprised I was still standing up.'

James smiled: 'No, you silly bugger, it's because you come from the Ukraine. Winston refuses to allow any of us who were at our training school to travel by sea. According to him people who come from areas well away from the sea don't have the stomach for sea travel because resistance to seasickness hasn't been built up over the generations. In the circumstances he doesn't want people breaking down and doing something stupid like talking in Russian. I used to think this theory was just one of Winston's foibles, but you certainly proved him right.'

He waited for me to continue the argument, but by this time I realised it was a battle I was unlikely to win and so I just shrugged.

James got up and walked around the room stretching his legs. Then with some irritation he suddenly said, 'It's getting late, I'm getting tired, and I still haven't touched on the most important issue, or at least the most important issue we need to cover this evening. It's essential before Sid Jones or one of his British colleagues turns up that I explain something in detail to you. The original intention was that our operation was entirely staffed by Russian-born personnel, for obvious security and other reasons. When I first arrived there were only Russian nationals in our team. However, as I explained, after the welfare state was created, Moscow started to lose interest in our work and reduced the number of people being trained. Unfortunately, this coincided with a dramatically increased workload as Winston thought up more and more ways to damage the British system. The only answer was to create a team of local volunteers. You had been told prior to coming here that you should never tell anyone of your origins— that's because all our British team believe that we are all British-born. They can accept the idea of fellow-British workers doing everything possible to overthrow the establishment and the bosses, but we think some of them would react differently if they knew that a foreign power was behind the scheme. Therefore, they're led to believe that you and Elaine, for example, are the children of die-hard socialists who sent their children overseas for training. To minimise the risk that they might think you've been totally indoctrinated by the Soviet Union, they've been told that your training took place in a variety of countries over a period of six years. The only downside in telling them this story is that people like Sid Jones think you're more privileged than the pupils at Eton.

'One other thing—you referred to the Trojan Hearse just now, so I suppose Winston must have given you the name on his last trip. You should know that this term was never written down, never accepted officially, and was only used when Russian-born colleagues were alone together. We have always been careful not to use the name when the British element was around in case they wanted to delve further into its meaning. Anyway, the name was thought up by one of my old classmates who has since gone native—so hearing the name does nothing for Winston's blood pressure.'

For the next few minutes he concentrated on convincing me of Sid's importance to the cause

'The first thing I want to say is that you should not be upset at Sid, he adopts the same aggressive attitude to all our new recruits. We're all conditioned by our basic beliefs and Sid is a communist simply because he resents people born with advantages. Our last two recruits in the Lancashire area both had a reasonable education and were southerners, which is in itself almost a crime to Sid. When he heard that you and Elaine were at special training schools he got really worried. Winston wants to keep Sid interested and that's one of the reasons why he was promoted to be head of the North West Section.'

I stared at James for some time and then said, 'How can someone like Sid Jones be so important?'

James stared back for an equally long period before replying: 'Sid performs a lot of tasks that are essential to our cause. One of them is that he creates jokes—he thinks up jokes denigrating the aristocracy, British manufacturing, et cetera—these are then sent to comedians and the press. His actions have helped us cause a great deal of damage to the British economy. Martin, you must realise that Sid is important and should not be crossed.'

I could hardly believe what I was being told and reacted irritably: 'He's important because he creates jokes?'

By this time James looked very tired but came up with a further explanation: 'Martin, you have just undergone one of the longest training courses in history, but for the reasons I have given you already your real training will not start until you've passed certain tests. If you do pass these tests you'll have the opportunity to study and use mind-blowing techniques that will result in the collapse of capitalism in this country and then throughout the world.'

I must have looked doubtful because he continued: 'I have not the energy or the authority to describe the techniques in detail to you tonight, but I will give you a clue to whet your appetite. If you were suddenly asked to reduce a British manufacturer's market share by twenty per cent, how would you do it?'

Before I could answer he added: 'With your training you'd probably think in terms of blowing up factories. However, experience suggests that this would be seen as sabotage and would indicate to the population at large that competitors had no other way of competing and had resorted to violence. Ultimately this action would therefore tend to increase the bombed manufacturer's share.

'But consider this. Just about a year ago two of us spent a week each going around distributors and agents of the Morris Motors' manufacturing group. We were looking for people who were having trouble with their newly purchased vehicles. From just watching these premises from the outside we were able to isolate the people who were having trouble and consequently were not happy with their purchase. Statistically, rather less than one per cent of Morris cars seemed to have a problem, which probably suggests they were very reliable when compared to their main competitors. Nevertheless, when we approached the people who did have problems, claiming to be journalists, we were both able to get half a dozen to agree to their complaint being given publicity. Then we gave these stories to freelance journalists who we knew dealt with major newspapers. The result from just two man-weeks of effort on our part was a probable reduction in Morris's market share of five per cent. Then one of Jones's jokes relating to these stories was aired over the radio by one of the leading comedians. The result then was a decline in market share of twenty per cent. Somebody about to buy a new car might ignore something he had read in a newspaper but he would think himself a bloody fool if he'd ignored the warnings in a joke broadcast to the entire nation.'

I had to admit I was impressed by what he had just told me but suggested that concentrating on one manufacturer could not be continued for too long before someone latched on to what was causing the problem.

He assured me that they gave all British manufacturers a certain amount of their time but added, 'I'm not certain your assumption is correct though. The British had hundreds of observers in western Germany at the time Winston was spreading stories about unnecessary bombing and I don't think any of them thought anything unusual was going on.'

I went to bed shortly after hearing this and quickly went to sleep, but not before considering my situation over the last three nights. When I retired to bed two nights ago I was a powerful prince about to take my place as a key player in the most important drama on the world's stage. Last night the drama was still as important but I had fallen from power. Tonight I find that the play is being rewritten. Oh hell, oh bloody hell.

CHAPTER FOUR

Over the next few days my morale gradually started to improve. From further discussions with James I began to realise that although we faced problems that I had not bargained for, most of these were due to the effect that Winston's team had already had on the British economy. Therefore I was hopefully going to be playing on a winning team, and even if the British-German partnership was no longer a potential danger, the team's work must be furthering the cause of world socialism. In addition, after hearing the Morris Motors story I was excited at the prospect of using Winston's misinformation techniques and had to admit to myself that the thought of an ordinary job or being some type of military specialist did not interest me at all. In the circumstances, I reasoned that it would be well worth putting up with a few problems to play a role that was available to very few.

The specialist in mental disorders that Winston called for was considerably delayed and it was towards the end of my third day in the farmhouse before he arrived. He introduced himself as Horace Phillpott, a name that amused me because he was clearly of eastern European origin. He was a fussy individual who insisted on looking at all the rooms in the farmhouse so that he could choose the most suitable one to use to interview me. After he had chosen a room he surprised James with his next comment:

'Mr Cameron, I'm sure you will understand that it's essential practice that I be alone with the patient during my investigation. Perhaps you would be kind enough to bring us coffee and biscuits in say forty minutes' time.'

Phillpott did not take long to get down to basics. 'Martin, please explain in as much detail as you can remember, everything that happened to you from just before getting on the ferry right up to the point when you started to feel better.'

It was in my own interest to get a full understanding of the nightmare I had experienced on the ferry and so I answered in as much detail as I could without holding anything back. He took copious notes and then said, 'Tell me, have any of the sensations or memories you experienced stayed with you or come back to you since?'

I answered truthfully: 'I can still remember some of the thoughts that came into my mind as a result of being seasick. One was being a young child again and being terrified of being on the sea because I was alone. I can also remember some adults telling me to forget the experience because it was upsetting me but nothing else has come back to me since.'

He came up very close to me before asking his next question: 'Tell me, do you think these memories are your own or do you think they hark back to some previous life?'

I could not believe he was serious at first and it was some time before I could bring myself to answer, but then I found myself saying, 'I have to admit that I don't see how they could be my memories.'

He took some more notes but I was intrigued by the possibility he'd raised: 'Do you believe in reincarnation, Mr Phillpott?'

He smiled and said, 'I'm playing it safe, I neither believe nor disbelieve, because although there's circumstantial evidence for reincarnation it could all be explained by some sort of shock that throws the brain into confusion. Coincidentally, I think that is exactly what has happened in your case, Martin. I think the horrible mixture of food you described eating before you got on the ferry, the intense excitement of a powerful new job and a natural aversion to being on the sea combined to give your brain a nasty shock and it took several hours before it could recover.'

James came in at this moment with the coffee and biscuits. Phillpott ignored them. He gathered his belongings together and addressed James: 'Mr Cameron, I will let you have a full report in due course, but I'm convinced of our patient's sanity and suitability.'

He then doffed his hat and left the building.

James watched him go. 'How did you fix that?'

'I didn't fix anything, he said my problem was probably due to something I'd eaten before getting on the ferry.'

James did not appear convinced but it seemed the only possible explanation to me and I began to feel much more hopeful about my future prospects.

The enforced extra time in the farmhouse resulted in James and me talking in far more detail than either he or Winston would have originally intended. Once he had started on his daily intake of whisky he was very informative about the running of the organisation and on his views of our various colleagues and the quest we were pursuing. At one stage he said his greatest desire was for the conflict between East and West to disappear.

I asked him what he would do in those circumstances and he lowered his head and said, 'Stay here.'

He saw that this surprised me and explained that his desire to stay in Britain was due to the fact that he was happily married to what he described as 'a highland lassie'. Although it was obvious that James had no strong political views I already saw him as a real friend.

Eventually the word came through from Winston that I had been given the all clear and I was to report for my first assignment after a few days relaxing on the Lancashire coast with Elaine. Before leaving for the holiday, I suggested to James that he was perhaps unwise to be so open once he had had a few drinks. He just nodded his agreement.

My reunion with Elaine turned out to be a major disappointment—at least for me. We had been joined on our weekend break by two of her new girlfriends who were sharing a room with her. This situation was clearly not likely to create the ideal setting for a romantic interlude. However, I felt that the presence of these girls could not entirely explain why Elaine was much cooler and diffident towards me than I expected. When I became affectionate she was quick to reject any small advance I made. Naturally I assumed that her feelings had been affected by what she had seen and heard of me during our first day in Britain. In the circumstances I decided to let her know Phillpott's conclusions and because I thought it was information that deserved a wide audience, I told her when the other girls were present.

'Winston sent a psychiatrist to examine me and he decided that the problem I experienced was due to the food I'd eaten before we got on the ferry.'

All three girls were silent for a moment or two, then one of them, a tall girl called Joan, started to giggle: 'Oh you poor devil, you're allergic to food. Our friend Mavis here is allergic to chocolate and I'm allergic to men.'

She addressed Elaine, 'I wonder what you're allergic to, let's hope it's not cotton.'

This remark was a direct reference to Elaine's first job, which was in the personnel department of a cotton mill in Leigh, Lancashire. Elaine had already told me that the job had been found for her so that she could look for ways to damage the cotton industry.

Joan and Mavis continued to joke about allergies and Joan then looked at me and said, 'Oh dear, your new job doesn't involve food by any chance, does it?'

Elaine was not as frivolous as the other two but I felt that the joke had gone on long enough and excused myself.

As it happens my new job required me to travel around the country as a commission-only salesman, selling books to householders and businesses. When I was first told about this role I was concerned that the constant travel would limit my opportunities to see Elaine. However, during our two-day break Elaine continued to keep me at arm's length and when our little holiday came to an end I was in some ways quite pleased that we wouldn't be meeting for a while on a regular basis. Part of my reasoning was that if she had lost interest as a result of what she saw as my indiscretions then a short absence could well make her remember happier times. Against that it occurred to me that she may feel that she now had a bigger pond to fish in and as a result I found myself comparing my appearance unfavourably with most of the young Englishmen passing by.

I had almost convinced myself that our relationship was over. But just before the end of our holiday break Elaine insisted that I telephone her the following evening and gave me the number of a phone situated on a landing in the block of flats she was living in. When I called, she told me the reason why she was acting out of character. Apparently, during the ferry crossing, she had become convinced that she had previously travelled on a boat with Stephen, our friend from the orphanage. Her voice became quite emotional:

'Martin, I'm sure the boat was sinking and I was clinging to Stephen. If I was, then I have to assume that my parents were not there and therefore Stephen must be my brother.'

I tried to interrupt but she continued, 'I realise that becoming slightly seasick may have caused me to dream that I had been on a sinking boat in the past and it would be logical for my mind to associate Stephen with helping me as he had been so supportive to us. However, thinking about it since, I cannot understand why he has not stayed in touch or why I accepted his sudden departure from the training school, without concern and further thought.'

Her story made me shiver slightly because in many ways it was close to my own seasick dream.

'Elaine, I had a very similar experience and you now have me wondering if we were on the same boat all those years ago.'

'Oh no,' her voice was harsh, 'I would have remembered a whisky-sodden young boy lying flat out on the deck.'

I almost dropped the phone at this point because it was obvious that she thought I was simply using her story in order to explain my own pathetic antics of a couple of days ago.

'Elaine, I really did have a similar experience to the one you've described, but you obviously don't want to believe me. Another thing, I did not drink whisky or anything else prior to getting on the boat.'

'I know that Jones told me you gulped down several double whiskies immediately after getting on the ferry.'

'Elaine, I did not drink anything on the boat, Jones is a liar.'

'Well, if you hadn't been drinking, what excuse do you have? And don't repeat that stupid story about food poisoning.'

I was depressed by her reaction and did not immediately respond.

Then I heard her say, 'Hello, are you there, are you there?'

I said, 'Yes, I'm just thinking about the mess we're in.'

She appeared to soften: 'Martin, I don't want to run the risk of losing another friend and as you'll be the one travelling, please telephone at least twice a week. I won't tell anyone else about my dream, if that is what it was, but at some stage when it's safe to do so I would like to trace Stephen.'

I was pleased to get her explanation and her desire to stay friends but I was made very much aware that she was describing me as an old friend and not her future lover. Later I too found myself wondering why Stephen's departure from the training school had so little effect on me—I must have been a self-centred little so and so.

I was not looking forward to knocking on strange doors in order to sell even stranger books but I was resolved to make the best of everything that was thrown at me and so I did not question my lot. In any case it was clear that I had to earn an independent living and consequently I was not in a position to turn anything down. When I thought about the future I realised that Elaine and I were trapped in a situation that was outside our control. Previously, the excitement and opportunities suggested by our assignment had prevented such negative thoughts from entering my consciousness.

On the brighter side the heavy security that had surrounded me since arriving in Chorley was removed and I was allowed to travel alone back to the town. At the bus station Sid was waiting for me. I got the impression he'd been told to improve his attitude towards me because he was almost polite and friendly. However, when I got out of his car he reverted to type:

'Don't expect me to act as your bloody chauffeur again.'

Two days later Sid made a telephone call from the farmhouse and then told me he had Winston on the phone.

Winston was curt and to the point: 'Martin, I don't have the time to enter into a long discussion, so pay attention. I want you to join your new company in London tomorrow. Be at the central door of the Midland Railway Station in Manchester by eight a.m. A man called Raymond Marshall will approach you at that time. He will have your travel tickets and will explain what's required of you during the journey.'

Before I could make any comment the line went dead—clearly I had my instructions and I was expected to comply with them.

Raymond turned out to be a small, dishevelled-looking individual in his mid-forties. As he approached me at the entrance to the station he stuck out a limp hand and said, 'Hello, Sonny Jim.'

Before we got on the train he made it clear that this door-to-door selling lark was new to him and he was not looking forward to it. We were on the train for over an hour before the compartment cleared and he was able to brief me. He told me he had been trained in what he termed the honourable profession of espionage. However, his career as a spy was curtailed when Winston discovered he had spent some time in Poland both before and during the war. Winston wanted someone who could infiltrate the Polish community in Britain and Raymond was apparently able to satisfy any doubts that the British Poles might have regarding his nationality, by claiming that his family had been trapped in Russia during the first part of his life. When I asked why he had accepted Winston's offer, he snarled back,

'Don't be bloody stupid, Sonny Jim, Winston had just reached celebrity status having created the indiscriminate bombing stories in Germany and Moscow gave him anything he asked for.'

Raymond's initial task had been to move around the Polish clubs being set up in Lancashire and elsewhere and try to overturn the tendency of Polish families to adopt British surnames. Winston apparently thought that children growing up in these families would be more likely to accept British history and join in with the flag-waving if they had a British name and he wanted to prevent that.

Raymond was openly critical of the concept and said, 'These families all became pro-British, whether or not they changed their names.'

'So it was not a successful exercise?'

'Winston will tell you it was very successful but I don't think it met any of our aims. Why waste our time on a group of people who are fanatically opposed to communism because of their recent history?'

If James was indiscreet when he was drinking, my new friend Raymond was even more so, and he didn't need a drink. As he talked it occurred to me that these criticisms of official policy might be being made to test my loyalty and consequently I ought to report these indiscretions as soon as possible. On the other hand it was noticeable that both James and Raymond appeared to enjoy a love-hate relationship with Winston. In the circumstances, I never reported any of these comments to Winston or anyone else.

Raymond went on to explain that our new job was simply a natural development of the work at the Polish clubs—it was all to do with immigration. Winston had concluded that what was required was a major influx of people who were not only of a different culture but would have long-term reasons for rejecting the so-called glory attached to British history. Raymond then said, 'So Winston organised the influx of people from the West Indies.'

This statement amazed me and I found myself saying, 'That's bloody silly—how could he have done that?'

Raymond was irritated by my reaction: 'Look, I don't always see eye-to-eye with him, but he did organise it. He used the same tactics he developed during the welfare state project and he definitely caused the influx of West Indians into this country.'

I thought for a moment and then said, 'But I have read that the immigration was necessary because of a labour shortage.'

Raymond looked at me quizzically and said, 'Yes, a chronic labour shortage, because in the welfare state no one wants to work. In a capitalist society it would normally be difficult to imagine a situation where a country cannot produce enough to pay its way and yet has a shortage of labour—but that has happened here in every industry. There's a saying that this country is made of coal and surrounded by fish, therefore it would take a genius to create a shortage of coal and fish. Thanks to the welfare state the British have achieved the near impossible—they not only have a shortage of coal and fish but of everything else. But given those circumstances why would any group of managers deliberately import labour that will also frequent the National Assistance Board rather that the Labour Exchange? Don't you think that responsible managers would have required guarantees of a minimum level of work and minimum skill levels if they had been responsible for the immigration?'

I was still confused and answered his question with another: 'So, are you telling me that this influx of West Indians is all due to Winston's desire to have black people in the country?'

Raymond was annoyed: 'No, that's not what I said—read your bloody history books and listen to what Winston is saying. It's all down to Winston's desire to create a sizeable section of the community that will always be against flag-waving imperialism. The direct ancestors of these immigrants were kidnapped by the British and other Europeans and sold for slavery. So they won't forget it in a hurry and neither will future generations of West Indians who are born here. Once the immigrant population reaches a certain level the British will have to change the way they teach history to children. If future generations in Britain are taught to be ashamed of their history then Winston has won. If you want to prosper in Winston's group then you should consider what makes him tick and you may conclude that it's not necessarily the desire for universal socialism.'

'What the hell do you mean by that, Raymond?'

He shook his head and said, 'Look and hear and you shall learn.' He finished my briefing by explaining that our covert activities during this project were all to do with the immigration issue:

'We are to travel in teams to various parts of the country. Where we go will depend on the level of immigrants moving into the area and the reaction of the locals. Our task is to observe, listen and report back. Winston is looking both for ways in which immigration can be increased and in addition measures to prevent widespread objections by the indigenous population.'

I tried to see the positive side of the situation: 'Well, it appears that Winston has got it all planned out and it might be fun travelling around the country.'

'Fun, Sonny Jim! I hope you still think so next year. I'm glad to say I'm one of five lucky sods who will only enjoy the fun for a couple of weeks because full-time jobs have already been found for us.'

Raymond then looked at me and said, 'So some of us will be around for a few weeks, others a few months, but you might be selling door-to-door for years.'

The thought of working in this business for years depressed me. 'Why do you think that's likely?'

'Good question, Sonny Jim, and the answer is that I can't think of any other job that provides an excuse for a team of people to travel the country in an apparently disorganised manner while earning an income.'

'Why is that essential?'

'Because our lord and master, Winston, is insistent that all of our people should deal honestly with the revenue. He doesn't want the whole organisation to be investigated just because one person is trying to fiddle his tax return. When Winston was told he had to return his tatty carpet recently I thought that he'd be forced to agree because I knew he was so keen to get on with the next phase of this immigration project, but could not do it without funding. Instead his fertile brain clicked into gear and he saw that selling these books would naturally result in people wandering about the country earning their own living. So now we have an ideal cover for our activities. One final thing, Sonny Jim, the company we're working for is in no way aware of our extra activities.'

'Believe it or not, Raymond, I had worked that out for myself, but one thing I don't understand is why you keep calling me Sonny Jim.'

He looked at me a little sheepishly from the other side of the compartment and grinned. 'I have nicknames for everybody and it seemed like a good name for you.'

'Why is that?'

'Oh, the name comes from a book I read a few months back. The central character was a young idealist, but everything went wrong for him.'

'You think I'm an idealist and things will go wrong for me?'

'Well, I'm sure you're an idealist because they wouldn't have burdened us with you if you weren't, but as to how satisfied you'll be with your lot in life depends on your character.'

'Could you elaborate on that point, Raymond?'

For a moment I thought he was going to refuse to answer my question, but then he became very serious: 'When Winston first took me away from my chosen profession I was very annoyed. But then when I saw the success he was having with his misinformation techniques I thought he'd given me a lucky break.'

'Did something go wrong?'

'Yes, you could say that—Winston does not need or want anybody to help him with ideas or the running of the organisation. So our role is that of the pawn on the chessboard or the labourer in the field. You may be able to accept such a role but I find it difficult and it has become very difficult now that the British group in the organisation has become so large.'

The train was coming into a large station, which I assumed must be in London, but it seemed like a good idea to seek further details from my companion while he was in a talkative mood: 'Raymond, I'm sorry to keep asking why, but why does the existence of the British members make your situation worse?'

'That's simple, since we have recruited the British people but can't tell them the real reason for our existence, we the Russian members not only have labouring jobs, we get the worst jobs, the industrial equivalent of lavatory cleaners. Take this crazy venture for example—the real aim of it cannot be disguised. There must be real doubts that any of our British colleagues would accept the nature of this assignment and so the entire team is made up of Russians. If next week Winston needs a dozen people to walk off a cliff, guess who he'll volunteer to do the job?'

There were eleven of us in the team and we were all booked into a large commercial hotel in the Kings Cross area. Having been told that this was to be an all-male and all-Russian affair, I was not entirely surprised to find my classmates Peter, David and Paul in the hotel. I had said goodbye to them about four weeks earlier because their travel arrangements were settled ahead of ours. In the circumstances I was looking forward to hearing about their experiences in Northern Ireland.

I would think it fair to describe my relationship with the individuals in this team during the last few years as one of friendly rivalry. However, I did not think of any of them as close friends. When we met in the hotel bar Peter and David maintained our previous relationship—they smiled, shook hands, said how are you, but then took their drinks over to a small table at the other side of the room. Paul, on the other hand, treated me like a long-lost brother. It quickly became obvious that his relationship with the other two was at a low ebb. During the next hour or so he explained that the change in attitude was due to the fact that he had fallen in love. The other two, and more importantly Winston, were apparently appalled at his lack of professionalism.

Paul was determined to get me on his side. He told me that a few days after arriving in Belfast he had met this beautiful young Irish woman and that it was love at first sight. He said repeatedly, 'They can't expect me to live like a monk—can they?'

I found it odd that this conversation was taking place, as I could not understand why this relationship was so bad. However, I suddenly realised that this apparently childish scenario had been played out shortly before my own unfortunate escapades. As Elaine was also behaving strangely I felt I could understand Winston's attitude towards me a great deal better. I tried both to sympathise and advise:

'Paul, I understand how you feel, hopefully they will not try to stop you seeing this girl, but bearing in mind the amount of time spent training us I think you need to concentrate on the job to begin with.'

My advice was not accepted, he suddenly got up and said, 'I can't get any sense out of anyone here, I'm going to bed.'

✐

We were drinking in a bar set up in a private room and having been left on my own I became aware that most of my colleagues were involved in a heated discussion. Apparently, it was now very rare for the Russian members of the organisation to be alone in a group without their British counterparts, and the opportunity for fact-finding discussions was too good to miss. I would have loved to join in these discussions, but as my standing with Winston was very low I reasoned it would be unwise to get involved in anything that might later be used against me. Accordingly, when the arguments intensified, I reluctantly decided to retire for the night. But then I found that I had been roomed with Paul, at his instigation, and consequently had to listen to his problem all over again. In order to change the subject, I asked him if he had met any of the IRA people in his short stay in Belfast.

He was obviously annoyed at my changing the subject but said, 'We have more people in Belfast than the IRA and none of our efforts has managed to spark them into life. If this crazy job had not come up we'd still have been withdrawn from Ireland.'

'What makes you say that?'

'Why the hell should the IRA people want to kick the British out? In the welfare state they can get dole money for doing nothing—the Republic of Ireland isn't going to give them that.'

With a show of irritation he then put the light out.

I woke early the next morning and to avoid further unrewarding discussions with Paul I dressed quickly and went downstairs. My intention was to get an early breakfast but I discovered I had to wait ten minutes or so for the service to begin. With a little time to kill I decided to look for the private room that we were due to be briefed in. I found the room and could see it was suitable, at least for security purposes, as it was set apart from other rooms by corridors and a back yard. A large wood-and-glass door led to the back yard and as I had the time to spare I decided to open it and satisfy myself that there were no unseen security problems. The door was locked and the key was missing but there were a number of metal coat hangers on the back of the main door. I quickly fashioned a key out of one of the hangers and opened the door. To my amazement, three men were behind the door, Winston and his two bodyguards.

Although Winston was not expected at this briefing, none of us would have been surprised if he had turned up while a session was in progress, because that was the sort of thing we all expected of him. However, meeting him like this was a little unnerving to say the least.

No one said anything for a few seconds, but then noticing that Winston's two companions were both holding guns under their coats, I looked down at the coat hanger and said, 'Mine has got more bullets than yours.'

I felt quite proud that I had handled the situation so far without any obvious show of fear or undue concern, but that was mainly because I realised I was unlikely to be in any danger if Winston was present. Winston spoke next, saying,

'Martin, what are you doing?'

'I am carrying out a security check while waiting for breakfast.'

This seemed to annoy him:

'Security is not your job at this function.'

'I would be ignoring all the training I had been given if I walked into situations without considering the security aspect.'

He had a look of disgust on his face: 'Still the bloody soldier— go and get your breakfast, Martin.'

During breakfast the word quickly spread that Winston would be attending our briefing. As a result we were all sitting down attentively at the appointed hour. James Cameron counted off the people present and then said, 'Winston will get the meeting underway.'

The door opened and Winston and his two minders entered the room. Winston's companions made a point of looking professional and tough and then left.

In an unusually downbeat manner Winston then explained that he had decided to attend this briefing after getting a report of our discussions the night before. This left most of his audience feeling uncomfortable. He continued by saying that something else had occurred that he wished to share with us.

'It is all to do with an odd incident I witnessed this morning. Hopefully you have all met Martin, our newest recruit.'

He pointed in my direction and there was a general murmuring. I was beginning to feel edgy as he went on: 'Before breakfast this morning, Martin decided to do a security check on these premises and eventually he bumped into yours truly and the two gentlemen who have just left the room. He was armed with a coat hanger, which he apparently thought was a gun because he insisted he had greater firepower than the three of us put together.'

The room erupted with laughter and I felt many of them were thinking that everything they had heard about me was true. All I could do was smile ruefully. Given time I might have come up with a suitable response but suddenly Paul said in a loud voice, 'We were trained always to check security.'

I had not mentioned my unexpected meeting with Winston to anyone, but Paul's comments were almost identical to the words I had spoken less than an hour earlier. It was not surprising, therefore, that Winston's gaze moved between Paul and myself and it was inevitable that he would conclude that I had complained to Paul about being ticked off and that we were supporting each other.

The room suddenly went very quiet and then Winston said, 'Yes, Paul, and you were also trained to be mature individuals dedicated to our cause, not spoilt children who sulk continuously at the first setback.'

However bad I had been feeling a moment earlier, Paul's

discomfort was clearly much greater and was there for all to see. Sadly it got worse—much worse.

Winston turned to James and said, 'Will you make sure that Paul and Martin are in different rooms tonight—they both need to be influenced by positive thinkers.'

Winston then flicked his fingers and said, 'That reminds me, the people I report to have just asked that one of our highly trained operatives be sent back to augment their other teams as they have suffered heavy losses recently. I will have to make a decision regarding the lucky person soon now.'

With a forced smile on his face he said, 'Perhaps the honour should go to whoever sells the most books—or the least.'

This time his joke produced a lot less laughter, which I took to indicate that not many people in the room were absolutely certain of their standing in the organisation.

We were expecting to hear the real reason for his visit but Winston decided to move the conversation in a different direction.

'Now, I would like to hear the briefing on how to sell the books, because if I had the time available I think I could outsell the rest of you put together.'

James Cameron intervened at this point: 'Unfortunately, Winston, I think we have to change the schedule for the day. As you know Angus Weir developed the relationship with the book company but he's sick in his room this morning. As it happens I was going to postpone the presentation on selling the books until the late afternoon session to give him time to recover.'

Winston smiled at him. 'So you think the fact that Angus has a hangover is a good excuse for holding up the move to world freedom, do you?'

James had to admit that it was not, to which Winston said, 'Well, you give the briefing, James.'

After a faltering start, during which he was at pains to explain that Angus had only partly briefed him on the subject, James began his explanation: 'We are working for a company based near Ludgate Circus, in London, called the Wavertree Book Company.'

Winston interrupted: 'No, James, Wavertree is the district in Liverpool where you used to live. We are working for the Waverley Book Company.'

There was limited laughter from the audience. Our unwilling lecturer apologised for his slip of the tongue and continued: 'We have two basic products to sell—a set of encyclopaedias called *The Book of Wisdom.*'

Winston corrected this to *The Book of Knowledge.*

Raymond thought he would get involved: 'Is this encyclopaedia anything like *Encyclopaedia Britannica*? If so it will be bloody heavy to carry around.'

This produced more laughter from all concerned and I even saw Paul smile. James said it was a much cheaper encyclopaedia than the one Raymond had mentioned, but added, 'We sell it for something like twenty-four pounds and we make three pounds or perhaps three pounds ten shillings, I'm not sure exactly. It's not heavy because we just carry a special book around with pages from all the different volumes. It's like *Britannica* in one respect though: it's full of imperialistic flag-waving rubbish.'

Winston stood up looking shocked. 'So, we'll be selling books promoting British imperialism—do you expect me to renounce everything I believe in for a three-pound commission?'

James was clearly taken aback and was unsure what to expect next. He almost whispered, 'No, I suppose not.'

Winston said, 'I should think not—but make it three pounds ten shillings and I'm your man.'

After a pause for more laughter, James continued by saying, 'The second product is a collection of large single-volume books written under the flag of the Good Housekeeping Institute. The advantage of this second string to our bow is that unlike *The Book of Knowledge* it can be sold during the day by leaving a copy in government and other offices and asking people to put their name and addresses on a list and leaving a ten bob deposit. The interesting part is that our commission on each of these books is ten bob and as they have to produce a ten bob deposit we get paid immediately. Therefore if we're required to do other work in the evening and

64

don't have time to call on householders we have the opportunity to earn money in the daytime.'

James said he couldn't really provide any more information than that and promptly sat down. Winston thanked him for his efforts but insisted he get Angus into a sober state during the lunch break, so that a fuller presentation could be given in the early afternoon.

Then Winston said, 'Now for the reason I'm here. Which of you would like my job?'

Not surprisingly, there were no volunteers to take over the leadership role.

Winston tried again: 'Let me put it this way, if I suddenly told you I was leaving and young Martin here was taking my place, would you be happy with that?'

Naturally I did not say a word but everyone else did and none of it was complimentary to me.

Winston said, 'Well, summarising all your reactions, you think it would be a disastrous appointment because Martin has none of the experience necessary to do the job. That leads me to the next question. Do any of you have the experience to do the job?'

There was general agreement that there was no one in our group with anything like the experience necessary to replace Winston.

Winston then said, 'When somebody has been doing a unique job for a period of time, then by definition it becomes almost impossible to find anybody with the necessary experience to replace them. Yet last evening several of you were claiming that Comrade Stalin had been in office so long that he must be a dictator. Apparently, someone quoted *The Observer* newspaper as a reliable source for this priceless information. My friends, don't you think it is possible that Comrade Stalin's senior colleagues all recognise the enormous experience he has gained as our leader and are reluctant to lose that experience? Can't you imagine that he must sometimes long to take a rest from all the pressure? I often wish I could take a rest, but the pressure of my much smaller job prevents it—what must it be like for Comrade Stalin?'

There were some very red faces present and during a thirty-minute discussion all concerned seemed genuinely to accept that the criticism of Comrade Stalin was unfounded. Winston brought this discussion to an end by saying, 'You should remember that we are here to change the way the British think, therefore when I am told that the British capitalist press is beginning to enjoy success indoctrinating certain members of this team, then I'm bound to get concerned. We should break for lunch now but please think before you speak on such matters in the future.'

I had not fully taken in the subject matter of last evening's argument and so all this surprised and worried me. It worried me because if some Russian-born operatives felt this way then there was a high risk that one of them, sooner or later, would blab to the British authorities. As I understood it all the people who had gone native so far had left behind promises that they would keep quiet about their past activities, but how long was that likely to continue? Over lunch though I began to realise that there was another cause for concern: which member of our group had reported the offending conversation back to Winston? From their reluctance to talk I could sense that most of my new colleagues were thinking along the same lines.

Angus joined us promptly for the afternoon session. He appeared to be very sheepish and concerned about getting drunk the night before. It was very noticeable that he was reluctant to look anybody directly in the eye. When everyone had sat down James got the session going by saying that Winston would like to say a few more words.

Winston slowly got to his feet and said, 'I am frequently told that I talk too much.'

He paused, probably expecting some laughter, but no one fell into the trap.

He went on, 'Well, I think I talk too much—I frequently find I have to talk a lot to keep everybody's mind on the job.

'I had intended just to listen this afternoon but I heard a comment over lunch and saw some reactions to that comment that makes it necessary for me to open my mouth again. The comment was made by our friend Raymond, who suggested that if we really succeeded in our present task then we might achieve the feat of transferring the population of Africa into Europe. Raymond might have been joking or he may have had some other motive but he certainly got you to move your brains out of first gear and it was obvious that some of you did not like the prospect he raised. I will just say this once and I don't want to find these words repeated at any stage in the future—we have no intention of promoting or allowing this extensive immigration to be repeated in mainland Europe. It will be confined, I repeat confined, to the island containing Wales, Scotland and England. We believe that the level of immigration we envisage is essential if the working people of this island are ever to throw off the shackles of feudalism and capitalism. To put it bluntly they need the benefits of new people, with new cultures and new ways of thinking to untie the locks.'

Winston started to sit down but he was subjected to two interruptions. The first was from Raymond: 'Winston, I would just like to say that I was simply making a joke. I wanted to lighten the negative atmosphere that was ever-present during the lunch break.'

Winston accepted this and acknowledged that it might be beneficial for all concerned in the long run that the comment was made. However, he added to Raymond's acute embarrassment: 'It was yet another instance of the mouth working before the brain got into gear.'

The second interruption was by the delicate-looking Angus, who disappointed me by not having a trace of a Scots accent. Angus was clearly very keen to make his peace with Winston by any means possible. He started by saying, 'As some of you know I have recently come back from a spell with the team in New York that is seeking support for the Catholic cause in Ulster. I can tell you that all the Americans I met are convinced that Britain is an undemocratic feudal society that will never change. All these Americans are appalled that only public school pupils can achieve worthwhile positions in Britain.'

Angus sat down and James stood up and prepared to get the session proper underway.

Then he noticed that Winston was still on his feet and in deep thought. Winston gathered himself and eventually vented real fury at Angus: 'After all the money we have spent on training you, how dare you stand up and spout American propaganda at us.'

Angus looked terrified and confused and started to raise his arms above his head in a pathetic gesture.

Winston did not allow him time to marshal his thoughts. 'Angus, where were you based in New York?'

The answer came back, 'Rye, sir, Rye, New York, sir.'

'Did you live in Rye?'

'No, sir.'

'Why not?'

Angus took a deep breath and said, 'It was too expensive, sir, only the rich can afford to live there.'

Winston sneered: 'Yes, it's expensive to live in Rye, and it's expensive because they and communities all over America like Rye make the cost of attending school high enough to keep the riffraff out. Did you live in the neighbouring borough of Port Chester?'

'No, sir.'

'Why not?'

'Well, it's where the blacks and the dropouts live.'

'Yes, it is, isn't it—so can't you see that America is the least democratic of all the capitalist countries—in this country the poor can at least live in the same town as the bosses. Okay, their kids will go to a different school, but don't believe all that crap about that type of elitism being confined to Britain—the private school system is much more in control of the top positions over there than it is here. Christ, Angus, we send people to capitalist countries to indoctrinate them on a different way of life—the communist way of life. You're in New York for five bloody minutes and they've indoctrinated you!'

With that, Winston stalked out.

Needless to say, James and Angus had a difficult time briefing us during the rest of the day. James concentrated on our activities on the immigration front. He explained that we would operate in teams of two, three or six depending on which part of the country we were operating in. Again he stressed that our task was simple and uncluttered. All we had to do was engage various people in conversation on the immigration issue. Although we would be effectively interviewing them, we had to make it appear that we were indulging in top-of-the-head comments to get a reaction. Therefore although it was essential that each conversation be reported accurately, we should not make notes in front of the people we were talking to. However, a full written report of each interview was essential and had to be completed as soon as possible after the conversation was completed. Angus joined James in a number of play-acting roles to suggest ways in which key individuals such as policemen, postmen and the immigrants might be approached.

On the book-selling front, Angus did provide us with some additional information, but the most memorable thing he said was, 'Remember, if you want to eat you must make sales!'

That night I went to sleep thinking about all the things that had happened over just a few short days. My relationship with Elaine was far from satisfactory, my position and prospects were even less satisfactory, but life around Winston was really interesting.

The next morning we woke to find that Paul had won the short straw on the repatriation front. He was already booked on a flight east and would be back in his homeland in a few days. The general consensus, or at least the one put forward by Peter and David, was that Paul was most suited to a military lifestyle and would be happier in a role where he could fight the capitalist enemy head on. I must say that this impression of Paul surprised me, but I had to accept that Peter and David knew him much better than I did. After breakfast, we split into two teams, one moved into the East End of London and the other set up temporary shop in Birmingham.

I joined James, Raymond, Angus and another man called Robin in East Ham, London. I was pleased to discover that for the first two weeks we were to concentrate solely on the selling aspect of our work. This was very necessary from my point of view because I had just a few pounds to my name when I arrived in London and

I had already been forced to borrow from James to pay the deposit on my boarding house accommodation. Three evenings later I was in very poor spirits, as I had not come remotely close to making a sale. During three concentrated days of selling effort, men, women, children and dogs had chased me from their respective doors without even listening to my sales presentation, and I had a cookery book thrown at me when I tried to leave it in an office. I did not want to appear defeatist but when I found James on his own I described to him some of the aggression I had suffered.

His only comment was, 'Now you know why you were trained in unarmed combat.'

My colleagues eventually took pity on me and pointed out that I had been concentrating in a rather poor area. Their advice to go up-market necessitated a great deal more walking than I had been doing. This was not easy because I chose to put a lot of cookery books out in offices and factories and the books were very heavy. Nevertheless, going up-market soon paid off and by the end of the week I had caught up in terms of sales with most of my colleagues. During that first weekend I received further good news when James said he had managed to get Winston to waive the twenty per cent surcharge on earnings for anyone working on a commission-only basis.

After the first month there were only four of us still operating. By the third month everybody had found other jobs or been assigned to other work, apart from Angus and myself, and we were both still operating in key areas of London. During this period we both earned at a rate far above the national average. When the money eventually started to flow in I treated myself to an expensive suit and then experienced the additional sales benefits from being well dressed. It was not always easy though. After the fifth month we started to travel to other immigration hot spots and sometimes found it difficult to pay our way. On one occasion a Mrs Thomas, who ran a guesthouse close to Cardiff Arms Park, kept our belongings in her kitchen until we had scraped together sufficient deposits to pay for our week's accommodation.

Angus proved an interesting companion on these journeys. In his own words, he was of mixed middle European race—his father originated in Georgia and his mother the Ukraine. He said he had a happy childhood on a farm until the Germans invaded but he then lost contact with his family. At one point he joined the German army but managed to escape with some minor secret information, which he took to the Soviet army. As a reward he was sent on various dangerous escapades to infiltrate the German lines. I had heard many similar stories to this and usually they included great personal heroism, but there was no real reason to doubt him. After the war, he tried without success to find his family. Eventually, on the basis of his war record, he was trained in various forms of espionage and was eventually recruited by Winston on the grounds that he looked very upper-class English.

When Angus told me this, it irritated me that he was clearly proud that Winston thought he had an aristocratic appearance.

I made a point of studying his features from a variety of angles and then said, 'Yes, I can see what he means, you do look like someone who is always getting drunk and doesn't have to get up for work the next day.'

For that, I had to withstand a barrage of peanuts, which only stopped when the landlord of the pub we were in at the time told Angus to stop behaving like a hooligan. The assault almost started again when I said, 'I think that proves the case for the prosecution.' Trying to stay ahead in this childish alcohol-induced one-upmanship game, I then said, 'Anyway, if he gave you the name Angus Weir you ought to look and sound like a Scotsman.'

The answer came back, 'Why should I sound like a Scotsman if I'm supposed to be a bloody Australian?'

If it had not been for this silly discussion, I may never have heard about another of Winston's extraordinary activities.

Angus told me a strange story of how he first met Winston in Moscow in early 1947. At this meeting Winston told him bluntly that although he would like to use him, his English was not good enough. As a result he arranged to send him on a course to improve his speaking voice. Apparently, when Angus finally arrived in Britain in early 1948, Winston was disappointed with the accent he had acquired and said he sounded more like an Australian than an Englishman. But being Winston he immediately thought of a way to use Angus's odd accent to good effect. When, in 1950, he was satisfied that there would be no hiccups with the introduction of the welfare state, Winston took four others, including Angus, for a six-month trip to Australia and New Zealand. During their time there, Winston claimed to be from Eire, Angus was portrayed as an Australian who had spent the period between 1938 and 1948 in the British army and the others were supposed to be Rhodesians. They travelled the Antipodes in various labouring roles. Whenever the opportunity arose they would tell stories about how the British were determined to send the shoddiest of the products they produced to the colonies down under. They claimed that while working on the rebuilding of a bomb-damaged government office in London, they accidentally discovered that the powers that be in Britain believed it was only right that inferior people should get the inferior products. Various well-known British politicians were said to have written memos saying that the rubbish should be sent to Australia and New Zealand. Angus told me that they would frequent a different pub each night telling these stories and the result was often violence when the locals began searching the neighbourhood for stuck-up poms.

Apparently, Winston really enjoyed this activity and he funded it from previous contributions made by Moscow. Then one day his controllers contacted him in Sydney and said they were surprised he had taken so many people on what they described as an extended holiday. Not surprisingly, the venture was brought to an end quickly. However, at the earliest opportunity Winston sent Angus back to Australia to continue the good work and over time he had built up a small team of helpers.

Angus really did seem to dislike Australians and insisted that he regularly pleaded with Winston to let him out of the country as often as possible. He was not looking forward to going back again but told me that he had got a maximum of three further months in the UK and then would be confined to Australia for at least another nine months.

His comments surprised me. 'Angus, I keep reading that the British are queuing up to go to Australia, what's your problem?'

'They may be queuing up to go, but when they get there they'll find that the typical Australian male is a moron who's forever bragging about how tough he is and then screams like a demented schoolgirl when anything goes wrong. In my opinion none of the bastards would last very long in the Soviet Union.'

I thought I could follow his reasoning: 'Let me guess, you think that the discipline and self-control needed in a communist state would be too much for them?'

He looked at me as if he was talking to a small child. 'Are you still a communist?' When I confirmed that I was he smiled and said, 'Ah, the innocence of youth. I'm even less interested in communism than I am in Australia.'

Not for the first time during the year I found a colleague expressing views I could not relate to and in the circumstances I found myself saying, 'Well, why do you do this job?'

The reply surprised me: 'Because Winston wants me to, old son. I don't think he's yet found the answer to the world's troubles, but if there is an answer he'll find it and because of that I will do whatever he asks me to do.'

The comment was made in all seriousness and was yet another indication of Winston's strange power over people. I could not think of a response and the evening came to a rather quiet end. Thinking about it later though, I realised that Winston had a similar hold over me—I was constantly trying to please him so that I could play a more important part in his grand plan.

After the first week or so my telephone conversations with Elaine were becoming increasingly painful. I would ask her if she was well and she would say, 'Oh yes.'

She would repeat my question and I would say, 'Yes, fine.'

I would ask her how the job was and she would say, 'It's okay.'

To try to cheer her up I would tell her that I was making good money and with luck I would get up to Lancashire in a few weeks' time. Then I would tell her how well Winston was doing and that I thought he might succeed in his task in just a few short years.

Each time I called, the response I got back was dull, as if she was not interested in anything I said, and sometimes I found it difficult to believe that this was the bouncy girl I'd grown up with. I began to resent the lost selling time and cost of telephoning her. This was particularly true when very few words were spoken in between inserting the coins. One evening she asked me to call her at the usual time later in the week but gave me a new number. This turned out to be a call box some distance from her flat. Calling her on this number was an improvement because she felt freer to talk but she was obviously very unhappy with life. Her main concern was that she hated the idea of damaging the cotton industry.

At one point she said, 'Martin, it's awful, we're already up against unfair competition and all the mill girls depend on the work to live.'

No matter what I said on this or any other subject I could not cheer her up. A few days later I called Elaine's box but the number was engaged and when I tried again a few minutes later an elderly lady beat me to the box and stayed inside it for fifteen minutes. When I finally got the telephone to myself, Elaine's number just rang and was not answered.

I called the number at her flat each of the next three nights before I managed to contact her. She was very angry with me and I told her that she was being unreasonable. She gave me a new number to call in future, which she said was in a less busy area, and the telephone saga began again without benefit to either party. Inevitably a month later I failed to contact her because her number was engaged. This time we had arranged an alternative and at ten p.m. that evening I called her flat.

Again she was angry: 'If you had called at exactly seven p.m. as we agreed I would have been able to answer it.'

I thought it was about time we stopped the mutual agony. 'Elaine, I don't think we're suited any more, we should stop hurting each other, I don't think I should call you again.'

I heard a little moan. 'Please, Martin, don't desert me—you don't have to love me, but please don't desert me.'

I got as far as saying 'Elaine' but she interrupted me:

'Please ring me on the other number tomorrow night.'

When she picked up the telephone the following night she told me immediately that she was worried that the previous night's conversation was being overheard and so reluctantly had asked me to call again. Before I could say anything at all she said, 'I have had twenty-four hours of hell in case you decided not to call again.' Then she almost whispered: 'Martin, if you don't love me I will understand, but we have to be the very best of friends, contacting each other regularly, because we have no one else in the world.'

I struggled to say anything at all for a few seconds and felt her concern at the other end. Finally, I got it out: 'Elaine, I love you and nothing else really matters, I will do anything you want me to do.'

I was expecting a cheque for over fifty pounds from the book company within two weeks of this eventful conversation and over the next few nights we agreed that I would hire a car and drive north to meet her as soon as I got my hands on the money. I called her every night from then on and our happiness appeared to increase with each call. Elaine even promised to get down to her covert job at the mill.

The dramatic improvement in my relationship with Elaine may have been responsible for my first real contribution to the cause. The day after announcing our love for each other I had approached a West Indian immigrant on the Commercial Road in Stepney with a genuine feeling of goodwill towards all mankind.

'Cheer up, you look sad, I hope you're being treated well.'

Within minutes the man had complained about everything from the weather to the treatment he received from his new neighbours.

'Ah, so you'll soon be on your way home to the sunshine.'

'No, I can't do that, I'm trying to get friends to come over here, so I'm telling them everything is fine, just fine.'

In answer to my question asking why he should tell a lie, he gave three reasons. They were: 'Eventually our families will be better off here, I know the British and most of them will be nice to us, but I would feel a lot happier with more West Indians over here.'

With that he roared with laughter and went on his way.

My report on this meeting led to a complete new activity that was soon being used in other areas apart from immigration. Within weeks of getting my report, Winston and his team had carried out various studies to see how my contact's misleading letters home could be developed to further the organisation's aims. Soon the team was producing fake newspaper cuttings in large quantities and sending them to social clubs and other similar groups around the world. Typically, the articles contained stories of how well the immigrants were doing in their new country. Some stories were attributed to immigrants and others to members of the indigenous population who were apparently happy to welcome them. A variety of themes were used including stories of immigrants who did not want to share their good fortune and so wrote negative letters back to their friends and relatives. Great care was taken to make the articles attributable to small newspapers, which may or may not exist, in small towns around the UK. Often towns like Newport were used, and as there are something like fourteen Newports in the UK the chance of an article being labelled a forgery was rather slim. Obviously, these fake articles were not distributed in the UK. Even so Winston thought that we might get three to six months before the British authorities started to look for the source of these articles. Not that he was concerned, because as he later explained:

'If the British government starts to make an issue of the subject, it will backfire on them because people will assume they're creating the story in order to limit immigration.'

As far as I know, no one ever complained about these fake articles. In any case Winston had another success.

Although it was obvious that I had not seen the potential when writing up the interview with the West Indian I did gain some benefit from the incident. I learned that Winston was researching ways of creating mass media misinformation techniques based on it at about the same time I got my big payment from the book company. In the circumstances I let it be known that I would be concentrating my efforts in Lancashire from then on and no one objected.

Therefore, when I finally called for Elaine and took her for a drive onto the moors I was able to tell her that we were unlikely to be separated in the near future. When I returned her to her flat later that evening she suddenly said, 'Do you think she would approve?'

'Who are you referring to?'

'That bitch?'

'Which bitch?'

'The one at the training school who said I was risking becoming pregnant.'

CHAPTER FIVE

lmost twelve months to the day from when we first arrived in Britain, Elaine was told that a new job had been found for her in a large hospital on the outskirts of Eccles, Manchester. I had been working in the Leigh area on the day she got the news and was waiting for her when she left work for the day. I could see immediately that she was upset and when we were on our own she let rip.

'Our beloved leader has decided that the cotton industry is in terminal decline and no longer needs our services. So he has now turned his attention to our health service. They have found me a new job in a hospital and now I'm supposed to damage an organisation that helps the sick.'

I tried to placate her: 'Perhaps it isn't like that, maybe it's just an ordinary job.'

'You always think I've got it wrong. No, I'm not wrong, Martin, at least six people including all my Russian girlfriends have been found jobs in different hospitals in the region and we're supposed to find evidence damaging to the service. Just so that bloody Winston can use his usual tricks to publicise problems that don't exist and bring gloom and doom to everyone.'

I could see that she was very angry and I was concerned that she might get herself into trouble because of it. I tried to play for time.

'Elaine, you have to accept that there could be some grand plan in Winston's mind. Perhaps he thinks that this tactic will demonstrate to the British people that the welfare state won't work under capitalism. Please promise me that you will be careful in what you do and say in the future.'

She walked on in silence for a while and then said, 'I promise to be careful, but I don't see how damaging something like the health service can bring communism any nearer.'

Three days after starting her new job she greeted me with the comment, 'I think I've solved my problem. I will just concentrate on errors that ought to be corrected. I will do it with enthusiasm and I'm sure that will be enough. If it isn't then that's too bad.'

Three weeks after Elaine started her new job, I obtained a shop-counter sales position with a firm of builders' merchants in Manchester. The change from door-to-door salesman came about in a rather odd way. At about eleven-thirty one night I returned home after an evening at the cinema with Elaine.

As I approached my digs I was aware of a fruity voice coming from a parked car: 'Oh, Your Majesty, do you have a moment for a poor commoner like me?'

I turned to see the unmistakable face of Sid Jones. He was sitting behind the wheel of his car with the window wound down. For the benefit of the elderly couple walking by I said, 'I would be careful if I was you, chummy, the police are hot on drunk drivers around here.'

He laughed and answered, 'Joking isn't going to remove your debt to me.'

I did not appreciate my neighbours being told that I was trying to avoid paying my debts and I made a grab to open the door of his car but it was locked. When I realised that I could not get at him I yelled, 'What debts—what the hell are you talking about?'

'You owe me twenty per cent of your earnings since you came back to my territory—Winston agrees with me, we really ought to tax your earnings from day one the way you have been fleecing the public. But I'm a kind soul, I want twenty per cent of your earnings for the last four weeks.'

With that he started to drive away but then stopped and threw a newspaper at me. He glared through the open window at me: 'We don't have an assignment that would suit a person of your delicate breeding, but you could get yourself a proper job. While you were frequenting the fleshpots of the city, I've read the *Manchester Evening News* from cover to cover. There are plenty of jobs advertised, for prats like you who make out that they're better than they really are.'

As he drove off I started to get angry and decided to go for a short walk to cool down.

During my first year it had been emphasised on a number of occasions that Winston and his senior managers expected me to back down and crawl before Jones. In fact James Cameron and others had gone out of their way to stress that Sid Jones was my superior and I should respect him. My reaction on each occasion I was lectured in this way was that I could never imagine respecting the man and as long as he threw insults at me he would get them back with interest. I realised that I was taking a risk in adopting this attitude but reasoned that each of them would do exactly the same thing if they were unfortunate enough to be in my position. All in all it was a bad relationship and I felt that Winston could either accept that or remove us from the man's control.

This incident made me realise that our careers and future prospects were always going to be at risk because of the silly vendetta with Jones, and I genuinely believed that this situation would not improve even if I went down on my hands and knees and begged forgiveness from the man. Since I had moved back to Lancashire I had not pursued any work with immigrants, therefore alone of Winston's team I was doing nothing to support the drive to create a communist state in Britain. I realised that this was probably Winston's decision but there had to be a strong chance that I was simply being held back by Sid.

Eventually, I came to a decision and next day outlined it to

Elaine. As Sid had suggested I find my own job, my idea was to look for a job that was situated as close as possible to Elaine's workplace, involved roughly identical hours of work and did not require any travel or undue stress. My motive was simple: if we were not in a position to benefit the cause and we had to pay a subsidy, then we should ensure that the jobs were conducive to our enjoying ourselves.

Elaine was in complete agreement. At one point she said, 'If those people just want money out of us then we will have to rethink everything.'

As we talked this over I got the impression that she would have agreed to a complete break from Winston's organisation at this time. To balance the situation I stressed that if we lost touch with Winston and his cronies we would not be in a position to play a part in defeating capitalism. During the next few days we looked for a flat and without telling anyone in the organisation we set up home together in Eccles.

No one objected to Elaine and me living together, but Sid Jones complained bitterly that I had found myself a job that was not beneficial to the organisation. I reminded him and everyone else who wanted to know why I had taken this step that Sid had told me to get a new job because they were unable to find an assignment for me. I half expected that because of this an assignment would be quickly created for me, but it did not happen.

In retaliation, Sid managed initially to involve us in all the organisation's various night-time activities, but this rarely stretched beyond two to three night a week and eventually, after one fortunate incident, our involvement in these escapades almost dried up completely. Most of these after-hours exercises involved us in rent-a-mob-type activities at industrial disputes. One evening a few months after starting our new jobs, a meeting in Blackburn turned unexpectedly violent. I decided I had to get Elaine out of the area as soon as possible and after departing the scene of violence in some haste, we stopped at a nearby pub for light refreshments and entered through the saloon bar. When I went to the bar to order our drinks, I noticed the unmistakable figure of Sid Jones in the public bar, and it was obvious he had been there for some time and had downed a few pints.

We went to a debriefing session the following weekend and were immediately confronted by an irate Sid who snarled, 'Where were you on Wednesday?'

Almost as one, Elaine and I claimed to be involved at the sharp end and added, 'Not like you in the public bar in The Fox and Hounds.'

Sid was visibly shaken. He did not say another word and thankfully during the next ten months he very rarely called upon us to share his evenings.

Elaine maintained contact with two of her Russian girlfriends, Joan and Mavis, during this time. From one of these girls she discovered that Winston was still negotiating on whether or not to return the carpet. In the circumstances we felt we were safer on the fringe of the organisation than at the centre.

For the later part of 1955 and for most of 1956 Elaine and I led a reasonably enjoyable lifestyle. Our respective jobs were by most standards of the day halfway between mundane and outright boring. However, we told each other that we should try to enjoy our work and by making the effort we both made plenty of friends from the various daytime colleagues of our own age. Several of these friends turned out to be avid Manchester United fans and after joining them on the Old Trafford terraces one Saturday afternoon both Elaine and I were permanently hooked. We turned up at most home games and even travelled to away fixtures.

Usually at least two evenings of the week were spent either at the cinema or the theatre and a further two were taken up by either eating in local restaurants or visiting friends. Initially our main problem was having the money to support this lifestyle. Between us we earned just over fifty-three pounds per month gross, but after stoppages we were left with slightly less than forty-three. We were aware that many families had to live on less than that but after paying our subsidy of just over eight pounds and rent on our furnished flat of fifteen, we were usually left with under twenty pounds for the month. This had to cover all our other living costs including travel to and from work. We usually lasted out until payday but never had anything over to put away for a rainy day. Not unnaturally, we both resented paying the subsidy, particularly as it had to be delivered by cash-in-hand once a month to the so-called duty officer. On those occasions when Sid Jones assumed this role I usually had a devil of a job getting a receipt from him. On more than one occasion we both threatened violence during these sessions.

As time went by our attitude to the unfairness of the subsidy hardened but we were not in a position to refuse payment if we wanted to remain at least on the fringes of Winston's grand plan. We were also becoming increasingly troubled by feelings of guilt. Our real friends now were all British and we were worried by the fact that although we were not currently taking an active role, we were still part of an organisation that was dedicated to bringing their country down. We first began seriously to discuss this situation while lying in bed one Sunday morning. Elaine raised the subject by first referring to the football match we had seen the day before and then jokingly adding,

'I hope we never do anything to harm Manchester United.'

We both laughed at this, but then as we talked it became obvious that we were both having doubts about the rights and wrongs of our situation. Over the next hour or so we discussed our feelings much more openly than ever before. We concluded that Britain was no longer the threat that Winston had feared but on the negative side we accepted that we might never succeed in converting the country to communism. From that point on it was a short step to questioning whether or not we were all wasting our time. Before long we were discussing what we would do if the East-West conflict ended and we were free to decide where we wanted to live for the rest of our lives.

In the end we agreed that if what the British newspapers said about the Soviet leadership was true, then we did not want to be a part of the communist system. However, we thought the capitalist press lied on a regular basis about almost everything. Therefore, by what we agreed was a narrow margin we concluded that in the event of a thaw in the cold war we would probably go home even though our homeland would be more foreign to us than Britain.

The next week our landlady unexpectedly brought in people to decorate our flat. This caused us some inconvenience and where possible we tried to eat out. One evening when we were getting ready to go out Elaine approached me with a worried look on her face and put her finger first over my lips and then her own. When we were well away from the flat she produced a small piece of white paper marked with a small green leaf and said, 'The decorators must have accidentally left it behind.'

I studied the paper and then shrugged my shoulders to indicate that I could not see the significance of her remark.

'Don't you remember, the bugging equipment we used during our training school sessions was wrapped in paper like that?'

I could not bring to mind what the packaging looked like, but I had to agree with her next comment.

'We are probably in deep trouble because she only told us about the decorating a few days after our Sunday morning conversation. So we have to accept the possibility that the decorating was done as a cover in order to plant listening devices.'

We did not enjoy our meal at all as we inevitably spent most of the time mulling over the various possibilities raised by finding the paper. At first Elaine thought that there had always been some type of listening device in the flat.

'I've always thought that Mrs Evans is a peculiar woman, I think she probably installed some primitive device in the flat for her own amusement. Then when she heard references to espionage she must have called in British Intelligence.'

Before I could react she had dismissed that theory: 'No, that can't be right, British Intelligence would be unlikely to use Soviet listening devices and even if they did they would not have retained the original Russian wrappings.'

I agreed with her observation. 'Yes, and as we chose the flat ourselves it's very unlikely that Mrs Evans would have known any of Winston's people prior to our moving in. I realise that does not mean that Winston's team are not involved, but I think that if they had doubts about our loyalty they would take the easy way out and give us the Pembridge treatment.'

Elaine grimaced: 'In that case I'm going to assume that it's Mrs E. After all, we must be a fascinating couple to study.'

In the end we decided to begin a slow systematic search for anything that looked like a listening device. This took several weeks of irregular effort but we found nothing. Nevertheless, we had to accept that something might have been concealed by clever decorating techniques. In the circumstances we never again discussed politics indoors.

Elaine and I spent most of our non-working time together, but occasionally only one of us was required for clandestine activities in support of the cause. One night Elaine joined girlfriends on a venture that was quickly called off and they did what all high-spirited girls do in such circumstances—they adjourned to a pub. When she got home, Elaine told me she would like to go for a walk, which I took to mean she had some information to impart. Once we were on the road she began her story:

'Joan was keen to get home and stayed for just a single drink. But Mavis insisted on buying another round and then in confidence started to tell me how we are seen in the organisation. Apparently, the key people now believe that we are both very difficult to work with. No one doubts our loyalty to the group, so that may rule them out as being responsible for the bugging, but there is a widely held view that our training has been wasted because we like the good life too much and are not strong enough mentally. Mavis said that Winston had now accepted that we could not be used in any significant way to benefit the cause.'

The news thoroughly depressed me.

'It sounds as if Sid has been successful.'

'Yes, Mavis has heard various stories of how Sid Jones was in despair trying to get us to accept reasonable discipline. He claimed that all we wanted to do was dress up and go to nightclubs. Mavis says she suffered a similar problem at Sid Jones's hands a few years ago and that's the reason why she passed the information on to me, but she made it clear that she was not prepared to risk openly supporting us.'

According to Mavis, most people in the organisation were amazed that Sid could operate from such a high position when it was clear for all to see that he was intellectually inferior. It was assumed that he must have a special relationship with Winston and if so was virtually fireproof. Nevertheless, to those in the know Mr Jones was being increasingly referred to as Nan, their abbreviation of Neanderthal. On the subject of abbreviations, Mavis told Elaine that everyone was now referring to the organisation as TH, but while the Russians understood it to mean Trojan Hearse, the British thought it meant The Help.

After considering the information we had been given regarding the way we were perceived in TH we decided there was nothing we could do about it. We might just as well carry on enjoying ourselves until an opportunity arose to fight back. In turn, members of the organisation increasingly ignored us and although this did cause us some concern we were also pleased not to have to do as much after-hours work as others. I have to admit that the ideal of a communist world now rarely entered my mind and it was noticeable that Elaine was tending to agree with the Conservatives when watching political discussions. One area where we did disagree however was in our attitude to Winston and his team. I usually argued that Sid Jones was the real problem and that we could enjoy a very rewarding life if only we could get closer to Winston. Elaine made it very clear that she did not share this view.

In the spring of 1957, Elaine and I, and for that matter all the other TH activists in the north of England, were instructed to attend a get-together in Yorkshire. When we got this instruction I pleaded with Elaine to join me in pursuing any opportunity this might provide to get back into Winston's good books. She took some persuading but eventually agreed to support any effort I made.

We were told to make our own way to what turned out to be a very pleasant guesthouse in the Yorkshire Dales. Many of the local guesthouses benefited in this way because almost 100 people had received invitations. Surprisingly, in each case, the accommodation was prepaid.

After spending the night in the guesthouse, our instructions were to make our way to a large hill in a nearby farmer's field. We realised that as the land was private we were not likely to be disturbed by passing hikers and therefore security was unlikely to be a problem. It was nevertheless an extraordinarily risky venture, from a weather point of view, to hold such a meeting in the open air.

It was obvious that somebody, presumably Winston, would address us from the top of the hill and consequently the early risers were seeking vantage points as close to the summit as possible. We saw Sid Jones in one group and naturally made our way to the other side of the hill to be as far away from him as possible.

Suddenly, I noticed James Cameron making his way towards us. He was as pleasant and as effusive as ever, even going as far as raising his hands above his head to register his delight at finding us. After the initial pleasantries, James said, 'Now, you two, I have something important to say.' He then went on and on for several minutes arguing that we must reach some sort of understanding with Sid Jones.

I listened politely for a number of different reasons but Elaine clearly wanted him to shut up. Suddenly, she said, 'I remember you now from the training school—you were the phantom bottom pincher, the Neanderthal bully with the one-track mind.'

James went as red as the proverbial beetroot, and with a higher than usual pitch to his voice he said, 'My dear young lady, I assure you that I have never… .'

He did not get any further because Elaine interrupted: 'I remember it very clearly now. You used to sneak over to where we were playing and pinch our bottoms.'

She tried to continue but then she started to giggle and eventually James realised that Elaine was pulling his leg and that she was doing so because she had not enjoyed his lecture. At that point, Elaine was called over to another giggling session with a group of her girlfriends.

As she left us I felt a little embarrassed and said, 'Please excuse her, James, I'm afraid that like myself she is frustrated at not being at the centre of things.'

To this he just shrugged and said, 'I keep telling you what you must do to improve your prospects in that area but the problem is partly due to not having suitable roles for you.'

I decided to change the subject, because the current one was clearly not going to lead anywhere. 'Well, what have you been doing recently?'

He surprised me with his answer: 'Oh, I've just spent several months in Australia and New Zealand with Winston and Angus.'

I was keen to learn how life was treating my old selling and drinking companion: 'How is Angus, is he enjoying living in Australia any more than he used to?'

James shook his head, thought for a minute and then said, 'I suppose his problem is that the Australians think and behave very differently from the typical Russian.' Then as an afterthought he added, 'But you have to wonder what our activity over there has got to do with promoting world communism.'

He saw my surprised reaction to his comment and partly under his breath murmured, 'Why do I feel the need to utter what should be private thoughts when I'm in your presence, Martin?'

'I hope it's because you feel you can trust me. Perhaps I could trust you with my views in due course.'

He just nodded and added, 'Perhaps so.'

At this point, Elaine rejoined us and to change the subject yet again I asked if they were still promoting the send-them-the-rubbish theme down under.

James said, 'Yes, and a few variations on the theme, which coincidentally will be part of Winston's address today. Winston is very concerned that despite all our efforts the British economy may be about to expand quickly.'

I told James of my surprise that TH was risking this presentation to the vagaries of the British weather.

Without hesitation, James said, 'Oh, don't worry, Winston

managed to get a guarantee that the weather will stay fine until twenty minutes after the meeting breaks up.'

At that moment a woman interrupted James by asking if there was any truth in the rumour that Tweedledum and Tweedledee would be arriving by helicopter.

James answered with one word: 'Possibly.'

Tweedledum and Tweedledee were the TH insiders' current names for Winston's two bodyguards. Later other names such as Pinky and Perky were used, but Bill and Ben or alternatively the flowerpot men eventually became the norm due to the fact that they rarely said anything.

When the lady moved on James said, 'That woman has asked me before about Winston's bodyguards. I wonder if she fancies one of them. If so, she's probably going to be disappointed, they rarely risk their expensive suits if there's rain about.'

Elaine looked at the sky and said, 'I think it's going to rain soon. Who did Winston get the guarantee from?'

James smiled. 'Ah, Elaine, it all depends on who God is and whether or not he reports to Winston.'

Elaine smiled back at him, 'One game all, but be careful—it's my serve next.'

The weather was not looking good but there was no sign of Winston—in fact we could not see anyone moving apart from a shepherd and his dog. The shepherd whistled at the dog and it moved away from him but he continued towards us. When he got to the bottom of the hill he removed his cloak and we all saw that it was Winston. Our leader then went up the hill to rapturous applause carrying two white books.

James said, 'Good grief, it's the Sermon on the Mount.'

For just under two hours, Winston kept us all spellbound. A weak patch of sunshine seemed to form a halo around him as he began his lecture. He started in his usual way with his hands slightly above his head:

'Friends, thank you for coming along today, I hope you enjoyed the accommodation provided.'

There was a murmur of agreement, but after that no one else

uttered a sound until he had completed his talk. After a while it became obvious that his aim was to get the British people present to take actions that they would normally not contemplate and to encourage others to follow their example. His theme was that the benefits of the welfare state were being eroded very quickly due to inflation and that as even more rampant inflation was inevitable over the next five years this would go a long way to halving the benefits that had been so painfully fought for. As an example of the dangers of inflation he announced,

'By the time those of you who are about thirty-five years of age come to retire, the state pension will amount to about one tenth of the average wage.'

As I looked around the assembled faces, I could see that he had total control over his audience and most of them were looking very concerned.

He went on to claim that we had all swallowed the stories put out by the BBC and the national press that inflation benefited no one. At one point he said, 'I believed those stories for a while, because I reasoned that it is surely just as bad for British bosses as it is for British workers if our products are too expensive to sell overseas and foreign products conversely become cheaper in this country. I assumed that the British capitalists must be very concerned about inflation because if the foreigner starts to sell in this country and we cannot sell in his then long-term problems will be created. Given a situation where we are too expensive for their market but they can undercut our prices in this country, then we will also have a problem that we may never be able to correct. However superior our products are now, eventually the situation will change and the foreign products will not only take over the cheaper end of the market, their growth advantages will be so great that they will take over the quality side as well. Therefore manufacturing in this country will not be possible.'

At this point he paused and continued almost shamefacedly: 'But I was wrong, as we all know the larger British companies are already getting products made overseas and this trend will continue. It would appear that their hatred of socialism and their greed is greater than their concern for their country. By getting the product made overseas they can not only ignore the welfare state, they can neutralise it. They are actually putting up their prices for home produced products by more than the inflation they are incurring in order to accelerate the problem. I keep asking myself the question, if by this ruse they increase the cost of a locally produced product now costing the purchaser ten pounds to twenty, in five years' time will they also double the workers' income? Of course not, and no one will expect it because with fewer sales, profit from UK production may be less than it is now. However, they will have halved or more than halved their contributions to the welfare state, and no political party will be in a position to stop them.'

He continued in this vein for a while and introduced a variety of examples aimed at convincing his audience that poverty was staring them all in the face. He looked around him and began the next part of his address with an apology:

'Friends, I'm afraid I have let you down. You joined our organisation in the belief that we were the most likely group to promote the interests of the working-classes, because we don't just talk—we take action. But I have let you down because I just did not expect that so many British bosses would be willing to sell their country and its people down the river out of hatred of their employees and personal greed. I am afraid that if the current trends continue then our people will become the paupers of the western world.'

Then raising his voice he said, 'Many of you will have heard me argue in the past that despite everything we should buy British products whenever possible. I now accept that I was totally wrong in suggesting this. James, Angus and I have recently visited other countries and witnessed first-hand a number of campaigns where the aim is to stop buying the products of companies that treat their workers badly. These campaigns have worked very well and quickly. They effectively forced the manufacturers to re-think their tactics and in virtually all cases this caused them to treat their employees as partners rather than slaves. I am therefore proposing that we take similar action here and do so in the certain knowledge that it will benefit workers, country and bosses in the long run.'

For the next twenty minutes or so he outlined how his scheme would work and emphasised the importance of following the rules he had laid down. Despite his passion for the subject his final comment surprised most of his audience: 'Friends, this action is so important that I am authorising three-quarters of total TH resources to be aimed in this direction until further notice.'

When he'd finished he was given rapturous applause and everybody watched as he made his way back along the path from which he had approached the hill. Just before he disappeared from view he was joined by two dogs that kept close to his heels.

A man close by said, 'That must be Tweedledum and Tweedledee.' From the look on his face he appeared to be convinced that Winston had turned his bodyguards into sheepdogs.

As the crowd slowly started to depart the scene, Elaine and I quickly decided that we would like to be involved in what Winston had termed 'the fair share of the rewards campaign'. Although we knew that Winston's real aim was long-term damage to the British economy and we felt increasingly guilty about damaging our British friends' prospects, we had no problem in getting involved with this campaign. By chance just a few days earlier, Elaine and I had agreed that the British bosses were far too confrontational and that it would be better for all concerned in the long run if someone taught them a short sharp lesson by boycotting their products. Taking part in this campaign would therefore enable us to get closer to TH in the most agreeable way we could imagine. The obvious way to make sure we played a part was to make a plea to James Cameron before he left the site.

We found him still gazing in the direction Winston had taken. Before we could say anything James started on yet another eulogy of Winston: 'Have you ever witnessed anything like that, not a word out of place—and he has given them all a deeply religious experience that will bind them to us for another year or so, at least.'

Then after checking that we were the only people in earshot, he continued, 'I just did not believe that this venture would work and I repeatedly told him so. You would never believe that only a week ago he convinced a group of us that the average person would take more than a lifetime of work to repay his country for the damage inflicted just by buying one foreign car.'

Before we could interrupt, he added, 'And all that rubbish about previously telling people to buy British products—I never heard him say that before and I don't know what sense it would all make to a competent economist. But it does not matter what he said previously, or what sense it makes, they have enjoyed a deep religious experience and will do as he asks.'

When he finally stopped talking about Winston's supreme skills he started to move away.

'Well, we must all be going soon now because Winston's moratorium on the weather will last only a further ten minutes or so.'

We then made our plea to be considered in the plans that were being put together and finally James promised to submit our plea to Winston. However, he took the opportunity to restate his earlier argument: 'I will see what I can do, but our case would be easier to sell if you would be less confrontational when dealing with the Jones man.'

Elaine then surprised me by saying, 'Oh, stop it, James, everybody in TH knows Jones is a Neanderthal.'

James was not pleased with this remark and so I felt I had to intervene: 'I'm sure Elaine is only joking and we will both do whatever we can to improve our relationship with Sid.'

As we left James and began our descent of the hill there was some tension in the air. Elaine broke the silence:

'Can I remind you that we are not married and we live in the twentieth century, therefore you have absolutely no right to play the heavy Victorian husband.'

'Elaine, I am very sorry but you were risking our relationship with the one person we both respect in TH.'

'I respect only people who talk sense.'

'Oh come off it, Elaine, he was trying to help us, but in return for his help you called him a bottom-pincher and kept using the word Neanderthal. Why in hell did you ramble on like that?'

To this last comment Elaine suddenly adopted the manner of a kindergarten teacher addressing a dumb pupil: 'Oh, I see—you don't know—oh, it's simple really, all men are Neanderthals, it's only the female half of the population that has actually adopted civilisation, and science has now proven that the most obvious sign of a Neanderthal is the bottom-pincher.'

I sensed that Elaine was sorry that she had reacted to James in the way she had but she was nevertheless preening herself on her last comments. I then reacted in a way that I was soon to regret. I suddenly stopped and let out a groan. Elaine was initially concerned that I may be ill, but I continued by acting out a scene I had witnessed at the cinema relating to the first movements of Frankenstein's monster. My final movements from this scene involved raising my right arm above my head, my thumb and forefinger twitching and a maniacal look appearing on my face. Elaine played her part well. She flung her handbag away and ran down the lane and around a farmhouse with the palms of her hands in mock protection of her bottom. I followed with twitching fingers and demented expression still in place.

As we rounded the farmhouse we ran into the main body of Winston's audience, which unfortunately for us had taken a different route down the hill. Thinking back on this incident, which has always been a painful experience, I think one or two people must have laughed. Most, however, were far from amused and I will always remember one woman saying, 'How could they behave like that after such a moving experience?'

Sid Jones had not been in the group that witnessed our embarrassment, but he would learn of it soon enough. It took us about five minutes to find Elaine's handbag and shortly after that the heavens opened. By the time we got indoors again we were completely soaked and thoroughly depressed. Quite clearly, our standing with the TH hierarchy would be even more difficult from now on.

After thinking over the situation for a few days we decided to fight back in every way we could. Shortly before I was due to pay our subsidy the next month we composed a letter to Winston.

Rather than pick out the individual incidents that had alienated us we simply assured him of our loyalty and pleaded for a chance to take part in his new campaign. My initial thought was to pass the letter over only if Sid was not the duty officer. Elaine thought that a better tactic was to pass it to our enemy anyway and say it was personal for Winston and if we did not get a reply we would keep writing to him. Her view was that Sid would not dare to hold anything back from Winston. If he did we would repeat the request through the next duty officer and Winston would want to know why the first one did not get through.

I accepted Elaine's reasoning and accordingly, when a few days later I found myself paying Sid the subsidy, I passed the sealed letter over and said, 'It's not for you, it's personal and private for Winston.'

He simply smiled and replied, 'You've come up in the world, haven't you, writing letters to the boss.'

I smiled back and said, 'Letters sometimes got lost in the post so we'll keep writing in this way until we get an answer and provide the time and date of previous letters each time.'

He smiled again. 'Oh, I'm sure Winston will be delighted to swap letters with you.' As I turned to leave he added, 'I understand you got a big rise—have you increased the subsidy?'

In reply, I told him that it was a small cost-of-living increment to my meagre salary and it did not come into effect until the following month. His reaction to that was, 'That's fine, BP, increase the amount next month.'

I did not ask why he called me BP but he told me anyway: 'It stands for Bottom Pincher.' He emphasised the two words as much as he could by spelling them.

I smiled as broadly as I could in return and said, 'You could strain your brain by attempting to spell words like that—don't forget to deliver my letter.'

We did not get an answer prior to making the next subsidy payment and so we repeated the letter and indicated that the original had been given by hand to Sid Jones the month before. We were still enjoying our social life but Elaine was getting bored with her work and so added to the letter a comment that she would soon look for a new job. The subsidy and new letter were passed to a different duty officer but again we got no response by the time the next payment was due. We were sick of everything to do with the organisation by now and on several occasions during this period I was close to agreeing when Elaine raised the possibility of escaping from TH's clutches. I resisted the final break because I was secretly still hopeful of playing an important part in Winston's future plans. But Elaine's hesitation was more basic. She wanted a proper wedding with all our friends present and she realised that was possible only if we stayed with TH.

The next month we repeated the second letter and Elaine then said she wanted to add a request that she be put in touch with Stephen. I convinced her that she should not refer to him as her brother and finally she agreed that it would be better if the letter appeared to come from me. Eventually I penned what I hoped was a pleasant note that indicated our contact with Stephen would be a one-off. I claimed that we had recently been talking about our time in the orphanage and we had both realised for the first time in adulthood how much we owed the fellow. Therefore we felt we ought to make up for lost time by writing and thanking him for looking after us.

I had not been entirely on the level with Sid regarding my salary increase. I had been given a substantial 17.5 per cent rise, not the meagre cost-of-living increase I claimed, but I had been truthful regarding when it took effect. Although originally employed on the trade counter, about six months after joining the company I had helped out with some admin work. As a result of my efforts, my boss decided almost immediately that I would be better employed in the finance department and at the point of writing our third letter to Winston I had just completed my first four months as a trainee accountant. The job and the salary increase had been made on the condition that I trained by correspondence course to be an accountant with the Institute of Cost and Works Accountants. I had readily agreed to this but decided not to inform TH until I was close to qualifying as an accountant. Now that Sid knew that I had got a salary increase, I assumed there was a fair chance he would also know of the conditions attached to it. In the circumstances I added a further note to our third letter saying how much I was looking forward to qualifying as an accountant and assuming this could be very valuable to Winston and his team. Finally we explained that we would like to get married and asked for Winston's agreement.

About three days after submitting this third letter, I received what I thought was a business call at my place of work. After getting me to confirm my identity a young lady passed me over to Winston. I was at first a little worried, but he was not unpleasant. He asked me to grab a pen and paper and take down some information. In quick succession he barked out the information. In a nutshell it went like this:

'Don't send me any more letters—we have found a very important job locally for Elaine and she will be hearing about it soon—write a letter to Stephen and we will make sure he gets it—continue as a trainee accountant but we will also have an important job for you in about three months—we will talk about your marriage after that.'

As I expected, Elaine was delighted with the news and we jointly concluded that our working life was about to get an awful lot better. In one telephone call we appeared to have got everything we wanted and we had demonstrated that we did not have to bow down before Sid Jones.

We carefully penned a letter to Stephen. In it we said we hoped he was well and enjoying life and that when he left us we were too young to realise that we would not see him again. We wanted him to know how much we appreciated his efforts to look after us. We asked him to write and acknowledge the letter but we gave no indication that we ever expected to meet him again. Common sense indicated that the letter would never get to him if we were to ask for anything more than a single written response. Finally we told him we were happy and we hoped he was. A month later we were told that the letter had been despatched by the usual means but it might take three months or so to get to him. We were also warned that even if he replied immediately it might take a further three months for his response to get to us.

In late November Elaine was called to an interview for an administrative role at the headquarters of the United Kingdom Atomic Energy Authority (UKAEA) at Risley, near Warrington. The ease with which she got the job suggested to me that TH or some other Soviet unit had managed to infiltrate the organisation and someone had managed to pull a few strings. When I mentioned this to Elaine she insisted she had got the job purely on charm and intellect.

Although Risley was only fourteen miles or so from our flat we realised that Elaine could not possibly commute that distance and eventually we found a new flat in a village called Culcheth, which housed a lot of the Risley employees. I tried cycling to work but January in Lancashire is cold and wet—not a good time to be exposed to the elements. Eventually, I solved the problem by acquiring an old motorbike. I asked that the cost of running the motorbike be deducted from our monthly subsidy and was delighted and surprised when this was agreed. As the weather improved we used the ageing transport for trips to Southport, but it also meant that TH could use us more frequently on errands and evening rent-a-mob activities.

In August 1958 I was found a new job and immediately I had mixed feelings about it. I was a salesman again and therefore I thought the chance to qualify as an accountant was probably gone. I had already signed up for the first year with the institute and they had a time limit of six years in which to complete the course. As the course normally took a minimum of three years to complete, it was a question of getting back into a suitable accounting role within three years or forget about becoming an accountant. I sat the first year exams before leaving the builders' merchants firm and was later delighted when informed that I had passed in all the papers.

The new job did have one major benefit—my new company car. To the motor trade, the car was simply an Austin Cambridge A50. To Elaine and me it was an object of great beauty that gave us enormous pleasure and enabled us to travel in relative luxury at someone else's expense. The car had only a few miles on the clock when we got it but it had first been registered a couple of years earlier. When I went to my first sales meeting all the other salesmen were green with envy because they were all driving around in the much more functional and cheaper Morris 1000 estate cars. The sales manager explained to them all that the purchase had been a mistake but I would be permitted to use it for a few months until an economical opportunity arose to make a change. This satisfied most of them but I had no doubt that we had planted someone in the organisation and that the mistake had been made for a reason. In the circumstances I would have bet anyone five pounds that I would still have it in twelve months' time.

The reason for the more up-market car soon became obvious. Winston needed someone who was reasonably presentable to chauffeur people around the north of England and to deliver important packages related to the campaign to depress the sale of British-made goods. In both roles, the organisation I was representing had to appear highly reputable. In the circumstances I was back to wearing high quality suits and I was told I had been given a British car to emphasise the fact that our organisation was a patriotic one.

The job that TH and I were being paid for was a simple one. It involved me calling on wholesale chemists and multiple grocers across most of Lancashire and selling a relatively new range of soft tissue paper handkerchiefs and toilet rolls. I had to record my orders and produce a daily report but I found that I could get by by just spending around half the working day on this activity. At first I found that with effort I could fit in this work and that of TH with some ease and still have time to spend with Elaine during most evenings and weekends. Gradually, however, the TH work increased to such an extent that Elaine started to accuse me of deliberately staying away from her.

The TH campaigns took many forms but they were all based on Winston's communication skills and his understanding and experience of using them for negative purposes. For example, one of the most successful of his tricks was based on his reasoning that in any large manufacturing concern, mistakes would sometimes occur that were potentially very dangerous or at least could be interpreted as dangerous by a devious mind. He therefore had his operatives frequent public houses and pretend to be workers from different departments of the company. Comments such as 'I hear there was another near disaster in the paint shop this week' would normally be sufficient to get employees talking about real near misses that had occurred in the past.

For each incident the TH people would find the names and addresses of at least half a dozen people who were either directly involved or who had spoken openly about it. A citizen claiming to care about public safety then submitted these names and the related story to a local newspaper. Hundreds of manufacturing workers were contacted in this way over the years. They never expected the contact and were amazed at how the journalist got hold of their name. Even if they objected to being named these people almost always confirmed that the incident took place and almost invariably damaging articles resulted.

We picked up copies of editions containing such articles and then other TH colleagues and I would take them to local newspapers in other parts of the country demanding that our fellow local citizens also be warned of the problems mentioned.

I pretended to be calm but irate during the first few minutes in each newspaper office. I always refused to give my name and address and left as quickly as I could, taking care to park my car some distance from the office I was visiting, to avoid the risk that someone would record the car's number. One of my colleagues had his car traced when a young journalist followed him out of the newspaper office and he had a difficult time explaining to his company why the subject was important enough to take him miles away from his sales territory. When this happened we asked that hire cars be used to minimise the risk and embarrassment.

Winston laughed at this suggestion, saying, 'I prefer the way we are currently doing it because it means that your British companies are not only paying your salary and keeping TH solvent, they are also paying all the direct and indirect costs of the exercise. Fascinating, isn't it—British companies paying us to damage the British economy.'

CHAPTER
SIX

By the end of 1959 the strain of doing two jobs at the same time was beginning to affect me. The company paying my salary got a new sales manager who not unreasonably concluded that even though I had obtained some useful orders in the past, I might do even better if I made a few more sales calls. Up to this point I had assumed that someone must have been protecting me from such criticism because I had to admit that it was certainly justified. I took this advice to heart and informed the TH duty officer that I would have to scale down my clandestine efforts in the future. Much to my surprise, two nights later I received a telephone call from Winston.

'I understand that you want to reduce your efforts on our behalf?'

'Yes, I have been doing so much of your work during the daytime that I haven't been keeping up to my sales targets.'

I was even more surprised by his next comment:

'We have been squeezing extra effort from you recently, but it will cease immediately. I don't know whether you both realise it but your girlfriend's job at Risley is an important one and indicates that we are satisfied that she is finally on the right track. After the chaos you caused when you first arrived here we were forced to put you both through a long apprenticeship for security reasons. As far as I'm concerned you have also completed your apprenticeship and a career opportunity will be found for you shortly.'

I just had time to say thank-you before the line went dead.

When I put the phone down Elaine said, 'That was the big bad wolf, wasn't it?'

I confirmed that her suspicions were correct and repeated Winston's words to her, adding, 'That's really good news, isn't it?'

'Good news, Martin, I sometimes think you're besotted with Winston. Can't you see that he's trying to separate us?'

However, when the letter informing me of an interview for the new job arrived we were both initially delighted that it was with the UKAEA and consequently I would be working in the same group of buildings as Elaine.

After she had thought about it for a few minutes though I heard Elaine saying, 'I wonder what the catch is?'

The role was in financial administration and, in theory, should present me with an excellent opportunity to continue my accountancy studies. However, when I was shown a copy of the typed CV that had been submitted on my behalf it was clear that it clashed in almost every way with the one I had previously submitted to the Institute of Cost and Works Accountants. Obviously, I was not going to be able to continue my studies through that organisation.

The interviews at Risley were relatively straightforward and it was obvious that someone had eased my path to joining this apparently important body. Losing the company car meant that we were slightly worse off than before but any negative feelings this aroused were soon overshadowed by a message from Winston suggesting that Elaine and I should get married as soon as possible.

That evening I heard Elaine talking to one of her Russian girlfriends on the telephone: 'I think that God probably tipped Winston off that I am already pregnant—but I fooled both of them.'

The ceremony was arranged for the first Saturday in April and we were allowed to invite some of our British friends from previous jobs. Much to our delight James Cameron and his wife accepted our invitation to attend the ceremony. Winston sent a message saying he was otherwise engaged but that he had asked Sid Jones to attend in his place. This development did not really surprise us and we secretly hoped that our uninvited guest would get drunk and make a fool of himself.

One evening Sid was waiting for us as we left Risley for the flat in Culcheth. He thanked us for the invitation and said, 'I will bypass the ceremony, that sort of thing doesn't interest me, I'll just turn up for the meal and drinks.'

Again we were not surprised at that statement but the next announcement did come as a surprise and was to have a lasting effect on us.

'Winston says don't allow anyone to take photographs at the wedding and make sure that photographs do not appear in any newspaper. Winston thinks you should tell all your friends that they should send the money they would have spent on photographing you to their favourite charity.'

Elaine, in particular, did not welcome this news but we could see that it made some sense and we had to go along with it. The wedding ceremony itself went ahead without too many problems. We had to remind a couple of guests at the last moment about the no photographs rule, but most people took our request as a quirky variation on the no flowers requests, which were quite common at the time.

James Cameron's wife, Helen, turned out to be pretty red-haired young woman from the Highlands of Scotland. She was excessively shy at first but when she began to feel more at ease she began to talk in the manner of an intelligent schoolgirl just out of a convent. Her innocence was a delight, she told us she had visited Aberdeen only twice in her life and she thought it was too big. Then she explained how exciting it was travelling down on the train to Manchester. She was at pains to warn Elaine not to let me become a stockbroker in London. She explained that James was a stockbroker and she rarely got to see him. Obviously, she had no idea what James's real role in life was. I watched James as she warned Elaine about the stockbroker's lifestyle and I could see that it hurt him deeply to mislead her.

Later, when he and I were alone at the hotel bar, I took a risk and said, 'We may both have to do a runner at some stage for the sake of our wives.'

He did not look up at me but simply said, 'If you're suggesting we do it together, then I think you should know I believe that would more than double the risk.'

I was just wondering how to react to this comment when Sid Jones suddenly announced over a microphone that he would like to tell some of his jokes. Those who knew him groaned out loud but it did not put him off. To his credit, he kept the stories clean or at least cleanish, but this was to be expected in a way because he was repeating the stories in the form he sent them to comedians or the media.

For the last few months Elaine and I had both heard references to the centre. This was a relatively new headquarters for TH and we were aware that Sid Jones and other senior people were now based there. However, no one had bothered to tell us where in the country it was located.

One of the jokes told at our little party by Sid went something like this: 'Did you hear about the Birmingham fellow who got beaten up in a racist attack?'

As with all such jokes the answer came back, 'No, what happened?'

Sid then delivered the punchline: 'He got beaten up by two white fellows.'

This joke got a good response because there had been frequent recent media comment on the number of West Indian immigrants settling in Birmingham. To me though the joke was a very strong indication that the centre was in Birmingham because Sid gave the impression that he was telling it as a Birmingham resident. James was still at my side as I said, 'So the centre is in Birmingham.'

James answered with a nod and added, 'That's very perceptive of you but don't say you know.'

I wanted to ask him why I should not divulge this knowledge but our wives joined us and the opportunity never arose again.

About three months after we were married, I received a pleasant surprise while delivering the month's subsidy to the duty officer. He told me that they had received a special letter for me and that it would be delivered by hand that evening. Elaine and I waited as patiently as we could and about eight p.m. the letter was duly delivered by Mavis, one of Elaine's girlfriends. Mavis was clearly surprised when we simply thanked her for her trouble but declined to invite her in for refreshments. We explained our lack of common courtesy on this occasion by claiming that we thought the letter would require us to do a great deal of work that evening and we would need to start as soon as possible.

Ever since we had first written to Stephen we had accepted that there was only a fifty-fifty chance of getting an answer and that if we did get one there would be a similar risk that it would be a fake. Obviously then our first thoughts after reading the letter through were to decide if our old friend Stephen was the author. About an hour after first reading it we concluded that it was almost certainly written by our friend. The letter made a number of references to situations that would have been difficult for anyone else to know. The most striking of these was a reference to a boy in our orphanage who was about five years older than Stephen. Elaine and I had both forgotten about this boy's existence but we did remember him after reading the letter. Apparently he made contact with Stephen about four years ago and told him he had discovered they were brothers. It was fortunate for Stephen that he did because he was helping to bring some normality back to his life. After leaving the training school, Stephen had attended an ordinary school and then joined the army. Very early in his army career he had been involved in an accident and as a result had the lower part of his left leg amputated. The letter went on to describe a life given over to alcohol and drugs but there was some optimism based largely on his brother's support. The letter contained an apology for not saying goodbye to us all those years ago. He gave the reason as embarrassment because he had failed the course. His concluding remarks suggested that he thought we lived in Moscow and for that reason we would not be able to write any further letters to each other.

Over the next few days Elaine and I discussed the letter frequently. There were aspects of Stephen's life that made us feel very sad, but Elaine now believed she had been wrong in thinking that Stephen was her brother.

Her final comment on this episode summed up both our feelings: 'When all things are considered I'm glad we made the effort to contact Stephen, but there is no point in trying to pursue it any further.'

During the remainder of 1959 through to the middle of 1961 we settled down as a typical married couple. With two salaries we were relatively well off despite the continuing aggravation of having to pay the TH subsidy. By the end of 1961 we managed to put together the £200 deposit necessary to get a mortgage on a modest new house in Culcheth and six months later we were also the proud owners of a battered old car. During this period our after-hours TH activities were at a low level and because we thought that this would only be a temporary lull, we took the opportunity to enjoy life while we could.

One day towards the end of 1962, an incident occurred that was to change our standing within TH dramatically. Up to this point we had been given only minor responsibility within the TH organisation, despite Winston's earlier statement that we had both completed our apprenticeship. Our situation had both positive and negative connotations—while we enjoyed the extra time and freedom this provided, we did not enjoy the second-rate implications that went with it. This was well illustrated by the fact that neither Elaine nor I was under any pressure from TH to do anything other than our nine-to-five jobs at Risley.

Although someone had gone to a great deal of trouble to plant us in the UKAEA offices it now appeared to us that the main reason had been to keep us occupied and to provide an income for TH via the subsidy. When we had asked if we should be looking for secret information we were told that as Risley was just the head office it was unlikely there would be anything useful to steal, but if we were tempted to take something, we should be very careful.

According to in-house rumour, security at Risley was a bit like the curate's egg—very good in parts but probably rotten in other areas. A week before the Christmas break I noticed that certain people whom I understood to have special security clearance were looking very stressed and overworked. Quite by chance I entered a copying area to do some work and was told by one of the stressed individuals that he was almost finished and that I could have access to the machine in about two to three minutes. In the circumstances I waited my turn at a distance, as he seemed anxious that I did not get too close. Then one of his superiors came in and asked him to do something in another office. At the same time he promised to finish the work the first man had been doing. A young girl then came in with a tray of coffee and biscuits for the second man, who thanked her and asked that the tray be placed on another table for him. The girl was a little flustered and in meeting his request she placed the tray over the last batch of papers that the first man had copied and then left the room.

I watched in total fascination while the second man first looked for the final batch of copies that he believed had been made and then went through the copying process again after assuming that his colleague had not completed the task. He drank his coffee without moving the tray and when he left, I carried out the small amount of copying work that I had to do. Then I removed the copies from under the tray, put blank paper over the top and my own originals and copies on top of them. Then I went into a sort of rest area close by for a drink of water and made a point of looking through my work. I realised that I might be being observed, so although no one else was nearby I expressed a certain amount of irritation when I came to the blank copies. After looking around, I placed these and the presumably secret documents underneath them among a pile of papers in an office that was not being used due to the illness of the executive who normally resided there. After that I returned to my work station.

My emotions were very mixed at this point. The more courageous parts of my make-up demanded that I collect the copies immediately and put them in my briefcase to take home at the end of the working day. Other voices told me that the whole thing was too risky and warned that undue bravado might result in Elaine and me spending years in solitary confinement. The negative voices eventually won through on the grounds that the incident I had witnessed might have been a deliberate set-up. At the earliest opportunity I contacted Elaine, reported what had happened and explained my conclusions to her. To my relief she agreed with my decision and for a while I relaxed.

Late in the day, however, my more courageous emotions started to gain ground again. I thought of the credibility we should earn just by taking private and confidential information from the building—even if the value was not all that great. In these changed circumstances I approached the office where I had left the copies. To my horror, they were no longer there. I was in a depressed mood when my working day finished and I was then even more depressed and irritated when contrary to our normal arrangement, I found that Elaine had made her own way home.

Elaine had been in the house for just a few minutes when I got home and was making a pot of tea. The first thing she said when I entered the kitchen was,

'Do you think I'm getting fat?' She then unzipped her dress to reveal the photocopied documents that had caused me so much worry during the day. Her explanation for taking it upon herself to remove the documents was, 'You clearly did not want to do it and I thought the opportunity was too good to miss.' She also left the building on her own so that I would not be blamed if she had been caught.

I was now consumed by two other emotions—a great love for this crazy young woman and a strong desire to get the documents off the premises as soon as possible. Fortunately, a call to TH resulted in one of the Russian girls arriving at our house at midnight. She was very nervous and left very quickly. We were also very nervous and did not get much sleep that night as we half expected that every car noise indicated the imminent arrival of British Intelligence.

We were both still apprehensive when we reported for work the next day and we found it difficult to concentrate on our jobs.

However, there was not the slightest indication from any source that anything was wrong and we celebrated that evening by booking a table at a top restaurant in Manchester. My own apprehension lasted to some extent for another few days but by the end of the Christmas holidays we were very confident we had got away with it.

A further two weeks went by without any feedback from TH. By this time we had resigned ourselves to the distinct possibility that the information we had acquired was worthless. Nevertheless, we had the satisfaction of knowing that our actions had demonstrated that we wanted to be part of the team and we were alive to any opportunity that might arise. Then another of Elaine's Russian girlfriends appeared at our home one evening and told us that two senior TH people would like to talk to us the following night in Manchester. A room had been booked for this purpose at the Grand Hotel in the city centre but first we were to join our hosts for dinner at the new Piccadilly Restaurant. On hearing this news we naturally began to feel that the information we had provided must have been valuable.

However, this impression was soon changed when our visitor made her final comments, which were: 'They particularly want to know why you thought the information was sufficiently valuable to take the risks you took?'

We spent some time later that evening mulling over what our answer should be to this question. As we talked we naturally reshaped the events in order to demonstrate our total dedication to TH and to maximise the impression of our courage and skill.

We arrived at the restaurant on time and were ushered to a table made out for four. After a delay of about five minutes our hosts appeared. We had not really expected one of them to be Winston because the messenger had emphasised two senior TH people, and no one else in TH was as senior as Winston.

Nevertheless, a smiling Winston appeared and was accompanied by a large plump man. Winston shook hands with both of us and said, 'I would like you to meet my good friend Abraham Stern, the well-known American investment banker.'

Despite this introduction, Elaine and I both realised that we were in the presence of a senior Russian agent.

Stern monopolised the conversation over dinner. Most of the time he talked generally about the great opportunities that existed in different parts of the world for experienced and enterprising husband-and-wife teams. Initially we gave only guarded responses to these comments because it was obvious that he was suggesting that we move to another country and we could not judge whether Winston was in favour of such a move—more importantly, *we* were not.

Eventually, I used a ploy that we had discussed the night before. Looking directly at Stern, I said, 'We are both ambitious and keen to make the most of our careers. We both accept that we got off to a bad start when we first arrived here but we believe we are learning fast.'

Then switching my gaze between the two of them I made what I hoped would be a successful pitch for senior roles within Winston's group: 'Although we have spent most of the last few years on the sidelines we're both amazed at the achievements of Winston's team and our only ambition in life is to assist him on a more full-time basis.'

Stern seemed reluctant to accept this statement at first but finally he nodded and concentrated on the remainder of his meal. When we reached the room chosen for our meeting at the Grand Hotel we were met by the now familiar sight of Winston's two bodyguards who quickly confirmed that the security had been checked out. When the door closed behind us we could see at least a dozen bottles of champagne and yet there were only four of us.

Both Winston and Stern then boomed out the word, 'Congratulations!'

We were both stunned and delighted, but then Stern made a grab for Elaine, which she easily avoided and she also quickly resisted his plea for her to sit on his knee. When he made another playful grab at her I moved to restrain him, but Winston stepped in front of me and informed Stern that he had to play by what he termed 'the local rules'. Stern finally roared with laughter and nodded his acceptance of Winston's decision.

Over the next hour or so we were informed that the information we had obtained was extremely valuable. It had nothing to do with secret formulas, and if it had the value would have been limited because, as Stern explained, 'We already know how to make bombs.'

Instead the documents contained key elements of the project management process in the setting up and maintenance of nuclear facilities. Furthermore, there were passages explaining key differences in the procedures adopted by both the British and the Americans. Mr Stern confirmed that the information was not only helpful to the Soviet engineers, but also chillingly added, 'It will also help us to create problems in Western installations.'

As the champagne flowed, Elaine and I embellished the planning necessary to bring about our coup. Not to be outdone, Winston informed Stern that he had recognised special skills in Elaine and me and that was why he had chosen us to work at Risley. Mischievously, he informed Stern, 'As you have heard from our two young colleagues here we have achieved miracles recently in undermining the British economy, so we thought we should spare some time to assist your struggling organisation.'

Stern answered this with a weak smile and started to say something in response. However, he had clearly consumed too much alcohol and decided to go to sleep instead.

Winston then ushered us to the door. He gave us twenty pounds and said, 'Spend this on a taxi home, and don't worry—you'll stay in my team for the foreseeable future.'

On the way home I felt on top of the world but I could sense that Elaine had mixed feelings on the outcome of our night out. When I asked her what the problem was, she replied, 'I just have a funny feeling in the pit of my stomach when I think about working closer to Winston.'

The next evening we were contacted directly by Winston via the telephone. He kept it short and to the point. 'I'm very pleased with the way that meeting developed. I promise that you'll be involved in senior roles from now on and you'll not be directly responsible to Sid Jones. But leave it to me to give that news to Sid—okay?'

I agreed to this request and then asked for an explanation for something that had surprised me.

'Winston, I was amazed that we were joined at dinner by a senior man from Moscow. I presume this means you've returned the carpet.'

I heard a chuckle at the other end when he answered, 'No, we're still negotiating on the final destination of the carpet or whatever it is, but both sides recognise that we must still talk because we need each other and our aims are the same.'

Before I could say anything else he moved the conversation on. 'During the next six to twelve months you should continue your work at Risley. This is a direct request from Stern because Moscow believes there is a reasonable chance you might accidentally pick up more valuable information. Obviously this will limit the amount of work you do for me. But it's essential that you do play senior roles for me because otherwise Moscow will be very keen from now on to use you in a different sphere of influence. So the way for you both to delay such a move is by doing good work on a continual basis.'

Surprisingly, he then added, 'Can you take any more good news?' When I assured him we could he said, 'Much to my surprise, Stern told me this morning that Moscow will make a substantial single payment to the TH coffers as a result of your efforts at Risley. Honest man that I am I have decided to authorise the return of your last two years' subsidies as soon as we get the money.'

Elaine had not spoken to Winston and as I therefore needed to relay his comments to her we decided to go for a walk and take in the local pub on the way. I was extremely happy about everything apart from the threat of being transferred to another country. We decided that if that ever became a real possibility then we would need to make alternative arrangements. Come what may, we were, by this time, determined to stay in Britain.

We reached that conclusion while we were in the pub, but I was not prepared for Elaine's next conclusion, which she reached while we were walking home: 'We stay in Britain—so that means we can start a family immediately.'

The idea of starting a family terrified me. If, as seemed very likely, we had at some stage to consider escaping from the TH sphere of influence then it would be doubly difficult with a baby in tow. I remembered James Cameron's words on this subject and the prospect did not appeal to me at all. Over the next few days Elaine and I discussed very little apart from starting a family. Our views were directly opposed and we both thought the other was being unreasonable.

A week after our meeting with Winston and Stern we were called to a meeting at the Birmingham headquarters. To my surprise Elaine was still sulking and refused to make the trip and in the circumstances I was forced to make ill-health excuses for her. Winston was upset by her absence but our stock was still clearly in the ascendancy and he confined himself to making me promise that she would see a doctor. He next told me that he had some bad news.

'I recently agreed the basis of a deal to return my carpet and I sent James Cameron to Moscow to thrash out some of the finer points. He was expected back today and was going to be involved in our discussions. But just a few hours ago I got a message from the bastards saying that they had decided to use James in another part of the world and he would not be returning to the UK.'

Winston was silent for a moment but then added, 'It's probably my fault for rubbing up Stern the wrong way. I told him he could not have Elaine or yourself, so he has grabbed James.'

I was shocked and appalled by this news and I found myself asking one question after another as they occurred to me, without giving him the chance to answer any of them properly.

Winston was clearly irritated by my barrage of questions, most of which related to James's wife. His reaction was to say, 'James married the woman without consent and for that reason he will have to live with it, because he certainly will not be allowed to contact her.'

Thinking that it might be possible to get him to agree to some sort of message being passed to Helen, I said, 'That's a pity, Mrs Cameron will probably die wondering what happened to her husband.'

His response indicated that his attitude was unlikely to soften: 'She won't be the first woman to suffer that predicament. As she understood he was visiting New York, she'll probably assume he met some film star or some other floozy.'

I could see that he was not intending to take any action that would ease Helen Cameron's worries and was probably again thinking that emotionally I was unsuited to a senior role. In an attempt to deal with both these problems, I thought up an elaborate lie: 'Winston, I admit that I'm sorry for James and his wife, but I'm also concerned about our security. I don't think you have met Helen Cameron because as I understand it, the first contact she had with TH personnel was at our wedding. Despite having the appearance and conversation of a young girl, I gained the impression that she was highly intelligent. I would imagine that a few days after she expected him back she'll begin talking to the various investment houses, which would be unfortunate, and after that I'd expect her to retrace her steps to our wedding and start making enquiries.'

Winston studied me for a while and then said, 'Martin, you may be a real help to me after all. I'll get our American operation to come up with some story that keeps her off our backs until you complete your task at Risley—after that it won't matter so much.'

I nodded and left the matter there. I may have made the situation worse for Helen by prolonging hope but it was obvious I could not expect anything further from Winston. I did, however, make a mental promise to myself that if I ever escaped the TH web, I would find Helen and tell her that James had not deserted her.

Later that day, I was told that the various duties that James had previously performed would gradually come under my wing and within eighteen months or so we should think of relocating to the Birmingham area. Of more importance I would no longer pay the subsidy and in addition a special bank account would be set up for me to reward me for special services. I was then told that the likes of Sid Jones had considerable pension monies already salted away in this manner. I have to admit that I was pleased with this news because it worried both Elaine and me that we were always struggling to live on our net income and were putting nothing away for the proverbial rainy day. It did immediately cross my mind that a system that rewarded the senior people at the expense of the rank and file could hardly be termed communism, but I quickly dismissed the idea from my mind. As a final point Winston made it clear that Elaine would still be subject to the subsidy until a new role had been agreed with her.

When I returned with my news Elaine put a rather different interpretation on events from mine. When I had told her everything I knew about the kidnap of James, I concluded with the words, 'That's a clear warning that we should not start a family at this time.'

'Rubbish, Martin, it makes it imperative that we start a family immediately.'

Our son Andrew was born in early December that year. He turned out to be a splendid little chap.

In the period leading up to Andrew's birth our lives and careers both turned somersaults. Initially, I found that Winston was confiding in me more and more. I had almost unrestricted access to the centre and began to feel that I was making a significant contribution to the cause. I still had a full-time job at Risley but I was spending about ten hours a week away from home on TH business. From this lofty position I could see the effect that the TH activities were having on both the British economy and the British way of life. One weekend I tried to explain to Elaine how effective the various activities were, and I must have done so with a certain amount of pride in my voice.

She listened for a while and then said, 'Do you realise what you're saying?'

Before I could answer, she snarled, 'We have committed ourselves to this country—this is the place where we want to bring up our children, and now you're proud to be trying to destroy it.'

I felt a little silly about my earlier comments but I was also beginning to feel that my situation was in a way quite hopeless. I was never going to find the right balance in my various activities.

Elaine was not always so unreasonable—at other times she agreed that we were in a very difficult position and frequently used a typical Lancashire expression to explain our predicament: 'We can't do right for doing wrong.'

She waited impatiently for an interview for her promotion, but the call never came. When I chased Winston on this issue he simply said Elaine would have to wait until some suitable part-time activity arose. He reminded me that it would need to be part-time because Moscow was expecting us to keep our eyes skinned for further opportunities at Risley. This seemed reasonable to me, but when I made this point to Elaine, she accused me of not caring about her career because I was doing well. She then reminded me that she had been the one 'that had pinched the secret papers'.

During the first few months following my promotion I began to see different sides of Winston. While he gloried in the fact that his efforts had devastated the British nation and the British people, he did modestly admit that the TH team had considerable help from other sources. When he first made this point during a heavy drinking session, I assumed he was referring to other activities sponsored by Moscow, but in fact he was referring to British organisations and institutions. The most help he thought came from the Labour Party. He argued that Labour politicians pursued policies that were very obviously damaging to the long-term health of the nation simply because it was the easiest way to get at the establishment.

He also acknowledged considerable help from the legal profession, which he argued had dramatically increased the crime rate for their own good. He kept a record of the number of murders in the UK in every year after World War II. In addition he recorded the total number of police and the total number of lawyers practising in each of these years. From this he was able to demonstrate that the murders and other serious crimes increased at a steady rate, the police numbers remained steady or fell, while the number of lawyers increased dramatically. He argued that it was all a great wheeze.

'Think about it—a significant number of MPs from all parties are lawyers, so they pass laws making it more difficult to get convictions and so ensure that the legal profession will always prosper. I reckon that by the end of the century it will be very difficult to keep anyone in prison for any length of time.'

Winston had regular question-and-answer sessions with his senior staff and we all enjoyed them, though our leader did almost all the talking. When one of my colleagues had the temerity to argue that our task would be much easier if only some country would just invade Britain, Winston tore this argument to shreds in a very aggressive manner and I drove home that evening with Winston's words still ringing in my ears.

'Basically,' he said, 'we have to hope no one attacks this country for a few years yet, because that might cause the people to unite as they did in 1939. In wartime everyone is a member of the club and in theory everyone shares the benefits of working together. In peacetime the workers realise that the benefits are not coming their way and they are easier for us to manipulate. If the British were subjected to another invasion threat they would also stop the influx of people from different cultures. Both the working-classes and our great cause benefit from this influx of cultures because their presence in large numbers will ultimately prevent the British government from indulging in any form of flag-waving based on the notion of being British. No, we don't need external help when we're all doing so well from inside the Trojan Hearse.'

When it was clearly apparent that Elaine was pregnant, I informed Winston at the earliest opportunity. He looked quite deflated when I explained that we would have a child in about four and a half months' time. His attitude towards me changed almost immediately and he asked two questions.

The first was, 'Let me guess, it was an accident and it is now too late to do anything about it—is that right?'

I confirmed that he was right.

His second question was, 'How should I explain to Moscow that our bright new stars have reverted to type and had an accident?'

I simply raised my palms in the air and said I was sorry.

His final comment on that occasion was, 'Go home to your pregnant wife, Martin.'

Elaine took the normal maternity leave for the birth and initially intended to go back to work about six months later, but she never did return to work. Despite giving birth easily and being completely overjoyed with her new baby she did experience some severe bouts of depression. Her doctor put this down to a minor case of post-natal depression, but we both realised it was most likely due to the apparent hopelessness of our position. Ever since I had informed Winston of the pregnancy we had been reduced to our former low-life role in the scheme of things. The special bank account was not actioned and the full subsidy at twenty per cent was required from our salaries. However, the worst effect of our fall from grace was that we fell under the direct control again of Sid Jones.

We had not seen much of Sid for a while, but now his bulky figure appeared frequently on our doorstep with demands for assistance in some way. When it became clear that Elaine was not well enough to return to her paid job, the TH people made sure that she was fully occupied by inundating her with administrative work of all types. When we could get out of the house for any length of time we could often be seen pushing a pram along the streets of Leigh or Warrington. Sometimes we were discussing the shopping we had to do, but mostly our conversation was confined to trying to find a way to escape the TH clutches. During these conversations I was very much aware that Elaine was in favour of a complete break and would take the necessary risks. For a variety of reasons, however, I could not bring myself to take this final step. When I tried to analyse my reasons I realised that the loss of the opportunity of playing a leading role on the world's stage was the most important factor.

About six months after Andrew was born Elaine wrote to our employers saying that as she was unlikely ever to be fit enough to return to work—she was forced to tender her resignation. Her salary had in any case recently been stopped, so the news did not come as a great surprise to anyone at Risley. The TH duty officer took the news calmly when I delivered the following month's subsidy, but a few days later we received a message informing both Elaine and me to meet Winston in Birmingham.

We travelled by train from Warrington and were met at the station by our old colleague Peter. He was reasonably friendly but then saw that we had Andrew with us.

'Why did you bring your baby with you?'

I could have anticipated Elaine's reaction: 'Because, dear Peter, there was no one we could leave him with. I know it's awfully difficult for you men to understand this, but babies have to be cared for.'

In truth though we had not looked for a babysitter, as we were very nervous about the implications involved in being summoned to Birmingham and were wary of being separated. Peter deposited us in a hotel room close to the station and said Winston would be along shortly. We waited almost two hours, feeling more nervous with every passing minute. We were both loath to say very much in case the room had been bugged but eventually we ran the bath taps full on, and assuming this would cause problems with any bugging device we reassured each other that Winston was delaying his entry in order to make us nervous.

Eventually, Winston made his entrance, and he also asked why we had brought the baby along. But as he had done many times before he carried on talking without waiting for an answer. 'I am very disappointed by your lack of commitment to our cause. Your irresponsible attitude has finally convinced me that you should not be considered for major roles within the organisation. In future you will be involved in only minor activities.'

He looked like a father telling his children how disappointed he was with their school reports. Then he said, 'So I suppose you've got what you've been looking for. You will have to pay the subsidy and will have to do some work for us in your spare time, but you can develop your own lives and find your own jobs in the future.'

He paused slightly, but before we could say anything, he added, 'In the normal course of events I would not have bothered to meet you at this time. However, I am afraid there is a strong chance that British Intelligence are on to you, or at least getting close to you, and in the circumstances it's important that you take the correct action at this time for all our sakes.'

We both started to say that there must be some mistake because we could not see how the British authorities could trace us due to the time that had elapsed since we obtained the documents from Risley.

Winston reassured us on that point: 'No, I accept that. Moscow has admitted that some action they took has let the cat out of the bag. For reasons that they have not explained their slip-up pinpointed Risley as the most likely source of the leak. They want to know whether any special security activity has got underway at Risley within the last two weeks.'

I would have preferred not to have added to Elaine's worries at that time but as I had gone into detail while we were on the train to Birmingham about a major security exercise I had witnessed the previous week, I could not disguise the fact. After I had given him a brief report on what I had seen, I found myself saying, 'Winston, what do you think we should do?'

He studied us both in turn and replied, 'It is unlikely you will come under suspicion in the short term, so it would be stupid to draw attention to yourselves by leaving too quickly. Nevertheless, Martin, I think you should resign in about four months' time using the perfectly valid excuse that your wife is ill and needs to move south to be close to her mother.'

CHAPTER
SEVEN

We sold up and left the north of England at the end of 1964. By then house prices had increased sharply due to the almost permanently high inflation levels that had existed since we bought our property in Culcheth. Consequently, after paying off the mortgage we had nearly £500 over, which we assumed would be sufficient for a deposit on a modest property in the south. However, the TH people insisted that we make several moves both north and south of London before settling anywhere on a permanent basis. This they deemed was necessary so that they could be sure that British Intelligence was not on our trail. We could hardly disagree with these tactics, but unfortunately it resulted in nine months of expensive living in rented accommodation during which time I could not find anything but the occasional temporary job to ease our financial problems.

The net result was that our intended deposit all but dwindled away and by the time TH agreed that we could settle down there was no alternative available to us but rented accommodation. During this period I was very concerned for Elaine. It was difficult leaving our friends and even more difficult dealing with a young baby on a hand-to-mouth basis in less than satisfactory accommodation. At first she was in a state of almost continual despair. Gradually, however, her resolve to win through and enjoy a normal life became stronger, but it was disconcerting to see that her determination was fed almost entirely by a hatred of Winston and all he stood for. At one stage I thought this anger and hatred would be damaging to her health. I tried to calm her down.

'Elaine, love, don't get too angry. In a way, Winston and his team are in the same trap we're in. Winston may be thinking that he has taken the only action open to him and may be expecting and hoping that our training will enable us to come up smelling of roses.'

There was silence for a moment and then she said, 'I appear to have married a bloody fool. You should be thinking about what your hero has done to us and in particular about the damage he and his people are doing to the country we now call home.'

'Elaine, you should perhaps be thinking about the traitorous comments that you now make on a regular basis.'

My last remark resulted in a strained silence that lasted almost an hour. After that, I could not stand the unpleasantness any longer and tried to apologise.

She interrupted my apology by saying, 'No, you have a point and I think it's suggested a solution to our problem.'

'Oh, good, what is the solution?'

'It's the obvious one. We go to British Intelligence, tell them everything and throw ourselves on their mercy. I think we should do that tomorrow morning.'

I did not hesitate for long: 'If that's what you want to do, Elaine, I'll come with you. If nothing else it will bring the uncertainty to an end and no other alternative comes remotely close to achieving that.'

We opened our last remaining half-bottle of wine to celebrate our momentous decision. A little while later, however, I found her in tears.

As I approached she said, 'It's a rotten idea. They'll put us in prison for years and we have a baby to look after.'

We spent the rest of the evening trying to work out Plan B.

Suddenly Elaine said, 'I'm not going to worry any more. It's finally dawned on me that once you get a good job we'll be in a position to escape from Winston's clutches and I'm certain that you'll get a good job soon.'

I was very pleased that she should have such confidence in me, but I had not the slightest idea how I would achieve these aims. Although I never told her this, my dream of a better life lay in the hope that one day soon Winston would invite us back into his senior team. I had only a brief time in the TH senior ranks but I had enjoyed every minute of it and would have grabbed the opportunity to return with both hands if it ever surfaced again.

While struggling to find temporary work I was constantly reminded of just how difficult it was going to be to find a worthwhile permanent job without either a background of work experience or professional qualifications. Common sense and TH demanded that I did not refer to specific experience obtained in previous years, therefore it was becoming increasingly obvious that I needed to invent past experience and qualifications. One of the temporary jobs I had taken during our travels in early 1965 was in the personnel department of a large finance house. After working there a short time, this temporary job gave me the opportunity to climb a few steps on the ladder to success.

To get into the good books of the personnel manager, I put in a few hours unpaid work one evening in order to clear a backlog of work. As I hoped, he made a point of thanking me for my efforts the next morning and promised that if a suitable permanent job became available in the next few months he would contact me. In the course of the conversation I made a carefully rehearsed offer: 'Would you like me to begin checking the qualifications and experience claims made by the people you're proposing to take on in the current recruitment drive?'

He smiled and said, 'When you become more experienced in personnel work you will discover that it's not practical or necessary to take up references for all new recruits.'

Further questioning convinced me that normal practice in industry was to check only ten to fifteen per cent of CVs. The candidates most likely to get their CVs checked out were those who claimed the most impressive qualifications or had senior positions in not very well known companies.

Over the next few days I created a number of CVs to suit a small range of advertised jobs that I thought were not only interesting but would also enable me to earn the most money in the short term. In doing so I gave myself a minor external university degree and an even more minor professional qualification. It was some time before I could use one of these CVs to apply for a permanent position, because the TH people had insisted on my changing my name from Martin Reeves, but for some reason they disagreed internally on what it should be changed to. Eventually it was agreed that I would become Mark Rogers from now on and that Elaine would change her Christian name to Elizabeth. As soon as this was finalised I began looking for jobs close to Hemel Hempstead. The TH people thought that this new town was an ideal place for us to live because hordes of people were moving into it from all over the UK and elsewhere. It was therefore an ideal location in which to hide away from prying eyes.

Using one of my special CVs I obtained a sales and marketing position in the late autumn of 1965, with a medium sized manufacturing company close to Hemel Hempstead. This company provided a car and this enabled us to improve our lifestyle enormously. About twelve months later I was surprised to be summoned by Winston. It turned out that he was concerned about my wife's lax attitude to security. Much to my surprise he recounted three instances where she had made what he termed dangerous mistakes. Two of these involved introducing herself as Elaine instead of Elizabeth. I promised to stress to her the danger she was putting us all under and he left it at that. I was pleased he had issued the warning in a friendly way but realised that the real reason for the visit was to inform us that we were constantly under observation by TH personnel.

Just prior to dismissing me he said, 'Martin, I think you should be congratulated on breaking all the sales records in your company and introducing so many excellent new marketing schemes.'

I was a little embarrassed by his comments and said, 'I'm sorry, I don't know where you got that information from, I've done well but nothing like as well as you think I have.'

He just laughed and said, 'You never learn, do you? I'm saying that after twelve months in any job I would make no more than six telephone calls to get my employer's biggest competitor chasing me with offers to double my salary.'

'How would you do that, Winston?'

'Our usual techniques—what else is necessary?'

It took me rather more than six calls and nearly six months to do it and I got only a twenty per cent increase. Nevertheless, following the TH system of manipulating both people and circumstances, I did manage to convince a large competitor that they should offer me a job. One way I achieved this was by going into major outlets away from my own sales territory that stocked our main competitor's goods. I always made sure I was talking to the senior person in the outlet and I always paid cash. Then, when I was collecting the goods, I claimed that I was surprised they were selling so much of our competitor's product. When I was asked why, I explained that I had an old school friend who was a salesman for the company in North London and he had told me that his sales had suffered enormously since a new salesman called Mark Rogers had joined the competition. According to the unwritten Winston manual you have only to do this six times to reach your goal, if it is done with the right flair and zest. In other words you convince the person you are talking to that they will win brownie points by immediately informing the competitor company. But I did it at least a dozen times just to be sure.

Two years later, in mid-1968, some similar techniques contributed to my getting a position as senior marketing consultant with one of the major accountancy-based management consultancies. I was now doing very well financially and we began to think of buying a high-quality property. Eventually, in early 1970, we did take out a large mortgage to get such a property. It took us a long time to make this decision, because in doing so we were effectively tying ourselves for life to TH, which in turn meant continuing to pay the subsidy, which had now reached almost eighty pounds per month. However, to escape now would not only mean that we would be on the run with a young child but in my mid- to late-thirties I would have to start yet another career and we would lose the money invested in the house.

This problem had been continuously in our thoughts ever since I had found my first job in Hemel Hempstead. At that very point Elaine and I realised that I ought to be able to create a CV for any suitable job anywhere in the country. Therefore, that would have been the ideal time to make our escape. The reason we did not was the same reason we had now bought the house—a lady called Mary Maher.

Soon after we first established ourselves in Hemel Hempstead, Elaine had the idea that if she could find a crèche close by then she might be able to get a part-time job and thereby help in getting us back on our feet. When she made enquiries she was told about Mary, who sometimes took in children for an hour or so each day. Mary was married to a relatively senior civil servant called John. She also had a good job on a freelance basis working from home. Therefore, she did not need the money, but she was unable to have children of her own and so helping young mothers in this way presumably satisfied some inner emotional needs.

Elaine's need for part-time work was soon satisfied when Mary subcontracted work out to her. The two women became very close friends and soon young Andrew was spending more time with Mary than he was with me. At various times I found myself getting irritated by this situation, particularly when after he learned to talk he invariably greeted me by telling me what he had done with Auntie Mary during the day. Inevitably, I found myself in John Maher's presence on a regular basis during leisure hours. Normally such meetings with family friends would be very pleasant occasions, but John Maher had a remarkable ability to bore me in a way that I had not experienced before. One day in 1968 I got the chance to join a local golf club. Elaine told Mary, who told John and he also decided to join the club. As we were both learners it was natural we should play together, but I soon found myself searching for excuses for missing our strolls around the course (as he put it). One day just after I had made the best putt I had ever achieved and was walking eagerly towards the next tee-off point, he asked me to define marketing.

In late 1969 John received a further promotion, which provided him with an office of his own well away from his subordinates. Elaine thought I was being very unkind when I said his subordinates must have organised it. This promotion set John and Mary on a quest for a better house and in due course Mary reported that they had found one on a new executive estate. A few days later, I arrived home to find a very excited Elaine telling me that another super house was being erected next door to Mary's. I never did get John's opinion on the matter, but Mary, Elaine and Andrew were all very happy when we all moved in.

Elaine's friendship with Mary and my considerably improved career prospects therefore conspired to keep us within the TH sphere of influence. There was, however, another reason for staying put and that was the possible disbanding of TH. Although we had only occasional contact with Winston and his team, we did hear the odd whisper in the late 1960s that the struggle was coming to an end and that we had won. In one way I thought this sounded very strange as the chance of Britain being converted to communism was clearly less likely now than in any of the previous post-war years. On the other hand, I had long accepted that I enjoyed the capitalist trappings and it would have been difficult for me now to plead for a communist state. On the assumption that the logic of the situation had occurred to Winston and his team, I thought that the winding down of TH might be completed in just a few months or years.

Towards the end of 1970 Winston invited me to pre-Christmas drinks with his senior team. As Elaine was not invited I told her it was a men-only session.

Her reaction to this was, 'So, apart from all his other faults, he's also a bloody chauvinist.'

Winston and his team had taken a private room in one of central London's newest wine bars. The first thing I noticed was that the TH management team, or at least those present, had shrunk to just eleven including Winston himself. The second feature of note was that, apart from Winston, I knew only four of them. The now very Australian-sounding Angus was back permanently as

Winston's number two, a position he clearly relished. My old school colleagues Peter and David were well into a drinking binge by the time I arrived and with them was Sid Jones. The presence of Mr Jones was in some ways surprising because all the other people present were, as far as I could tell, Russian-born.

As I got involved in their discussions I began to be less surprised by Sid's involvement as all the talk was that from now on they were working to build up their pensions. My long-term enemy was now a plump, slow-moving creature in late middle-age, but he tried very hard to be friendly.

After making a little speech in which he thanked everybody for their efforts during the year, Winston took me to one side and nodded towards Sid. 'I noticed you were surprised to see Sid. You should know that he's now aware that the rest of us are Russians, but it makes no difference to him. He would lose a considerable sum of money, which he has worked very hard to accumulate over the years, if he shopped us—so don't worry, there's no chance of that happening.'

I did not want to make any sort of comment positive or negative about Sid, so I just nodded and changed the subject by saying, 'I see Angus finally escaped from Australia.'

Winston then enthused for almost ten minutes about how successful the TH campaign had been in both Australia and New Zealand. His eyes were glazed as he started his explanation: 'I first got the idea for the campaign down under from reading about the American War of Independence. Apparently the vast majority of colonists involved in the revolution considered themselves to be loyal British subjects right up to the time the British government refused to grant them representation in the British parliament. When that mistake was made they became violently anti-British to the last man and woman. I assumed that the Australians and New Zealanders would react in the same way if I could manufacture problems and blame them on the British people or government.'

As he recounted the successes they had achieved on the other side of the world, I got the distinct impression that Winston's personal hatred of the British went deeper than the simple desire to convert the country into a communist state. He then told me that he had withdrawn Angus and his team because the job was done.

'Britain will have to join the Common Market soon and that will be the last straw to both the Australians and the New Zealanders—they will feel deserted, because we've been telling them that the poms were planning to desert them.'

Having heard of these successes from his own lips, I reacted positively: 'Winston, I am pleased it has worked out so well for you.'

In response to my comment he just gave me a quizzical look. Then as if to counteract what he clearly assumed to be a sarcastic and untrue compliment he added, 'Anyway, I needed a good number two because after I lost James Cameron and you let me down I've suffered from too many inexperienced helpers.'

Perhaps unwisely, I tried to take advantage of the situation: 'I've always regretted what happened, Winston, and would really like another chance in your core team.'

He just stared at me for a moment and not wanting to lose the opportunity, I added, 'I might be able to help in other ways, because I now have something of a reputation as a finder of both legal and illegal money-making schemes.'

He seemed surprised at this and said, 'Well, let's talk about it in the new year sometime, and in the meantime as a gesture of seasonal goodwill you're excused from paying the subsidy until we meet again.'

I had been intending to ask him why his team was talking about the imminent winding down of TH but Angus called him over and I did not get the chance. Nevertheless, I drove home thinking that 1971 could be the start of something really big. I had an excellent career and now I suddenly had the prospect of earning extra from TH for perhaps a few years until it was wound up.

CHAPTER EIGHT

January went by and so did February and March and I did not hear from Winston. His silence did not concern me too much because I had been struggling to complete an extensive study of the UK meat industry for a major client and the demands of a new house did not allow me too much leisure time. In addition not having to pay the subsidy and meet up with TH personnel at least once a month provided some consolation for being ignored by Winston.

Early in April, however, I got a call from him. He was terse and to the point and instructed me to meet him at a hotel in the Midlands at nine a.m. the following morning. I started to tell him that I had an important meeting in London at that time, but he just said, 'Be there, your life depends on it.'

I did not take this threat literally but all things considered I realised I had no option but to obey. Consequently, I made excuses to my business contacts and duly met Winston at the time and place he requested. When I first saw him, I almost failed to recognise him. He had obviously been ill and he confirmed as much in his first words to me. Then he started to look around the lounge of the hotel we were in. I could see his bodyguards out of the corner of my eye and asked, 'Are you looking for Pinky and Perky.'

He laughed and said, 'You're out of date, everyone calls them Bill and Ben or the flowerpot men now.'

Then he told me that the lounge was too crowded and he went off to book a private room.

Once we had settled down in the room, he began his story. 'I have been very ill. I was rushed into hospital in January with a problem that the medics insist is due to my passion for whisky. In theory, I have fully recovered but it must be obvious to you that I ought to take it easy for a few months. But I can't take it easy at all because we have a major problem. In my absence Angus took over and made some very serious errors. The first was to give the TH team the impression that the winding up of the organisation was imminent.'

He stopped talking when he saw the look of surprise on my face: 'I see you did not know anything about it but most of the others did.'

'No, Winston, that's not correct, I had already heard that TH would be disbanding prior to our last meeting in December.'

The effect of my words on Winston was startling.

He suddenly screamed out at the top of his voice, 'Jesus Christ— Holy mother of Moses, I don't deserve this!'

He looked as if he was going to collapse and I tried to get him to a chair but then I had to move quickly to open the door because it was about to come off its hinges. His henchmen burst into the room armed to the teeth and I had to move at my top speed to avoid a wild lunge from one of them.

Fortunately, Winston was quick to react and shouted, 'Calm down, all of you—calm down.'

Inside the room we had calmed down but outside it I could hear the sounds of panic. I rushed over to close the door but because of the serious damage done I had difficulty closing it.

Reacting quickly, Winston ushered his bodyguards out and said, 'Tell the hotel management that you tried to break the door down when you thought you heard someone shouting fire. Give the manager fifty pounds for the damage caused and say I will confirm your story.'

After giving a rambling explanation to the hotel management a still shaken Winston waited until we were alone and then said, 'Explain to me in detail what you heard about the winding down of TH and when you heard it.'

'In truth, Winston, I heard only brief references to the subject and the first would have been around October or November.'

'Did Angus tell you?'

'No, it was just part of a conversation several of the team were having when I joined them on one occasion.'

This news depressed Winston even more: how could Angus have been so stupid—how could the rest of them be so stupid? He sat back in his chair and was silent for a while.

When he looked as if he'd recovered I took the opportunity to satisfy my inflamed curiosity. 'So it's not true then that you intend to disband TH?'

The response was enlightening: 'Yes, it's true, the British will never be a threat on a global basis again and they will never again be able to threaten their neighbours, so effectively the job is complete, but that's no reason to risk all our lives.'

I tried to interrupt but he would not let me.

'It's one thing to close the operation down, but where does that leave you and me and the rest of the team?'

I was enormously pleased to hear that the assignment was completed and we could, at long last, look forward to a normal life. As a result, I ignored his 'where does that leave us' question and instead started to heap praise on him and the organisation he'd created.

'Winston, as far as I am concerned you have earned your place in history. Almost single-handedly you have brought this nation to its knees.'

'Thank you for your kind words, Mark. I accept them even though we both know that for the rest of us the demise of TH will leave a hole in our lives, whereas for you and your wife it's the end of a nightmare—you'll accept that, I'm sure.'

I couldn't deny it:

'Yes, but that's because we were excluded from your core team and had to create separate careers. You and the others will now be able to do that.'

He grinned at me. 'Perhaps some of the others will look for new careers but I would prefer a long and happy retirement. But before you get too carried away with success and happiness, you need to understand certain things. The first is that we in TH succeeded only because the British politicians allowed us to. When I started my activities over here I expected the fight would be long and hard because I assumed the government here would manipulate the media to fight back, but they have done nothing to stop us.'

Then almost as an afterthought he added, 'I am convinced that somewhere in the British government or establishment there is a major group that supports our aims and that they know of our existence.'

I was so surprised by this last comment that for a moment I could not think what to say. Before I could question him further he said, 'Close your mouth, Mark, you look like a goldfish. I have not told anyone else of my fears in that area but if both the Russians and certain British connections know of our existence then that dramatically increases the risk we run in our daily work. That by itself is an incentive to stop as soon as we can.'

After the first shock of hearing about what I assumed to be a communist cell within the British government, I decided it was probably the figment of a sick and worried man's imagination. However, I could see that if Winston believed that such an organisation existed then it would provide him with an incentive to disband TH sooner rather than later, and so I was not about to challenge his view. He was thoughtful for a moment or two and then said,

'Now is probably not the right time to discuss the British government's assistance. In the circumstances I want you to forget my reference to their involvement, do you understand?'

Then he returned to his original theme. 'All right, we disband TH, but what do we do then? Our original sponsors in Moscow have disowned us so our people have nowhere to go. We would all become virtual paupers whether or not we returned home to Russia.'

The only answer, he argued, was to build up what we had been calling pension funds, so that our people could relax in reasonable comfort somewhere and at least obtain a degree of benefit from the enormous efforts they'd made over the years.

'Some of our people have got reasonable pots of money, but nowhere near enough to retire. I think all our efforts for say two to three years should be put behind creating these well deserved pensions and then we can all go our separate ways confident we have enough money to do whatever we want to do. In most cases that will mean escaping from this country and I would suggest you get your young son away from here just as soon as you can.'

Overall the news that I had been given thrilled me and I was in the mood to agree with anything he said. 'I agree with you, Winston, it would be very unfair if people who had given the best years of their lives to the cause should end up destitute.'

At this point in time, however, I had not given any thought as to how we would go about raising the money. I then asked him what he wanted me to do.

To my surprise his answer was, 'I want you and your wife Elizabeth to assist me with the control of the operation over its last few years.'

When I asked where this would leave Angus, he replied, 'Angus is dead, my bodyguards misunderstood a heated argument we were having because of the mistakes he had made and knowing I am quite fragile at the moment one of them shot him. Believe it or not though it was a horrible mistake. I don't think any of us ever expected anything like that to happen—it really was an accident.'

After pausing to get my reaction he added, 'You should accept that I need not have told you how Angus had died. But I want to be completely up-front with you because a complete and open relationship is essential if we're to make it through the next few years. My own health will not stand up to all the demands of the job any more and you and your wife are the only people with the necessary in-built discipline, financial experience and intellect to fill the gap. You won't suffer from this arrangement, you will still be able to keep your current jobs and instead of paying the subsidy you can look forward to building up a sizeable additional pension.'

I confirmed that I would like to accept the offer and I could not see any reason why my wife would decline it. Bearing in mind the changed role being given to TH, I was reasonably certain that Elaine would be happy with this arrangement. I was horrified by what had happened to poor Angus but had to accept that his death was probably an accident. However, if you employ armed bodyguards I suppose such accidents are always likely to happen.

After some further explanations as to why it was essential to continue activities until suitable pensions had been created he got himself a drink of coffee and said he needed to relax for five minutes before going on. As he relaxed I took my coffee over to the window and saw one of the flowerpot men in the distance with a camera and other gadgetry trained on the room we were in.

Winston must have seen me step back from the window because I heard him say, 'Don't worry, Mark, they're there for your safety as well as mine.'

I nodded and said, 'That's nice.' Yet I felt distinctly uncomfortable.

He went on, 'I notice that you haven't asked me why I've been calling you Mark and your wife Elizabeth—can you tell me why you have accepted me using these names?'

The only response I could think of was, 'I suppose it's all to do with the old argument that those setting out to deceive will leave a tangled web. In the circumstances we have to be very careful not to trip ourselves up—so I have become Mark Rogers and I think of myself now as Mark Rogers?'

The reaction to this comment was, 'Excellent—there have been occasions in the past when I could quite happily have strangled you, but I have always accepted that you have been very careful in matters relating to security. Events over the past few months suggest that I can rely on no one else in the organisation, with the possible exception of Sid Jones, to give the necessary attention to security. In a nutshell, that's why I need your assistance, but I will give you and Elizabeth the job description in about a month's time.'

I assumed that this last statement meant that the meeting was about to break up, but I then discovered that the real reason for our meeting had not yet been aired.

After pacing around the room for a few minutes, Winston gave me a very serious look and then said, 'Mark, however conscious you are of security you can have only the briefest notion of the struggle I have had to keep us all safe over the years since we have been in this damned country. Originally we just had the British counter-espionage people to worry about, and because we were all new and nervous our operatives were less likely to take risks and make mistakes. Then people became over-familiar with their surroundings and the mistakes started to creep in. Until recently, though, none of our mistakes, including some you and your wife made, has been critical.

'But in recent years we have faced an additional hazard. As you know our one-time friends in Moscow decided some time ago that our job here was finished and ever since then they have been pressuring me to transfer our staff to them. I'm sure you'll remember that they snatched James Cameron and we have returned one or two people who were quite happy to go back. I think I am right in saying that the rest of the team, and that certainly includes me, would hate to return and that very fact puts us at risk. We will all be safer when our operation is disbanded and that will happen just as soon as everybody's pension pot is filled. In the meantime, however, the pressure continues to increase. When we asked you to leave your atomic energy job we told you that there was a good chance that British Intelligence agents were on your track. I believed that to be the case at the time but I also thought that unfriendly Russian elements were also looking for you, and for a variety of reasons it was in my interest as much as yours to stop them contacting you. I have continued to deal with Moscow but we have been forced to keep changing the address of the centre every few months to keep ahead of them. Before you ask, I have not returned the carpet and now I don't intend to. It is mainly a matter of honour now and although we now think it's not politically valuable it is an excellent negotiating tool if I ever need it.

'Anyway, back to the story. I'm afraid that a week after I was taken into hospital one of Moscow's bright boys tracked us down again and Angus quite stupidly gave him a great deal of information that I would have preferred them not to have. If Angus had an excuse it was that he was inexperienced and was confronted by a team led by Gerry O'Donnell. This man is supposed to be from Eire but is in reality one of Moscow's top thinkers and achievers in the dirty business of espionage. In the course of their discussions Angus explained the situation concerning you and your wife and O'Donnell reacted by referring to you both as cripples. The significance of the term cripple is that in their world it means an agent who is no longer useful. As cripples you are valuable commodities because you can be swapped with British Intelligence.'

At this stage fear got the better of me and I asked several questions one after the other regarding the extraordinary statement he had just made.

Winston waited for me to calm down. 'You have to understand that people involved in espionage are subjected to achievement targets like everyone else. At some stage in the past, some unscrupulous agent must have got rid of one of his own cripples by shopping him to the opposition and in return gained valuable brownie points when the favour was returned later. So, swapping cripples has become an acceptable practice.'

As this information began to sink in, I blurted out, 'So at any time my wife and I could be arrested and imprisoned by British Intelligence?'

The answer came back, 'Not imprisoned, just arrested and shot—cripples are almost never brought to trial.'

'How can you be so sure that we would be shot?'

He responded with a smile on his face. 'Oh, think of it from the other side's point of view—if I shopped you to the enemy they would have a difficult time in the courtroom with you and your wife having a child. The prosecution would have to admit that you were no longer active and the media would ask why they could find only ex-spies not current ones.'

'You seem to be enjoying giving me this information, Winston.'

'As it happens, Mark, I am sure you are not in immediate danger, and just as you have to thank Angus for creating the problem, you should know that he also accidentally found a way to protect you. He told O'Donnell that you are a top management consultant and for some reason added that your wife assists you in your work.

Finally he told him that you had just completed a year-long study into the British meat industry. The net result is that for now at least O'Donnell is desperate for you to work with him on a study in Northern Ireland. When you understand the circumstances you will realise that you and your wife are very safe from GOD—which incidentally is what his colleagues call him. You need to understand that the term comes from his initials—no one is comparing him to a religious deity and certainly not to me.'

I ignored this second joke, if it was one, and asked him to explain why he thought my family was safe. His reaction to this was measured.

'You are much safer from O'Donnell and his henchmen than anyone else in TH, because of chance—a series of coincidences. During his early training in Russia it was noticed that O'Donnell, or whatever his real name is, was very good with figures, and a plan was hatched to try to get him into a British government internal audit unit. It was assumed that if he could eventually get to a senior role in this environment then he would be in an ideal position to obtain valuable information. However, by the time he got to this country other Russian groups had managed to infiltrate the internal audit system and it was decided that they did not need any more cooks to spoil the broth. For some reason that I am not aware of it was decided to reinvent O'Donnell as an Irishman and he eventually joined a large international accountancy firm in Dublin. The original intention was that after a few years he would transfer completely to London. However, when he did eventually transfer, his superiors asked him to work for some of his time out of Belfast. He did well and within a few years he had been made a partner. In the normal course of events our friend Gerry would have grown old flitting between Belfast and London in a mixture of audit and taxation roles. He would have earned a good living with only minimal risk of being exposed as a spy, and once in every blue moon he would have passed on some questionable piece of information to keep the men in Moscow happy. A little bit like the part-time role you and your wife have performed for me over the years.'

I ignored the jibe. 'But what has changed and how does it all affect me?'

Winston looked very tired but he carried on: 'It's all to do with Britain's impending entry into the EEC. The powers that be in this country are slowly accepting the need to join the European Community. In recent years the British government has called in the big consulting firms into an increasing number of government departments usually with the European issue in mind. O'Donnell was instructed by Moscow to get involved and because he was a partner in a big firm he was able to pitch for and lead consultancy assignments without getting permission from anyone else. Effectively, Mr O'D now gets called in to help himself to espionage riches that would otherwise take years to uncover. There is a downside though, and that is he has suddenly been pitched into a high-profile role where the risks increase each time he passes on information. However, he is confident he can last out for at least three years, by which time the UK should be in Europe and the golden age for central government espionage will be at an end.'

'That's very interesting, but I don't see how it affects me.'

Winston grinned back at me. 'O'Donnell now gets so much central government consultancy work that he's constantly fretting that he's missing opportunities in all sorts of areas because he has hasn't got any other Russians among his consultants. Consequently, he's desperate to recruit any Russian agent who has high-level financial or consultancy experience. Before completing his interrogation of Angus, he asked if we had such a person. It must have seemed like Christmas to O'Donnell when Angus told him that Mr and Mrs Cripple fitted the bill. Not only that but you have just completed your long study into the meat industry, and that has already enabled him to secure a massive assignment to estimate the effect of entry into the Common Market on Northern Ireland's biggest industry—the pig industry.'

From the look on Winston's face it was clear that he thought my immediate future was cut and dried.

'Sorry to disappoint you, Winston, but what you're suggesting is impossible, because O'Donnell and I work for competing firms.'

Winston looked at me with an element of surprise in his eyes. 'Don't be bloody stupid, Mark, I told you yesterday your life depended on meeting me today. It also depends on a meeting you and I will have this evening with O'Donnell in Birmingham. He'll offer you a job, you'll accept and you'll start work in Belfast with him in two weeks' time. Your present employers will initially complain but will have to accept the situation. O'Donnell has told me that he'll prevent any ill-feeling being directed at you by getting government ministers to explain to them that you're essential to the success of the assignment. It's simple really. You do this and you're on easy street—refuse and your lives are not worth much.'

I shrugged my shoulders and said, 'Well, it's all settled then.'

He had to have the last word: 'Not quite. I want Sid Jones to be with you all the time you're in Belfast, and before you ask there are two reasons for insisting on it. First, I don't want them to do a James Cameron on you, and second, it must be obvious to you by now that O'Donnell is a major threat to us in the medium and long term—so we must find a way to dispose of him.'

Although I was immediately resigned to being accompanied to Belfast I saw no reason to hold back my feelings.

'I cannot for the life of me see how Sid Jones would match up to either of those requirements.'

In answer to my question all I received in return was a knowing smile.

Winston had claimed we were in no danger from O'Donnell's group in the short term, but he was obviously taking no chances. He and I sat in the back of a car driven by one of the bodyguards as we pursued a less than straightforward route to our meeting. At various times I saw that the other bodyguard as well as David, Peter and Sid, were all driving individual cars and were attempting to provide some protection for Winston. When we eventually met up with O'Donnell it was obvious he had provided himself with a similar level of protection.

Winston introduced me to O'Donnell with the words, 'Mark, this is Gerry O'Donnell, and he would like you to do some work for him in Belfast.'

O'Donnell greeted me with a few words in Russian and then reverted to English to explain his requirement. He was a bouncy dapper man in his forties and he exuded all the qualities you would expect in an Irish gentleman. In fact if I had not known other details of his background I would have unreservedly enjoyed his company. Over the next hour or so he explained what was required of me but interjected various questions designed to uncover why I occupied such a strange role within TH. Winston and I had anticipated most of these questions and so my answers were well rehearsed.

It was obvious that O'Donnell had also prepared himself well and was asking questions from a set of notes. At one point he said, 'Ah yes, Mark, an important point, can I ask if you have studied the bacon imports scheme negotiated between the UK and various European countries such as Denmark and Holland?'

As it happened I had recently looked at this and could not understand why the arrangement was so slanted against British bacon producers.

I got as far as saying, 'Yes, I have looked at it,' when Gerry interrupted:

'Can you explain to me why British civil servants have agreed to a scheme that stabilises the share of Danish and Dutch producers when consumption is low and therefore only penalises the home producers?'

I was about to say it was unfair but suddenly realised that, in his effort to understand why I was not taking a more active role in TH, O'Donnell was probably asking me this question to judge the level of my sympathy towards Britain. In the circumstances I simply said, 'I suppose it's a bloody good job for us that they make these crazy arrangements.'

After a number of other questions and answers O'Donnell tried to sum up: 'I think we'll make a great team but we have to move fast and you'll have to join my firm in two weeks' time.'

I shook my head: 'No, the minimum period would have to be four weeks—I have a great deal of work to complete so even four weeks is cutting it fine.'

Despite his protestations I refused to join earlier and appealed to his professionalism by stating that I would only damage my reputation if I tried to rush through the work in order to get out sooner than that. Eventually, he accepted my stance but insisted on an assurance that it would be no later than four weeks. In holding out on this point I was, in part, looking out for extra time so that Elaine and I could sort out our options.

After we left the meeting, Winston appeared satisfied. 'I was very pleased that you refused to join in less than four weeks because it gave me a chance to study the man when he was under stress. It was a very useful exercise because it clearly demonstrated that he gets flustered when people disagree with him. But what the hell was that bacon quota discussion all about?'

'Oh, I think he was trying to test the level of my sympathy towards Britain.'

'Was he really? Just the sort of thing I would do.'

CHAPTER NINE

In the first few days after the meeting with Winston and Gerry O'Donnell I thought long and hard about my family's safety. Eventually, I decided that just two possible scenarios were worth considering. One of these was negative and the other positive. The negative argument initially had the strongest voice. It screamed out that we would have to begin a new life once more some time during the next few weeks, because even if Winston managed to dispose of O'Donnell, our personal details were already on file with his colleagues, therefore we would still be in danger. In this scenario, however, we would be long-term losers. It may no longer be necessary to inform TH of our whereabouts but we would, nevertheless, be virtual paupers once more because we would not be able to sell the house in the time available to release our money, and I would have to create a new career in some other area.

The positive line of thinking began when I realised that Winston was clearly correct in saying that we were safe as long as O'Donnell thought I could be of assistance as a consultant. Finding and placing another Russian consultant inside British government offices would certainly provide him with more kudos than any other action he could take. I remembered that O'Donnell had talked at length of the work we could do together when the pigs job was completed, and that job alone could take eighteen months from beginning to end. Finally I concluded that I could string my relationship with

O'Donnell out for a year or so and by then TH may be a distant memory. In addition it would provide me with the time necessary to create another family identity and to transfer funds to it.

Given these circumstances I decided not to worry Elaine unnecessarily by going through any of the cripple story with her. She had not been at her best for a few weeks and it would hardly have helped at this time to start her worrying about changing both our identity and address—not to mention the loss of friends and capital that that would entail.

At the first opportunity I told her of my meeting with Winston and O'Donnell but gave her the impression that Moscow had transferred O'Donnell to Winston's team.

Her reaction was low key: 'I presume that means he's given them their damned carpet back?'

'I don't know the answer to that, but listen, I've got some good news. O'Donnell is a senior partner in his firm and he's offered me a ten per cent increase in salary to join them. I know that we normally talk over important decisions between us but I had to give him an answer on the spot, so I've agreed to join them in about a month's time.'

I was relieved by her reaction: 'Oh, you know what's right for your career and what's not. A ten per cent increase will be handy but I hope it doesn't mean more travelling than you're doing now.'

I tried to reassure her: 'No. The amount of travel will always depend on the assignments that come up and in the future that will be as hit and miss in terms of location as it has been in the past. But I'll need to spend ten consecutive days in Belfast just two weeks after joining my new firm.'

On hearing this, Elaine suddenly burst into tears and said, 'Oh no, not for two weeks.'

I thought she was worried about my going to Belfast and with my arms around her I laughed and tried to joke her out of her concern. 'I promise you that my visit has nothing to do with the IRA.'

'No, I don't think you're daft enough to get mixed up with the IRA, it's just that I don't want to be on my own for such a long period.'

She had never been worried about my travels before and consequently I became convinced that something fundamental was worrying her. However, all my questions on the subject both then and over the next few days were answered with the words, 'It's just a mood I'm going through.'

I did manage to improve her spirits when I told her that Winston had confirmed that TH would be wound up in the next year or so and I thought my next comment would please her even more.

'Winston says he wants both of us to take over the role of his second-in-command during the remainder of the time that TH will be in existence.'

I expected her to be pleased at least to get this offer, but I was soon to be disappointed.

'I can't raise any enthusiasm for that job. If you want to cheer me up, promise me you won't go to Belfast.'

I did want to cheer her up, but I could not refuse the Belfast trip and I did not want to tell her why. In the circumstances I simply promised to try my hardest to reduce the length of our separation. The next day, I suggested we take a weekend break at the earliest opportunity. She readily agreed and two weeks before I changed jobs we managed to get a late booking at a family hotel on the east coast. We had an excellent time, most of which was spent eating and talking while Andrew played with other children. Even though her spirits did improve I was very much aware that the periods of silence and depression always returned.

On the way home, while Andrew was sleeping in the back of the car, Elaine suddenly said, 'Whichever way you look at it, our lives are just one big lie'.

'Yes, they are, but what's brought this on?'

'While you were collecting the car, that little girl Anne started showing Andrew some of their family photographs, and guess what? He then started asking why we have no family photographs.'

This had always been a contentious issue and it put me on the defensive again.

'Elaine, we both previously obeyed the no-photographs edict because we could see that it made some sense.'

'Well, I've been thinking and I don't believe it makes any sense now. If we were ever investigated it would look very suspicious if we didn't have family photographs.'

I found myself agreeing with her: 'Yes, you're probably right, and in view of the changed circumstances at TH there does not appear to be any sound reason for not getting our photographs taken.'

A few days later we had several copies of a family sitting, which we immediately treasured. Elaine and I kept one each in our wallets and we put the others in one of the more secure parts of the house.

The weekend before I changed jobs Winston telephoned to see if Elaine and I would like to be briefed on our new TH responsibilities during the next week, but quickly added that we could put it off until I had returned from Belfast if I was still too busy. I was keen to find out what the role entailed but because for the first time ever he had given us a choice, and in the hope that Elaine would get more interested once I was home again, I opted for the later date.

Fifteen minutes after joining my new firm I was engaged in a heated private conversation with Gerry O'Donnell.

He welcomed me on board and then immediately said, 'Please describe the background and credentials of Sidney Albert Jones.'

I found this an extraordinarily difficult question to answer, as my normal reaction would just be to describe him as a pig-faced thug. Clearly, however, this was one occasion when I could not be truthful. But as Winston had told me that he had admitted to O'Donnell that Sid was neither a consultant nor an accountant, I simply said, 'I know him but I haven't worked with him, nevertheless I know that Winston believes him to be his best operative.'

O'Donnell persisted, 'Why do you need a bodyguard while you're in Northern Ireland?'

I was reasonably certain that Winston would not have said that Sid was my bodyguard, so I assumed he was just fishing for information.

Accordingly, I reacted with a chuckle: 'I don't see Jones as a bodyguard in any circumstances, but if his presence worries you then you should discuss it with Winston.'

The next question was, 'Jones is obviously not one of us: where does he come from?'

Tiring of this line of questioning, I simply said 'Yorkshire' and eventually O'Donnell dropped the subject, though he made it clear that he wouldn't be paying for either Sid Jones's time or expenses.

It was arranged that Sid should pick me up from my home early on the morning of our flight to Belfast. Elaine didn't want to meet him so we said our goodbyes before I left the house. I was amazed when I first saw my travelling companion because he was wearing an expensive suit. But he looked very uncomfortable in it and his body seemed to be doing its best to slip out of it. Nevertheless, he was pleasant and friendly and I was pleased at that because it was clearly essential that we should avoid any unpleasantness on this trip. When we got out of his car at Gatwick I was immediately impressed with his expensive new suitcase and a rather up-market briefcase.

I complimented him on his accoutrements and added, 'What's in your briefcase?'

He showed me—just a few pieces of blank paper.

'Just plain white paper, Sid? What's that for?'

'It's to write jokes on. The Irish are very good at creating jokes and I intend to interact with them over the next couple of weeks to create a few beauties.'

I immediately wondered what Gerry O'Donnell's reaction would have been to that statement.

The work over the next few days was very interesting but after a while I became uncomfortable with the bias that O'Donnell was building into the notes on which the final report and recommendations would be based. Much of our effort up to that point had been taken up with interviewing the main civil servants and other key players in the local industry. These individuals ranged from farmers to managers of slaughterhouses and meat product manufacturing plants. It was natural and proper to ask these individuals what they believed were the pros and cons of entering Europe, but O'Donnell was writing up the pros much more strongly than the cons. Winston would have been very impressed with his performance in this area because the technique used might well have come from the TH handbook. The net result was that no individual reading the report later could have argued that false impressions were given. Nevertheless, the arguments in favour were exaggerated to indicate that entry into the Common Market was in line with this particular industry's wishes. In actual fact, I thought that on a sixty-forty basis the opposite was true.

The significance of O'Donnell's tactics lay in the fact that the pig industry was extremely important to Northern Ireland and given the political problems in the province it was conceivable that a resounding no vote by these people might have made British entry into Europe very difficult. Obviously, I had to follow O'Donnell's lead in this area, but for professional reasons I tried to be less biased than he was. When he looked at my notes, however, he appeared satisfied with the results.

On the other hand he was clearly unhappy with Sid's presence. On several occasions he appeared irritated when Sid joined our discussions. Eventually this irritation got the better of him.

'Sid, what do you imagine your role is in this assignment and why do you insist on following Mark around?'

We were both taken aback by Sid's response:

'My role is to write jokes and I keep close to Mark because looking at him gives me inspiration.'

I burst out laughing and Gerry O'Donnell actually laughed so much that he fell off his chair. From that point on he accepted Sid's presence without further adverse comment and frequently tried to supply him with punchlines. Later when we were back in the hotel I said, 'Sid, did Winston think up the joke you made at my expense?'

He looked slightly hurt and said, 'I told you, *I* write the jokes.'

O'Donnell's main Belfast office was in the inner city area that included the largest and most frequently used offices and shops. The British army had created a large metal net around this section of the city and everyone entering or leaving was subject to scrutiny, if not a full-scale search. About a week into our time in Northern Ireland a visit was arranged for us to meet with management and staff at an American-owned pig processing plant at Enniskillen, a town close to the border with the Irish Republic. O'Donnell arranged for a limousine so that we could go there in comfort and did not seem to be too unhappy when Sid insisted on making it a threesome. Just as we were leaving the office O'Donnell said, 'Don't you need your briefcase, Sid?'

Sid had to run back for it and again this led to a great deal of banter when he caught up with us.

The pick-up point arranged with the limousine owners was immediately outside one of the heavily guarded gates in the metal netting. Two young army privates and a corporal were manning the gate area. It seemed to me they were in a very exposed position despite limited protection from a half-wall of sandbags. There were some tall buildings not more than thirty yards away on the other side of the road that could have housed any number of snipers.

While waiting for the transport I walked about twenty yards down the road looking in the shop windows and came upon a branch of Burton's the tailors. In the window was a tailor's dummy dressed in a reasonably smart suit. There was a large sign shaped to go around the top half of the dummy and it featured the slogan 'Can you beat this price?' I laughed because there was no price marked anywhere in the window. Guessing that I might have come across something that could be used in one of his jokes, Sid came scampering towards me and as usual he'd discarded his briefcase before setting off.

The corporal assumed the squat position and pointed his rifle at Sid and screamed out, 'Pick it up—pick it up.'

Given the possibility that our actions might have been a ruse to plant a bomb, most people would have seen this as a perfectly reasonable request. Sid, however, decided that he wouldn't back down and just folded his arms. Recognising the danger Gerry O'Donnell moved towards the corporal with the palms of his hands pointing down in a conciliatory gesture and said,

'It's all right, Corp, he's just an ignorant Yorkshire sod.'

The corporal, while still in the squat position, turned the rifle on O'Donnell with the bayonet finishing just inches from his stomach, then snarled, 'Yes, and here's another Yorkshire sod.'

After that O'Donnell, the corporal and several passers-by were convulsed with laughter. Sid, however, retained a silly defiant attitude and it was fortunate that the limousine arrived at that moment and we were able to bundle him into it.

From memory, the journey to Enniskillen took an hour or so. Most of the time was taken up by Sid trying to compose new Englishmen-Irishmen-Scotsmen jokes. O'Donnell insisted that a new impetus would accrue to such jokes if Yorkshiremen were substituted for Englishmen, and eventually Sid warmed to this possibility. When we got to the outskirts of the town our driver indicated that he would have to ask someone where the factory was. He chose an old man who insisted on describing four different routes before he had finished. This led to my two companions going into further fits of laughter and generally taking the mickey out of the Irish. I looked at the driver's face and concluded from his expression that if he had been a terrorist, then whatever his religious beliefs we would have been in real trouble.

Later in the day I began to realise that O'Donnell was trying to get close to Sid in order to find a weakness he could exploit. This became obvious when the factory manager almost proudly claimed that some of the leading IRA men were working in the next building we would be visiting. Sid immediately made an excuse for staying outside and as I knew he had spent some time with the IRA, I, rightly or wrongly, assumed he was simply trying to avoid the problem of suddenly coming face-to-face with someone he knew. I'm not sure what conclusion Gerry O'Donnell drew from Sid's reaction but he mischievously tried to get Sid into the building concerned on a number of occasions before the end of the afternoon. They were not on speaking terms during the drive back to Belfast.

Two days before we finished our stint in Northern Ireland, the girl O'Donnell had provided to do our typing and administration asked me if it was okay to leave some of my work until the next day. She claimed she was under pressure and needed to do various things for Mr O'D before he left—and he was going at three that day.

Sid said, 'Oh, is he going back to London?'

The response was 'No, he says he's got a lot of work to get through before he has dinner with you tonight at your hotel, and he works better when he's at home. But his flat is not far from The Europa.'

Gerry had chosen to have dinner most evenings with us in our hotel and usually left just before midnight. As the army had a general curfew running after dark he effectively ensured we could not follow him back to his flat without being under the gaze of the army of international journalists who spent most evenings drinking and hanging around the hotel lobby. Sid gave me a knowing look and quickly left the building carrying his briefcase.

I left the office at about five-thirty and went straight to The Europa. After making myself a cup of tea, I followed my usual practice on these occasions and phoned home. Young Andrew answered and so I initially engaged in a general discussion on life as it affects eight-year-olds.

When I finally spoke to Elaine she said she was looking forward to me coming home the following night. I asked her how she was feeling and she replied, 'I feel much better, I've been very silly but it's all right now—I'll tell you about it tomorrow.'

I wanted to ask more but accepted it would be better to carry on the discussion when we were face-to-face and I left it at that.

A little later I phoned Sid's room, partly because I was curious as to what had happened during the late afternoon and partly because I was hungry and I could hardly go to the dining room without first asking him when he wanted to eat. He was not in, so I left a message at reception for him. I checked my watch and saw that it was nearly six-thirty. I was surprised that Sid had not returned and started to fantasise that O'Donnell and Sid had beaten each other to death. In this dream world I realised that I would not benefit from O'Donnell's death at this time because that would mean that his associates would be free to trade in Elaine and myself as cripples. On the other hand, as far as I was concerned, the grim reaper could take Mr Jones whenever it was convenient, but the sooner the better.

My dream was shattered within minutes. First O'Donnell called to say he'd be over at about seven-fifteen, ready, willing and able to eat.

Almost immediately afterwards Sid Jones knocked on my door. He had a silly grin on his face and informed me, 'We've got the bastard.'

During the next half-hour or so he gave me chapter and verse of his brilliant detective work. Apparently, he had waited for O'Donnell to leave his office and followed him to a small block of flats. Then by watching the windows intently he finally got lucky and was able to pinpoint the exact flat.

As he left my room he whispered, 'So, if he stays in Belfast he'll meet his maker no later than the end of next week.'

It crossed my mind that it ought not to be too difficult to track down O'Donnell in London but I did not say so. Instead, I asked Sid why he had taken his briefcase with him.

He was deadly serious in his response to this request. 'Oh, I realised I might get hungry while I was waiting for O'Donnell to appear, so I took my briefcase so that I'd have something to put a pizza in.'

During dinner O'Donnell informed us that he'd be staying in Belfast for the next few weeks and insisted that I return without Sid in no more than ten days' time. It had previously been agreed that I could do a certain amount of research in London, but I thought that would only take four or five days and so I was happy to agree with this request. I certainly did not want to be in Belfast when an attempt was made on O'Donnell's life. For his part, Sid just shrugged in response to the statement that he should not accompany me on the next visit.

I found it difficult to get to sleep that night. On the grounds that Gerry O'Donnell had once referred to Elaine and me as cripples, I was now virtually sanctioning the death of someone who was enormously important to my country. In theory I might benefit from his death by assuming the senior role on the consultancy assignment, but that counted for nothing when balanced by the fact that my family would then be exposed to danger from his colleagues.

Eventually, I decided that the best solution was to postpone the death sentence until the current consultancy project was completed. It was no use discussing this with Sid but I resolved to argue for a stay of execution as soon as I got home and could talk to Winston.

Next day Sid and I left the office for an afternoon flight from Belfast to Gatwick. Being anxious to get home, I was again irritated by flying in and out of Gatwick when Heathrow would have been much more convenient. However, I had not originally concerned myself with the travel arrangements, so I had to accept that I had not helped myself in this respect. Security was very strict at Belfast and after checking in our luggage we found that access to the flight was achieved by standing in a single-file queue that snaked backwards and forwards around a room and all the way out to the steps of the plane. I was standing just behind Sid and when we were ten yards or so from the plane's steps a young lady made an announcement. From memory her words were,

'Will the person who left a briefcase in the reception area please collect it immediately.'

She repeated this request several times before we got on the plane and the urgency and pitch of her voice increased in unison each time she said it. There was some nervous laughter from the people around me but I was not really nervous at all because I knew the briefcase did not contain a bomb.

I sat next to Sid and carefully avoided his gaze until we had taken off, but then we both burst into fits of laughter.

When he managed to control himself, Sid said, 'I shouldn't be laughing, that bag was expensive.'

'Yes, but Winston will be pleased at the trouble you'll have put the intelligence services to. Just imagine the bomb disposal team's reaction when they find that the briefcase contains just pieces of stale pizza and numerous bits of paper with strange coded messages each beginning with the words "There was a Yorkshireman, an Irishman and a Scotsman." They'll be forced to involve the best minds in the secret service and the pizza will be subject to hundreds of tests.'

The remainder of the flight was uneventful and Sid managed to get through central London's early evening traffic without too much trouble. I was anxious to get home and was therefore further irritated when Sid said he needed to stop at Scratchwood Services. My irritation was due to the fact that this particular motorway service area was less than twenty minutes' drive from my home. Sid, however, told me that he had no choice because Scratchwood was a key meeting place for senior TH people and he had been told to report to an office in the building when we got back. When we arrived there I joined Sid in a small office that was apparently rented by TH. There was a telephone on the desk and while Sid went to the toilet I decided to phone home. I had just started to dial when my TH colleagues Peter and David burst in. Peter grabbed me by the shoulders and David found a seat for me.

Looking very concerned, Peter then said, 'Martin, we have some bad news for you—your wife and son are dead.'

My brain could not initially make sense of these words and when Sid entered the room all bright and breezy I thought they were playing some sick joke on me.

However, when they repeated the news to Sid I began to realise that they were serious and I found it difficult to control my emotions. In answer to my many questions I was told that my house had burned down about eight-thirty that morning but the first they had heard about it was at lunchtime when it was announced on the radio. It was also announced that the police were looking for the owner and my name and description were given.

Peter then said, 'Martin, you and probably all of us are in danger, the local police let it be known that a young boy's body was found in one room and a woman and a man were found in each other's arms in another room. They think the man was a neighbour and that you found them together and killed them while in a rage.'

I started to say that I could prove that the story was untrue but then realised that although I could prove I was in Belfast at the time of the murder I would be subject to a line of questioning that would eventually result in my exposure. Then I began to feel guilty about even thinking of my own safety and decided that I had to go home and see for myself.

'Please, will someone get me a car so that I can drive close by my home to try and understand what happened. I promise I will not get close enough to get caught.'

Peter intervened: 'We're waiting for instructions from Winston, but I expect he'll agree to your going to your home. But you'll have to calm down first because I don't think you could be trusted to drive safely in the state you're in.'

Just then the telephone rang and Peter answered it. It was Winston, and eventually he asked to speak to me.

'Mark, I'm afraid it's true, your wife and son have both been killed during a fire at your home this morning. I have been trying to use my various contacts to get information ever since I was given the awful news a couple of hours ago. I have not got to the bottom of it yet, but all the signs indicate that it is the work of British Intelligence.'

Winston's statement removed the last little bit of hope I had that my loved ones could still be alive, but I had to see for myself.

'Winston, I need to go home, will you tell your people to provide me with a car?'

After further pleading he agreed that I could go to the site immediately but insisted that Peter, David and Sid accompany me in one car.

The others fashioned a sort of disguise for me with Peter's heavy spectacles and a scarf purchased in the shop at the service station. They drove as close as they could to the remains of the house and I could see that the police had also boarded up part of the Maher house. This proved too much for me and I tried to get out of the car with the idea of discussing what had happened with the Mahers. As I was getting out of the car I felt a needle enter my backside and hands began dragging me back in the car. I must have gone to sleep very quickly.

CHAPTER TEN

When I regained my senses, I was lying on a bed in a small room. I was stripped down to my underpants and vest and covered by a single blanket. Then, as if reliving a nightmare, I gradually remembered being told that my wife and son were dead and I screamed out my anguish at the top of my voice. I heard somebody unlocking a door in a hurry and David entered.

'David, was it you who drugged me, you bastard, where am I? How long have I been here?'

David was not a big man and he appeared to be on his own, which may have explained his apprehension as he approached me and answered my questions.

'You're at the centre and you've been here for about twelve hours. I'm afraid there's no doubt about it, old friend, Elaine and Andrew both perished in the fire. There is considerable confusion regarding what actually happened. The police either don't know or they're not telling, but Winston and the boys are desperately trying to find out what they can. We did drug you but you'll soon realise that it was for your good as well as ours.'

Then as if he expected me to be surprised by his comments, he added, 'After all, if they can get to Elaine they can get to any one of us.' He brought me a cup of tea and said, 'You know it really is essential that you control your feelings over the next few days.

Your only recourse now is to fight back at British Intelligence and you won't be able to do that if your emotions get the better of you.'

There was not much chance of my getting over-emotional for the next hour or so because the tea was drugged.

When I finally recovered from the effects of the tea, I was subjected to profuse apologies from Peter, David and Sid regarding their use of drugs to control me. David was doing most of the talking.

'I must have over-done it with the original dose but honestly I only put a mild sedative in the tea. I had to make sure you didn't do anything stupid like rushing down south to your home. If you lose your rag we'll all be in danger.'

In the circumstances, I tried to control my emotions. I could see that for my own safety it was necessary that I appeared outwardly under control. My colleagues had given me strong indications that my period of mourning should now end and I recognised that I needed some help from them if I was to fight back in some way. I did not know how I was going to fight back or who I would be fighting against but it was becoming obvious to me that I had to play for time and hope that a way forward would eventually present itself. Accordingly, I tried to appear steadfast and determined from that point on. Inwardly, however, my mind was racing in a variety of directions as I tried to find answers. When I retired to my bed, I had the greatest difficulty in getting to sleep, and the same questions kept coming into my mind and then leaving it without the semblance of an answer. Among these many unanswered questions were, who murdered my family, why were they killed, who was the man found with Elaine and why had the police assumed I had been responsible? Additionally, when she said the night before her death that she'd been silly—was she referring to an affair she had tried to end, and what, if anything, was O'Donnell's role in the matter? However, the two questions that really kept me awake were, did her concern about my being away from home indicate that she was frightened of an attempt on her life, and would their lives have been saved if we had made a run for it when I first heard the cripple story?

Early on the third morning of my stay in the centre, Sid Jones appeared and announced that we had to leave the premises in just under two hours' time. As he was speaking a large vehicle pulled up outside and we were told to grab everything that was useful or incriminating and load it in the van. I left in Sid's car and was surprised to find him doubling back on himself in central Birmingham.

Eventually we pulled into what had previously been the offices of a defunct manufacturing business not very far from the centre of the city and not that far from the premises we had just vacated. The building had a large wall around it with two big doors built to allow large vehicles easy access. When these doors were closed we were safe from the prying eyes of the outside world.

As I got out of his car to close the doors, Sid said, 'Welcome to the new temporary centre.'

Before I could ask why it was so close to the old one he said, 'We need to stay near Birmingham for a while.'

When we entered the main office, Winston, the flowerpot men and three other people I did not know were already making themselves at home. There was a lot of lively banter already going on but a stern-looking Winston, seeing we'd all arrived, asked for our attention and addressed us like a schoolmaster.

'You will see your name on the door of the room set aside for you, put your kit in your room and then get yourselves prepared for lunch in fifteen minutes.'

For the second time in my TH career I noticed that to get from my room to the main exit would require me to pass almost everyone else's room.

Lunch was served in what had been a despatch area. The food was laid out on an old worktable and packing cases made do as chairs. The fare itself had been hastily put together from a number of local takeaways, but it was well received.

For obvious reasons, my attention span had been very limited during the last few days. In fact unless I was being addressed face-to-face my concentration tended to lapse and I would revert to brooding on my loss. Joining in at this strange meal, however, I was suddenly aware that my table companions were adopting a siege mentality—they were genuinely worried about their safety. Bearing in mind their background and experience, this surprised me, because as far as I could tell they were all active, therefore they were not cripples and as such they were presumably safe from swapping.

When we had finished eating, Winston began what turned out to be an extraordinary diatribe. 'My friends, I am sure you will join with me in offering our sympathy to Mark on the loss of his family and in promising our active support in killing the bastards who carried out these crimes.'

Then he produced some newspaper cuttings relating to the fire that had killed Elaine and Andrew. The sight of these cuttings depressed me further but I forced myself to read them.

As I struggled to make sense of what I was reading, Winston put his hands on my shoulders and said, 'Mark, you could read it all through a dozen times but I'm afraid these reports do not add anything to what we knew yesterday. But I promise we will continue to monitor any media developments. I have got two people from outside TH to keep an eye open for future reports on the incident.'

After his usual break for a puff on a cigar and a sip of whisky, Winston continued, 'Friends, I have some more bad news. Just over a week ago our old friend Robin was also killed in a house fire.'

He then produced a further set of newspaper cuttings to prove it. It turned out that he was referring to Robin Woods, whom I had worked with briefly during my time as a door-to-door book salesman, but had seen only rarely since then. I did not previously know it but Robin had been retired by TH after being badly injured in a job that went wrong. These facts appeared to incense Winston's audience and comments such as 'we must get O'Donnell' were soon flying about.

Surprisingly, Winston then shook his head. Producing a further newspaper cutting he explained: 'This as you will all be able to see later is a headline report from a well-known Irish paper and it refers to an explosion in a house two days ago. It explains that three men and a woman were killed by a bomb blast in the house and that two other people were injured by it. I can tell you that all the people in the house were members of O'Donnell's elite group of Russians and that O'Donnell himself was one of those injured.'

I had noticed that Peter had been very upset by the announcement of Robin's death and from his next remark he was obviously reluctant to let O'Donnell off the hook: 'How can we be sure that it was O'Donnell's group that was blown up?'

In response Winston produced cuttings from a number of newspapers. One from *The Times* had a small headline reading 'Business consultant targeted by IRA' and it mentioned that O'Donnell was seriously ill.

After studying the articles there was a good deal of confusion.

Finally Peter broke the gloomy silence: 'I suppose we have to consider the possibility that O'Donnell arranged Robin and Elaine's killings and then faked his own involvement in the bombing.'

Winston shook his head: 'I've thought of that, but think what O'Donnell has lost. The newspapers say he is seriously ill so that means that someone is in hospital and will be subjected to police and press investigation if he gets better. In the circumstances, even if it's not O'Donnell in the hospital, he still can't surface; he's lost his job, his fantastic once-in-a-lifetime opportunity for easy espionage pickings and the benefits that Mark would have provided. No, it doesn't make any sense to assume that O'Donnell and his team were directly responsible for the two separate murders of our people. So who do you think *is* responsible?'

After a brief pause, Peter again was the first to react: 'I think that only leaves British Intelligence, but if that is the case then we're still faced with the two questions. Why did they do it and how did they track our people down?'

At this point almost all those present began to voice opinions and most of these referred to the slip-up Angus made when dealing with Gerry O'Donnell.

Winston agreed and gave his considered answers to both of Peter's questions. 'I think we're safe in assuming that they have our details because of the error Angus made. Whether they got the information because some renegade within O'Donnell's team gave it them or they succeeded in infiltrating O'Donnell's group, we may never know. But on the assumption that they got the information from O'Donnell's group can anyone suggest a reason why they have chosen to start liquidating us?'

There was a general shaking of heads and so he continued: 'Imagine you're with British Intelligence and you care desperately about the well-being of your country. Then through the O'Donnell group you discover details on a number of people working against the interests of your country. If you abide by the law you're likely to waste an enormous amount of time and effort trying to bring these people before the courts. Let's face facts, many of the actions we have taken in the past are not crimes. It is not a crime or even an offence under the Official Secrets Act to tell politicians to vote for a welfare state. Neither is it an offence to encourage people from overseas to come and live here. It certainly isn't an offence to criticise goods made in this country. Therefore, it is always going to be difficult to form a worthwhile case against TH personnel. This is particularly true when you consider that most people will not accept that we can have had a marked effect on the British economy from just employing communication skills. So in your position as one of Her Majesty's top counter-intelligence experts, what do you do? I know what I would do; I would liquidate the conspirators and I would start with the relatively inactive people because with a little bit of luck their deaths wouldn't be noticed immediately. Gentleman, they have decided to do the obvious thing, they have declared war on us. I think the bombing of O'Donnell's group came about because Mark had already been targeted and then Sid and Mark met up with Gerry and they indulged in long discussions at The Europa Hotel in Belfast. I have tried to put myself in the position of the British Intelligence people. These discussions between two enemy groups in Belfast would worry me, particularly if I knew that some of these conspirators were working on important government projects. Given these circumstances the O'Donnell group getting together for a meeting under one roof would be too good an opportunity to miss, and I could then deal with the individual members of the other group on a piecemeal basis.'

The effect on Winston's audience was electric. Within minutes we had agreed that where possible all personnel would return each night to the centre. There were two reasons for this: firstly to maximise individual security, and secondly to ensure that the latest information on the enemy would be available to all. We accepted that we could not put names or faces to individuals within the enemy's ranks. In addition, although Moscow might be able to fill in some gaps in our knowledge, we could not risk making contact with any Russian group in the foreseeable future. Therefore as we were operating blind it made little sense in trying to go on the offensive by attempting to identify individual targets within the intelligence services. My hatred was intense. I was convinced that the British security forces had killed my family, and whatever the circumstances were leading up to the fire, the only ambition I had left was revenge.

The three TH members I had not met before were all quite young. Two, John Lynch and Daniel Lambert, were most probably Irish. They both had cultured accents and I got the impression that they had worked previously as a team. The third man was called Simon. He was a very strange individual who seemed to have a permanent twitch and found it difficult to concentrate for long. When I asked Simon for his surname he told me he did not have one. A few hours in this character's company and you didn't need to be a brain specialist to know he was dangerously mad. Collectively, these three people appeared to me to be out of place at the centre. When the opportunity arose later that first evening at the new centre, I asked Winston what their backgrounds were.

He considered my question for a moment or two and then said, 'In the present circumstances I think it best that we know as little as possible about each other's background—I think it's safer that way.'

When I could tear my mind away from my personal sadness, I felt totally bemused that I was living in a factory in Birmingham,

England, with nine other men. As far as I could tell only four of us, Winston, Peter, David and I, were Russians. That meant the other five were probably Irish or British and therefore they were part of this strange team out of personal choice. I hoped that their involvement, at least in the beginning, was due to a passionate desire to spread communism around the world, or failing that a hatred of the British establishment. For my part, I no longer had any interest in communism but I did have a growing hatred of the British establishment.

Our second day in the new centre was given over to an intense discussion on our future activities. Winston started the discussion by repeating that all our efforts from now on should be directed at increasing our personal pension pots and that damage to the British nation should simply flow from these actions. Then he announced that some people, most notably his bodyguards Sid, David and Peter, had been contributing to their pensions for almost twenty years. Looking directly at me he said, 'When Moscow stopped subsidising the TH efforts we had to find other sources of income and to achieve this it was necessary to create an incentive scheme whereby those bringing in the most money got the largest commissions. I hope Sid does not mind me saying this but his pension is already over £150,000. One of the reasons for this is that Sid has lived on very little over the years, preferring to see his pension maximised so that at a relatively young age he can settle down in comfort at the seaside.'

Sid certainly did not mind Winston giving us this information; in fact he looked very smug all the way through the explanation. I tried hard not to look too surprised at what was being said but I realised I should have guessed that Sid's importance to Winston lay in some highly illegal way of bringing in much needed funds. Despite my other troubles I inwardly winced at the thought that while Sid was earning money from spurious sources, Elaine and I had been contributing to his well-being via the subsidy.

Winston was at pains to say that previously only about ten per cent of the TH total effort had gone into building up pensions, so he felt he had a good idea how much we could earn if all our efforts were in this direction. He suggested some targets, which ranged from £300,000 for Sid, down to £125,000 for Simon and £175,000 for me. Apparently, I had already got £25,000 in the pot, which was my allowance for the success Elaine and I had gained by obtaining information from the UKAEA. This news intensified my personal hurt when I realised that I would now gain from Elaine's valiant actions.

Surprisingly, there was only a little argument about the targeted personal shares and Winston was able to bring this part of the discussion to a conclusion. I think all present were surprised when he said he was sure we could make all the targets within nine months. He explained that he and therefore his bodyguards would spend as much time as possible in the centre for safety reasons and that everyone else should return to our new base each evening.

Winston then turned to the subject of how we would earn a net £1,000,000 over the next few months. He looked at everyone in turn and said, 'There are many ways to earn money but if anybody has scruples about indulging in certain activities then they should voice them earlier rather than later.'

It was obvious from the reaction of most of the people in the room that the question was really being directed at me.

Although I was not looking forward to hearing about these activities, it was obvious that I had to play for time and that meant convincing all of these people that I was prepared for anything. Therefore, I reacted quickly to Winston's question with another question: 'If someone declares war on you, how can you have scruples about anything?'

My comment went down well and I felt that these people immediately warmed in their attitude to me. It was, nevertheless, a strain to keep my body language under control when I learned over the next few minutes that TH was already a major player in the illegal drugs industry.

Peter said, 'Welcome to the drugs trade, Martin.'

Winston immediately chipped in by saying, 'Mark is going to get very confused if some of us call him Martin and others refer to him as Mark. We will probably all have to change our names within

165

the next few months but until then let's maintain our discipline and refer to him as Mark.'

Sid thought he'd be helpful: 'We could solve the problem by using the special name I have for him.'

I gathered from the laughter that other people present were aware of this name. I reacted rather weakly by saying, 'I'll bet it's not as good as the one I have to describe you.'

The proceedings were brought to order when Winston made another comment that put an even greater strain on my ability to control my body language.

'Mark will have to do his share of pick-ups and deliveries of the various products but that's not where he's going to be of the greatest use to us.'

To my amazement he then went on to say, 'In recent times Mark has made a special study of how to make big money on the side out of the finance industry. I will be working closely with him in this area and for that reason he will act as my number two in matters of general organisation. Sid will act as my number two in all other areas.'

All I could think of doing at this stage was to nod in agreement with the comments being made. My colleagues were clearly impressed that I was going to make a lot of money for them by manipulating the financial markets in some way and for the second time in a few minutes I could see that my rating was on the increase. It was immediately obvious to me that Winston had misunderstood me at the Christmas meeting when I had told him I had become an expert in both legal and illegal money-making schemes. With hindsight I should have explained that I was referring to methods to counteract illegal schemes, but the statement had been made in a hurry when I was trying to impress him. When lying on my bed that evening I agonised over what this misunderstanding might have led up to. Certainly he would not have been so keen to get me on board again if he had not thought that I might be a source of new income. It was therefore possible that my error had led to the murder of my wife and son. However, Angus would probably have still given our details to O'Donnell and that was the real cause of the tragedy. Eventually I had to accept that I could not undo the past and had to live in the present. In the circumstances, I would just have to play for time but try my hardest to come up with a suitable scheme.

Over the next few weeks I tried very hard to create money-making schemes. I sketched out a few ideas in draft and after about a month I discussed them with Winston. I pointed out that they all had positive and negative implications. It was clearly a case of increasing our personal risk to increase the reward. In some ways I was quite pleased with what I had been able to put together, but Winston was disappointed and asked me to renew my efforts and speed up the process. Eventually, however, he came back to me and asked me to explain to the entire team how one such scheme would work. The idea was to trick our biggest customer for heroin. This was a complex and risky scheme but as we would have brought TH to a halt shortly after completing the scam we did not need to worry about future business being curtailed. If it worked we would net an extra £400-£500,000. Initially there was some doubt that our customer could raise this amount but I reminded my colleagues that they frequently claimed that the two key individuals running this organisation were looking to launder millions of pounds at any given time. As a result this particular objection was removed but the idea was eventually voted down. Later I pointed out to Winston that the people who voted against the idea, namely John Lynch, Daniel Lambert, Simon and Peter, were all heroin addicts and that they probably had their own reasons for not wishing to double-cross any important players in the drugs trade. Winston's reaction to my comment was not to react at all. He did not say anything and he did not move a muscle.

Two months after the idea was rejected, John and Daniel used parts of the scheme I had put together to double-cross TH. Effectively they got away with around £470,000, and even after pulling back their pension allowance the rest of us had suffered to the tune of almost £220,000. In addition, for obvious security reasons, we had to go through the inconvenience and trauma of finding yet another base or centre, which at Winston's insistence was also in Birmingham. There was a great deal of ill-feeling in the remainder of the team and most of it was directed at me. Winston's declining health meant that I was taking on more and more of the day-to-day running of the organisation and if it had not been for this fact, I might have been in real trouble. I was free to come and go at will from the centre and as I had no real income or wealth of my own I did not really have an alternative. Nevertheless on occasions I got the distinct impression I was being followed. On one such occasion I decided to take an alternative route back to the latest centre. In doing so I accidentally witnessed one of the flowerpot men entering a lock-up workshop. I made a mental note of the premises and the street name but walked on, hopefully without giving the impression that I had seen anything unusual.

Within the next six weeks we pulled in a further £60,000 and I was responsible for about £23,000 of it. Even so I kept hearing sly remarks that I had cost them a quarter of a million. I thought about confronting Winston on this issue by pointing out to him that it was his idea that the detailed planning of the scheme should be outlined to all concerned. Fortunately, common sense prevailed and I kept my mouth shut. I could see that Winston was struggling to work on even a part-time basis and this gave me hope that the TH saga might be over in weeks rather than months, and that I'd have a reasonable amount of money with which to begin a new life. The warm feeling that the impending death of TH gave me was, however, negated by a growing fear that perhaps the pensions, or at least my pension, was an illusion. I had noticed how easy it was for Winston to confiscate the monies theoretically due to John and Daniel, and what was more Winston knew that I had taken this important issue on board. It had also become obvious to me that Winston was taking at least sixty per cent of the income from the combined activities and probably had taken an even bigger slice in previous years. Some simple arithmetic indicated that the man had to have at least £10,000,000 salted away.

The ill-feeling coming my way as a result of the defection of John and Daniel was not helped by my chief accountant role in the organisation. As we got closer to the £1,000,000 net target that Winston had set I found that my less mathematically alert colleagues believed that we had got more money than my accounts were showing. Winston asked me to keep these accounts but let me take all the flak when complaints were made. To fight back I kept a list that I called Winston's Rules. This was kept reasonably up-to-date and simply showed income less expenditure. From then on when anyone complained I went through the figures with the person complaining and pointed out that *they* were spending the money not I.

I suppose it was natural that as the team members felt richer they would be increasingly inclined to indulge their desires. Eventually, I was forced to point out that total purchases in month eight was more than three times that incurred in the first month of our enforced commune. Winston decided to study the figures and was horrified to find that Simon had incurred over forty per cent of the expenditure on his own.

When confronted on this issue, all we could get out of him was: 'For Simons's stinger.'

Although quite mad, Simon did have some extraordinary skills and most of them involved designing new weapons. The idea behind his stinger was to devise a method of firing a drugs capsule out of something the size of a small revolver. As the weapon was intended to be silent in operation or at least did not sound like a gun going off, he had mostly experimented with powerful clockwork systems. So far he had managed to create a stinger powerful enough to penetrate human skin with a drug pellet from a distance of about nine inches.

His expensive purchases included a mass of clock and other mechanisms and some electronic components. I argued that as we were so close to completing our task, this type of expenditure was unnecessary. Surprisingly, Winston did not agree and a relieved Simon immediately decided that I was an enemy.

Later, when I was on my own, Simon sidled up to me and said, 'Winston says you're showing your true colours now—you don't like weapons and you created a scheme to damage drug dealers rather than the government.'

There was not much I could say in response but I felt more nervous than I had for a long while.

Several nights later, Simon and I were in a car with Sid and David. We were supposed to be engaged on an east coast drugs pick-up but the boat we were due to rendezvous with had failed to materialise at the appointed time. Rather than draw attention to our presence by parking in one spot, we chose to keep moving and took it in turns to drive the car by differing circular routes in order to return to the drop site at fifteen-minute intervals. Recent pick-ups on the east coast had been risky and for that reason we felt it necessary to work as a heavily armed team of four.

After ninety minutes on this roller-coaster had failed to sight the boat, tempers started to fray and Sid decided to leave it for a further forty-five minutes before returning for the last time to the drop site. He took the wheel himself and decided on a longer circular route that took in some built-up areas. Simon and I shared the back seat and as we passed a parked police car with two men inside I noticed that he started to take his gun out of his pocket but then put it back.

Almost immediately, Sid said, 'Jesus, I have taken the wrong bloody turn.'

Within minutes we approached the parked police car again but this time it was on our side of the road. As we got close Simon wound down the window slightly and started to point the gun at the policemen.

Fearing that he was trying to kill them I knocked his arm up. My action must have pulled his arm back in inside because the bullet went through the roof of our car.

Sid screamed out, 'What the hell!' and immediately turned the car lights out and put his foot down.

The policemen must have been very shocked because by the time they had reacted we were a long way off. With a bullet hole in the roof it was obvious we had to abort the operation and we made our way back to our base as quickly as possible. Much to my surprise Sid and David both apportioned blame for our failure that evening on a fifty-fifty basis between Simon and myself. I heard this for the first time when they were recounting the episode to Winston. It aroused such anger in me that I attacked both of them and a bruising scuffle developed that was only stopped when the flowerpot men intervened. As we were pulled apart we continued to throw insults in each other's direction.

Surprisingly, Winston appeared unmoved by the furore but he brought an end to it by banging the table. He called for silence and then said in a weary voice, 'I have some news for you. Our suppliers did not even attempt the trip tonight because of unforeseen weather problems—so you've not really lost anything. But on the positive side we have arranged two jobs for next week, which should increase our capital substantially and enable us to close down the operation within ten days.'

He followed up this news with a report on the state of the individual pension pots. As I had given him the details two days previously, the figures did not come as a surprise to me. Basically, all but Simon and I had reached their targets. If the night's escapade had been successful then Simon and I would have got closer to our targets and the others would have bettered their expectations.

The mood in the room improved with the news of the extra jobs and Winston had to bang the table again to make his next announcement.

'I have some important work to do later in the week, which requires me to visit Scotland. When I return I'll be bringing a large amount of cash so it's important you are here when I get back—because otherwise you'll miss the share-out.'

I found it difficult to join in the shrieks of delight that this news produced because I thought it would be a simple matter for Winston just to disappear now with all the money. However, Winston then produced a range of documents that appeared to be transfers of large quantities of stock and shares to each of us. Before placing them in the main safe he allowed all concerned to study the transfers. Then he explained what would happen on his return.

'Each one of you has got transfers made up to the full value of the pension you have earned up to this point. When I return I will buy back stock for cash on a pound-for-pound basis, up to a maximum of £10,000 per person. Any further pension earned as a result of further work will be paid in stock. I am limiting the cash element to £10,000 each because I think it would be dangerous to have too much cash floating about in the short term. But as you will all be going your separate ways, you'll be able to make further cash withdrawals within a week or so of receiving the transfers. For those of an untrusting nature I suggest that you choose just one of the stock transfers and check out its legality before I leave.'

His final comment on the subject was: 'As Mark has the greatest experience in these matters and is certain to be the most suspicious of my motives, I suggest that he might check out the legality. And as a double safeguard, in case anyone thinks that Mark and I are pulling some sort of fiddle, someone else should choose the actual stock transfer at random.'

This little task was accomplished with ease the next day and I was not really surprised that the document was legal. However, I had to accept that it might be the only legal document in a rotten bunch because I noticed that Sid immediately decided he would choose which document to test. If they had similar doubts no one else appeared to show it as Winston and his bodyguards were waved off on their visit to Scotland with glee.

Later that day I sat in my room and questioned the logic of my actions over the past nine months or so. I could not be sure of getting my pension even now but the situation had not really changed during this period. I reasoned that I had no obvious alternative to the life I was leading and there was at least a chance I would get a substantial fund if I just held on a little longer. It was a question of holding on for a short period, though, because my hatred was on the decline and correspondingly the guilt at what I was doing was on the increase. I must have dozed off at some stage because I was surprised to see that Simon had entered my room and was pointing his stinger in the general direction of my stomach.

I made an effort to get out of the way but this only resulted in the dart entering my body just above the waist. It must have taken at least thirty seconds before all my lights went out and in this time I experienced the sensation of sliding to the floor in slow motion while a madman appeared to be delighting in the fact that his toy had broken all previous records.

Once more I woke up in a TH centre having been drugged by one of its inhabitants. This time I was lying on a cold floor without even a blanket over me. I was angry the first time it happened but this time my anger was almost uncontrollable. I was nauseous and in pain from a swelling where the dart had hit me but despite this I dragged myself through the various rooms looking for Simon and screaming insults at all and sundry. Gradually, it dawned on me that I was alone in the building and most of the contents had been removed during the time I was unconscious. Using what little strength I had available I then vented my anger by smashing some of the remaining bits of furniture.

Common sense then prevailed and I tried to take stock of my situation. I assumed that the others had absconded with all the money available for the share-out. My attempts to work out a plan of action were shattered when the front door was opened and Sid walked in. His reaction completely took the wind out of my sails.

'Oh, good, you're okay. That silly bastard Simon shot you with his stinger—he seems to think that it was acceptable to experiment on someone and for obvious reasons he chose you. Winston says that even at this late stage we're going to have to do something about Simon, because he's too crazy to be left on the loose—too crazy for all our sakes.'

I grunted: 'That must have been obvious to the lowest level of moron on first sighting the man.'

Sid's reaction was typical: 'Winston will be pleased to hear how highly you rate his leadership.' He went on, 'But we need him and you both tonight. The last two pick-ups were supposed to have taken place last night when David and Peter were available but got postponed once again until tonight. Winston has already got both of them on IRA duty tonight and so they won't be able to help make these pick-ups, and I want a minimum of two at my rear as back-up support.'

He then left the building to buy some pizzas and other

173

refreshments but before leaving he told me that Simon would be back shortly and he didn't want any trouble between us. His final comment was: 'Leave the fight till tomorrow night and I'll buy ringside seats.'

His reference to IRA duty was to a limited bombing campaign on various targets that was to take place as a diversion when we finally left the centre and closed down TH. The authorities would not blame the IRA for long but just long enough to draw away the attention of anyone beginning to take an interest in us. The news that this would take place tonight meant that I had probably been unconscious for anything up to forty hours. More importantly, the payoff was very close and I ought not to risk everything at this late stage by warring with Simon. Nevertheless, I was unarmed and it made sense to try to rectify this situation well before I left on the night's work.

I went through all the rooms, starting with the front door cupboard where weapons were normally kept, but couldn't find any form of gun that I could secrete about my body. There were two sturdy safes that were dragged around when we moved from one centre to another. I knew that Winston had keys to both and apart from that only Sid had a key to just one of them. I tried to open each of the safes but I made no impression on either of them. It seemed very silly trying to open these safes in the hope of finding a gun when on other occasions weaponry of all types had been left lying around.

I made a special search of Simon's room because after all, he was the self-styled weapons officer. There were a few of his experimental stingers around but I was not convinced that such a weapon would be of any value in a gunfight at share-out time. I carried on looking for a more conventional weapon and was so engrossed in this task that for the second time in a matter of hours I did not see Simon enter the room. He screamed insults at me in a language that I did not understand and then rushed at me with his hands raised. I had previously assumed that I would have little difficulty in overpowering Simon but that turned out to be a mistake. As we rolled together around the floor he was beginning to get control of the fight, and I began to realise that his youth and my poor condition would work increasingly in his favour. I was also under no illusions about his intentions—he would kill me if he could. As we struggled I tried to reach for any weapon that might be at hand. Eventually, I grabbed a telephone that had been pulled to the floor and hit him repeatedly around the head with it. When he stopped struggling I was at first relieved but then horrified at the damage I had done. He was not only very dead but I was forced to accept that anyone seeing his condition would assume that the attack had been carried out by a homicidal maniac.

His blood covered me, so I washed and changed into the only other clothes I possessed—a tee shirt and jeans. I thought about leaving the premises and TH for good, but all I had was ten pounds in my wallet and the fear that Winston and his team would take revenge by leaving evidence of my involvement for the police to find. The alternative I decided on was to carry on with TH to the end and hope that by getting rid of Simon I had solved the problem that Sid had referred to.

When Sid returned and saw the body I thought he was going to have a fit. I tried to explain what had led up to the mayhem but he kept interrupting my explanation saying he had to think. Eventually, it became clear that Sid did not see any real problem in Simon's death.

'Look, you stupid bastard, forget about him being dead, I'm more concerned about protection for this evening's activities. I think I need to telephone Winston for advice.'

He was about to make the call but I reminded him that a call from the centre could be traced back later if a murder enquiry was started.

My advice seemed to add to his confusion. 'Bloody hell, I suppose the same holds true for the local boxes—I'll have to find a telephone a few miles away.'

During Sid's absence I continued my search for a weapon but failed to find one. When Sid returned he was more cheerful.

'When I told Winston what you'd done he just said how bloody typical of him. But he doesn't think it's necessary to do anything with Simon's body because we'll be torching this place within the next few days.'

I was relieved to hear this. 'Thank God for that, but we do have another problem—I can't find a weapon.'

Sid seemed unworried by my announcement. He looked at his watch and groaned, 'We don't have time to search for a weapon, we have to leave immediately to get to the pick-up points in time.' As I got in his car he looked at me and said, 'You'll just have to try and look fierce.'

After travelling for about an hour we stopped for takeaway pizzas and coffee and I moved into the back of the car to make it easier to eat and drink on the move. I must have dozed off because the next thing I remembered was Sid cursing and swearing because he couldn't find the seafront café where the first deal was to be completed. When he did find it I could see that he'd become extremely nervous. I enjoyed seeing his discomfort and decided to add to it.

'Blimey, I'm glad I don't have to go in there, I'll lie down on the back seat to keep out of sight until you get back.'

He waved the gun in front of my face. 'You cowardly bastard, you're going in first.'

I surprised myself with my reaction: 'Fine, tell me whom I have to negotiate with and give me the money and the gun.'

My fat colleague clearly thought he had thwarted a plot I was hatching.

'Not so bloody fast, I want you to stay with me until we're in the café, but keep a distance from the negotiations. I want you to keep looking out of the café window and give the impression of nodding to someone outside to indicate we have additional back-up.'

When we got inside the café I adjourned to a table by the window. I suppose because my life was already in a complete mess I didn't feel particularly nervous in this situation and decided to add to Sid's discomfort by laying my head on the table and pretending to go asleep. Through my half-closed eyes I delighted in Sid's fear when he thought I had gone to sleep. When he turned towards me again seconds later he saw that I was wide awake and smiling at him. Eventually Sid and three swarthy-looking individuals left the café for another destination. I followed but walked back towards Sid's car in the knowledge that I had deliberately left the passenger door unlocked and that in all probability I would find another key in the car if he did not return within half an hour or so.

Sid returned to the car after about fifteen minutes, carrying a bag and sweating like a pig. He threw the bag at me and drove off at speed. When he was certain we had not been followed he stopped and opened a can of lager.

It was obvious he was not going to offer me a drink, so I said, 'No thanks, Sid, I never drink on duty.'

His reaction was to say, 'Smart sod, aren't you!' but then he passed me a can.

Before starting on the next pick-up he took the opportunity to berate me for not staying close to him to protect him when he left the café and for not obeying his instructions to keep looking out of the window. He was almost pleading for an answer when he finally said, 'What sort of game are you playing?'

I totally confused him with my reply: 'Sorry, Sid, I thought it *was* a game—it must be the effect of that drug Simon gave me.'

Whether he believed me or not, I don't know, but once we were underway again he told me the deal he'd done was a very profitable one but that he thought it would become increasingly difficult for anyone to play our traditional 'middle man' role in future. Apparently it was not only the TH overseas contacts that had enabled them to get started in the illegal drugs trade, it was also the original willingness to work on low or zero margins. Winston took this step as a way of doing additional harm to the British people, but he had always refused to allow anyone to get closer to the actual users. Sid was in effect arguing that the suppliers and dealers would continue to get closer to the users and so force out the middle men who were taking only minor risks.

I told Sid that I was still feeling dopey from the effects of the drug that Simon had inflicted on me. In truth I had recovered surprisingly well, but this ruse gave me the excuse to doze in the back seat while Sid searched for the next pick-up point. I expected some opposition from Sid because it was a foul night with very heavy wind and rain, but he seemed quite happy to do all the work on this occasion. In addition he appeared to be very considerate by keeping quiet and allowing me to sleep. Eventually, however, I started to hear muttered curses and deduced that he was having difficulty finding his target.

'Where are we, are we close to the pick-up point?'

'I think we're getting close but you can make yourself useful for once by keeping a look out for signposts and telling me what they say.'

This turned out to be a difficult task because we were on a dimly lit coast road.

I could not make sense of any of the signposts I saw over the next few minutes but it was clear that we were approaching a large bay.

Rather childishly, Sid then said, 'I've found it despite your assistance.'

He continued on the coast road and reached an area where houses were few and far between. On the left-hand side of the road was the sea wall. The tide was coming in and the combined effect of the tide and the wind was causing water and pebbles to litter the road. It crossed my mind that we ought to get off this road quickly before the authorities closed it for safety reasons. The other side of the road was mainly scrubland and this extended for several hundred yards uphill before buildings of any sort could be seen.

At the middle point of the bay were two shelters containing seats facing out to sea. These were about a hundred yards apart and in better weather they must have been pleasant places to relax. In the conditions we were currently encountering, however, they would provide only limited comfort.

Sid stopped between the two, opened his door and shouted, 'We'll both have to get wet.' He pointed to one shelter and said, 'Pick up the bag under the seat, I'll get the bag from the other shelter.'

I did not argue and to avoid getting too wet I rushed towards where he had directed me. Within seconds of setting off though, serious doubts entered my mind—why would anyone leave drugs under a seat without first getting payment? I stopped and turned to look at Sid. He was standing by his car door, gun in hand, and it was pointing at me. I then realised that one bullet had already been fired at me. Presumably, it missed, because Sid had been taken aback by the speed I had left the car, but he was taking aim carefully this time. The sea wall was only about fifteen to twenty feet away and so I ran towards it and jumped over into the sea.

Later I realised that I may have been better advised to run in some other direction, because no one would normally survive in the conditions I suddenly found myself in. I was immediately dragged under the water at great speed. When I surfaced it was still difficult to breathe but the force of the incoming tide then threw me against the sea wall. Fortunately, as I bounced off the wall, I rebounded onto a large wooden groin. I grabbed this structure and held on until the tide ebbed. I managed to move to another groin that I assumed would give better protection from the next wave. Then as I looked along the wall I saw Sid on all fours at least seventy yards away. He was looking over the wall at the point I had entered the water, and even in such dire circumstances I remember thinking how fortunate I was that my enemy was a complete idiot.

I kept as still as I could and eventually a small car drove by. This caused Sid to return to his own car and soon he drove off in the same southerly direction he had pursued when we first entered the bay. I was incredibly cold and I determined to get back on the road just as soon as Sid's rear light became faint and the wave conditions allowed. Suddenly, however, Sid's brake lights came on and I could faintly see that another car had drawn abreast of him coming from the other direction.

The drivers of the two vehicles obviously spent a few moments talking. Then Sid drove on without changing direction and the other car approached me very slowly. I was filled with dread at this ominous turn of events because it clearly indicated that a combined TH effort was being made to liquidate me. Consequently, I was not surprised that when the car stopped both Peter and David emerged and they were both armed. Their car was less than fifty yards from me and they were shouting to each other. The wind and noise was so strong that I caught only snatches of their conversation, but I thought I heard David saying, 'Where are you, Martin?'

Unlike Sid it was obvious that in their efforts to locate me they were trying to allow for the direction of the waves. Accordingly, David started close to where the car was parked and Peter jogged a couple of hundred yards along the road. I assumed that they then intended to work towards each other making a careful examination of anywhere I could be hiding behind the sea wall. I quickly decided that if possible I would follow the direction that Sid had taken but it meant that I either had to avoid David seeing me or overpower him in some way. I was having a difficult time holding on to the groin when the big waves occurred, because I had very little feeling left in my hands. David adopted the policy of waiting for the waves to subside and then leaning over the sea wall and peering down. He was doing this about once every ten yards. I kept myself still on the side of the groin away from him and when the opportunity arose I picked up a heavy stone. I thought that with luck, when he finally got close to me, I would see him before he saw me and I would aim the stone at his head. At the moment when I expected him to appear almost above me there was another substantial wave and David wisely kept his distance. The added tension I experienced during this delay was almost too much to bear, and when his face suddenly appeared not more than eighteen inches from my own I was less prepared than I should have been. Fortunately for me the experience of seeing me so close virtually transfixed David and with a little effort I was able to smash the stone into his skull. He had been in a squatting position and the effect of his head being smashed back knocked him back on his haunches, but then he slipped forward into the sea.

For a moment or two I found that I could not release either my grip on the groin or the stone. Then I managed to put the stone on the sea wall and pull myself onto it. The effort nearly caused me to pass out but I quickly recovered and looked northwards. I saw a figure, which I assumed to be Peter, on hands and knees, looking down into the water some 150 yards away. I made a brief search hoping to find that David had dropped his car keys or his gun, but this proved fruitless. I then adopted the same squatting position as Peter but moved towards the car. I opened the car door but the keys were not there. Then I remembered it was standard TH practice to tape spare keys, money and sometimes weapons under the carpet in the boot. I was able to unlock the boot from inside the car and I found thirty pounds, which I pocketed, but no spare keys and no gun. I continued to search for anything that might be useful to defend myself. I saw a container, which indicated that they had been involved in a drugs pick-up. Then I saw a box that I knew contained small explosive devices, which they had presumably used in their 'IRA' activities. From behind the car I could see Peter getting closer and from his general demeanour I sensed that he was thinking it was pointless continuing the search.

I set the timer on two devices for three minutes and when Peter again squatted down to study something in the sea, I ran to the only cover I could see on the landlocked side of the road. I then watched with mounting fascination and horror as Peter got closer to the car.

To this day I am convinced that my original intention was to destroy the car and so force Peter to run away. But it did not work out that way. He was nervous when he got to the car because he couldn't see David. He was tentatively opening the driver's door when the explosion occurred and I saw that he was killed instantly. I suddenly realised that I was sobbing and it took a few moments before I could compose myself. I ran south in the direction Sid had taken but then I saw headlights approaching me so I threw myself into a ditch.

The car passed me and then stopped. The driver got out and ran towards the conflagration. Looking over my left shoulder I saw from the exhaust fumes that the engine was still running. At the same time I realised it was Sid's car and he had now stopped running and was studying the sight in front of him. I also noticed that he had a gun in his hand. The noise from the elements was deafening and Sid obviously did not hear me approaching the car. In fact I had put the car in gear and closed the door before Sid realised what was happening. He fired at me and hit one of the wing mirrors, but he then took fright and ran around the burning car keeping close to the sea wall. At the same moment I accelerated around the burning vehicle, intending to put it between Sid and myself. I took this risky action in the belief that it was my best chance to escape from the gunfire. If I had taken the southern route, I would have been forced to do a three-point turn and would have been a sitting duck.

As David's car had been parked on the left-hand side of the road the only safe route past the flames was a small gap close to the sea wall. Therefore, as we were both trying to keep well away from the burning petrol, it was perhaps inevitable that I should run over him. The car dragged him along for about fifty yards before it was safe to stop. Immediately I got out of the car it was obvious he was dead. I did not hesitate for long—I dragged his body over the sea wall and into the sea. I then spent some time in a fruitless search to find his gun, but when I saw headlights coming from the south I quickly drove off in the direction we had both come from such a short time earlier.

CHAPTER
ELEVEN

Within a few minutes I was clear of the bay area but was then faced with a decision as to where I should head for. Eventually, I decided that my best option was to drive away from the coast and then find a place to rest and take stock of the situation. I had to control a very strong desire to put my foot down because it was obviously important that I should not draw attention to myself. After about fifteen minutes I came across a sign pointing the way to Norwich. Some distance along this road I stopped at a lay-by. It was three o'clock in the morning and there were very few cars on the road.

I stopped the engine and stepped out into the heavy rain. Up till that point I had been reasonably in control of my emotions, but now I became very sick and began shaking violently. Eventually, I got some control back and after cleaning myself up, decided to be on my way.

Before starting the car again I mulled over my options. I probably had safe use of the car for three days because even if Sid's body was found within the next few hours, the car was not registered in his name. Therefore, associating his body with this car was by no means automatic. It could be that the police might conclude that all the participants in the bay area violence were dead and would not look for anyone else. However, I could not rely on that assumption. As far as I knew, only Winston and the flowerpot men remained of the TH team. It could be that Sid, David and

Peter had tried to kill me without Winston's permission so that my pension would go to them, or they could have been acting on Winston's orders. It was probably an evens bet that Winston was involved, in which case I still had the chance of a sizeable pay-off. Alternatively, I had something over thirty pounds to my name if I decided not to risk meeting up with Winston's team again.

As this last thought came into my mind I caught sight of headlights in my mirror. Instinctively I turned the engine on and became aware of the mass of keys on the key ring. It then dawned on me that by using Sid's car and keys I would be able to get right into the centre and one of the safes would almost certainly be opened by one of the keys nestling in my hand. Sid had told me that Winston would return to the centre later that day. In that case I probably had twelve hours between now and when Winston was likely to get there. If I could find money and a gun in the safe then I could decide on future options at that point.

I worked out that it would take me no more than three hours to get to Birmingham, so I had the opportunity to pay my very overdue last respects to my wife and son by stopping off to visit our last home. As I started on my journey again I was suddenly aware that I had no idea of the east coast town or district where my late colleagues had ended their lives.

By five-thirty in the morning I was making very good time and decided to stop for breakfast at an all-night café. While eating and drinking I mulled over the fact that I had killed four people in separate incidents in the last twenty-four hours or so. I knew that all these killings had been in self-defence, but accepted I had no right to expect anyone to believe me. Quite clearly, I could not expect any mercy in a court of law if I was ever charged with these offences. It was obvious that with or without a TH pension it was essential that I should disappear from sight in some remote region for the foreseeable future.

As I was filling up with petrol at an adjoining petrol station, I suddenly realised that I had not looked in the boot of Sid's car for under-carpet goodies. I pulled up in a quiet place and eagerly searched through the boot. Sadly, I found no money or guns, but just as I was about to close the boot I saw the bag containing the drugs Sid had collected a few hours earlier. I realised I ought to get rid of this as soon as possible. At the first opportunity I pulled up by a large culvert at the side of the road and undid the fastening. The rain was coming down heavily again and so without studying the contents, I tipped them into the culvert. The next moment I saw a gun drop into the culvert followed by the drugs. I spent a few minutes trying to raise the top of the drain system but I couldn't move it at all. I marvelled that the gun could have got into the drain and then realised that it must have fallen into the one damaged area where this was possible. Mr Murphy's law worked again.

At about seven o'clock I got to the M1 area and because I didn't want to get to my old home before it was in full daylight, I made a detour to Scratchwood Services. My intention was to see if the TH office was still there. From talking to a group of workmen in the building I discovered that some strange start-up company had hired an office for a few weeks about a year ago but the experiment did not work and the company had quickly pulled out of the deal. There was no other trace of a TH office anywhere in the building. Obviously, as I drove away, I wondered if the limited hiring of the office space had something to do with the murder of my family.

Just driving up to my old home was emotionally taxing. It became even more stressful when I realised that the house was being rebuilt. The Maher house had presumably been sold to new owners because it had been completely redecorated in a style that was out of keeping with Mary Maher's taste. I parked about a hundred yards away but stayed in the car to limit the chance of anybody recognising me.

A middle-aged woman that I did not recognise soon appeared riding a bicycle. She was delivering newspapers to some of the houses in the area. When she got close to me I wound down the car window and called to her: 'I wonder if you can help me. I'm told that there is a house for sale around here but I can't see one that matches the description I've been given.'

Before she could answer, I added, 'Well, the one that's just being built matches the description, but I was told that the house up for sale was at least two years old.'

Her face immediately took on an all-knowing look and she came up close to the car window. Over the next few minutes she treated me to what had clearly been an exciting piece of local gossip and she obviously enjoyed the opportunity to enlarge upon a story she had told many times before.

She started by announcing, 'It's not a new house—it's being rebuilt because the last owner murdered his wife and her lover and then ran off with the next door neighbour. No, I wouldn't live there for all the tea in China, but some people enjoy living in morbid circumstances.'

I needed to get her in the right frame of mind so that she'd develop the story, and so I said, 'That's a pity, we're almost running out of options in trying to find a house. But I can imagine living in a house where there has been a murder would be a problem.'

Before I could say anything else she enlarged on the story: 'You see the Rogers and the Mahers were well known swappers—they were at it all the time. But Mr R decided to pretend he was going away on business and came back and found her with Mr M. The police think he knocked them both unconscious and then set the house on fire. Why Mrs M ran away with such a man I'll never know.'

At this point she announced, 'Well, I can't stand here gossiping,' and started to ride away.

I just had the time to ask, 'Were any children hurt?'

To that she answered, 'Several, I think.'

I drove on to a sparsely populated area about five miles from my old home and parked the car while I fought to control my emotions. It was not just the loss of my family that was troubling me but the fear that I might never find out why my wife and son were killed. In the last nine months or so I had taken some comfort from the notion that when I finally escaped from the clutches of TH, I would be free to find out what really happened to them. Now I began to feel that I might be facing an impossible task. I realised that I had talked to just one local person and several of the facts she had relayed were incorrect. It was obvious that if I could talk to other local people I might hear slightly different versions. Nevertheless, it seemed likely that they would all report that I had run off with Mary Maher. I could not understand this at all—why had Mary left in a hurry and allowed the neighbours to denigrate her memory? I eventually forced myself to set off for the centre but I was now resolved to risk everything to establish the truth.

Using Sid's keys I got into the centre and quickly established that there was no one else present. Even so it was with enormous trepidation that I opened the individual doors. It took a special effort on my part to look into Simons's room. His body was still there and it was not looking any better than when I last saw it. I opened the safe that Sid had access to. Inside were the stock transfers but nothing else. After some thought I decided to leave them inside and closed the safe. None of the other keys would open Winston's safe and so I had to accept that my journey had so far been fruitless.

I suddenly realised that one of the keys on Sid's ring was for a large padlock, and there was no such lock in the centre. Then I remembered the lock-up building that I had seen one of the flowerpot men entering. I couldn't think of anything else to try and I did not fancy confronting Winston without a weapon, so I carefully locked all the relevant rooms again and made my way to the lock-up. As I put the key in the padlock I realised I was being scrutinised by people in neighbouring premises. There was no point in backing down at this stage though, and in any case the key was a match and from then on entry was straightforward.

The premises turned out to be much larger than I would have guessed from the outside. The main room was a large warehouse and from the number of tables and chairs I imagined that up to twelve people at a time had worked in there in the past. As I walked around the rooms it was obvious that TH had used the place for many years and its presence explained why the control function had to remain in the Birmingham area. This is where they made and stored the tools to damage the British nation. There were bits and pieces of literature and equipment that I remembered using and other things relating to situations that I had no idea that TH were involved in.

Then I saw the tool that both enlightened me and made me feel very foolish. It was a very old printing press and lying around it in neat piles were the posters, newspapers and articles that had been printed on it over the years. The early ones were mainly associated with the mock articles intended to encourage immigration. But right from the first moment I saw the press I knew that this is where they had printed the newspaper articles relating to the murder of my family. When I finally saw copies of the articles that had been produced for my benefit nine months earlier, I could hear my heart beating very loudly and I knew I must do something to reduce the stress I was feeling. To some extent I achieved this by adopting a strategy that accepted that weapon or no weapon I had to meet with Winston and wring an explanation from him and then kill him.

I locked up the premises and decided to walk back to the centre and so abandoned Sid's car in the car park where I had left it. To some extent this move was a way of reducing my own options and thereby ensuring that I would confront the demon. On the way I decided it would be much better if I entered the building when Winston was already present, as I would appear less threatening that way. As a result I took the opportunity to stop for a meal and eventually got there at about four p.m. A few nervous minutes after entering the building it was clear that Winston had not yet returned and I had to accept that there was a possibility he would never return to these premises. Despite this possibility I had no option but to wait and I busied myself in a further search for a gun and suitable ammunition. I had no more success in this search than I had the first time and eventually decided that although Simon's stinger might be useless in most circumstances, it was better than nothing. I experimented with three different versions and decided to choose the smallest one, even though I estimated its ability to penetrate human skin with a dart was limited to a maximum range of about five inches. The other two, including the one used on me, were probably effective up to eight inches, but they were more difficult to conceal. The repeating firing mechanism was also more reliable on the smaller version but I found that I could load and fire a maximum of five dart pellets. I had no idea what the pellets contained but I hoped and assumed that whatever it was it would be sufficient for my needs.

I knew that both Simon and Winston had considered the stinger to be a weapon that would be used to inject poison in some unsuspecting person as you walked past them and therefore it could simply be housed in a coat pocket. My enemy or enemies were likely to be on their guard at all times and this was the factor that made the stinger far less suitable than a gun in my circumstances. In the end I decided that it could be useful as a surprise weapon if my foe was convinced that I was not conventionally armed. After thinking about this for some time I decided to tape the stinger to the skin on the inside of my left thigh. After some further experimentation, I added padding to my inside leg before taping on the stinger to limit the chance of the pellet entering my own body in an accidental firing. When I replaced my jeans, though, I appeared to have one thigh much thicker than the other. I solved this by reducing the padding around the stinger and adding more to my right leg. When I finished this exercise I waited as quietly as I could with the light on.

Just after eight I heard the front door opening and I went to meet whoever was about to join me. At first I couldn't see anyone and I shouted, 'Is that you, Winston?'

Eventually Winston emerged from behind a door, gun in hand and with a very surprised look on his face.

I raised my arms to show that I was not armed and said, 'Winston, we need to talk.'

Then I was hit hard on the back of the head.

CHAPTER TWELVE

Some time later I became vaguely aware that I was in the boot of a car that was moving very quickly. My hands and feet were tied with what appeared to be parcel tape. In addition there was a large pencil separating my teeth and my mouth was partially taped up. Gradually it dawned on me that someone, presumably Winston, was trying to keep me alive for a little while but had also taken steps to prevent me from shouting out until they got away from the built-up areas. In coming to this conclusion, I reasoned that the fumes from the car would have made breathing difficult for an uninjured person, particularly if they had their mouth taped up. But I had received damaging blows to the nose and my left eye, which made my situation much worse. Whoever trussed me up in this way must have assumed that I would be violently sick at some stage during the journey and realised that if my mouth was completely sealed I would be forced to swallow the vomit and the result would probably be fatal. I took some comfort from this conclusion, because it meant that someone wanted to talk to me and I dreaded the thought of being tossed into a river in this condition.

I was already feeling very sick and as I did not want to rely entirely on the pencil, I tried to make sure that my face was always facing downwards. I concentrated on breathing slowly and steadily to control the feeling of nausea but I realised that I could not prevent the inevitable for very long. Suddenly, the car stopped, the boot was opened and a hand checked to see if I was still breathing. I had kept my eyes closed during this time to try to convince the person examining me that I was still unconscious. Then I heard Winston's voice:

'What condition is he in?'

The answer came back, 'He's not been sick.'

'Then release his mouth, it doesn't matter how loud he screams now.'

The boot was then closed and the car continued on its way. I was violently sick and then went to sleep.

I awoke to what initially appeared to be a pleasant dream-world full of magical farm animals and in which I was a small boy again. Gradually, however, it began to dawn on me that I was looking at mock farm scenes painted on various cabinets in a very large kitchen, and I appeared small because I was lying on the floor. I was horrified to find that my feet were tied together with parcel tape and my hands with a mixture of rope and parcel tape. Previously my hands were tied behind my back, but this time they were tied at the front. I was still feeling nauseous and my head ached but I realised that as I was still alive I must have some chance of surviving even if it was only a small one. I tried to move but the effort was painful and so I decided first to think out what options I had. I assumed that the only reason I was kept alive was that Winston wanted to know what had happened to Sid and the others. Therefore it made sense to feign unconsciousness when my assailants returned to give me longer to dream up a situation that might keep me alive.

I twisted my body to see if there was anything in the room that could help me and discovered that the stinger was still strapped to my leg. I was surprised at this but I thankfully assumed that my assailants must have missed the weapon because of the padding I'd applied. Then I realised that using the stinger in my present circumstances was not going to be easy. My hands had been tied together in front of my body but this still made it virtually impossible to reach and pull the trigger mechanism. After a certain amount of experimentation I discovered that with my little fingers pressed together I could unzip my jeans and then was able to get at the trigger of the stinger quite easily. However, this was of limited value because leaving the zip down would draw attention to the fact that I had something strapped to my leg.

In the circumstances it appeared inevitable that if I was going to use the stinger I would need at least thirty seconds to go through the unzipping and firing sequence, and then be within a few inches of my foe. Feeling deflated again I zipped up my jeans and hoped that the incredible luck I had experienced during the coastal violence would still be with me when I came to need it again. Trying to think up alternative defensive tactics was not helped by the fact that both the pain and nausea were getting worse and I kept drifting in and out of consciousness.

Suddenly, I heard the noise of someone entering the room and I braced myself for the expected kick. When it came I was relieved that it was not too violent and I was able to keep my eyes closed and feign unconsciousness. The kicker cursed and went into a room alongside the kitchen but left the door open. Then another person joined him from yet another room and from their conversation I realised it was the flowerpot men. Although they were renowned for saying very little, I had heard them speak a few times over the years and the one I always thought of as Bill was the one who drove me up to Chorley on my second day in the country. He was the first to speak:

'Don't tell me he's still in bloody lullaby land.'

'Yep, sleeping like a big soft kid.'

Bill was very irritated: 'Why did you have to hit him so bloody hard?'

'I didn't think it mattered how hard I hit him, his nibs wanted him dead.'

'Yes, he wanted him dead, but not before he'd asked him a few questions.'

'No one told me that.'

'Well, you discovered it soon enough when the boss had his heart attack. Common sense should have told us we'd have to take this creep with us until he could be interrogated. But you go and give his head and guts a good kicking and so make it bloody certain all our arrangements are delayed and we're in deep trouble.'

'I keep telling you, I assumed the boss was dying from his attack and we'd lose everything. I was angry and so because he was responsible I gave him a little kick.'

Bill was not going to let him off lightly: 'Well, let's examine what you've achieved with your bang on the head and little kick. The boss is now with the doctor and won't be back for forty-five minutes, I should think. Even if our friend here recovers in time it'll be another forty-five before he coughs up the information and we've dealt with him. Then remember, we have to escort the boss to Salisbury, hang around until he's done what he has to do, complete our deal with him and wave him off to Heathrow. It's all right for bloody Winston, he's not going to miss his bloody flight whatever happens, because everything we're doing is based on serving him.'

Ben was confused: 'I thought our flight to Spain was later than his?'

'Yes, it is, but unlike you and the boss I still have some chores to do. It looks as if I'll have to take the risk of returning here in the next few weeks and all because of a bash on the head and a little kick.'

Ben suddenly sounded contrite: 'I'm sorry, but why didn't you mention it earlier? You could have hired a car from little Tom in the village this morning and then we could have got some of your jobs done.'

This brought on another blast from Bill: 'Are you being deliberately stupid? If Winston returned and we weren't here, he could pick up his bloody great rug and the other bits and pieces he agreed to leave behind as security and bugger off without us. Why do you think I spent so much time negotiating with him to leave these things with us?'

Ben was annoyed at being called stupid and questioned Bill's acumen in regard to the securities concerned. 'How can you be sure he's coming back anyway? The rug thing may be worthless.

I'm sure I could buy a better bloody rug for a few quid down Petticoat Lane and it'd be worth more because it hadn't been given by Stalin.'

'That's interesting. You reckon you could buy a carpet valued at £10,000,000 for a few quid do you?'

Ben was clearly impressed. 'How do you know it's worth that much, why didn't you tell me? Hey, we ought to take it now and get out of here.'

'That's why I didn't tell you. It's worth millions only because the boss has negotiated its sale to a group who are trying to break away from the Soviet Union. We couldn't do that. To us the bloody thing is worthless, except it will be in our hands until we say goodbye to him. If he wants the carpet he has to pay us the remainder of what we're due.'

Eventually, their mutual anger declined and Bill said, 'Let's get him to the front door so that our sick friend doesn't have to traipse through the house to talk to him.'

When they got close to me Ben said, 'Christ, he's beginning to stink to high heaven, I don't want to touch him.'

After some discussion they wrapped me in what appeared to be the loose cover from a large settee. Bill picked up my feet and Ben held me under my arms. The cover was not pulled tight around me and my hands were inside it, therefore I had an ideal opportunity to undo the zip and fire the stinger. However, in the position they adopted to carry me, their bodies were too far away for the stinger to be effective.

It suddenly dawned on me that if the stench I was giving off was not to their liking, then by being violently sick I should become even more offensive. Before they had carried me more than a few steps I started to vomit and I wasn't acting—it was just a case of letting the inevitable happen. They quickly dropped me back on the kitchen floor and lying on one side I repeatedly pulled my legs up to my chin and then down again in a motion that I hoped indicated great discomfort. This gave me the opportunity to undo the zip, but it took me longer to do it than when I was experimenting, probably due to the fact that I was lying on my side. When I managed to get my finger around the trigger, I stopped the convulsions.

Seeing that I had calmed down, Bill approached me and said, 'Have you finished being sick?'

I indicated that I had and they picked me up even more cautiously than the first time. This time Bill put both his hands under my left knee to avoid the mess I had created on the covering over the right-hand side of my body and Ben again put his hands under my armpits. In this position Bill's hands were within five inches of the stinger but my left knee was occupying the space in between. As they lifted me, I deliberately forced my right leg downwards and Bill had to compensate by grabbing my left knee with his right hand.

I pulled the trigger and I heard the yell as the dart penetrated Bill's hand.

He dropped me and screamed, 'What the hell!'

He must have pulled the dart out quickly because it wasn't to be seen as he made a pathetic effort to inform Ben what had happened. As he slowly collapsed it brought back memories of my own dying swan interpretation a few days earlier. Ben clearly had no idea what had happened but he got down on his knees to loosen Bill's clothing and conveniently placed his right thigh within range of the stinger. The dart got home and Ben slowly turned towards me with a look of absolute horror on his face. Considering everything Ben had done for me recently I thought he deserved something in return and I fired a second dart at him. He began to collapse and I had to move my body to avoid him falling on top of me.

As everything went quiet the initial feeling of relief was immense and strangely within seconds I had to fend off the desire to sleep and ease my aching body. I resisted the temptation, got on my knees and searched the two men to try to find a gun, but they didn't appear to be armed. Searching them was difficult with my hands bound together and I realised that there would be knives available in the kitchen drawers with which I could cut myself free. However, Winston and perhaps others would soon return and I would prefer to have a loaded gun and my hands tied together than have my hands and feet free but be without a weapon to defend myself. Clearly, I could not rely on the good fortune of being in a position to use the stinger again and in any case there was probably only one dart left in it. Then I remembered that at each of the TH centres, we had all parked our guns on entering the premises in a cabinet close to the front-door coat cupboard. Assuming that must be the case here I struggled to my feet intending to find the front door. Then I heard one of the flowerpot men groan.

Panic swept through me when I realised I would have to kill the flowerpot men or at least put them out of action for several hours because I couldn't be sure how long the effects of the drug would last. I looked around and saw several ornamental plant pots on one of the kitchen cabinets. These were about two feet tall and each contained a small orange tree. With difficulty I lifted one of these pots by one of the handles on the side and then shuffled over to the prone figures. From a height of about four feet I dropped the pot on Bill's head and then went through the same routine with Ben. I then made the mistake of looking down to see the effect I had achieved. The damage to Bill's face was much more extensive than I had imagined and his blood was already running onto the floor. The sight of this must have made me unsteady because I slipped on the mess below. When I scrambled up again my legs were covered in blood. Then I noticed that one of the broken pieces of pot had a sharp edge and I tried unsuccessfully to use it to remove the binding on my hands. However, it was a relatively simple task to cut through the tape binding my legs together.

The elation at being able to walk reasonably well again was balanced by the horror at what I had done with the plant pots. In the circumstances I stood for a moment on very unstable legs, my lower half covered in my own vomit and someone else's blood and my heart pounding so loudly that I feared any further movement would give me a heart attack. Having movement in my legs made me reconsider my earlier intention to head for the front-door area to look for a gun. Instead I moved around the kitchen looking for a suitable knife. I quickly found one but with my hands tied together

I had great difficulty in placing the knife in a position where I could cut through the rope and tape. When I finally succeeded I also managed to inflict a deep cut in my left hand. Then I removed the stinger from my thigh and stuck it down the top of my jeans just over my spine. At that moment I heard the sound of a car approaching the building.

On hearing this sound, extreme tiredness and the negative elements of my make-up combined to insist that I stop and refuse to take any further part in this ongoing nightmare. Fortunately the will to live was stronger and after only a second or two's delay, I rushed to find the gun cupboard before the occupants of the car entered the premises. As luck would have it the house was enormous and I had to go through several corridors before I could even see the front door and I was delayed by falling over a can of petrol outside one of the doors. The car engine had stopped long before I had got within twenty feet of the door. When I heard footsteps outside the door I realised that I was not going to have time to search for a weapon and decided to adjourn to a living room attached to the hall. Once in there I sat down on an armchair and was immediately seduced by the comfort it provided.

My original idea in entering the living room was that whoever was opening the door might walk through the house without looking in this room and I might then get the opportunity to search for a weapon. I was wrong in this assumption. Within seconds of closing the front door Winston entered the room and was clearly very shocked and surprised to see me sitting in one of his chairs. After putting a hand to his chest as if to ease some pain he turned and moved away as quickly as he could. His medical condition was such that a fit young man would have probably caught up with him before he could have moved more than a few yards. Sadly, from my point of view, I was no longer that young and my current condition was bordering on disastrous. After about thirty seconds during which time sheer physical and mental exhaustion had prevented me even getting out of the chair, Winston reappeared, gun in hand.

Winston appeared to sense that I was not likely to be an

immediate danger to him. He moved to a corner cabinet and poured himself a large whisky with one hand while holding the gun in the other.

He sat down in a chair opposite me and finally spoke: 'Where are my bodyguards?'

By this time I felt almost too weary to speak let alone think, but when he repeated the question, I muttered, 'Gone out.'

He looked both quizzical and nervous at hearing this comment and I realised I had to say more. After a little thought I added, 'They said they had some chores to do and were going to get a car from someone called little Tom in the village, but I heard them saying they'd be back in two hours.'

I could see that my mentioning little Tom had almost convinced him I was telling the truth, but then I could see him staring at my feet and hands. Therefore, I was not surprised to hear his next comment:

'So they left to do some chores but thoughtfully released the binding on your arms and legs so that you'd be free to walk about the neighbourhood, did they?'

At that point he put his drink down and with two hands on the gun pointed it in a very threatening gesture at my head. Then it slowly but surely dawned on me that I had not moved since he'd first entered the room and I had blood all over my jeans and my hands.

With a painful expression on my face, I slowly ran my hands down my shins, raised my blood-soaked palms in the air and said, 'Oh, they made sure I wouldn't get too far.'

Winston visibly relaxed after this and joked, 'They really are a couple of rascals.' But he then qualified his enthusiasm for their qualities by adding, 'But I promise to make them suffer for leaving their posts.' He took another long drink of whisky and also lit a cigar.

I shook my head and mockingly played the caring role: 'You know that's not good for you—why do you bother to see the doctor if you're going to carry on smoking and boozing?'

He ignored me but tersely asked, 'What happened to Sid, David, Peter and the drugs?'

I heard his question but could not originally think how to answer it. After considering my response for a moment or two, I tried the reasonable-man approach.

'Winston, you look as if you don't have much of your life left and my own luck will surely run out soon, so why don't we swap information honestly? You want me to answer the question you have just asked and I have just one desire left—to find out why you've been trying to kill me?'

Winston smiled and responded in his philosophical mode: 'But they're not of equal value—mine is just a question about three unfortunates and a couple of pots of gold, but your question relates to issues like the meaning of life.'

I thought that was the end of my reasonable approach but suddenly a look of delight appeared on Winston's face.

He stood up and walked around the room waving his gun as if he was conducting an orchestra. 'Martin, you have just made me realise that for the first time in decades I can share my secrets with someone and not have to worry about the consequences. You being here at this time provides a golden opportunity for me to see someone marvel at my achievements, because whether I tell you or not, I'll obviously have to kill you before my wayward helpers return.'

He appeared to wait for me to react but I couldn't think what to say so I closed my eyes and said nothing. I had not enjoyed hearing him announce that he would shortly kill me but part of the reason for closing my eyes was the pain and weariness that I was experiencing.

He appeared to think he was in danger of losing his audience and almost shouted, 'Martin, do you know what it is like to have achieved enormous success yet have to disguise the fact?' Before I could answer he added, 'No, of course not, you've never achieved very much.'

He then tried a different approach. 'Whom do you think is the greatest person of the twentieth century, and don't say Comrade bloody Stalin?'

I struggled to reply. 'Don't know—don't care.'

He seemed to be disappointed in my reaction and volunteered an answer to his own question: 'Well, if only the published data currently available is considered it would have to be Churchill, for his part in turning the tide in the war. But when eventually my memoirs are published it will be seen that Churchill's achievements do not compare with my own. So prepare yourself for a treat— you're going to hear a mind-boggling story, but first you answer *my* question.'

I tried to think through my limited options. He might listen to my explanation of what occurred during the previous day or so and then kill me without bothering to keep his side of the bargain. On the other hand he did appear to be very keen to boost his ego by telling me his story and as he said, he believed he'd nothing to lose by letting me into his secrets. In addition, he appeared to be convinced that I did not have the use of my legs. It was therefore reasonable to conclude that if I was going to take advantage of that it was more likely to happen when he was indulging in self-glorification than when he was attentively listening to my explanation of recent events. I was also very much aware that I had to bring the proceedings to a finish soon because my remaining strength was ebbing fast.

I therefore went through an honest explanation of events up to the point where I poured the drugs down the drain. It was clear that Winston had already obtained some information regarding the events on the east coast and his reaction indicated that he believed my explanation.

When I had finished he said, 'You were a lucky bastard, weren't you?' He was more concerned about the fate of the drugs than his TH colleagues but finally accepted the inevitable by saying, 'Yes, it would be just like you to chuck money down the drain.' Chillingly, his final comment on my story was, 'You robbed them of about twenty-four hours of life—I had no intention of letting them live in luxury.'

When I asked if the same fate awaited the flowerpot men he just smiled. He then asked why I returned to the centre, when I must have realised that I was risking my life. I again answered him truthfully and added that my desire to know what was going on was increased after visiting his Birmingham lock-up.

He sat back in his chair with a smile on his face and said, 'We torched that place as well as the centre last night, but I can see now why you're desperate for me to answer your question.'

He leaned further back in his chair and for a moment or two I thought he was going to renege on our agreement, but then he began his story with a statement that amazed me. 'I am an Irishman—I was born near Dublin.'

I did not initially react to this statement but inwardly I assumed I was about to hear an off-the-cuff fairy story.

He smiled when he saw the look of surprise on my face and continued: 'Although I have a poor general view of my fellow-countrymen I have always been intensely patriotic and grew up with a deep hatred of the British.'

I realised that it was the wrong time to interrupt him but as long as he was going to tell me a fairy story I thought I had the right to join in: 'Why do you have a poor view of the Irish?'

He did not appear irritated by this interruption and quickly answered, 'Mainly because although they may hate the British they have a strong tendency to support them in front of other nationalities.'

I thought for a moment and then said, 'Yes, I've noticed you do that on several occasions.'

This time he was irritated: 'Shut up and listen, my associates are likely to return in about half an hour, so you've a maximum of twenty minutes left to hear the most amazing story ever told.'

I realised I was more likely to catch him offguard if I didn't upset him any further. 'Sorry, Winston, I do want to hear your story.'

He smiled again: 'I was seventeen in early 1939 and when the conflict became inevitable I moved to Germany to assist them in their fight against the British. However, I hadn't been there long when I realised that the Irish Republic would suffer badly if and when Britain collapsed. In the circumstances I decided that the best solution from an Irish viewpoint was for the Germans to stop short of outright invasion of Britain and the best way to ensure that would be for the Russians to start a second front in the east. So I managed to get out of Germany and aligned myself with the Soviets. I found it very difficult learning the Russian language but this forced me to develop my extraordinary communication skills. Using these skills I found I could manipulate situations to my own advantage and I became very useful to the senior Soviet hierarchy. Then when it was obvious that the Germans would be defeated, I convinced my contacts that a British-German axis was a distinct possibility and that I should be funded to prevent it happening. The funny thing is that I didn't believe any of it myself at first but then I realised that if the British leaders had shown any sense at all, it would have happened.'

Winston then got carried away with his own storytelling and couldn't resist digressing into other aspects of his time in Russia that demonstrated his superiority over other mortals, and so the basic story was being stretched out agonisingly. Obviously, I didn't fear the flowerpot men coming back but I did wonder what Winston's reaction would be when he realised that they were long overdue. In addition I was concerned as to how much longer I could stay awake and I wasn't sure I believed much or any of the story that was unfolding. Weighing all these points together I decided to interrupt him again.

'Winston, I'm enjoying the story, but could you tell me at this point why it was so important to kill me?'

He looked at me almost pityingly and snarled, 'Well, you'll be dead and in hell shortly so now you'll never hear the end of my story.' Then he looked at me again and said, 'But as the answer to your question will drive you crazy, I'm happy to tell you—I hate you because you're British. But I hate you even more than the rest of the British trash because of the problems you've caused me.'

I found his statement ludicrous. 'You forget that my wife and I were recruited from an orphanage near Kiev.'

'Yes, you, your bloody wife and her toady brother were taken from an orphanage. I made the mistake of my life when I was told that a number of British kids had been picked up in the early part of the war and had been put in an orphanage. I thought it would be very fitting to train you to damage the British economy, a sort of revenge for your nation's divide-and-conquer tactics in the past. In the orphanage, your wife's brother kept all three of you alive but you still lived among rats and in filth. For that reason my Russian colleagues were against using you but I insisted and in due course you and the Russian kids from other orphanages were all subjected to brain-washing techniques to remove your early memories and make you ideal candidates for our needs.'

Although I had not completely believed the early part of his story his last comments were delivered with such vehemence that I realised there must be a possibility that they were true. However, my mind was in such turmoil that although I was hearing the words clearly enough, they initially failed to affect my emotions. At one stage my mind must have switched off completely but when it switched back on I heard:

'Someone thought it'd be a good idea if Stephen and the two girls of his age from your year joined the older class at your training school for physical training. As luck would have it he was sent on a sea survival exercise and became seasick. When he recovered he remembered that he and his little sister were British and confided this information to the two girls. Apparently, the two girls then started to remember some of their own pre-brain-washing memories. The local management panicked and for imaginary security reasons all three were immediately shot and buried in the grounds. The result was that for the first time my image was damaged and all because I had insisted on using British scum.'

I didn't want to believe that Stephen and the girls had been treated in this inhuman way and I tried to think of something to disprove it. Then I remembered that relatively recently we had a letter from Stephen and challenged Winston with this fact.

His reaction was, 'I enjoyed writing that letter—I knew about the older boy in the orphanage because we originally thought he was British.'

Winston was clearly enjoying seeing me suffer—the exercise appeared to be giving him strength, but it was definitely sapping my already poor energy level. I waved the back of my hand in his direction and told him I didn't believe a word of his story.

Winston smiled and said, 'If I'm telling porky pies how do you explain the fact that both you and your wife reacted so badly when you made the sea crossing to Dover? You should also consider the coincidence that Sid Jones was promoted that very day. His predecessor ignored my instructions that you were to fly from Ostend because he thought he knew better, and you saw what happened to him.'

He waited for his words to sink in; he was confident now that I had no alternative but to believe the awful story he was telling me. I felt totally numb in mind and body and although I desperately wanted to destroy this evil man I doubted if I could even get out of the chair in my present state. He gestured with his gun that I should make an effort to get to him. At first I assumed that some perverted notion of gallantry by giving his enemy a last chance was behind this gesture, but I couldn't respond.

He laughed and said, 'Well, who's a cowardy custard then?' Then he added, 'Oh silly me, I forgot the punch-line—you probably don't know it but your stupid wife had begun to remember her British origins but couldn't be sure of your allegiance to Mother Russia. Being bloody stupid she confided in her next-door neighbour who just happened to be one of Moscow's sleepers assigned to look after an important potential convert by marrying him. Obviously, we had to eliminate your wife—you do see that, don't you?'

On numerous occasions since I have tried to analyse my immediate reaction to these words. I should have leapt from the chair and attacked him with the strength of a madman. But initially I couldn't move at all and for a while my mind almost ceased to function. Looking back over time it now seems to me that my problem was due to something akin to overheating of the brain, probably caused by a combination of tiredness, pain, horror and the unanswered questions that were flooding through it. Winston was studying me closely. At first he took my inactivity to be a sign of weakness but then he clearly began to wonder if my failure to act was due to some other reason. He was still urging me to attack him but his demands were getting weaker.

I have heard that when badly wounded in battle, grown men frequently cry out for their mother to come to their assistance. I couldn't remember my mother, but I sought a similar type of help. At odd moments in the relatively short time that had passed since my fight for existence with Sid, David and Peter I had marvelled at how in each case the circumstances had allowed me to get through almost unscathed. And today, just a short time ago similar luck had enabled me to defeat the flowerpot men. Nothing miraculous had occurred during any of these incidents, I had simply used the weapons and situations that happened to be available. Nevertheless, I was under stress on each occasion, yet something had drawn my mind to the solution. I thought this might be my guardian angel and he or she must have had a direct telephonic connection to my brain. Now I couldn't really think at all and so I feared that the connection had been broken.

Then Winston suddenly stopped urging me to attack him. He stood up and waved the gun at me. 'Come on, we're going into another room.'

I didn't move, it was obvious he was planning to kill me, but he didn't want to do it in this room. This puzzled me for a moment, but it either allowed my brain to get into gear again or my guardian angel re-established a connection. At first I couldn't see Winston's problem because from the number of petrol cans around they were clearly planning to burn the place down before they left, so he was unlikely to be worried about damage to the furniture.

I looked down and saw that my chair was placed on a large elaborate carpet. It dawned on me that this must be the famous gift from Stalin and that with time running out before his departure, Winston would have difficulties trading it in the short term if it was badly stained with blood. It also explained why he had entered this room first—he wanted to be sure his treasure was still there.

I pushed the chair backwards, a task I was able to complete quite quickly despite my poor condition.

Presumably because I finished up on top of the carpet Winston didn't fire, he simply screamed at me, 'If you get blood on it I'll make you wish you were never born.'

I stood up, holding the carpet to my chest with my left hand, while grabbing the stinger with my right hand and screamed back, 'I already wish I'd never been born.'

For a moment or two we faced each other like warriors of old but neither making an effort to shoot. I could see the increasing strain on Winston's face and realised that sooner or later he would shoot me—carpet or no carpet. I tried to move closer to him so that I could bring him in range of the stinger, but he didn't fall for that and kept his distance.

Remembering that he'd collapsed from anger when Ben had hit me over the head, I realised that I had to capitalise on what I assumed was his heart condition. To achieve this aim I had to make him very angry but keep him from shooting at me for as long as possible by feeding him new information. Up until this point he'd regaled me of an almost non-stop barrage of insults, to which I had intermittently responded in kind. Now I smiled at him and embarked on a tactic intended to bring about a heart seizure.

'Winston, you were right about Simon's stinger, it worked a treat on the flowerpot men.'

He stopped and suddenly looked even more frightened, and I realised that he had not taken drastic action up until this moment because he'd assumed his bodyguards would soon ride up to rescue him.

I went on, 'They're both stone-cold dead in the kitchen back there. I don't know what's in the stinger pellets, so I finished them off by dropping the orange trees on their heads. So, I've destroyed all your team and you don't have to pay them anything—you should thank me for that.'

I could see that his eyes were bulging and he must have been only seconds away from shooting at me. I quickly threw in what I hoped was the punch-line:

'But you didn't need the flowerpot men at all. I've rigged the place up and poured petrol everywhere, the place will explode just as soon as you pull the trigger. You'll lose everything, no retirement, no fame and no memoirs, and I'll win because I've no future outside this building.'

As he struggled to understand this statement, he started to suffer an attack. I lunged at him intending to use the stinger when I got close enough, but I dropped it. Fortunately for me he couldn't hold on to the gun either and the result was that I finished up on top of him on the floor. As we struggled I managed to sit on his chest and pull Stalin's present over his face. Initially, he put up a struggle but then he weakened considerably and even in my own poor physical condition I realised he was going very fast. To finish him off, I sang to him. Winston died listening to my first public rendition of *Rule Britannia*.

CHAPTER
THIRTEEN

Although I was reasonably sure he was no longer breathing I continued to press the carpet over his face for several minutes until I obtained the courage to move away from him. As soon as I did I made a grab for the stinger and fired the remaining dart into his lifeless body. I stared for a while at the body until I was convinced it wasn't going to move anymore.

A very tired feeling of elation came over me and I whispered, 'You're dead, you're dead—you're all dead.'

Then I crawled to the door of the living room and tried to think what I should do next. In turning the tables on Winston I had eventually marshalled my thoughts very successfully in order to utilise the resources available to me. But now I couldn't concentrate long enough to map out any sort of plan of action. My brain was simply filled with thoughts that I had killed Winston, he said I was British, I had been brain-washed and I needed desperately to sleep.

Gradually, I forced myself to concentrate on the needs of the moment and concluded that as it was possible that some other friends of Winston could materialise at any minute, I needed a gun. I picked up Winston's gun, checked that it was loaded, and with a considerable feeling of relief put it in my trouser pocket. Then I decided I needed to find a bathroom. While in the bathroom I looked in the mirror and didn't immediately recognise myself.

My nose was badly broken, I had a nasty swelling around one of my eyes and my hair was full of congealed blood. In my present condition I was going to stand out from the crowd as someone who'd recently been involved in violence, when what I needed was the ability to melt into the background. I turned the shower on in the belief that running it cold I would not only obtain a thorough clean-up, I might be able to wake myself up a bit. However, the noise of the shower and the thought that I could be approached unawares once inside it frightened me off. Instead I washed my body down bit by bit over a vanity basin.

Clean towels had been thrown on the floor of the bathroom and when I moved into other rooms I saw that clothes, paper and other combustible materials had been liberally scattered around. It was obvious that this was all done to aid the fire that Winston had been planning. In one of the bedrooms, which I assumed to be Winston's, I found new underwear, socks, shirts and trousers that had been scattered around with their packaging materials. Some of these had been deliberately cut before being discarded but I found sufficient clothes to make myself reasonably presentable, though both the trousers and loose jacket I chose had small cuts in them and they'd been intended for someone an inch or two smaller. Unfortunately, I couldn't find any shoes that fitted me and I was forced to spoil my appearance and feeling of comfort by using the blood-spattered pair I had just taken off.

Throughout this attempt to prepare myself for the world outside I had been hindered by the cut on my hand and so I fashioned a bandage of sorts from bits of white cloth scattered about. I had filled one of the vanity basins with cold water and returned to it frequently to insert my face in the hope it would help to keep me awake. After doing this for about the third time, I suddenly woke up to the fact that my wallet was missing and with it my only family photograph. Normally, I would have gone to great lengths to avoid any further contact with the three bodies on the premises but now I was forced to go through their clothing to search for the photograph. I didn't find it on the flowerpot men but between them they had about forty-five pounds in sterling and roughly four times that much in Spanish pesetas. A search of Winston's body didn't produce the photograph but I did find £170 in sterling and a substantial quantity of travellers' cheques. Stealing from the dead wasn't a factor, I desperately needed money and in any case Winston owed me considerably more than the amount I had found.

The thought that the photograph might be lying around somewhere caused me to search the rooms systematically. As there were at least twenty rooms in what I now discovered was a massive dormer bungalow the task took me a considerable amount of time. I even searched through the rubbish bins, but all to no avail. When I saw from the kitchen clock that it was two-thirty in the afternoon I realised I had been searching for the photograph for fifty minutes. Very reluctantly, I abandoned the search and prepared to leave. I opened some of the cans of petrol and tipped the contents out. I collected the guns parked by the flowerpot men and opened the front door. Outside I saw Winston's Mercedes and a separate garage complex. After a further fruitless search in these buildings I started the car to make sure it was in working order. Then I returned to the bungalow for the last time, removed a large curtain and dowsed it in petrol. I fed part of the curtain out through the letterbox on the front door, removed the house keys from the key ring and put them on the mat inside, then exited. Using Winston's cigarette lighter I lit the cloth and rushed for the car.

I had probably gone no more than fifty yards in the car when the bungalow appeared to explode behind me. When I had first started up and tested the car I had assumed from studying the land in front of me that the drive to the house was no more than seventy yards long and would open up directly onto a road. Now I discovered that the drive extended for at least a quarter of a mile and at the end of it was a large set of security gates. I cursed myself for not anticipating this but decided to approach the gates slowly at first to see if it was possible to open them manually. If not, I would have to risk crashing through at speed. When I got close to the gates I was relieved to see them opening. Whether this was due to some control gadget in the Mercedes or the electric system failing in the bungalow I would never know, and it wasn't something I intended to lose sleep thinking about.

Once through the gates I saw that the driveway continued for another fifty yards or so before butting up to a country lane. From the references I had heard to Heathrow, I assumed I was still in Britain and that I should drive on the left-hand side of the road. I turned left on to the country lane and began to feel a sense of freedom. In order to stay as wide awake as possible I lowered all the windows and drove at a relatively low speed. After about five minutes I saw a sign to Barnstaple and then other indications that I was in North Devon. I decided to head for Barnstaple but once in the town I couldn't see a safe place to stop. Although I was having difficulty concentrating on my continued predicament, it was obvious that the most likely danger to my newly obtained freedom came from the car I was driving. Once the police were alerted to the fire I had just started they would try to trace the owner of the property and although Winston would have been careful to cover his tracks, it was possible that someone would remember the number and type of vehicle that the owner used.

I decided to keep going until I could see a place to hide the car. Eventually I came to a signpost saying Croyde Bay and I realised I was driving into the equivalent of a cul-de-sac. Turning round and retracing my steps might also create dangers and so I decided to stop somewhere in the town. I discovered that Croyde Bay was a prosperous little seaside resort but it was out of season. However, it had been a nice day in the area and rather more shops and facilities had opened than would normally be the case at this time of year. Consequently the main car parking area was reasonably full and I was able to park the Mercedes in a spot where it wasn't that conspicuous. I got out of the car with the intention of finding something to eat, then finding some boarding house with a garage big enough to hide the car and then going to sleep for a week.

As I walked towards the shops I felt pain and discomfort throughout my body and although I hoped that a good night's sleep would put me right I began to think that my health problems might go a little further than that. The first shop I came to was selling

211

shoes and a few other items of clothing. I stopped and bought a comfortable pair of shoes and an anorak-type coat.

The elderly sales assistant gave me my purchases and then asked, 'Who declared war on you?'

Without thinking I mumbled, 'I was attacked by a gang of louts.'

Almost immediately the words were out I regretted saying them because the salesman almost shouted, 'Not in Croyde Bay—have you reported it to the police?'

I was startled by his reaction and mumbled, 'No, it happened in Barnstaple, I didn't report it because the assault was partly my own fault.'

I left the shop listening to a lecture on the need to report all crimes and I realised I had to think up an excuse for my appearance that didn't include an assault by a third party.

Half an hour later I had finished eating a plateful of sausage and chips in a small café. The food was quite good but I realised with every mouthful I was going to have difficulty in keeping it down. While settling my bill the young waitress couldn't resist asking how I'd got my injuries.

Having noticed how rocky the coast was I said, 'I fell while climbing on the rocks.'

With a note of genuine concern in her voice she said, 'Oh, that can be very dangerous, have you seen a doctor?'

I lied again: 'I saw a doctor in Barnstaple and he advised me to stop somewhere locally to rest up. I've come to Croyde Bay in the hope of finding a room.'

'Oh,' she said, 'my Auntie Maude has a holiday flat, which she sometimes lets out of season.'

After further discussions between the waitress and myself face-to-face and the waitress and her aunt on the telephone, I discovered that the flat didn't have a garage, but it did have an enclosed yard attached to it. Thirty minutes later I collected the keys of the flat from Aunt Maude after paying her for a week's rent in advance.

Just before she left the flat she said, 'I don't spend a lot of time here because it brings back too many memories. My late husband used the flat for his ice-cream business in years gone by and he kept his van in the yard. I've not looked in the yard for a long time but it might contain some packing cases and other rubbish.'

After she left I looked longingly at the bed, but as it was getting dark I realised it would be a good time to get the Mercedes away from view and decided to look in the yard. There was rubbish everywhere and with my physical problems it took me about forty minutes to stack it in such a way that I could get the car inside. However, when I did finally insert the car I realised that the effort had been worthwhile, because the rubbish almost completely disguised its presence. With relief I re-entered the flat, washed my hands and collapsed on the bed.

Sleeping for a week was a nice idea in theory but I woke up in the early hours of the morning feeling very sick and weak. When I got up to go to the toilet I had difficulty in taking even a couple of steps. Later, as I lay on the bed, I began to realise that I needed medical help and that without it I was in real trouble. However, if I allowed myself to be hospitalised, then problems regarding my identity would arise. I could claim to have lost my memory but in my pocket I had travellers' checks that were clearly not mine. In addition I had arrived in Winston's car and I was in no condition to dispose of it. Worse still, there were guns with my fingerprints on them in the glove compartment and my own blood-soaked shoes under the front seats. Then I realised that there was likely to be even more damaging evidence in the boot and I had not yet looked in there. Given the evidence in the car it was likely that the police could easily connect me with three killings and would probably be happy to leave it at that. If I tried to tell the whole story it would sound so far-fetched that no one would take the trouble to investigate it. Why should they? Winston's last words had left me in a confused state as to what my life was all about—so, if I couldn't sort out fact from fiction, why should anyone else believe me? In between my limited bouts of sleep I made my mind up that I had no alternative but to keep going without seeking medical help.

Then my guardian angel switched on again in the guise of Aunt Maude. I felt a hand on my shoulder and heard a voice saying, 'Are you all right, Mr Marks?'

At first I couldn't understand why she was calling me Mr Marks, and then I remembered that in searching for a new name I would not forget, I had reversed my previous name and introduced myself to her as Roger Marks.

'Sorry if I've disturbed you but it's eleven-thirty in the morning and the curtains are still drawn. You were very poorly yesterday so I thought I'd better check how you are.'

I was still confused. 'How did you get in?'

'Oh, I have a set of spare keys, but did you sleep all right?'

I replied truthfully: 'I slept only fitfully during the night and I had no idea of the time.'

She started to fuss about my condition and said, 'Shall I get a doctor?'

I tried to laugh off her concern: 'Please don't worry, I'm not as ill as you think.'

She didn't look convinced by my comments but got me a drink and said she'd return with some soup in about half an hour. When she returned with the soup I did my best to appear a lot healthier than I really was.

Then she asked another difficult question: 'Where are your antibiotics? You'll be needing one by now.'

I told her that the doctor in Barnstaple had given me a prescription but I must have lost it soon after leaving his surgery. I expected a further discussion on this subject but she just shrugged and left without another word.

She returned a couple of hours later with more food and drink and an assorted selection of antibiotics. She explained that these were the remnants of antibiotic courses that she'd obtained from her doctor over the years.

I took the opportunity to appear caring: 'Didn't the doctor tell you? You're supposed to complete each course specified.'

'Oh, I know that, but I don't like taking anything unless it's absolutely necessary, so once I feel better I just put them on one side for a time when I might need them.'

I thanked her and when she reappeared with food for the third time in the day I gave her fifteen pounds and said, 'That's for your nursing services.'

This routine continued for a further four days because despite the antibiotics and her care and attention I was in no fit state to leave the flat, though I tried my best to appear to be recovering when she was present. Aunt Maude, for her part, appeared to be pleased to have someone to look after and clearly appreciated the extra money.

On the morning of my sixth day in the flat I started to feel well enough to look after myself and after lunch I told Maude that I would leave that evening. She had obviously hoped that the rental income and the fifteen pounds a day would continue for some time and made one or two comments indicating that she thought I might be in trouble with the police. When I ignored the implied threats, she became more forceful:

'Are the police looking for you?'

I smiled at her. 'Maude, you've been very kind to me and I really appreciate the help you've given me. But if I'd been in trouble with the police you would have put yourself in danger by asking that question. I think I know what's worrying you but I promise you I'll never tell anyone you've been selling me your antibiotics.'

Her reaction to this comment convinced me she would keep her mouth shut. During the afternoon I went into the village and booked myself into a motel on the border between Devon and Cornwall. I took the precaution of telling Maude I was heading for London, but I drove into the motel forecourt about an hour later. After paying cash for a first night's stay and buying some essential toiletries, I had just over thirty pounds left.

Once I had put my personal belongings in the room, I returned to the car. This was my first real opportunity to open the boot in reasonable safety and privacy. I had previously removed the house keys from the large bunch of keys I had taken from Winston's body, so that I wouldn't be confused by them when it came to unlocking items I might find in the car. However, there were still a great many keys left to choose from and in the dark it took me a few minutes before I found the correct one. The light came on when I opened the boot and from the strong smell of disinfectant that greeted me I realised I'd once had a close encounter with the

215

boot of this vehicle. I was fascinated by what I might find in the luggage, but my initial thought was to look under the carpet for money. I was disappointed to find just fifty pounds but hoped there might be more in the luggage. The boot was tightly packed with three suitcases and two briefcases. I took out the briefcases, locked the boot and returned to my room.

I didn't sleep much that night or the next. In fact I must have spent about eighteen of the thirty-six hours after I had opened the briefcases studying the contents. James Cameron had once told me that Winston's ability to speak for hours on end without getting a word out of place wasn't matched by his written communication skills, and here was proof of that opinion. Much of the paper inside one briefcase contained either aide-mémoire or planning notes. I found the hairs on the back of my neck twitching when I read notes made just a few weeks back. He claimed to have kept me alive during the previous months because he hoped that my illegal financial skills might benefit him, but once I failed to match his expectations in this respect he outlined various ways to kill me. This made unpleasant reading, but there was a lot for me to take pleasure in.

I had assumed that Winston was planning to leave Britain for good when I heard he was heading for Heathrow. But from his notes I now discovered he was departing for heart surgery in South Africa and after recuperating there for about six months he intended to return and settle in what he called the Celtic country of Cornwall. More importantly, he had spent considerable effort over many years planning for his retirement in Cornwall but he had been careful not to buy a property. In order to achieve a long and happy retirement he had put enormous effort into creating a new identity. This effort became apparent when in the second briefcase I found evidence of long established bank accounts in the name of Norman Owen Thomas. He had taken money out of his accounts in this name from time to time but mostly paid considerable sums in. I realised I was probably only seeing the tip of the iceberg but I could see that £160,000 was readily available to Mr Thomas. I could also see he had made transactions of both types from different parts of the country without too much difficulty.

Strangely, I also saw he had used the same three initials, NOT, for two other aliases over the years and he had always used the same signature. Then I began to realise why he might have done this. He was, for example, still making rental payments on the lock-up in Birmingham under his original alias and the rates on the bungalow I had burned down under the second one. Presumably, he used the same signature to avoid the risk of making a mistake.

From one of his most recent notes I saw that Winston had hired a reputable security firm to look after him at a hotel close to Heathrow while he transferred his carpet to the people he'd been negotiating with. Apparently, he had previously been offered one and a quarter million for the heirloom but was holding out for £2,000,000. In the same series of jottings I saw that he had pre-sold his Mercedes to a garage close to Heathrow. They had already arranged for the car to be shipped with several stolen cars to the continent. It occurred to me that even though almost a week had gone by since Winston was due to make the flight, I could take the car to the garage when it was closed, leave the keys in it and then inform the police that it was likely to be stolen. If the garage owners were involved in the scam, then with a bit of luck this action might enable the police to make arrests. But it was obvious I would need to erase my own fingerprints to ensure I wasn't the one arrested.

Then I discovered a driving license in the name of Norman Owen Thomas and realised that if I could forge his signature, I would not only inherit Winston's money but I could immediately buy a different car. The idea of dumping the Mercedes at the garage then became very appealing, because although the car remained the biggest threat to my continued freedom, I needed a vehicle of some description at this time. The next day was spent buying a second-hand microscope, examining Winston's signature in detail under the lens and then practising my own version of it. Late in the afternoon I had obtained £200 from one of the bank accounts now in my possession and I doubled it the next morning. I then bought and insured a second-hand car, which I arranged to pick up two days later. The car was a Rover of British manufacture—I had remembered Winston's comment that few people could ever achieve enough for their country to compensate for the damage caused by buying one single foreign car. Winston's calculations had been based on buying new cars but I thought that the principle still applied. Not that I was totally convinced that I was British, but until I was sure that Winston was lying I was determined to act as if I was.

By late evening the next day I had disposed of the Mercedes and made a phone call to the police. In it I suggested that they watch the garage and see what happened to the car. Then I travelled back to the motel by train and taxi—it was very pleasant not to have to worry about money even though I still couldn't be sure if I had really reached freedom. I had to wait a further day to pick up the Rover, so after my evening meal I planned to continue my studies of the contents of the two briefcases. However, I had also brought Winston's three suitcases into the room because I had not previously had the time to investigate them properly. I made a cup of coffee and watched the television news to see if there was any reference to my activities. Fortunately, there wasn't anything reported that concerned me and I decided to get on with my task. It seemed logical that I should repack the suitcases putting the things that I needed to hold on to or study at my leisure in one of them. Then I would be able to dispose of the other items once I had picked up the Rover.

Having seen the quantity of clothes, both new and old, that Winston had scattered around the bungalow, I was surprised how much more he had packed into these three suitcases. I sorted through the clothes with the intention of dropping them off at various charity shops on my route into Cornwall. The idea behind this was partly altruistic but I also thought that the dumping of a relatively large supply of good quality clothes anywhere else might result in the police taking an interest in them. In one of the suitcases I came across a pile of bed linen and was surprised that anyone would bother to take such items when leaving the country for a period of time. Then it became apparent that the bed linen was there to protect a pile of paper nearly five inches thick. Within seconds of removing the last linen covering, I realised what it was and then experienced the proverbial shivers running down the spine.

CHAPTER
FOURTEEN

Winston's draft autobiography, for that is what I had in front of me, had been put together over many years. It took the form of an unstructured diary and was made up from notebooks and scraps of A4 paper. There were some typed pages but most of it was handwritten. Many of the sheets had newspaper cuttings or snippets from books attached to them by pins or staples. Winston clearly intended that at some more leisurely time in the future he would write his memoirs with the help of these notes. There was an almost childish note on the front page, which read, 'Must not be published while I am alive, but ought to be completed before I die.' For some of the events he referred to he had already written up two or more versions of his story, presumably so that he could choose the most relevant later. Quite clearly, he never intended anyone else to read the draft.

Although it was immediately obvious that a story was being told and that it was sequential, I began my study of it by flipping through the pages until I came to the part that dealt with the murder of my wife and son. I realised that just reading this section was going to be traumatic, but I wasn't prepared for the level of hurt I was about to experience. When I came to the relevant section, the first thing I noticed was my missing family photograph, but it had been cut into two pieces. The image of Elaine and Andrew was stapled to the left-hand edge of the paper at the top of the page and scribbled underneath were the words 'objective achieved', and this was followed by the date on which they died. An inked line ran down to the bottom of the page where my photograph was attached. Underneath the photograph was the handwritten comment 'he failed again, no further value'. The date had not been entered and no other comments made.

All the pain associated with the death of Elaine and Andrew came flooding back and it was some time before I was able to bring myself to read anything else. I put the two pieces of the photograph in my wallet with the intention of taping them together when I was in a better frame of mind. I tried to gain comfort from the fact that I had killed the evil man who wrote these words and I would certainly make sure this filth was never published. However, any comfort I might have derived at this moment from killing him was seriously reduced by what I now saw as my stupidity in previously treating him like a god.

From the scribbled notes in this section, I learned that Winston hated Elaine and me because of the horrible incident he told me about involving Stephen at the training school. From his own words, it was clear that his Russian masters were very critical of the fact that he had lost so many of the people who had been through the training school at great expense to them. Apparently this fact alone kept us alive during our first years in the country because he couldn't risk losing too many more people.

Then I read that Elaine had been murdered because of a combination of an awful coincidence and an understandable mistake she made. Elaine had first come into contact with Mary Maher because she was looking for a reliable babysitter. Mary Maher was keen to oblige because it was the only way to satisfy her maternal instincts, but almost unbelievably she was also a relatively low-ranking Russian agent who'd been ordered to get close to and marry John Maher. Moscow saw John Maher as a brilliant man with extreme left-wing views who was certain to achieve great things either as a civil servant or as a politician. He was one of many influential people being targeted in this way by Moscow and apparently at least one of his promotions was fixed by them.

If the notes were factual, then the two women initially developed a genuine friendship and knew nothing of each other's background. Unfortunately, however, while feeling very depressed one day Elaine had blurted out to Mary Maher that she was fed up of living a lie and intended to do something about it.

When pressed on what was bothering her, Elaine had apparently replied, 'Some people went to a lot of trouble to convince me that I wasn't born in this country, but I know I was and one day I'll prove it.'

Although Elaine would not elaborate on what she had said, Mary Maher was intrigued and managed to get a photograph taken of Elaine when they were out shopping together. Moscow confirmed from the photograph that Elaine was in Winston's group and instructed Mrs Maher to find out more. Being questioned further on this subject obviously frightened Elaine and I think this was responsible for her acute depression in the weeks leading up to her death. On the night before her death she had indicated to me that she was no longer worried, but there wasn't anything in the notes that suggested a reason why her fear had reduced.

Winston wrote that he was horrified and embarrassed when one of his senior Russian contacts told him that Elaine was close to defecting. If his notes told the truth, the Russians agreed with him that Elaine had to be silenced and they provided two operatives who bludgeoned her to death and set the house on fire. They also made sure that Mary Maher was away at the time so that she wouldn't be implicated. What they had not bargained for was John Maher arriving home unexpectedly, just as the fire was taking hold. John had attempted to save Elaine but had not managed to drag her outside when the fumes overcame him. Winston had added the comment, 'The Russians botched the job, but they blamed me anyway. Apparently they were convinced that John Maher would have been increasingly useful to them.' Further notes indicated that Winston was amused by John Maher's attempt to save Elaine and clearly believed that it provided a convenient sexual motive that prevented the authorities from looking for any further reasons for the murders. One of the most hurtful aspects of this story was that there wasn't a single reference to Andrew—clearly the life of an innocent young boy wasn't worth the ink.

When I could bring myself to do so, I read through the pages in sequence. The first five pages were alternative forewords or introductions to the intended book. They were in fact invitations to future readers to place the author's life in historical perspective by comparing his achievements with other acknowledged 'heroes'. It was clear that in each of these comparisons Winston was at pains to make sure the alternative hero didn't receive too much praise. For example one of them was a man called Richard Heenan, a New Zealander of Irish origin whose traitorous acts had apparently helped the Japanese to capture Singapore in World War II. Initially, the text claimed that Heenan wasn't a traitor but an Irish patriot, but then by various crossings out and additions it was clear that the writer thought he was giving too much credit to a competitor.

Winston went into detail about his early life near Dublin. The name Winston was an anagram of part of his real name, but I have no intention of risking giving him his place in history by providing that name. In fact, although I reluctantly decided soon after I first set eyes on the manuscript that it might eventually be in my best interests to keep it, I very quickly removed any evidence that could accurately identify him.

The story he had told me about joining up with the Germans and then transferring to the Russians was repeated early in the notes. Thinking about it, I suppose some of it had to be true or otherwise he would never have got into the position of importance he had achieved when I first set eyes on him.

Despite having lived with the notion for several days now that I might be British, it still came as a shock to read about the problems he eventually overcame in order to add three British orphans to the training course. We therefore had to be British—the story would not make sense if we weren't and in any case it was totally out of character for him to accept he had made a mistake by insisting we should be involved. In addition, although Elaine had never told me directly she was remembering her early life, I knew that for some time she thought of herself as British and had once said, 'We're orphans, so it's possible our parents left Britain for the Soviet Union because they were socialists.' At the time I thought she was so upset at our ongoing dilemma that she was simply indulging in wishful thinking, but now I could see she was probably hoping I would adopt a more positive pro-British stance before letting me into her little secret. Thinking back, I realised I had switched from being against TH to being very much in favour of it on many occasions. It must have been obvious to her that for much of our time in the country my greatest wish was to be given the opportunity to serve the cause. It repeatedly entered my mind over the next few days that if only I had adopted Elaine's approach, my wife and son might still be alive.

In the same set of notes it was also confirmed that Stephen was Elaine's brother. According to the text I was reading young Stephen was a useless, slow-witted moron and that was the reason his mind finally rejected the brain-washing it had been subjected to. To me though Stephen was already an impressive human being when his life was cruelly taken away from him. He would have been outstanding had he lived to adulthood. If he was a moron for rejecting the brain-washing, where did that leave me?—it was still working on me. Poor Stephen, poor Andrew, they knew nothing of the senseless game that was being played out but they suffered just the same.

It was clear from the final words in this section that Winston felt he would never be able to trust either Elaine or myself and had convinced himself before we left the training school that bringing in these three British kids was a serious mistake.

There were several paragraphs dealing with a number of team members who had let him down badly over the years. James Cameron had told me a long time ago that several people had gone native, often after marrying local women. The words now dancing in front of my tired eyes told a very different story. Winston claimed to have exterminated these people at the first sign that they had any doubts about his supreme authority. The pages contained several graphic descriptions of what he termed unacceptable insubordination or stupidity. Paul, the original partner of Peter and David, had been executed and put in the Thames within hours of my last conversation with him. Angus had not been killed by one of the flowerpot men but by Winston himself. This had happened when Winston went into a fit of rage on discovering that information had been leaked in his absence. Worst of all, James Cameron had not been retained for other work by the Russians. Winston had guessed that his number two was close to defecting and had arranged an ambush for James and his wife when they were driving in the Scottish Highlands. The last words relating to James and his wife were, 'They burned all the way down to hell.' Discovering the Camerons' fate in this way made me physically sick and for the third or fourth time since I had discovered the manuscript, I had to put the papers down and rest before I felt capable of taking in any more.

The more I thought about it, the more I liked the idea of being British until, that is, I realised that I now had to accept all the consequences of my past actions. The guilt that I now felt increased the more I thought about it. As a result I read through the complete notes again hoping I would be able to conclude that the overall efforts of TH had little or no effect on the British economy or the British people's way of life. Sadly, when I completed the exercise, I was forced to accept that even allowing for Winston's usual exaggeration, the real effect on Britain was far greater than I had previously imagined.

For a brief period of time the knowledge that I was now free and relatively wealthy went some way to help combat the effects of the beating I had taken from the flowerpot men. However, reading the draft manuscript set me back considerably and I was forced to confine myself to the motel for much longer than I originally intended. Learning how my family and friends had died was bad enough but the guilt I felt about the damage I had caused to the country of my birth was affecting my behaviour. For the next few days, I had the greatest difficulty looking anybody in the eye and when shopkeepers smiled at me I wanted to turn and run.

Over a period of about ten days I moved from hotel to hotel along the north coast of Cornwall and eventually took a long-term rental on a spacious furnished house overlooking the sea. The house was ideal for the reclusive life I now adopted. In the first few weeks I left the house just twice a week to collect my provisions. I watched television and listened to the radio, but most of the time I sat in my first-floor conservatory.

I spent most of my time going over the draft manuscript and the contents of the briefcases. Quite early in this exercise I decided that my day job should be split into three projects and that I should do some work on each of them most days. The first was to establish the extent of my newly discovered wealth. Within a matter of days, I was sure that I could spend up to £173,000, but further study of the information available only increased the amount a little further. I had no doubt that this was only a fraction of what Winston would have been able to call on had he lived to become Norman Thomas. My problem was that some of the information necessary to dig further was missing. For example, one of the keys I had taken from Winston was still a mystery to me. I suspected that it opened a strongbox somewhere but I had no clues as to its location. Within a matter of weeks from settling in the flat I had given up hope of finding more money.

My second project was to work out how I might go about establishing the real identities of Elaine, Stephen and myself. I had to accept that this would be a daunting task for even the best detective because I had no idea where to start. I had no real clue if the shipwreck we had been involved in was pre-war or during the hostilities or whereabouts the shipwreck had taken place. Come to think of it, I didn't know the nationality of the ship in question, or even if I had been in the same shipwreck as the other two. It struck me that there might only be a minute chance that there were records in existence that reported us as missing. Then, of course, there was the little matter of why a certain Norman Thomas would seek this information—what was his relationship to the children? I considered the possibility of using a private detective or a legal firm to advertise in the newspapers so that I could remain anonymous. If I was going to take this action it was presumably going to be easier to look for someone who might remember a young brother and sister being lost and then if successful I might get a lead to my own real identity a little later. I agonised over the thought that any relative, who might remember us, would be in advanced old age and if I delayed action too long the opportunity might be lost. Against that I had to accept that the advertisement would probably be seen by one of the many Russians active in Britain and if they got interested they would get my name and address whatever precautions I had taken to achieve anonymity. After considering the options for several days, I decided that any action I took should be delayed until I was in a better position to judge the implications of such a search.

Within a few weeks of starting the projects I was left to concentrate on the one that was the least appealing. This was to establish what I could possibly do to fight back against the Russian invaders and any remnants of Winston's group that might still be working against British interests. I couldn't postpone or see an end to this project but equally I couldn't take any worthwhile action because I didn't know if any TH people were still operating. In the end I wrote anonymously to British Intelligence giving all the information I had on Gerry O'Donnell's group. I drove to Bristol to post the letter and hoped it would do some good. After that I couldn't see what else I could do and I spent most of the rest of my first three months in the house gazing out to sea and reading books. Somehow, it seemed easier to look at the sea rather than look in the other direction where millions of my countrymen and women were struggling with the problems I had helped to create, and that I was doing nothing to correct.

When spring arrived and the weather improved I forced myself to be a little more adventurous and got into the habit of going for long walks, but I still took care to avoid contact with other human beings whenever possible. However, any dog or cat that crossed my path was very welcome and usually got rewarded with a tit-bit. One reason for taking long walks was the desire to tire myself out in the hope that my recurring nightmare was happening only because I wasn't taking enough exercise. In this nightmare I was alone in the sea and I was drowning. Each time the dream occurred, an adult arm pulled me up from the freezing cold water and on to an upturned dinghy. Each night I hoped that the dream sequence would be extended and I would see the face of my saviour, but it never happened.

My house was only a few miles from Tintagel and one day I decided to visit the area. One of the books I had been reading had referred to the almost magical atmosphere that the Tintagel cliffs created. I was aware that the area was associated with Camelot and other legends but I wasn't prepared for the long-term effect the place was to have on me.

When I first reached the cliffs I was immediately influenced by the atmosphere and I can remember thinking if this place wasn't the site of Arthurian legend, then it ought to be. After a meal and a single pint of bitter in a pub that evening I returned to the cliffs just to soak in the atmosphere again. I hung around for a while and suddenly realised I was alone. I was about to leave when I heard a low-pitched noise that seemed to emanate from the rocks I was standing on. My first thought was that someone was trying to play a silly trick on me, so I started to walk away. Then it dawned on me that a visitor could have slipped on the rocks and be lying injured close by. In the circumstances, I kept still and tried to locate the noise.

The noise got louder and louder until it seemed to engulf me. With a mixture of fear and fascination I slowly became convinced that long dead souls were making contact with me. I heard the voices of Celts telling me of their struggles with invading Romans and Anglo-Saxons. Then I heard Anglo-Saxon voices telling similar stories about their trouble with other invaders. In what must have been a matter of a few seconds my brain absorbed hundreds of their stories. There was no language problem and days later many of these stories were flooding back into my thoughts. The collective message they had for me was that these islands were special and had to be protected. They made it clear that they had helped me when I needed it and now it was up to me to take the fight to the enemy. Suddenly, the voices stopped and all I could hear was the noise of the wind and waves.

I felt elated during my journey home, partly because the experience had convinced me that there was some form of afterlife to look forward to and that eventually I would meet all of my family again. Not surprisingly, I slept well and I didn't experience a recurrence of my drowning nightmare. Although quite frightened at the prospect of taking on the enemy, I continued my studies of Winston's notes the next morning with renewed vigour. Several days later, however, I had to accept that I had no idea how I could begin any sort of fight-back. There seemed no point in just walking into a police station and telling my story. Eventually the seven deaths in two and a half days would come out and that would put an end to any further investigation. For some time I toyed with the idea of approaching the UKAEA security people directly and asking them to go back over their records to find details on Elaine and myself. From fingerprints and other records I assumed they could be convinced of my identity, accept that we had taken information out of Risley and begin a detailed investigation. At the same time I could donate Winston's fortune to the British government in return for a promise that they would investigate my story. While never discounting this combined approach altogether, I eventually put it to the back of my mind. The main reason being that I might find myself approaching someone who was working indirectly for Russian Intelligence. After all, Russian Intelligence had helped Elaine and me to get employment at Risley and for all I knew the security section there could now be 100 per cent Russian.

When leaving Tintagel on the night I had heard the voices, I'd expected to be a constant visitor to the cliffs, but now I almost didn't dare to return. Instead I looked for other reasons to explain my failure. Originally, I had been hopeful that the shipwreck dream was a sign that my brain-washing was finally coming undone. But then I realised that I ought to be remembering a little bit more each day and that wasn't the case. If my brain was playing tricks on me because of my need to know what had happened to me and my parents in the late 1930s or early 1940s, then the same thing had probably occurred with the Tintagel voices. In overcoming Winston and the other TH thugs everything had gone my way and it was natural to assume that I had received some supernatural help in doing this. However, I had to accept that imagining voices from the past could be a direct result of the brain-washing techniques I had been subjected to. In the circumstances I resolved to return to the real world.

About four weeks after my experience at Tintagel I decided to try a more conventional approach to solving emotional problems of the type I was experiencing—I went to church. I had not bothered to find out what particular religious denomination the church represented. It was a friendly-looking place that I had passed from time to time on my way to the shops. It was almost empty when I went in and I found myself a seat at the back. I closed my eyes and tried to imagine the same sort of atmospheric conditions that I had found at Tintagel. Concentrating hard I eventually heard a voice calling to me, but it turned out to be the local priest. For a minute or two I was deluged by words of comfort from a friendly Irishman who clearly saw the opportunity to help a tortured soul. As soon as I could I excused myself and left. I had nothing against any Irish person other than Winston and I had to accept that in common with millions of other British citizens, I probably had Irish blood in my veins. Nevertheless, I took it as a sign that I should avoid religion. The net result was that for the next four and a half years I devoted myself to study and writing my memoirs. In doing so I drastically reduced my contact with other people.

CHAPTER FIFTEEN

The industrial disputes of the 1970s were constant reminders to me of the damage I had done to my country and they didn't do anything to encourage me to change my hermetic lifestyle. Watching scenes on television of the coalminers' strike, for example, made me feel very bad and just the mention of the conflict was usually enough to ruin what might otherwise have been a good day. Obviously I had played no part in organising this very damaging strike and I didn't know anyone who had. Nevertheless, I knew that all the seeds for the dispute had been set many years earlier by a combination of TH activities and weak government. In the circumstances I restricted myself to watching the national news just once every three days. The rest of the time I concentrated on getting adequate exercise, doing the chores, reading and trying to understand nuclear physics and computing. Unfortunately these two areas of study were both very difficult, if not impossible for a recluse to become expert in. Despite this restriction I read widely on both subjects and by the late 1970s I had acquired several basic computing systems.

In early 1979 an event occurred that did eventually lead to a change in my lifestyle. The owners of the rented house I was living in put it up for sale and I decided to buy it rather than move on. As I didn't want to take out a mortgage, the natural result of this purchase was to reduce my capital significantly. However, not having to pay rent also reduced my modest outgoings and so I probably could have continued into advanced old age without worrying about money. But I was now in my mid-forties and I could see that it made sense to add to my capital in the next few years rather than find that I needed extra money for something when I had reached normal retirement age. In addition I was forced to accept that I would get a great deal more out of computing if I could work with others on larger systems. I realised that getting a job in computing would not be easy because of my age and my lack of experience. It was reasonable to assume that a curriculum vitae that admitted to forty-six years of age but claimed that private means had removed the need to get a job until now would probably result in a belly laugh and a short trip to the waste basket.

I could, of course, revert to my old tactics and create a CV that matched the desired experience, but my life had changed and now I didn't want to live any more of a lie than I had to. After considering my circumstances I decided that to get a suitable job I would have to make personal contact with one or more of the relevant executives looking for staff, try to impress them face-to-face and then plead for a chance. From studying the computing trade press, I decided that the ideal position for me would be with one of the software companies selling financial systems to large companies. I was certain that my accountancy background would enable me to pick up the technicalities quickly and if I could obtain a consultancy-type role I would be able to work directly with the company's clients. The desire to work in a number of premises rather than in one office was directly related to the problem that had limited my contact with other people for the last five years. From the moment I had escaped from Winston's bungalow I had found it difficult to answer questions about my background. I'd told the first person who had asked about my appearance the truth—that I had been attacked—and then when I realised that was likely to draw attention to myself, I switched to saying that I had fallen down the cliffs. Months after leaving Croyde Bay for the last time I wondered why Aunt Maude had assumed I was in trouble with the police. Then it dawned on me that the two versions relating to my injuries could have been circulating in the village.

Most people in my predicament would probably solve the problem by sketching out an imaginary past life and then keeping to it. But I'd managed to get through several past lives already, which would complicate matters. More importantly, I thought that any future attempt I made to discover my real origins would have a better chance of success if Norman Thomas's background wasn't cast in stone until I got close to the truth. As I wanted to leave this option open, it was obvious that I would have to avoid extensive one-to-one contact with other human beings.

Getting face-to-face interviews with the software companies turned out to be easier than I expected. I attended a software show in London and made personal contact with a number of executives responsible for recruitment in their companies. Most lost interest when my background was discussed but one American-owned company situated in the Thames Valley area eventually gave me an opportunity on a trial basis. Although I experienced one or two difficult moments during my trial period I was eventually employed on a permanent basis as a post-sales support specialist. In theory this role could be carried out by helping clients who had recently purchased our software either by answering questions from a home office base over the telephone or working directly on the implementation of the software at the client's premises. As it happened I spent most of my first year's employment working on two major implementations at client premises. In doing so, I found that my assumption that this lifestyle would enable me to avoid getting too close to my colleagues was totally wrong.

Typically, most assignments would involve two or more company specialists working long hours on client premises for the duration of the system implementation. Despite our customer's natural desire to complete the work as quickly as possible, it was rarely done in less than six months. I had therefore entered a world where I was spending around ten hours a day with my colleagues at client premises and then going back with them to the hotel where in all probability we would have a meal together and then finish up in the bar. In such circumstances I found it difficult to avoid asking my colleagues questions about their lifestyle and couldn't complain when they reciprocated. I was quite prepared to talk generally but always made it clear that as my wife and son had recently died tragically, I wasn't ready to enter into an emotional relationship with anyone else. For a while this was accepted and usually prevented further questions being asked. Gradually, however, I began to hear or imagine oblique references regarding my sexuality and my preference for my own company.

During the middle of 1980 I spent a period based in the UK head office and I came into contact with Pricilla West, a woman of about forty who had a similar job to my own. I suddenly found myself working with her in a team of two for a client that had recently completed a long and difficult implementation. The system wasn't working as well as the client had hoped and we were spending up to two days a week in their offices trying to tweak the system into top gear. That we succeeded at all was entirely due to Pricilla who was a veteran of around thirty major implementations completed for different employers over the last dozen years or so.

We started to go out together, but before asking her to have dinner with me for the first time, I told her that my wife and son had been killed in a house fire and that this experience had made me wary of future relationships. She was very understanding on this point and I was pleased that she didn't ask me any other questions at that time. In turn she told me that she was separated from her husband and was seeking a divorce. She then went on to say that her husband had left her for another woman and that the experience had almost destroyed her. She added that she had only recently returned from sick leave caused by the experience and then she promptly burst into tears.

After composing herself, she apologised and said, 'It's really the fault of the Mills and Boon club. Every time they see me they sympathise with me on my loss and I burst into tears—it's silly really, I don't want the bloody man back.'

The Mills and Boon club was made up of three young women from the administration section at head office. In recent times they had obtained a growing reputation for making highly emotional dramas out of commonplace situations.

Our relationship developed and we agreed to go on a two-week holiday together to Spain. Travelling overseas wasn't a problem for me as I had been put on standby to visit the US head office about six months earlier. The American trip had not yet come off but it meant that I had a nice new passport and was therefore able to take advantage of a cancellation for the week following our decision to go on holiday. The flight out was on the Saturday morning and I had taken the Friday off to make sure everything was in order at my home in Cornwall. Thursday was therefore going to be a very busy day for me and consequently I arrived at the office early.

I stopped for a coffee in mid-morning and vaguely became aware of the Mills and Boon girls floating around the place.

Eventually, one of them approached me and said, 'Isn't it wonderful? Pricilla's husband has come crawling back and she's decided to forgive him.'

I was amazed at this turn of events but managed to mutter, 'Yes, very good.'

As the girl left to spread the good news, I suddenly felt very foolish but I didn't experience any other strong emotions. A little while later, Pricilla approached me with the sort of look on her face that I had previously assumed was never used outside Victorian melodramas.

'Be happy for me,' she sang, 'and be brave.'

I assured her of my support on both of these issues and continued to do so until she left the building. As I watched her go I felt even more foolish.

About ten minutes after she had left I realised that I should cancel our bookings but I had reckoned without the club members. At various stages all three girls insisted that I should make the trip on my own because 'Now more than ever you need a break.'

One of them added, 'The omens are good—you're sure to meet someone special.'

I tried being rude to them but in the end I decided I would make the trip because I needed to get away from them. As it turned out the omens were truly excellent.

I got to the airport in good time on the Saturday morning and after answering numerous questions as to why I was travelling alone, I booked my luggage in and eventually proceeded towards the departure gate. Along the walls of the corridor leading to the departure gate was a series of pictures. These were placed there by the Trust House Forte group and were advertising some of their hotels in Britain. I briefly noticed that the first picture depicted a hotel in Winchester, and it crossed my mind that I had never been to Winchester and it might have made more sense going there today instead of Spain. The next picture was of a town I had visited and had no desire to visit again and the third detailed the company's offering in Salisbury.

Suddenly I remembered the flowerpot men talking about Winston making a detour to Salisbury. After all the hours of investigation into Winston's notes I now knew why he had to visit Salisbury on his way to Heathrow. I also knew which bank would hold the strongbox that the key I had inherited would open. The mass of bodies behind me propelled me towards the gate but as I reached it I turned to retrace my steps.

The startled girl on the gate did her best to hold back the wave and shouted, 'Sir, sir.'

I returned to explain my actions: 'I've changed my mind about travelling today.'

Other airport staff who seemed to appear from nowhere joined the girl and all assumed that the fear of flying had got the better of me. To all their assurances that flying was the safest form of transport, I kept repeating, 'I have just remembered another engagement that I'd forgotten when making the booking.'

'But sir, your luggage is already on the plane, and leaving at short notice would create a security problem and horrible delays for thousands of passengers—all the flights following will be affected.'

In the circumstances I reluctantly boarded the plane and was immediately singled out for special treatment by the cabin crew who were clearly concerned that I might be a very difficult passenger. When the seatbelt sign went off, I summoned a stewardess and asked for a seat on the next available flight back. She returned very quickly with a number of alternative flights and said I should choose one when we landed. Assuming I was looking for special treatment, two young couples behind me decided to have some fun at my expense and one young lady passed me a small teddy bear for comfort. I smiled and told her she could have it back when we got off the plane. When the stewardess went around offering alcoholic drinks, she looked briefly in my direction but didn't say anything.

I secured her attention: 'Young lady, could I have a very large— lemonade.'

I would have welcomed something stronger at this time but my gesture appeared to reassure the cabin staff and the fussing stopped.

During the rest of the flight I tried to appear calm and in control of myself, but I was inwardly elated and excited because I anticipated some momentous days ahead. Nevertheless, I was also disgusted with myself for my failure to remember the reference to Salisbury until fate intervened in the way it had. Without doubt, if Pricilla had been with me I would not have looked at the picture of Salisbury and the connection might never have been made.

The cabin staff had been simply trying to placate me by giving me the times of return flights and suggesting I choose one. For one reason or another I endured a further frustrating couple of days before I got a flight to Heathrow. On arrival I returned to my house in Cornwall to collect the strongbox key and plan my next steps. I reasoned that the passage of time between Winston's last visit to the bank in Salisbury and now ought to work in my favour, and I had only one problem to overcome. However, that was a major problem because it concerned the alias Winston had used when setting up the strongbox arrangement. I quickly decided he would not have used the name Norman Thomas but this was based solely on the assumption that he'd be cancelling the Salisbury arrangement as soon as he had picked up whatever was in the box. After another frustrating twenty-four hours investigating the briefcase notes I decided to use the alias he had been using up until the time of his death. My reasoning was based on the opening and closing of past accounts that I had already a great deal of experience with. Even so I had to accept that I was only sixty to seventy per cent sure that I was correct in this assumption.

Two days later I walked into the bank in Salisbury feeling very nervous but expectant. I had dyed my hair and made other changes to my appearance to make me look more like Winston. Fortunately for me, though, there had been considerable staff changes in the branch during the last few years and this subterfuge wasn't really necessary. The procedure was quite straightforward and I eventually left with the contents of the strongbox—two black notebooks.

I realised it was unlikely I would have been allowed to walk off with the contents of the strongbox if my words or actions had caused concern to the bank's employees, but old security habits die hard. I had parked on the outskirts of the town and now used a taxi to get part of the way back to the car. Then I walked the rest of the way stopping off at two pubs en route. My intention in taking this action was to make it difficult for anyone who might be following me, but these stops also gave me the opportunity to satisfy the overwhelming desire to look at the notebooks. From just a few minutes' examination it was obvious that I had found something important. However, it was also very clear that much of the information couldn't be unlocked without appropriate codes. I knew where the codes could be found—they were in the original notes I had acquired from Winston—but frustratingly I had put them in a safe at home.

When I was confident that I wasn't being followed, I set off on what I hoped would be no more than a four-hour journey to my home in Cornwall, but the traffic was very heavy and it took over seven hours. The frustration in not being able to decipher the notebooks immediately was almost too difficult to bear and when I eventually reached home I started on the work without stopping for refreshment.

Something like five hours later I was close to complete exhaustion and called a halt for the night. By this time I knew I was richer by over £3,000,000. A few days later I estimated the final total to be over £7,000,000. Ten days after first seeing the picture of Salisbury at the airport I wrote a letter of resignation to the software company. It wasn't because of my new-found wealth that I resigned—I had a much more important job now.

CHAPTER
SIXTEEN

From the notebooks, I discovered that Winston had maintained direct relationships with a number of the individual Soviet agents operating in the UK. Initially, I was very surprised at this because such contacts automatically increase the security risks for all the parties concerned, and he was dealing with some of these people during the time he was at odds with Moscow. However, after going through all the entries a number of times it became obvious that Winston was using codenames and had recorded these without contact details in one of the books I had picked up from Salisbury. The telephone contact numbers were kept under a single letter code in one of the books I had taken from his Mercedes.

Eventually, I was able to match the telephone numbers and codenames. This resulted in a list of nine contacts that Winston had dealt with during the three years before he deposited the notebook in the bank in Salisbury. This list didn't include anyone from the O'Donnell group. One of the last entries was dated just over a month after Elaine and Andrew had been killed and it stated that O'Donnell had finally died from his injuries. This note went on to claim that the O'Donnell group had been virtually wiped out and that there was detailed 'proof' that British Intelligence was responsible. Unfortunately, he had provided no clues as to what that proof was, but it did appear to indicate that Winston really believed that British Intelligence had been responsible for O'Donnell's demise.

I therefore had an interesting challenge—nine potential targets to assassinate. However, these contacts were at least six years out of date and all nine of them had probably changed location and telephone number in the meantime. Even worse, I had only codenames or nicknames to go on.

When I had written to British Intelligence regarding Gerry O'Donnell, I had hoped to read that members of his group had been arrested and put on trial. When that didn't happen, I assumed that my letter had failed to get to the right people. Now I thought it was distinctly possible that my letter was ignored because they believed they had already dealt with the problem. Finding this information on Winston's contacts was exciting and it gave me a purpose in life—the opportunity to do something to help my country by destroying those enemy agents that were still working inside Britain. The possibility that the counter-intelligence service had already destroyed O'Donnell's group also gave me the opportunity to do it the easy way. In the easy scenario, all I had to do was give the contact details anonymously to the right people and they would take the appropriate action—but would they?

I mulled over my options for a day or two without coming to a firm conclusion. Eventually, I telephoned two of the contact numbers but wasn't really surprised when the response I received was that the person I was looking for wasn't known. Nevertheless, in each case I established the address of the premises where the telephone was located. Therefore, anyone following up the lead with serious intent would have a starting point and it was just possible that clues might be obtained by asking questions in the locations concerned that would lead to one or more of the Russian agents. However, it was also reasonable to assume that anyone who thought there was a fifty-fifty chance that they were on a wild goose chase would give up when they discovered that some innocent individual answering the contact telephone had been *in situ* for up to six years.

I agonised over what I should do for several days but gradually as time went by I was forced to accept total responsibility for getting rid of this cancer in the body of the country. I couldn't risk passing the responsibility to anyone else in case they ran into the proverbial brick wall and decided that they were wasting their time. The most that I could hope for was that I might manage to find and exterminate one or two of these enemies and then involve the authorities. I assumed that once I had provided two dead bodies and supporting evidence the authorities would not be in a position to ignore the remainder of the list.

I had not been back to Tintagel since I heard the voices and failed to act on their wishes. Months after experiencing this strange sensation I had tried to convince myself that the voices were a trick played on me by my brain due to the emotional stress I had been under and the brain-washing treatment I had endured as a child. Inwardly though I never completely accepted this conclusion and I felt I couldn't go back to the cliffs as I had failed to match their wishes. However, once I had decided to take direct action against Winston's Russian contacts, the guilt had gone to some extent and I decided to experience the atmosphere again. I drove to Tintagel and waited until the light faded and few other people were present on the cliffs. Then I tried to concentrate on the noise.

I must have spent fifteen minutes in deep concentration but nothing happened and I heard no voices. Nevertheless, I found the atmosphere extremely heady and I decided to lie down on one of the dry grassy parts of the cliff and rest. After a while, a strange sensation came over me. I knew I was asleep, but I also knew where I was and what my mind's eye was going to see next. First I saw little Elaine at something like seven years of age. She was barefoot, very dirty and looked terrified. Then I saw that she was being held by the hand and gently pulled along by her brother who looked equally dirty and frightened. Stephen then appeared to put his hand out in my direction and I could see that we were being encouraged to move quickly by a group of adults who didn't want to get too close to us. Quite clearly we were being taken from the orphanage and we were destined for the training school. Then I witnessed the brain-washing techniques and marvelled that so many adults could be so cruel to children in the pursuit of a socialist ideal.

The images left me and I woke up feeling strangely refreshed and contented. As I got to my feet, I turned for a last look at the cliffs before leaving for home and wondered why the place should have such an extraordinary effect on me. Not that I was surprised to have had the dream—I had after all gone to the cliffs expecting or hoping for another meaningful emotional experience. Therefore, I tried not to place too much significance on what I had seen. Certainly Elaine's face was an accurate representation of what she looked like when I first knew her, and I had not been able to picture her at that age for many years. However, I also knew that in times of stress the human brain can bring accurate images up from the past, but I realised that an accurate image of the young Elaine in no way proved that the brain-washing scenes were factual.

During my early training school days, I imagined or hoped that I would grow up to be brave and fearless in carrying out the tasks that fate had in store for me. In truth though I had always possessed a strong sense of self-preservation. Prior to experiencing the brain-washing dream at Tintagel I had been terrified of the risks I would be facing in the near future. Some time after I left the area to go home, it dawned on me that I had become a very different person. I was now looking forward to the task and for some reason I wasn't frightened of the consequences.

I had retained only one of the three guns I had taken from Winston's bungalow. Now I had to find a quantity of ammunition and a silencer for it. This meant taking some risks, as I assumed that the best place to make initial enquiries about a source of supply was the East End of London, an area I didn't really know.

In the circumstances I thought it would make sense to seek the help of an expert and who could be more of an expert in such matters than a private detective that specialised in the East End. Eventually I was put in touch with a man called Ted Ferris who sounded appropriate because he had at one time spent many years as a police constable on the beat in the East End. I telephoned Mr Ferris and introduced myself as Sid Jones –the name seemed appropriate somehow. He invited me to visit him at his home in

East Ham that evening. When I arrived there I was surprised to see that he lived very well.

He invited me in and offered me a drink. 'What can I do for you, Mr Jones?' Before I could answer he suddenly said, 'I know you, don't I? Didn't you spend some time as a copper at Leman Street nick, but your name wasn't Sid Jones then?'

I laughed and said, 'I'll bet you've used that opening gambit many times before, but I promise you, I've never been a copper, but you're right, my real name isn't Jones.'

Then I gave him a photograph of a smartly dressed young boy of about fifteen that I had taken from an up-market Italian magazine.

'This is a picture of my nephew taken about eighteen months ago. Have you seen him around by any chance?'

Ferris shook his head and said, 'What's the problem?'

'The problem stems from his fascination with guns. We believe he's been in this area for several days now trying to buy weapons.'

Ferris interrupted me, 'Why haven't you given this information to the police?'

'There is a simple answer to that. His parents are well known and if this news gets out it'll be very unpleasant for them. If I haven't found him in two days' time though they'll go to the police.'

'I understand. What do you want me to do?'

'I promised you £100 just for talking to me and here it is.' I passed over the notes and then continued, 'If during the rest of our conversation I think you've helped me, I'll pay you cash up to a further £150, depending on value.'

'This is the sort of job I like. What do you want to know?'

'Quite simply, Ted, I want to know who you would contact if you wanted to buy weapons.'

'You could try a gun shop.'

'Yes, but my nephew may be after specialist weapons.'

Over the next thirty minutes or so Ted Ferris described several groups in the area who supplied weapons illegally. I was surprised at the number.

'Are the police aware of all these groups?'

'Oh yes, but every year that goes by the politicians make it more difficult for them to do anything about it.'

I looked at the list again. 'This is going to take me longer than expected. I'd better start with those that would be the most risky for him to approach, could you list them in that order?'

When he completed this task I gave him £150 and left. As I was leaving I noticed he was studying the photograph intently before passing it back to me.

I smiled at him. 'I wouldn't try talking to the newspapers, Ted.'

A few days later I had successfully completed my shopping for the desired items.

I started with a blank piece of paper for all of the contacts and tried initially to fill in as much information as I could on each of them. It didn't take long to establish that none of them were answering the phone at the numbers given. With some difficulty, I managed to pinpoint the location for seven of the contact numbers but in two cases the telephone number was no longer in use. Information on the various contacts was limited to say the least. The most hopeful concerned the code name Belly who was based in Bristol. Winston's notes had referred to this man at one point as the Jimmy Edwards double. It struck me that if the Jimmy Edwards in question was the television comedian, then Belly probably had a handlebar moustache.

I drove to the location in the Bristol suburbs that I had been given over the telephone and found it was a slightly run-down area of mixed shops and offices. The telephone I had contacted was in a unit now being used as a greengrocer's shop. I made contact again with the greengrocer but he wasn't of a helpful disposition.

'I told you over the phone that I've only been in the premises for four years and I can't help you.'

Despite his surly attitude he seemed to be enjoying a reasonable amount of custom and this created a lot of activity inside and outside the shop. I waited outside the shop and as they were leaving asked his customers if they knew the whereabouts of a man known as Belly and typically finished each question with, 'He had a big handlebar moustache.' Eventually, I got very lucky when one man said, 'Oh, you mean Michael Belham—he used to get mistaken all the time for Jimmy Edwards. Strange you should mention him. Hadn't seen him for years, but I saw him recently in Cardiff of all places.'

I couldn't believe my luck and it took me a moment or two before I responded, 'Did he remember you?'

My informant looked at bit sheepish: 'Well, he always was a stuck-up sod—when I said hello he peered down his nose at me and said I must be mistaking him for someone else.'

'You're sure it was him though?'

'Yes, I'm sure, and it wasn't just the moustache. I recognised Belham from his voice and walk as well as well as his appearance.'

I could imagine why a Russian agent would not want to meet an old contact in this way and so I continued to question him.

'Did he look as if he was living in Cardiff?'

'I've no idea, mate.'

'Well, was he carrying a bag of any description?'

'No, he was in his shirt sleeves and vest, so I'm sure he didn't have a bag with him.'

'Could you tell me the street or area of Cardiff that you saw him in?'

This resulted in a considerable amount of head-scratching, but twenty pounds turned out to be a perfect cure for a bad memory and it produced a street name in a pleasant suburb of Cardiff.

It took a further three hours of asking questions in and around the street that I had been directed to before I found someone who knew of a person with a handlebar moustache. The moustache belonged to a Graham Bingham who lived alone in an up-market property. Three days running, I saw my prey leave the house at around noon and return at various times in the evening. On the fourth day I waited for him to leave and then entered the house by breaking a small window at the rear of the premises. I assumed that I had at least four hours to establish whether the man really was a Russian agent. I had already decided that if I were not in an enemy agent's house, I would leave fifty pounds in compensation and a few tips on how to improve the security systems.

However, it was soon obvious that the man I had observed for three consecutive days wasn't only a Russian agent, he was also a person of very nasty character who was intent on feathering his nest by all possible means. He had fifteen-year-old newspaper cuttings relating to attacks on young women during the time he lived in London and one reporting a violent robbery in Dundee. From the way in which these cuttings were mounted in an album there was no doubt that they related to his activities and he was proud of them. To my delight, Belham also turned out to be a poor agent in that he had kept notes of his relationship with his colleagues. There were several early references to conversations with Winston, whom he described at one point as the 'most frightening man on earth'. His notes contained over thirty names but some were clearly plumbers, dentists and so on, and they may or may not have been Russian agents. Winston had provided a codename and a telephone number, but Belham gave the full name and simply crossed out old telephone numbers and put in the new ones. From this I was able to obtain full current contact details on all my eight other targets.

Most interestingly Belham had evidence that four of these targets were already dead. Three were named in a newspaper article and were said to have died when the boat they had hired for a fishing expedition had capsized. Belham had written on the cutting 'they never went near the sea.' The other had died when a gas canister he was using in a caravan exploded. One of Winston's contacts, codenamed Big Horse, turned out to be a Mr Len Cartwright, and he was also based in Cardiff. From Belham's notes it was clear that both he and Cartwright were worried by these deaths and it was clear that they suspected that one of the British counter-intelligence agencies was responsible.

Just before half-past six Belham returned and immediately went to his drinks cabinet. He was in the process of pouring himself a vodka when he noticed me approaching him, gun in hand. I thought he was going to have a heart attack when he first saw me and a second one when I said, 'Good evening, Mr Belham.'

Seeing his distress, I invited him to sit down, which he did. Up until that point, my intention had been to try to scare whatever information I could out of him and then kill him.

However, he started to ramble: 'There have been too many killings of innocent people by you security people and you've no real evidence of wrongdoing.'

His comments gave me an idea. I spat out a few insulting words in Russian and then said, 'I walk in here, say two or three words and immediately you're willing to sell your comrades down the river. This is amazing. Moscow send me over here to find out if our people are being executed by the British and I find that one of our agents is willing to confess all at the drop of a hat.'

Belham, or whatever his real name was, appeared terrified and started to plead with me: 'No, you've got me wrong, you've no idea what it's like knowing that the security people may be looking for you.'

Belham kept trying to approach me with upturned palms. I spat out my next comments:

'Sit down, damn you, I don't want to hear any more excuses. I'm already short of time if I'm to stop the British from taking any further action against our people.'

I walked around the room in silence for a minute or two. Then I looked at him in a way that I hoped would indicate my disgust.

'I was always taught that the essence of good espionage was security, but the first agent I make contact with keeps records.'

With that I pulled from my pocket some of the papers I had taken from his desk. He was distraught and again started to make excuses. As he rambled on about the pressure he was under he gave me another idea.

I snarled at him, 'Listen, Belham, I don't know who to trust, so I want Cartwright over here now; that way, if you're lying to me, he'll have to risk his life by supporting your story.'

He readily agreed to get his colleague to come immediately. Before letting him make the telephone call I stressed that as I couldn't trust him I would kill him immediately if he gave any clue that there was anyone else in the house with him.

He made the call and managed to convince Cartwright that he had something urgent to discuss but it couldn't be done on the telephone. When he put the phone down I asked him to write out for me all he knew about the three remaining contacts on Winston's list—all but the four who were already dead and the two who would shortly follow them. He wrote a number of things down over a period of about forty minutes, but I kept asking for more. Suddenly, his attitude changed and I realised that either from something I had said or he thought I had said, he no longer believed my story.

He looked down in horror at the notes he had made, then screamed, 'No, no, no,' and made a rush at me. I didn't hesitate. I shot him twice to ensure there was no chance of survival and then waited for Cartwright.

Len Cartwright had told Belham he would be with him in about fifty minutes. After pocketing Belham's notes and dragging his body behind a sofa, I looked at my watch and discovered I had about ten minutes left if my visitor kept to the time he had indicated. I decided that the safest option would be to wait outside the house near to the spot where I had originally gained entry. From that position I could hide in the shadows but would also be in a position to get close to someone approaching the front door without being seen. It was lucky for me that I took this precaution because instead of the noise of a car driving up to the front door I heard the unmistakable sound of someone climbing over a fence. Presently a tall figure approached a side door and then noticed the window I had broken earlier. I introduced myself to the tall man by pressing my gun into his back and invited him to step inside, with the words,

'I presume you're Len Cartwright.'

The answer came back, 'Yes, I'm Len Cartwright, but that's all the information you're going to get out of me, whoever you are.'

I took him over to the body and tried to gain his confidence by speaking in Russian.

'Len, I need your help. I've been sent over to try and stop the British killing our people and have discovered that one of these three must be staying alive by selling information to the British.' I then gave him a piece of paper on which I had previously written the names of the three remaining agents. 'One of these must be a traitor, and it's essential that you help me to find him.'

He looked at me calmly and said in English, 'Why did you kill this man?'

I answered in English: 'I didn't intend to. I told Mr Bingham— or Belham, if you prefer—that I needed his advice on which of the three was the most likely traitor. But then he screamed out something about too many killings without evidence to back it up. He made a mad rush at me and I shot him in self-defence.'

I showed him Belham's notes and said, 'When I first found these notes I thought that they confirmed that I had got the right person, albeit by accident. But I accept from reading them again in detail that they prove only that he was careless and stupid and not necessarily a traitor.' I tried to look contrite: 'If Belham wasn't the traitor it must be one of these three.'

Cartwright looked at the three names again and then said, 'Sorry, I don't know any of these people, I'm just a burglar.'

He was clearly a very brave man who didn't believe a word I was saying. In the circumstances, I shot him and left.

I boarded the first bus I saw going towards the centre of Cardiff, but before getting into the centre of the city I got off and phoned the police and told them where they would find the bodies. I took this action to prevent a cleaner or some other unsuspecting person from going through the trauma of unexpectedly finding the bodies. I gave no reason for the killings because I didn't want to frighten my last three targets into increasing their personal security. Then I boarded a train for Reading where I had left my car. Once seated on the train I started to read the notes that Belham had made for me on my remaining targets. I was surprised at the detail he had gone into in just over half an hour. The trouble was that I didn't know how much of what he had written was true.

I took a break for a couple of days intending to rest and refresh my batteries. However, I found it difficult to sleep or rest without going over and over the execution of the two Russian agents. I was still determined to complete my task but I had to suffer the constant thought that no one had appointed me judge, jury and executioner. Strangely, although I didn't fear for my own safety, there were moments during these two days when I seriously wondered whether I might crack up mentally in carrying out the next execution. In addition, it was obvious to me that sooner rather than later the last three of my targets would hear of the demise of Belham and Cartwright and as a result they would either dramatically increase their personal security or change their location. In the circumstances I had to get to all of them and finish the job as quickly as possible.

My next intended victim was a man called Frederick Seaford who resided in Dartford, Kent. Belham's notes indicated that this man had specialised in causing labour problems in the car manufacturing industry using Winston-type tricks, ranging from spreading dissatisfaction among the workers, to sabotage. Winston had referred to his contact in Dartford as Bobbo. Over the years Winston claimed to have given Bobbo considerable help in stirring up trouble in the car industry, and so I assumed that Bobbo and Seaford were one and the same. However, I wasn't completely sure because this was the only case where Winston's contact telephone number wasn't repeated in Belham's notes.

It took me just over a week to carry out the necessary research into Seaford and his activities. I discovered that Bobbo and Seaford were two different people. From further study of Winston's notes I saw that Bobbo had been a senior engineer, but then I discovered that Seaford worked in a marketing activity and had never been an engineer. Further research uncovered evidence that an engineer and left-wing activist called Bob Robinson had retired three years earlier and had gone to live elsewhere. The fact that Robinson had left the scene three years earlier made me realise why Belham had discovered that I was lying when claiming to be a Russian agent. When going through Belham's notes after first entering his house I had seen that he had crossed through Robinson and entered the name Seaford. I had assumed that this had been a change of name and so in asking for information from him on the three agents I had just used the name Seaford. But just before realisation dawned on Belham I had tried to get more from his memory by reminding him that there had been a name change. Obviously, I had made a bad mistake because no one from Moscow would have had reason to assume that Robinson had become Seaford. Nevertheless, I had lived through the mistake and I could forget Robinson.

Seaford had been on holiday during the week I had spent investigating him. It disturbed me to discover that he was a well liked individual of about forty and that he lived locally with his wife and daughter. The more I considered killing Seaford the less I liked the idea. It was certainly true that there was little or no evidence that he was harming the country and I tried to convince myself that Robinson had been my target and that Seaford could have been on Belham's list for some innocent reason. Against that Belham had readily discussed Seaford's role as an agent until he became suspicious as a result of my slip-up. Given such circumstances, I was forced to accept that I ought to investigate the man in more detail than I had originally intended.

I drove over to his house with the intention of waiting until he went out and following him to see if that led to anything. But as soon as I got close to the house I could see that something was wrong. The curtains had been drawn and serious-faced neighbours were talking in little groups. I asked one of the neighbours what the problem was.

'Poor old Fred Seaford has just been pronounced dead in the hospital.'

'How did it happen?'

Further information came out gradually and I discovered that Seaford liked to cook and that edible fungus was his speciality. Apparently he'd been preparing a meal for his wife the previous evening and had sampled the delicacy at some stage in its preparation. Although he was experienced and very careful in his choice of fungus, he must have included some substantial quantity of non-edible matter in his mix because he died quite quickly. His wife had found him in a coma on the kitchen floor when she returned from shopping. The neighbours seemed to think it must have been an accident, but assumed a police investigation would be set up just to make sure there was no foul play involved. I couldn't accept the accident theory and assumed that some unit in British Intelligence had caught up with Seaford and disposed of him using a plot from an Agatha Christie novel.

Once I was convinced that Seaford was dead I drove towards Lancashire, because the eighth person on my list was resident there. I was really pleased that I had not had to kill Seaford and hoped that British Intelligence would get to my final two targets before I did. It would be nice to think my task was over and I could get on with the rest of my life. However, I had no reason to assume that the strange accidents would continue and in any case British Intelligence, or whoever was engineering the accidents, might not know of the existence of my final targets.

Prior to setting out to eliminate Winston's contacts I had already got some doubts about Richard Grimshawe, the eighth target. Winston's notes had simply described him as an ageing queer. From this I deduced that Grimshawe was homosexual and much older than Winston was six years ago. Therefore, it was possible that this target could be in his sixties or even seventies. Belham's note included the statement 'for sexual reasons is against all authority'. Richard Grimshawe lived in St Helens and I began to wonder if I might have met him during my rent-a-mob days. Certainly I remembered a tall gangling man from St Helens who was always prepared to shout out anti-capitalist slogans at the front line of any dispute.

When I got to the area around his run-down home and began my research I initially formed the impression that Grimshawe was strangely unconcerned about his own security. His windows were full of left-wing posters and according to one local man he had at one time advertised his services on the picket line in local journals. The same local man told me that Grimshawe had been in hospital for the last couple of days but didn't know what was wrong with him. I visited the hospital ward that Grimshawe was in but at first I had difficulty in locating him. Then I noticed a white coat on a hook and after slipping it over my jacket, I walked the length of the ward dispensing encouraging looks as I went along. I recognised

Grimshawe as soon as I saw him, even though something over twenty years had passed since I last witnessed him preaching from the head of a picket line. He was situated in a bed in the middle of the room and around him were a number of small tables containing dozens of books and newspapers. He was taking up much more space on the ward floor than other patients and was clearly enjoying special privileges. The man was asleep and normally I would not have risked disturbing him and drawing attention to myself. But I needed to complete my task as soon as possible and it didn't make sense to leave without establishing his intentions. In the circumstances I decided to wake him up. Surprisingly, he seemed pleased to get a visit from a doctor that he had not seen before and when I questioned him on the subject of his health, he simply said,

'Oh, I'm just a bit run down.'

When I asked how long he was planning to stay he looked a bit furtive and didn't answer directly. So I thought I would help him with his answer.

I winked and said, 'Well, I think we agreed another two months, but take as long as you like,' and I winked again.

He winked back and said, 'Okay, I will.'

I smiled and left the building. It was clear to me that he was using the hospital for security purposes, presumably because only a madman would try to kill him while so many other patients surrounded him. Certainly it wasn't the sort of situation I would ever take on.

The human traffic buzzing about the ward was so intense that there was a very good chance that my visit would go unnoticed and unrecorded—if so, then Grimshawe was never likely to think of me as anything other than an 'in the know' sympathiser. On the other hand if by some chance he discovered he'd been visited by an impostor, then it might result in him panicking and changing his location. However, I would just have to live with the extra work that would entail, and in the meantime I had to go on to the next target and return to St Helens when that job was completed.

The last name on my list turned out to be an Edinburgh-based professor of psychiatric medicine, David Duschinsky. The brief notes that Winston had left only ever referred to him as Dussy, but they indicated that he had used this man's services on a number of occasions over the years. There were no negative comments added, which in itself indicated that Winston must have been pleased with the services provided. For his part, Belham had translated Dussy into Duschinsky and added the words 'very senior—very effective'. On first seeing the note Belham had made I realised that I really did have to succeed in removing Duschinsky from the scheme of things, but on the assumption that he'd received similar warnings to Grimshawe I anticipated he would be very heavily protected.

When I got to Edinburgh I discovered that my intended target had a private practice, which he operated from his very up-market home on the outskirts of the city. However, he spent at least half his working life in an office attached to an Edinburgh teaching hospital. From my first visit to look at his home, I could see that recent security improvements had made uninvited entry a very difficult task, and in the circumstances I decided to concentrate on getting to him via the hospital. Security at the hospital was also better than I anticipated and it was some time before I could pinpoint the offices he used. Then I had a frustrating couple of days waiting for him to make an appearance. When he did appear on the scene I got a couple of surprises. The first was that Duschinsky was my old friend Horace Phillpott, the man who'd pronounced me sane and suitable during my first few days in the country. For a moment or so I was confused about the name change and then it dawned on me that he had probably been known as Duschinsky since he arrived in Britain.

It was equally likely that he had adopted a Polish rather than a British name because he couldn't completely disguise his original accent. If that was so then he probably used names like Horace Phillpott only when he was called out on jobs where he didn't want his basic identity divulged. The second surprise was the number of people who accompanied him into his office—the first day it was five men and a woman and the second day it was just four men. I presumed that some members of this entourage were likely to be security people and that started me worrying about where such security guards would come from. If they were Russian and they got in the way that would not cause me any increase in the number of sleepless nights that I was already suffering. But my target was obviously very influential and he could have made up some threat to his life that would result in British people being involved in protecting him—perhaps even members of the Edinburgh police force. I decided that somehow or other I had to get him on his own to prevent anyone else from getting involved.

After considering my options I decided to try to get into his office at the hospital complex during the night. My intention was to study his notes, diary and anything else that might give me a clue regarding both his importance to the Russians and any weakness in his protection that I might exploit. This proved easier to say than do because the hospital staff proved to be very protective of the keys in their possession. Nevertheless, I eventually gained access to the key cupboard and managed to get impressions of what I thought were the relevant keys. The first time I went through this exercise I must have got hold of the wrong keys because it took me another frustrating three days before I was able to gain after-hours access to Duschinsky's offices.

It soon became obvious that he didn't keep all his records in this office, but there was sufficient information available to indicate the continuing threat he posed to the British nation. For a start it was clear that he'd been very instrumental in deciding who got many of the top jobs in politics, business and even religious organisations over the last fifteen years or so. He had achieved this by developing a reputation for analysing an individual's suitability for given jobs.

His working papers were reasonably well organised and looked as if secretaries maintained them, but then I noticed a selection of pocket diaries going back over the years. I found one for 1954 and saw a December entry that read 'Big W asked me to go to Chorley—difficult rush job, both jailer and prisoner brain affected.' Other later entries indicated that Big W had been instrumental in developing Duschinsky's reputation. In the diary for the year after Winston's death there were references to attempts made to find out where he was. The last reference to Winston assumed that he'd retired and severed all his old contacts to enable him to do so, but added rather ominously 'his ideas are only now being accepted and developed by the core'.

Dawn was breaking and I realised I would need to leave the office in another thirty to forty minutes to be reasonably sure I could exit the building without being seen. For the previous half an hour or so I had been working on the idea of taking the place of one of the well-heeled patients he saw from time to time. To do that I was searching through his appointment book to find evidence of a first-time appointment for a male patient, but I wasn't having any success in finding one.

I was very stiff from crouching and reading documents by torchlight under a tablecloth all night and so I got up to stretch and relieve my aches. As I did, the light from the new dawn illuminated the room and I noticed for the first time a sheet of paper in his in-tray. It was from a senior colleague at the university and it was wishing him all the best for his lengthy sabbatical. Looking at the dates mentioned I suddenly realised that this was Duschinsky's last day in the office. I had only one option now; I had to finish the job before I left this room.

After exercising to remove the aches from my body I eventually settled myself in a tall cupboard. To get in the cupboard I had to transplant various items to other parts of the room and I hoped that this would not be too obvious to Duschinsky when he entered his office for the last time. The dawn had been with me for a few hours when he eventually made an appearance and unfortunately for me he was accompanied by several other people. Gradually, I became aware that his visitors were leaving but I was only sure that there was no one else with him when I heard him telephoning his bookmaker. I stepped out of the cupboard, gun in hand, as he was completing the call but I had difficulty steadying myself because of the cramped conditions I had been enduring. He was startled and made several movements with his foot, but put his hands in the air to signify surrender.

For the want of saying something, I said, 'You were wrong, Horace Phillpott, I am not sane or suited to the job.'

He mumbled, 'What are you going to do?' and made another desperate move with his foot.

I saw that he was aiming for what was presumably a security warning button on the floor. Then I realised that he had already pressed the button more than once, so help was presumably on its way. I shot him twice, established that he was dead and made to leave by the main door to the office. Just then a figure entered by a side door and a shot was fired but it went yards wide of me. In panic I fired twice in the general direction of the person firing on me and was relieved when my bullets sent my assailant to the floor. I was horrified that I had been forced to shoot a security guard and didn't want to fire again. But I kept my eye on the guard's crumpled figure for self-defence reasons as I moved towards the door. Both the guns fired had silencers attached so although I expected curiosity to be rising outside the office, at this stage it had presumably not degenerated into fear and panic.

As my hand reached for the door a sickening realisation came over me. The security guard I had just shot was a woman. Self-disgust was now my paramount emotion and at first I just stared at her in horror and disbelief. Then I saw that my victim was Mary Maher and other emotions took over. I moved towards her and established that she was just about alive.

When she saw me she mumbled, 'Why?'

My broken nose had never been reset and I realised that she either didn't recognise me or was in too much pain to do so.

I said, 'Because you murdered my wife and my son Andrew.'

She was clearly dying but managed to shake her head slightly. I wasn't sorry to have brought Mary Maher's life to an end but partly to further excuse my action I added, 'And you claimed to be Andrew's second mother.'

Her only response to this was to repeat the word mother in a defiant way and then she died.

It occurred to me that the investigation into this incident would be more thorough if the police found a gun on her and so I took it from her hand and put it in one of my pockets to remove it from the scene. Then I put my own gun in another pocket and left the office adopting what I hoped was the normal demeanour of someone who had just spent a small fortune with his shrink.

Several people had gathered outside the office but didn't appear too concerned when I walked between them. I did notice, however, that one man of late middle-age had stared at me intently and then departed the scene as quickly as I did. I concluded that he was a security man and he was looking for help.

I left Edinburgh as quickly as I could and stayed in a border town guesthouse for a few days on my way back to St Helens. Staying relatively close to Edinburgh enabled me to pick up the first local news reports about the shootings. After three days of such reports I formed the opinion that the police had not found the bullet fired by Mary Maher because the incident was being reported as a double murder resulting from an attempted robbery. According to these reports, Mary was Mrs Margaret Macintosh, Duschinsky's housekeeper. She had apparently answered an advertisement to work for Duschinsky and relocated from the Norwich area of East Anglia nearly four years earlier after her husband had died.

CHAPTER
SEVENTEEN

My mind was now in almost constant turmoil. I was still determined to eliminate the last of these foreign subversives and I was sure that these executions were both unavoidable and morally correct. Nevertheless I suffered agonies as I relived the scenes of mayhem whenever I relaxed. The memory of killing Mary Maher was particularly painful as it meant that I would never be able to question her on the death of my family. As I drove from the borders towards St Helens, I told myself that I was nearly at the end of the road. I had to complete the job that fate had placed in my court but then I would never have to get involved in violence again.

Fate, however, decided that it would not be as simple as that. When I got to St Helens I found that Grimshawe was still in his very special bed at the local hospital. I phoned the hospital pretending to be one of a group of concerned neighbours who were worried that he might not be getting better.

The nurse on duty reassured me: 'Please don't worry, Mr Grimshawe is doing very well and I know he's expecting to go home in a fortnight.'

In view of that statement, I decided I would take a break myself for a couple of weeks and booked into a hotel in Southport. Over the next week all thoughts of being apprehended for the executions I had carried out had virtually disappeared. I couldn't see any way that the authorities would be able to prove that I had been involved.

I had used gloves all the time and therefore I was pretty certain that I had not left any fingerprints in incriminating places. There were no cameras around Duschinsky's offices because I had checked all that out before getting duplicate office keys made. True, some people, particularly the man I thought must be a security guard, had got a good look at me when I left the office, but my disguise was probably sufficient to give anyone serious doubts if they saw me now. In any case the security guard was probably embarrassed by his failure to take action at the time because none of the reports on the incident mentioned him. The one problem area might be the gun I had been using, because if that were found in my possession at any time it would be quite easy to match it to the Edinburgh shootings. In thinking this through, I regretted the fact that I had already dropped Mary Maher's gun into a river from the middle of a bridge. However, I couldn't change that and once I was in a position to deal with Grimshawe, the gun I had been using would be destined for the middle of an even wider river.

After a few days relaxing I began to feel a little better, but then my brain sought and found something else to worry about. Whether sitting in my hotel room, eating in a café or walking along the sea front, the main question taxing my brain during the next few days was what did Mary Maher mean when she repeated the word mother to me? Initially, I had assumed she was near death, and was referring to or calling to her own mother. The more I thought of it, the more I asked myself if it was as simple as that why did she use the English word 'mother' when her mother was Russian, and why did she appear to be challenging me with that word? Over the best part of three days I covered several sheets of paper with ever more ludicrous interpretations of what she meant. When I had finished the exercise, however, it was very obvious what I wanted her single-word statement to mean. I wanted it to mean I took him away and saved him—and I am his mother now!

On another piece of paper, I wrote out the words 'Is there any evidence that she saved him?' To this I was forced to write down a single-word response—'No'. Then I wrote down 'What evidence is there that he is dead?' I never did come up with a written answer to this question because I realised immediately that there was no conclusive proof that he was dead. The one newspaper article that had mentioned the death of a small boy in an adjoining room had since turned out to be one of Winston's creations. In addition my failure to search for a grave, I now realised, was based on comments by TH personnel that the fire had been so intense that there was no possible trace of a small body.

I decided Mr Grimshawe would have to wait for me now and I booked out of the hotel and headed for Cornwall. When I got home I spent about six hours going over what little evidence I had regarding the fire at my home nearly ten years ago. There was little doubt that Elaine had perished in the fire but the same certainty wasn't true regarding Andrew. I tried to get some sleep that night but I found myself agonising over the fact that I had previously failed to realise there was no clear evidence that my son was dead. This brought back memories of how I had failed to remember the flowerpot men talking about Salisbury and the fact that I never picked up the signals that Elaine was giving me. The only explanation that seemed plausible was that the brain-washing techniques I had been submitted to had affected me in some way. Whether or not this was the correct explanation, my hatred of the Soviet Union reached new levels of intensity.

Sleep proved impossible and at about three o'clock in the morning I got up and drove towards my old home. I entered the offices of the local newspaper as soon as they opened for the day and finally obtained access to copies of newspapers covering the period in question. The story had obtained coverage, on and off, for several weeks at the time of the fire. But only one small section in a paper about a week after the event mentioned the fact that Mark and Elizabeth Rogers had a son, and that report erroneously stated 'it is understood he is being looked after by grandparents.' Quite clearly, the so-called journalists working for the paper had missed an important point, the missing child, in their desire to create a non-existent sex scandal.

This new evidence or lack of evidence didn't mean that Andrew had lived through the fire but it did justify a complete examination of the possibilities. It also justified risk-taking on a scale that I had not previously contemplated. I created a new identity for myself as Arthur Cairns, an Australian cousin of Elizabeth Rogers, and in due course entered the local police station and asked where I could find the graves of Elizabeth and Andrew. This threw the constabulary into confusion.

The sergeant on the desk said, 'I am certain the mother was cremated because some wag commented at the time that she had been cremated twice, but I've no idea what happened to the boy.' He then apologised for his unthinking comment and put me in touch with various people who he thought would be in a position to help me.

None of them could help at all—there was no grave and no evidence of even a single cremation. I dropped the Arthur Cairns identity after just one day because I assumed that sooner or later some police officer would remember that they had an unsolved murder on their books.

At this stage in my investigation I was reasonably sure that Andrew had not died in the fire. Nevertheless, I had to accept that there was a good chance he'd been killed some time later—after all both Winston's team and his Russian counterparts had murdered children before if they got in the way. On the positive side though, there was no specific mention of Andrew in any of Winston's documents, but the note he had attached to his draft manuscript, with the torn photograph of Elaine and Andrew, appeared to indicate that he believed the boy had perished in the fire. From these few facts, it seemed logical to assume that if Andrew had lived then his removal from the scene was achieved without Winston's knowledge and the most likely person to have got the boy out of the way was Mary Maher.

I tried not to get my hopes up too much and accepted there was probably no more than a one-in-five chance that Andrew was still alive, and even if he was I might never find him. Nevertheless, I couldn't give up now and consequently I tried to imagine how Mary Maher must have felt ten years previously when told that

Elaine would have to be eliminated. In doing this, my aim was to try to establish the options open to her at the time and see if any of them was worth following up. Obviously any investigation of this type must start with some basic assumptions. My starting point was to assume that the two women were genuine friends. Therefore, if she had discovered Elaine's origins by accident as suggested in Winston's notes, then she must have been horrified when her curiosity signed her friend's death warrant. Perhaps in the circumstances she decided that the only way she could make up for her mistake was to ensure that Andrew was saved.

Out came the pen and paper again as I tried to put myself in the position of Mary Maher trying to find some way of saving the boy—what would I do in the circumstances? The first thing I thought of was to invent maternal grandparents. If the boy's father really were a homicidal maniac it would make sense for the maternal grandparents to take the child, change all their identities and relocate. Perhaps Mary thought of this and that might explain the reference I had seen to grandparents in the local newspaper. But where would she take the boy and how could you prevent an eight-year-old from making a fuss when taken away from his mother?

I decided to contact one or more of the local orphanages and see if I could get a clue from the way that they operated. To my surprise I found that the orphanage concept had largely disappeared and that children unfortunate enough to lose both parents were either fostered out or housed in residential homes. Obviously, that was one of the social changes that had passed me by as a result of living like a recluse. Several attempts to locate Andrew by asking to see lists of foster parents and young people in residential homes drew a blank. It soon became obvious that pursuing this line of approach too strongly would bring unwelcome attention on me and so I changed my tactics. Andrew would now be eighteen and several people had told me that a sizeable percentage of young people without parents join the armed forces when they're released from care, which was usually at the age of seventeen. However, I quickly discovered that not having a definite surname to go on made any such enquiries with the relevant services a waste of time.

Initially, I had been reasonably certain that Mary Maher would not have been in a position to allow a child to live with her. Nevertheless, a couple of weeks into my search for Andrew, I ran out of alternatives and so I drove over to Norwich to see if I could trace her movements during the period before she moved to Edinburgh. I started by looking through a six-year-old telephone directory at the entries under the name Macintosh and its variations. I was reasonably sure that Mary and her husband would have been on the telephone, and so I assumed that this was a logical place to start. Using the telephone, I began each call by saying, 'I'm looking for a Margaret Macintosh who used to live in Norwich a few years ago.'

After about six negative calls one lady said immediately, 'I'm Maggie Mack.'

This response surprised me and I mumbled, 'Oh, do you have a son in his late teens?'

'No, my sons are twice that age, but come to think of it I was introduced to another lady with the same name as me a few years ago and I think she had a young boy with her.'

My hands were shaking by this time, but I had difficulty getting any further information out of her. Then just as I had almost given up expecting any further help, she said,

'You could try my friend Doris—she was the one that introduced me to my namesake.'

Doris was out when I phoned her and I experienced several hours of mental anguish before I finally got to question her.

She was expecting my call. 'Are you one of those reporter men?'

'No, I'm not a reporter.'

Not believing me she went on, 'I expect you're a reporter because you people never tell the truth and I wondered if one of us would get a call when I heard she'd been done in.'

'I'm sorry, you're right, I'm a journalist, but I didn't want to start unnecessary rumours at this stage. I'm simply trying to decide if it is worth visiting your area to follow up the story. I'm also trying to find out if Margaret Macintosh had a son in his late teens.'

Doris depressed me enormously by saying no, but then added, 'She had a nephew called Andy living with her at one time.'

On hearing this, my mouth started to dry up and I was having difficulty in concentrating. But I managed to concentrate on the job.

'I will try to get to your area in the next few days. If I do would you be willing to let me quote you?'

'Oh yes, I have nothing to hide.'

'You said she was done in, do you mean she was murdered?'

'Yes, she was murdered by a burglar at her office in Scotland.'

'How do you know that?'

'Because one of my friends had been a next-door neighbour of hers when she lived in Norwich and had been due to visit her the week after she was murdered. My friend called Mary at her home and got the fright of her life when a policewoman answered it.'

Doris's final comment was, 'She wasn't no good anyway—leaving her nephew in care when he was just sixteen, so she could be with her fancy man.'

My hands were shaking violently as I replaced the telephone. I had to move fast though because it was getting distinctly possible that Doris and her friends might alert a real reporter or the police to look for Andrew. The following night I discovered that a young man called Andrew Macintosh was living with a group of other young people in a basement flat. When I got to the flat a neighbour told me that the inhabitants were probably in the local pub. I recognised Andrew immediately and it took a tremendous effort on my part to stop myself rushing over to him. I noticed that he didn't say much and tended to defer to older and bigger men in the group. However, at one stage I heard him say,

'I would like to work in the insurance industry. My uncle always said it was full of nice people and it was possible to get on even if you weren't born with a silver spoon in your mouth.'

He got a good deal of ribbing for this comment, some of it good natured and some less so. Then one of the group thought he would develop the story:

'Andy is desperate for a job in insurance. He has written to all the insurance companies and all the recruitment agencies in the area at least twice pleading for a chance to become a top insurance man. I'm convinced that the managers in these companies think anyone who actually wants to work in insurance must be mad so it's not surprising that he's not got any replies.'

That night I developed my strategy. I had to get Andrew on his own so that I could go through a long and difficult story with him. In the circumstances it was essential that his friends were not present during this meeting. It would also be necessary to choose a wide open space where he could cry, lose his temper and scream. However, it should not be so isolated that he became fearful when I told him that I was his father.

I thought of a way that I might get him to such a location and the next day I visited a number of local printers and informed them that I was looking to purchase a large quantity of business letter headings for a major start-up company. I told them it was essential that I had evidence that they had worked for a major company and I also needed to see evidence of the quality of their work. On my third call I found one printer who had done some work years earlier for Norwich Union, the large insurance company. After juggling with dozens of examples of the printer's work I dropped the lot on the floor and in the confusion managed to transfer two sheets of the Norwich Union paper to my briefcase.

During the afternoon I typed a letter to Andrew saying that I represented a new division of Norwich Union called Well Insured and would be looking for new premises in the area very soon. In the meantime I was looking for trainee managers and could see that he was keen on the insurance industry because of the number of recruitment agencies I had got his details from. I went on to say that because I had got his CV from so many sources I had decided to bypass the agencies in setting up the interview and I would decide which agency to pay the commission to, when and if I decided to take his application further. I told him to call me at the hotel I had booked into under the name of David Evans. I had paid cash in advance to avoid using my credit cards at the hotel and gave myself the title of managing director of Well Insured.

I arranged a meeting with Andrew at the hotel for the following morning, but just before he arrived I told the hotel staff that I had to go and meet an important customer and would not be able to keep the appointment I had made for that morning. I explained to them that I had to leave more or less at the time the interview was due to start. Therefore if the candidate arrived on time I would re-schedule him. On the other hand if he were late I would appreciate them apologising on my behalf and getting him to telephone me that evening for a further interview. I created this complicated story to avoid anyone becoming suspicious when they saw me driving off with the boy instead of interviewing him in the hotel.

As I expected, Andrew arrived about ten minutes before the agreed interview time. I joined him in reception and introduced myself.

'Andrew, I'm David Evans, and I'm afraid I have an apology to make for wasting your time. Late last night I got a call from an important client who insists that I meet him in about an hour's time. The irritating thing is that my meeting with him will only take a few minutes but he hates confined spaces and refuses to meet me in Norwich. So, I have to drive out to the nature reserve and that will take me at least half an hour's journey time each way, and I can't expect you to hang around until I get back.'

'Oh, don't worry about me, Mr Evans, I don't mind waiting till you get back.'

I pretended to be slightly doubtful: 'Well, if you really don't mind waiting then I'm sure they'll make you comfortable here.'

The receptionist confirmed that ample supplies of coffee and biscuits would be available to him in my absence and while she was still involved in the discussions I pretended suddenly to have an idea.

'Look, I have a better idea. We're all busy so why don't you come with me? We could complete at least part of our discussions on the way to my meeting.' I added, 'Once my client departs, I'll be free to complete the interview and after that I'll drive you home.'

Andrew readily agreed to this arrangement and I hoped that my subterfuge would reduce any fear or worries that he might experience once he set off with me in the car.

The journey to the nature reserve didn't take long but the traffic was heavy. It wasn't an ideal situation in which to begin a formal interview and so I asked that we delay the serious discussions until we got to our destination. Instead we filled in the time with idle chatter, which ranged from cursing the traffic to comparing our views on the merits and demerits of Norwich City Football Club.

When we got to the car park at the nature reserve I took my briefcase from the boot and said, 'Believe it or not we now have to take a walk in the countryside.' When we reached an area about a hundred yards from the main path I said, 'This is it, I'm afraid we'll have to sit on the grass. Andrew, when my client arrives, I'll introduce you but then I'll ask you to park yourself halfway back to the path so we can have our private discussion.'

Andrew was clearly amused by the situation. 'Why would anyone want a business meeting in the open air and so far from other people?'

I touched my nose with my finger and said, 'He probably thinks it's the only way to guarantee a really private discussion.'

I made an effort to make myself comfortable and with notebook and pen at the ready asked him to start the interview off by telling me something about himself.

He began falteringly: 'When I was eight years old my father left home after my mother had died in a fire. I then lived with my aunt until I was sixteen. My aunt married an important man in Norwich when I was about ten years old but this man—my uncle—died when I was sixteen. We moved around Norwich for a while but then my aunt got a job in Scotland and she was unable to take me with her. I was put into care for just over a year until I reached maturity.'

He stopped at this point, presumably to study my reaction to his story but I couldn't bring myself to look at him. After hesitating for a moment or two he continued in a positive vein.

'Since I have been looking after myself, I've worked hard and passed my university entrance examinations. I hope to go to university one day when I have put a little money on one side.'

I found it very hard to listen to what he was saying and when he finished telling me about his hopes for university, I stood up and looked away from him so that he wouldn't see the tears running down my face.

He asked if he should continue but I said, 'No, Andrew, it's my turn now.' I was surprised by how few members of the public were on the path. I had been hoping for a few more to lessen Andrew's worries once I started to tell him my story. Then suddenly I saw a group of about six adults and guessed they'd be within a hundred yards of us once I had told Andrew who I really was—I was therefore ready to begin. At that moment Andrew had assumed that I was staring at the path in order to see if my client was approaching.

He suddenly said, 'Why would a rich man want to keep out of the towns and cities?'

I turned to look at him and I could see his surprise at the sight of my tears. For some reason his question caused me to go off half cocked.

'Well, Andrew, I'm a rich man and I have had to keep hidden for most of the time since I was wrongly accused of murder.'

He was obviously taken aback by my comment and looked nervously about him. My introduction to the saga had not gone as I planned so I sat down to appear less threatening and carried on.

'Andrew, I arranged our meeting in this place so that we were free to talk without fear of being overheard, but I wanted people to be reasonably near so you would not be too frightened.'

Like any young man he reacted to the suggestion that he was afraid.

'I'm not scared of you,' he announced.

'Andrew, you have no reason at all to fear me, but I need to tell you who you are and as a result you'll be very upset for a while— but if you react badly you'll be putting both our lives in danger. If, however, you react calmly your life and mine will be enriched.'

I saw him studying my face.

'You're going to say you're my father, but I don't believe you—you don't look anything like him.'

I was pleased that he had kept reasonable control of his emotions so far but I could see he was very upset.

Suddenly, he cried out, 'If you're my father, then you murdered my mother.'

I pointedly looked about me to indicate that he had just taken a great risk.

'I am your father and I can prove that I didn't kill your mother. If you'll keep calm I'll provide all the evidence necessary to convince you from the documents inside my briefcase. Andrew, it is possible that I have placed you in danger by approaching you, but it is also possible that through no fault of your own you might have been in more danger if I had not intervened.'

I invited him to sit down and discuss the situation calmly but he reacted strongly.

'I would prefer to stand, I can listen to your story standing up, but if it doesn't start to make sense soon you can tell it to yourself.'

I was about to tell him how his mother and I had met in an orphanage when he interrupted me:

'You don't look anything like the man in the photograph.'

I realised that he must be referring to the only photograph we had ever featured in and pulled my copy from my wallet. I passed it to him and he immediately became emotional.

'Why has it been cut up?'

'Andrew, once you have read some of the documents you'll find out why, but to answer your question, a very evil man took the photograph from me.'

It was obvious that he didn't believe me.

'Oh yes, and how did you get it back?'

I hesitated a while before answering but it was obvious that even white lies at this stage in our relationship would do more harm than good.

'I was hoping to tell you the story in sequence so that it made the best possible sense, and you would understand the reason for the violence that took place. But the main reason why you don't recognise me is due to the fact that I was very badly beaten up by men working for the man who took my photograph away and I only got it back after I had killed them all.'

Andrew looked at me and appeared to shudder. Then with tears in his eyes he said, 'If you're my father and you didn't kill my mother then you obviously don't care about me—you never bothered to come and see me!'

This interview was getting more and more painful for both of us and I tried to think of some way that I could make him more receptive.

'Andrew, for reasons that will be clear to you when I take you through the documents I've been trying to show you, I was told you died in the same fire as your mother. I only discovered that there was a chance you were alive a few days ago and I then moved as quickly as I could to find you.'

I could see that he wanted to hear more but wasn't even close to believing me. This was confirmed when he muttered, 'But that still means that ten years ago you didn't bother to find out if I had died in the fire.'

At this point I decided it was time to shake him out of feeling sorry for himself and chose to do it by giving him as much of the bad news as I could manage in the shortest possible time.

I sat up straight and said, 'You're making the natural assumption that I was free to move around the country. The truth is that I was under house arrest for nine months from the day your mother was killed and during that time I was shown press cuttings claiming you were dead.'

He had backed away slightly when he saw me sit up straight and from the movement of his eyes I could see that he was making sure that other people were still in hailing distance. I couldn't see any easier way of introducing my next point and so I simply said, 'I wasn't free to move around, I have no real identity, I don't know what my real name is and therefore I don't know your real name. Your mother and I came to this country in 1954 as agents of the Soviet Union—we had been taken from an orphanage at an early age and trained to damage this country.'

The look of amazement on his face must have mirrored the shock he experienced on hearing my words, but I had to continue: 'Many people had been trained in this way but your mother and I were unique because we were born in Britain.'

I paused because I thought I saw the trace of a smile on his lips, but it didn't develop.

'Andrew, as I'm saying this I realise it can't possibly sound true, but it is. In addition, your so-called Aunt Maher was also a Russian agent, but of a different type.'

The story was sounding more and more ludicrous but I continued, 'We agents were so thick on the ground that your mother and Mary Maher struck up a friendship without either of them realising the secret life that the other was leading. Then your mother said something she should not have done and Mrs Maher was suspicious and arranged for a photograph to be taken when they were out shopping together. This led to your mother's death.'

I looked at him, half expecting a beaming smile by this time, but he was looking very serious.

'This photograph of them together, what was it like?'

'I don't know, Andrew, I've never seen the photograph and only read about it twelve months after your mother's death, when I found some papers.'

I was about to say I could give him a ten-to-fifteen-minute run-through of everything that had happened since we arrived in Britain, but he interrupted me again: 'Can I see something about the photograph?'

I thumbed through Winston's manuscript until I found the relevant passages, gave Andrew a quick overview of the writer and warned him that simply reading half a dozen paragraphs was going to be very traumatic. To put him at his ease I moved further away and sought a piece of dry ground to sit on. The land was very marshy and so I finished up some thirty feet away from him. At first he seemed quite composed as he was reading the notes, but then he burst into tears and held his head in his hand. I thought it better to let him recover by himself but I hadn't noticed an elderly couple approaching us when Andrew became emotional. They immediately offered comfort to Andrew and with half an eye on me the woman asked if they could help.

Andrew assured them he was fine and to my surprise said, 'It's all right, but my father has just given me some bad news.'

I thanked the couple for their concern and they wished us both well and departed. As I turned to look at Andrew again I could see he was taking something out of his wallet. I was pleased to see that he appeared to have lost some of his fear of me because he walked right up to me with the item he wanted to show me and stood shoulder to shoulder with me to examine it. It turned out to be a photograph of Elaine and Mary Maher out shopping.

Andrew pointed at the photograph: 'Look, my mother is clearly looking straight ahead but Aunt Mary's eyes are looking at the camera. I asked her why she was looking at the camera but she never told me.'

My eyes filled with tears again and I heard Andrew say, 'That must be the photograph because it was the only one I ever saw of my so-called aunt and she only gave it me when she left me in Norwich.' He went on to say, 'I wondered if she might be in trouble with the police because she was very secretive and frightened after Uncle died and she wouldn't give me her address in Edinburgh. She always said it was better that she contacted me from time to time.'

Then he began an understandable emotional tirade against the woman who until a minute or so ago had been his closest friend.

We were both hungry and in need of refreshment but I walked him around for half an hour trying to explain that in all probability Mary could have done nothing to save Elaine once her curiosity had got the better of her and she had asked for the photograph to be taken.

'Andrew, I believe that Mary must have risked her own life in saving you and probably performed a minor miracle in getting you to live with her when she married Macintosh. I would imagine that this man Macintosh was either an agent himself or someone they were trying to manipulate. It's also obvious to me that when

Macintosh died Mary would be reassigned to other work and there would be no way she could have a sixteen-year-old boy in tow.'

I then told him how Mary had died and that I believed she had given me the vital clue to let me know my son was alive. Eventually, I think I convinced him that she was as much a victim as we were and that we should remember her favourably. I probably went too far in supporting Mary Maher at this time because poor Andrew was virtually numb with shock and kept saying,

'But why did you have to kill Aunt Mary'?

I went through my reasons several times and concluded, 'Would you accept that if I am telling the truth then I had to kill these enemies of our country?'

He looked confused but answered, 'I suppose so.'

'Would you also agree that you are in no danger here and that you should not make a fuss even if you think I'm insane, until you've read the various papers I want to show you?'

He nodded and said, 'It all sounds crazy but I can see I have to be very careful in what I say to anyone else until I understand it better. I can also see you're trying to strike a balance between not wanting to frighten me and yet providing the space to talk like this and I accept that these are not the actions of a madman.'

I was extremely pleased with his reasoning and quickly relaxed. 'Then let's find the local pub, but while in there we should remain silent until we're alone again.'

He found it both difficult to eat and to remain quiet but he struggled through the meal and we continued our intense discussions outside until it started to rain. Then we drove off and found a small hotel where Andrew was able to read through the assembled documents in a small but quiet reception area. From time to time he would ask me what various points meant and I did my best to answer them.

Eventually he said, 'I don't think I can take any more of this today. I would like to go home now because I'm going to a party with friends this evening.'

I saw that he was uncertain about getting into the car with me again and I offered to get him a taxi. My gesture seemed to reassure him to some extent and he said confidently, 'I'm happy to travel in your car.'

Before starting the engine I told him of my conversation with the redoubtable Doris and we agreed that it was just possible that he might get a visit from either a journalist or the police. I asked him what he would like to do if that happened and he said he wasn't sure. It was obvious he wasn't completely convinced that I really was his father and that I was telling the truth. In the circumstances I used the journey to his home to remind him of places we had visited and things we had done as a family in his early years. I could see that he was still doubtful but fortunately this session resulted in him recounting an incident that I had long forgotten and involved just the two of us. When I remembered the incident and added additional information, he grabbed my arm on the steering wheel and started to cry. By the time we reached his flat he was totally convinced both of my authenticity and the fact that I was telling him the truth.

Before he got out of the car, he made to shake my hand and then gave me a quick hug. We were both very happy but I realised the danger in making this too obvious to the rest of the world.

'Andrew, given the situation we're in, it would not be wise to tell anyone that you've been reunited with your father.'

We agreed that I would pick him up at nine o'clock the next morning. He got out of the car and we continued to chat for a while but then one of his friends approached holding a piece of paper so I excused myself and returned to my hotel.

When I arrived to collect him the next morning I was full of the joys of spring and assumed I would find him in the same condition. However, as I approached the door it was obvious he'd been watching for my arrival. He closed the door behind him and indicated we should walk away from the house. He then passed me the piece of paper that he had been given the night before. It was from a local journalist who wanted to give him some news. Andrew was nervous.

'What do you think I should do? The journalist could arrive at any time.'

'Do you have any ties to the area, any reason for staying?'

'I have one reasonably good friend who is currently asleep in the flat but he's going to join the army in a couple of weeks' time.'

Within a matter of minutes it became clear that he would like to leave with me before the journalist arrived. We agreed that he would wake his friend, tell him he was leaving to try his luck in London and promise he'd write to him in a few days' time. Twenty minutes later Andrew put a rucksack, containing all his possessions, in the boot of my car and after I had collected my suitcase from the hotel we drove to my house in Cornwall.

On the way we naturally asked each other a great many questions in order to fill in the remaining gaps in our respective knowledge of the other's life and times. I wanted to know how Mary Maher had given him the news of his mother's death and how she had managed to get him to remain silent over the years. He told me that on the day of the murder, Mary had taken him out for a trip to Whipsnade Zoo so that his mother could prepare for my return from Belfast. As the zoo was closing for the day she bought an evening newspaper and showed him the report that his mother had been murdered and the house set on fire. Mary insisted that they should stay in a hotel for the night because his life was in danger. Next morning she was able to show him the speculation in the morning newspaper and it was made clear to Andrew that as I had murdered my wife and Mary's husband, I would also be looking to kill both of them. In this way Mary was able to control Andrew and prevent him from ever telling his story to anyone. From time to time she indicated that either the type of madness that had overtaken me would wear off or I would be caught and then they could return to Mary's old home. Andrew started to give me this explanation on the outskirts of London and the effect on me was such that I had to pull over to the kerb until I had stopped shaking.

Over the next three weeks we moved around the country attending sporting occasions and visiting historical sites that he wanted to see. For the long term, however, it was obvious to both of us that he needed to live his own life and he eventually decided he would settle, for a while at least, in Bristol—because he was interested in going to the university in that city. Just over five weeks after our reunion I left him in his nice new flat in the city. In addition a new car had been ordered from a local dealer and we had an agreement that he could collect it once he had passed his driving test. In view of his ambition, I made him a generous allowance in the belief that he had enough determination to make his own way in the world and would not be tempted to sit back and take it easy just because he had an independent income. In my final comments before leaving him in Bristol, I stressed that he should never attempt to contact me from his home. We agreed a one-word code that I would use if he called me and I was in trouble. The code word would mean don't ever try to contact me again. In addition I made him promise that he would not interfere under any circumstances if he heard that I was arrested, hurt or killed.

For the next few days I tried to relax at my home in Cornwall. With me for most of the time though was the nagging thought that I had unfinished business with Mr Grimshawe. If I could have conveniently forgotten this task, I would have done, but the voices in my head convinced me that I had to destroy my country's enemies and this man was likely to be a continuing threat to us all. Consequently, I drove north again somewhat reluctantly, but this time I found that Grimshawe had been out of hospital for several weeks. This news galvanised me into action and I made what I hoped were discreet enquiries in his home location, because I didn't want to risk frightening him back into his hospital bed. Then to my surprise I discovered that he was due to talk at a left-wing rally the following evening in Liverpool.

It proved to be a simple task to gain access to the rally—money at the door. The building used for the meeting had originally been a large church and I found myself a convenient seat close to the back of the hall. At first I couldn't see Grimshawe in the place where I expected him to be, that is, the top table facing the congregation. Seated behind this table were just two people, a middle-aged lady chairperson and a dishevelled and elderly man. I kept my hat on and my coat collar turned up just in case Grimshawe was getting a good view of me and recognised me as a friendly doctor from his local hospital.

I found it difficult to follow the proceedings because the chairperson had a very soft voice and the old man with her seemed to be intent on ignoring the agenda to concentrate on muttered stories of the old days. Despite this or perhaps because of their leader's ineptitude, there were frequent outbursts from the floor. The hatred of the establishment that came tumbling out during these outbursts was intense and one fellow appeared close to a heart attack before he was dragged back into his seat.

It then dawned on me that there were other people beside myself in the hall who were not extreme left-wing socialists. In particular, I noticed one group of about a dozen men and women in their twenties who although cheering every statement that the establishment bosses should be shot at dawn, were actually enjoying a night out. To them this meeting appeared to be an alternative to a day at the zoo or a night at a traditional music hall. This became very obvious when the star speaker for the evening was introduced to the audience. Grimshawe appeared wreathed in smiles and it was obvious that the group I believed were out for an evening's entertainment knew he was a homosexual. They clapped and cheered him but made gestures and comments ridiculing him even before he started speaking. Then I noticed individuals and groups in other parts of the hall were having fun at Grimshawe's expense and to a large extent this situation didn't appear to be understood by the older socialists present. For a while I thought some ardent Tories had gate-crashed the meeting but then one of the ushers addressed several of the loudest merrymakers by name and asked them to be fair to the speaker.

It was suddenly very obvious that Grimshawe would not be a serious threat in the future and I had no desire to execute him purely out of revenge. At a convenient moment I got up and left the hall feeling very relieved and looking forward to the future. Before picking up my car I entered the nearest pub and downed a double whisky by way of celebration and relief. Then I drove down the East Lancashire Road towards the motorways, but made a detour to the town of Warrington. I had previously noted that a high cantilever bridge spanned the Manchester Ship Canal in Warrington and I decided on a special ceremony to dispose of my gun and ammunition. After buying a loaf of bread I walked towards the centre of the bridge and commenced throwing some of the bread into the waters below. Then at a convenient break in the traffic I let the bag containing the gun, ammunition and the remainder of the bread fall into the water below. A little later I was on the motorway south heading for a hotel in the Midlands where I had booked in for the evening. After dinner in the hotel I phoned Andrew to find that he'd become acquainted with the best and most beautiful girl in the world. He asked me to break my journey to meet her but I said I would call him again in a month's time and if she was still the best and most beautiful girl in the world, then I would certainly like to meet her.

CHAPTER EIGHTEEN

I had arranged an early wake-up call for the next morning with the intention of getting back home at about noon. However, as it turned out my mind and body had different agendas. The thoughts occupying my mind were much more pleasant than of late and concerned issues such as what to do with the millions in the bank and the remainder of my working life. My body on the other hand wanted to do nothing—presumably it was reacting to the sudden absence of stress. After breakfast, I returned to my room and dozed off for a couple of hours. Despite this additional slumber I had to take two further breaks to rest my eyes before I got to Cornwall. Then by the time I had stopped off at the local supermarket to update my provisions it was getting quite dark. Eventually, I drove my car into my integral garage and was followed in by three men in dark suits.

I started to reverse but then saw guns pointing at my head from both sides of the car.

A deep voice said, 'Turn off the engine and put your hands on the windscreen.'

I reluctantly did as I was told and then followed further instructions and got out of the car. My high-pitched question— what the hell is going on?—was ignored. I noticed that the men were all in late middle-age and appeared to be smartly dressed. In the circumstances, I assumed that they were members of British Intelligence. They carried out a quick search of my clothes and my car, presumably looking for weapons, and then the deep voice said,

'Now, open the door to the house but keep one of your hands in the air until I tell you to lower it.'

As I moved inside two of them held on to my coat and pressed their guns into the small of my back. Once inside, one of the men took my keys and went to the front door. He opened it and from the noise of their foot movements I guessed that three more people had entered my home.

The now familiar voice continued, 'Don't attempt to look at the people who have just come in.'

Then with a gun prodding me I was forced to sit down in the dining room and instructed to keep both hands on the table.

During recent months I had tried on several occasions to imagine what action British Intelligence would take if they ever tracked me down. Without doubt I would be an embarrassment to them, but nevertheless I assumed that they'd want to recruit me rather than kill me, and for my part I would not now object to joining their club. In the circumstances I believed that my death was unlikely to be imminent if I co-operated with them. On the other hand, I had to be careful until I could be sure who they were and I had to avoid any sudden action that might result in a bang on the head and a house fire.

Two of the three who had entered by the front door moved away from my line of sight and returned to the room only when the lights were dimmed. As a result, I had no opportunity to study their faces. The other person walked up and faced me. With a pleasant smile on his face he introduced himself.

'Good evening, Mr Thomas, my name is Gordon.' To my surprise he went on, 'I do apologise for the crudeness of our entry into your home, but hopefully you'll come to see that it was necessary.'

I didn't initially respond because two factors regarding this man were both puzzling and very worrying. The first was his age, because from his appearance I estimated him to be at least seventy. The second factor was that he had one of those up-market cultured Scottish accents that I normally associated with Edinburgh. I assumed therefore that I might be facing senior members of the

Edinburgh police force and I would have to be guarded in my comments until I was very sure who my captors were. British Intelligence would probably react very differently from the police force on hearing that I had gone around executing foreign agents.

The man calling himself Gordon waited for a moment or two to see if I had anything to say for myself. 'Cat got your tongue, Mr Thomas? Oh, no, I realise my mistake—now that's not your real name, is it?'

I decided to act like a totally innocent man until I could be sure which camp they were in. 'My name is Thomas but I didn't say anything earlier because the fear and anger I feel from being attacked like this is balanced by my sorrow for you all.'

Gordon sat down at the other side of the dining room table. 'Why do you feel sorry for us?'

After looking down at my hands for a while, I tried to sound compassionate. 'I had never imagined that the old age pension was so inadequate that you have to go around the neighbourhood stealing in this way.'

There was some laughter from other parts of the room but Gordon silenced it with his next comment. 'Oh, I don't believe for a moment that you think we're burglars, but I promise you you'll answer our questions before we leave this place.'

He looked as if he was going to say something else in the same vein but then stopped himself and came out with what I thought was an extraordinary remark in the circumstances.

'Sir, we believe there is a very good chance that we're all on the same side, but you're correct in saying that none of us are spring chickens. We've been waiting for you for a long time and are naturally in need of refreshment. I'm told that your refrigerator contains various items and that there are other foodstuffs in your car. We will not steal from you but we'd all be grateful if we could make ourselves a cup of tea and a light snack, for which we'll reimburse you on leaving.'

'Please excuse my lack of basic hospitality, take all the food and drink you need, and I'll top it up with ten pounds for each of you so you can be on your way immediately.'

Again there was some laughter at my attempted joke but my offer of money at least was ignored.

Gordon decided to relax in one of my more comfortable chairs while the tea and snack were being prepared. His place directly in front of me was taken by one of the strong silent types who had grabbed me in the garage. This man kept his finger on the trigger of his gun and pointed it at my head in a very threatening way. I was, therefore, thankful when a thoughtful Gordon returned to face me with tea, toast and biscuits. He thanked me for the food and drink.

'It was good of you to provide refreshments and I'm only sorry you have not taken anything yourself.'

'I don't mind feeding you but I'm damned if I'm going to risk being poisoned.'

Gordon ignored me and decided to get down to the real issues. 'Why did you murder Professor Duschinsky and his lady assistant?'

I had half anticipated a question of this nature but it still came as a shock. A few minutes earlier this man had used what I had always been told was a favourite ploy by British Intelligence—we are probably on the same side—and now his last statement sounded like the start of a police interrogation. It was clearly important that I played for time until I could establish exactly who my visitors were.

'Gordon, or whatever your name is, I don't have the remotest idea what you're talking about.'

He then ushered forward one of the two people I had not yet got a good look at. This man faced me and then moved behind Gordon to get out of the way. Because of the lack of space behind Gordon's chair the man moved his legs from side to side in an exaggerated way.

'Mr Thomas, do you recognise my colleague?'

'No, I don't.' Then because I thought it would help my cause if I continued with my joking responses, I added, 'I don't associate with people who do the military two-step.'

Again, I was pleased that my remark got some laughter but my forced bravado was about to weaken dramatically.

Gordon didn't join in the laughter. 'That's strange because my colleague was outside the professor's door when you made your escape, and we have been very interested in you ever since.'

I couldn't resist casting another look in the direction of Gordon's colleague, and I had to accept that he matched the general image my brain had retained regarding the person I'd assumed to be a security guard. Seconds later I realised that I had an even bigger problem than being interrogated for murder. If they had been following me since the Duschinsky execution then there was a strong possibility that they were aware of my connection with Andrew and consequently I had exposed the boy to danger. Gordon could see that my resolve had weakened and invited me to tell him what happened. All I could think of was that if they had done their jobs properly they would have arrested me before I had involved Andrew.

It was obvious that I had to find out what they knew about my movements since leaving Edinburgh.

'When did this murder take place?'

Gordon looked exasperated. 'It was several weeks ago.'

'Well, if you think I carried out the murders, why didn't you arrest me before now?' At first there was no response to this but when I repeated the question his answer was limited:

'You are making a lot of assumptions that may be way off course.'

With my head in my hands in a gesture of partial surrender, I tried to move the discussion to some sort of conclusion.

'Gordon, in certain circumstances I would be prepared to talk for hours but I need to know who I'm talking to.'

He smiled and said, 'That's also our problem, but let me say that you appear to think we're the police and that may not be the case.'

I hesitated before answering because I was desperately trying to think of some way of establishing exactly when they had picked up my trail. I couldn't think of anything and so I finally reacted to his last comment.

'Who else but the police would enter my home and start questioning me about a murder?'

Gordon looked at me and raised his hands in mock despair. 'Think about it. If we are policemen, why did my colleague not attempt to arrest you at the scene of the murder and why did we enter your home in the way we did?'

I had to accept that he'd made some valid points and the odds were against them being police officers. However, I could still think of ways in which Andrew would be in danger if they were with British Intelligence and so I persisted in my attempts to establish their identity.

'If you're not the police, why are you here?'

Gordon looked completely exasperated but finally said, 'Well, treating your question hypothetically, we could be here for many reasons, including the fact that you appear to have been duplicating our work and we would like to know why?'

These comments did stir the first glimmer of hope that I might come through this ordeal, but I told myself to be careful because in reality he was simply repeating his earlier statement that we may be on the same side.

From Gordon's demeanour it was clear that I needed to start answering his questions soon, so I made a further attempt to find out if they were aware of my contact with Andrew.

'Gordon, I repeat that I am prepared to talk but I need to clear up a couple of points that confuse me.'

'Okay, ask your questions but do it quickly.'

'If you're so curious about me and half a dozen of you break into my home in this way, why has it taken so long to make contact with me?'

The septuagenarian looked irritated. 'I don't understand why that should bother you but the answer is that my colleague, let's call him Arthur, got out of your way in Edinburgh because he wasn't armed and you were, so we had no idea how to trace you. Then a couple of nights ago, Arthur saw you at a meeting in Liverpool, followed you to a pub and then to your car. He obtained your car number and we traced your car to this address and arrived here by lunchtime today.'

My relief at hearing this was such that I couldn't completely disguise it and the change in my demeanour wasn't lost on Gordon.

'Is that it?' he said. 'Can we get down to business now?'

'Okay, Gordon, ask your questions!'

'Let's start with your real name.'

'I'm afraid that I have to disappoint you there, I honestly don't know my real name.'

Gordon began to get angry again, but a voice in the darkness called him over for a brief conversation, which I couldn't hear. The break made me realise that the relief that I experienced when I discovered that my captors couldn't know of Andrew's existence had to be controlled if I was to avoid giving too much away too soon. Gordon returned to his seat and came out with the next question:

'What nationality are you and where were you born?'

I replied, 'I am British and I was born in Britain.'

His response to that was, 'Are you sure, are you really sure of that?' Without waiting for a further answer to his question he threw another into the arena: 'Why did you kill the learned professor and his equally innocent assistant?'

I hesitated but then said, 'Speaking hypothetically…'

He stopped me: 'No, not hypothetically, we want the truth.'

'Can I take it from your last comment that your original statement was a lie?' I didn't get an answer. There was a silence for about thirty seconds and then I started again: 'Speaking hypothetically, the only circumstances in which I would consider killing anyone would occur if I was sure that they were dangerous enemies of my country.'

Gordon's anger and irritation was now a thing of the past and he took a moment or two to assimilate my words.

'In referring to enemies of your country, may I ask which country you are claiming allegiance to?'

Now it was my turn to be irritated and I hissed, 'I am British and I have always been British.'

There was some garbled discussion in the background, but Gordon held up his hand to request silence and continued his interrogation.

'If, hypothetically speaking, of course, you could kill those two because they were dangerous enemies of your country, then presumably you might kill other such enemies?'

'That would appear logical in light of my earlier statement.'

He broke for a further out-of-earshot discussion and then returned with another question: 'Why in that case did you allow Grimshawe to live?'

I found the question very difficult to answer, but eventually found the words, 'In certain situations, the executioner might remove the death sentence if he decided that his target was no longer dangerous and he didn't want to kill someone purely out of revenge.'

Gordon was now subjected to whispered comments from several parts of the room and as a result decided to call a temporary break. He suggested that under supervision I could make myself a cup of tea and refreshments in the kitchen. I accepted this offer but first visited the bathroom. Two of my captors accompanied me as far as the bathroom door and one of them made a thorough search of the inside of the room to make sure there were no weapons inside.

The same level of security was maintained all the time that I was in the kitchen and when I used a knife to butter my toast they both adopted a squat position while ensuring that I wasn't in an ideal position to attack them. They were not to know it, but I was now so intent on finishing the discussion with Gordon that thoughts of escaping were not on my agenda.

When I got back to the dining room I could see that Gordon had a list of questions written on a piece of paper. Without looking at me he said, 'Do you know the whereabouts of a man who calls himself Winston?'

By this time I had decided to be more relaxed and open with him. 'If you're religious he's in hell, if you're not his remains are probably still blowing in the Devon wind.'

From the reaction to my words around the room, it was obvious that they were surprised to hear this and naturally I was asked how I knew that he was dead. I wasn't ready to admit that I had killed anyone and so I remained silent. Gordon seemed to understand my predicament:

'I believe that you still think we could be with the police force or some intelligence organisation. If I was in your shoes and I believed that the people grilling me were from a government body, then I would react as you are doing. Our trouble stems from the fact we are not an official body and consequently we must know who we are talking to.'

He saw that this confused me and elaborated: 'If the police get it wrong and interrogate an innocent man then they may have egg on their faces but no real harm is done. If, however, we make the same mistake we either have to eliminate the innocent man or risk exposure, and we don't look forward to either of those eventualities. I can now tell you that much because you are clearly not innocent in the truest sense of the word—we believe that for some reason best known to yourself you have been killing foreign activists in this country. We know that for certain because in some cases we have been targeting the same people. When we first realised that you existed we concluded that you were either a senior member of the intelligence services and in that guise we termed you "The Other Eye" or you were a renegade Russian agent most probably from this fellow Winston's group. Frankly, you still worry us because you do not match either of the specifications—you have no background in intelligence and you say you were not born in Russia.'

I was now reasonably sure that I was among friends and with increasing euphoria I blurted out, 'Gordon, you have convinced me—we're on the same side.'

Gordon cut me short: 'Tell us how you come to be involved in this matter.'

Many years of not being able to tell my story resulted in my explanation being delivered at a very fast pace. 'My wife Elaine and I were among many children taken from orphanages in the Soviet Union and trained to disrupt the British economy. The whole thing was organised by this man Winston and he hated this country so much that when he discovered that Elaine and I had been born in Britain he insisted that we should be included in the training scheme. He did this so that he could enjoy the added pleasure of getting British people to destroy their own country. About ten years ago he arranged the murder of Elaine and put the blame on me. Eventually he decided to close down the operation and he arranged for me to be killed. By chance I managed to kill the people he had sent to kill me but then Winston's bodyguards beat me up. Again I was extremely lucky and killed them and finally I killed Winston.'

I finished the story at a faster pace than I started it and waited for their reaction. As I did so I realised that Gordon was bemused by the speed with which I had told my story and I began to feel a little foolish.

The lights went on in the dining room and I saw that the person I had yet to meet was very badly disfigured. Gordon forced me to concentrate my thoughts again by asking me to name all the people in TH that I had killed.

When I finished he said, 'What about Angus Weir'?

'No, I promise you, Winston killed him in a rage when he discovered that Angus had foolishly given information to a Russian agent. Angus was a decent man, he was very different from the others.'

Gordon replied by saying, 'Yes, I suppose he was the only good apple in the barrel, but James Cameron was a bad lot I believe.'

I had got as far as saying, 'No, James was my friend—he was a good man,' when the disfigured man hit Gordon on the back of his head with a newspaper and said:

'Hello, Martin.'

My uninvited guests had all got smiles on their faces now, but they deferred to the man who had just said hello and waited for him to finish talking to me.

His next comment was, 'I won't shake hands, Martin, because it's too painful.'

I looked down and saw that his hands were badly burned, but it slowly dawned on me that I knew the man.

'Is it you, James, are you James Cameron?'

He nodded and said, 'Yes, but don't hug me either because I'm now a delicate creature. I see from your face that Winston got to you as well. He probably improved your looks but nowhere near enough to interest me.'

The others laughed at his joke and it was quite clear that they were all pleased with the outcome of the discussions that had taken place. James went on to say that he had not recognised me when he had first entered the room and added, 'You'd have saved all that questioning if you'd not got your face bashed in, had not changed your name and not insisted you were born in Britain. Even so I recognised you a good few minutes ago but Gordon's a bit fussy you know.'

For this comment he received a tap on the head with the newspaper from a smiling Gordon.

James wasn't finished: 'I have just two further things to say to you, Martin. What was all that baloney about killing seven TH people in two days and where in hell is my whisky?'

Whisky and other alcoholic drinks flowed freely for the next few hours and to avoid the risk of drinking and driving we made makeshift beds up around the house. I utilised various items including carpets, towels and curtains so that my guests were made as comfortable as possible for the night. After the first round of drinks, Gordon made a telephone call that was very brief—it sounded to me as if all he said was 'friend'. Then he announced that he hoped I would join their little group, which he said was called Eyeglass. Apparently, the aim of the Eyeglass organisation was to seek out groups and individuals inside Britain who were trying to damage the country and stop them.

Gordon raised his glass and called for a toast: 'To the queen, God bless her, and to Megan, God bless her.'

I went along with the toast and then said, 'Who is Megan?'

It was immediately noticeable that sadness came over my new colleagues and it was some time before I received an answer. It was Gordon who spoke and he did so in a slow stilted manner.

'Megan Thomas, who is she? Well, she's the daughter of a Welsh farmer, the widow of a leading civil servant and at one stage was a high flyer in counter-intelligence. Megan Thomas is our leader; the one we call "The Eye". In a country where everyone has been blind to the danger from within our shores, she was the only one with eyes to see. Megan believed that certain elements of life in this country were being manipulated but she struggled to convince people—there are only sixteen of us now and we fund all operations out of our own pockets, a fact that you'll need to consider if you decide to join us.

'But still—we have grown and as you have seen, if we have a project to complete we have willing hands to carry it through. In the beginning though she was entirely on her own and she had executed three Russian agents before anyone else joined her. If she'd been caught she would have been remembered as a mad woman. The reason we are all sad is that Megan is dying—she probably has no more than a few days to live. I called her a few minutes ago and to avoid taxing her strength I simply said you were a friend. However, she asked that I bring you to see her and if you agree, I suggest we set off early tomorrow.'

I confirmed that I would make myself available for the journey the next morning.

James added some further comments about Megan. 'She found and saved me—she would follow up anything she thought was suspicious and managed to get certain hospital groups to inform her of any unusual reaction to violent accidents. One day she heard that a hospital in Aberdeen had a delirious patient with seventy per cent burns who had occasionally screamed out Russian words. She visited me, helped to nurse me and won me over. I told her about Winston and his team and other Russian groups that I had contact with. I've been helping her to eliminate them ever since, partly because I feel as British as you say you are and partly to make up for contributing to my wife's death.'

I wanted to demonstrate to James that I was British and had, albeit accidentally, accounted for the seven TH members within a couple of days, thereby gaining revenge for both of us. To achieve this aim, I took the various documents I had acquired from Winston from my safe and passed them around the group. Gordon read several items and then announced that some of the information contained in the pieces he had been through was 'mind-blowing'. He asked me to put everything back in the safe for the night but asked that I should agree to the papers being analysed by their experts. I agreed to his request and the celebrations continued.

For the first time in my life I had real friends from outside my immediate family.

CHAPTER NINETEEN

Our journey to Megan's Buckinghamshire nursing home provided ample opportunity to discuss the future, because it took well over four hours. Shortly after setting out I raised the subject of the money I had inherited from Winston.

'Gordon, last night you invited me to join Eyeglass, and I accepted immediately. I was going to add something else at the time about money but then I thought it would sound better if I raised it in the cold light of day, and when we were alone.'

'And you're now having second thoughts because we have to fund ourselves?'

'No, you're on the wrong track, I'm prepared to back you in every way I can and that includes money. To be precise I would like to fund the Eyeglass operation to the tune of £5,000,000 in the short term and possibly up to £8,000,000 in the medium to long term.'

It was a good job he wasn't driving when I told him this because the offer almost left him speechless and motionless.

Eventually, he said, 'I had no idea you were so well off.'

'It's not *my* money, Gordon, I inherited it when I took over the identity that Winston had set up for his retirement. It's money he stole from British people and institutions, so it's very fitting that it should be used in this way.'

Despite my explanation as to where the money had come from he thanked me at least half a dozen times.

Finally he said, 'The news will be an enormous boost to Megan because it means we can upgrade our activities and plan things without worrying where the money is coming from.'

After a brief stop Gordon dozed for a while, then when he was fully refreshed he became very serious.

'Norman, I need to tell you something and as the traffic is light at the moment, I might as well tell you now. I'm sure that Eyeglass will benefit enormously from both your personal involvement and the funding you're going to provide, but on balance I believe we're in a much worse position now than I thought we were in twenty-four hours ago.'

This announcement surprised me but then I remembered his reaction to his brief reading of Winston's notes.

'Is this because of something you read in Winston's papers?'

'Yes, it is—I thought the situation was bad last night but this morning Arthur told me about something he'd read during his brief examination of the documents. I'm afraid that the scale of the problem facing the country is far greater than even Megan had imagined and we have only read a few of the bastard's notes. I don't want to worry Megan with this news but I would like to set up a study group as soon as possible and I think we should both be actively involved so we can quickly understand the scale of the problem and get to grips with it.'

Megan was sleeping when we arrived and we sat by her bed for about twenty minutes before she woke up. Asleep she was a frail old lady in her seventies with the pain from her suffering twisting her features. Once awake she appeared to gain strength by the second and soon she was smiling at me. Gordon was obviously intent on feeding her with good news.

'When we were convinced of Norman's suitability I told him that the fee to join Eyeglass was £500, but he said that was just pocket money to him and suggested a slightly larger sum.' He whispered the amount to her and she giggled in delight like a child when I confirmed my offer.

For the next few minutes Megan and I talked about our shared experience of knowing that our country was under constant attack from inside and not being able to enlist anyone else's assistance.

Her final comment on the subject was, 'Oh, I was so lonely.' Then she decided it was time to change to a more cheerful subject matter. 'Which branch of the Thomas family do you belong to?'

'I'm sorry, Megan, but I'm afraid I belong to the impostors' branch.'

I gave her a brief outline of my history in Russia and Britain and when I had finished her eyes were full of tears.

She thought for a moment and then announced, 'You poor thing, I'm going to adopt you so you can be a genuine Norman Thomas—do you understand, Gordon? I've adopted Norman from now on.'

Gordon smiled and said, 'Yes, ma'am.'

A nurse appeared and suggested that Megan should rest, but she was having none of it.

'Gordon, apart from Norman's arrival on the scene is there anything else I should know?'

'No, Megan, nothing substantial, tomorrow we'll begin analysing the documents that Norman has provided. It's already clear that the information they contain will make our work easier but it will be some time before we can put a revised strategy together.'

I was surprised at her next comment:

'Well, there's only so much we can do to counteract the damage caused by Winston and his friends.'

'Sorry, Megan, as a new member, can I ask what you mean by that?'

She thought for a moment before she answered: 'Well, can you think of a way to undo the damage Winston caused to British industry without some help from the government when we know they have no intention of helping in that way?'

'No, I can't, but there must be some way to force our views on the government.'

'Okay, suppose I tell you that I'm getting an army together to march on Whitehall to force them to listen, would you join me?'

Her eyes were fixed on mine as she waited for my answer.

'No, Megan, I would not join you in that venture. I think our so-called representative democracy is a disaster and attracts all the wrong people, but it would be even more disastrous to overthrow it or even risk overthrowing it in that way.'

She didn't respond to my comments but instead asked another question. 'All right then, we turn Eyeglass into a political party and sweep to power in Westminster, would you then throw out all the immigrants?'

'I would throw out all those who had entered illegally for purposes that were directly against the interests of the British people.'

She smiled and said, 'That's not what I mean. Would you repatriate the immigrant families who have settled here?'

I answered truthfully, 'No, I would not want to do that.'

She smiled and said, 'Norman, we find the same problem in trying to correct all the situations that Winston and his friends have bequeathed us. The British people will have to live with the problems because the vast majority of the population is too decent to take full corrective action.' She smiled again and added, 'I'm glad you answered in the way you did otherwise your adoption would have been the shortest on record.'

Gordon joined in with, 'Almost stillborn in fact.'

Then the two of them burst into almost uncontrollable laughter. Moments later Gordon and I were being encouraged by irate nursing staff to leave the premises so that Megan could get the rest she needed.

I never saw Megan again because she died a few days later. Gordon arranged an invitation for me to attend her funeral, which took place at a church in the mid-Wales village where she grew up. The family and locals were amazed at the number of people who attended. There were not only the Eyeglass members and their families but dozens of other people who had played a part in her long and valuable life. The number of mourners was in fact so large that along with many others I had to listen to the ceremony from outside the church. Fortunately, not all the mourners accepted the invitation to visit the family farm afterwards for refreshments.

Having met her just once I felt that I should decline the offer, which had been issued to all and sundry by Megan's brother, David. Gordon, however, insisted I attend by saying, 'What will people think if her only adopted son declines the invitation?'

Megan's family did everyone proud and David made a brief speech, which ended with the words, 'We are all very pleased that so many important people respected my big sister so much.'

He was, however, less pleased when he discovered that his sister's last will and testament asked for her cremated ashes to be scattered the day following the funeral from the top of Snowdon and that only the immediate family and individuals selected by Gordon should be present at this ceremony. For a while it looked as if David was determined to insist that the ashes should be left at the farm. He claimed that the main reason for his stance was that it was a very busy time on the farm and that no one could be spared at such short notice. Eventually he realised that he had to abide by his sister's wishes but then insisted that the only family members he could spare to take part in the ceremony were his two grandsons. These two boys were aged about fifteen and sixteen and they visibly winced when they heard their grandfather imply that they were surplus to requirements.

It was arranged that I should pick the boys up the next day and drive them to Snowdon. When I called for them, it was immediately clear that they were not looking forward to their day out because they were moody and fidgety. But their attitude changed when they saw the uniforms worn by most of the Eyeglass members. My colleagues had military service rankings ranging from army sergeants right up to senior officers in the RAF and Royal Navy. I wasn't really surprised to see that Gordon wore the uniform of a British army general. The uniforms impressed me, but the two boys were on cloud nine and when later they saw and heard a twenty-one-gun salute and heard speeches in both Welsh and English eulogising their great aunt as an important figure in British history, they became ecstatic. Although they had largely ignored me on the journey to Snowdon I now found myself the target of questions I couldn't answer. Gordon came to my rescue and spent about twenty minutes with the boys, after which he arranged for another non-uniformed colleague to drive them home.

When I was alone with Gordon I said, 'It's possible that questions might be asked in high places when the boys get home and tell their story.'

He just smiled, shook his head and replied, 'No, I don't think so—they'll tell their grandfather first and he'll just assume their imagination went wild as a result of visiting a pub or two.'

'How can you be sure of that?'

'Because I've arranged for them to visit a couple of pubs on the way back. But don't worry, they won't come to any harm.'

During the first five weeks following Megan's funeral I spent at least ten hours a day in discussions and work with other Eyeglass colleagues. I learned much from their interpretation of Winston's papers and I had a lot of catching up to do in regard to knowledge they had independently acquired. For their part it seemed that the information I had provided was causing them to re-evaluate the conclusions they had previously come to and their new conclusions were increasingly worrying. Gordon had called a meeting for the end of this five-week period to plan for the future. When we assembled, however, it was immediately announced that there was still much work to be done in a number of areas and we were split into various teams to bring these efforts to fruition as soon as possible. A new meeting was arranged for two weeks' time and Gordon promised to have reached some conclusions by then.

Gordon started the rearranged meeting with a very negative statement:

'When we finalised our agreement with Norman Thomas at his home a couple of months ago, I think most of us were of the opinion that between us we had completed the difficult agent elimination phase of our work. In fact I can remember Megan telling Norman the next day that our work would concentrate on maintaining the status quo from then on. That is what she believed and that is, I think, what we all believed—then. But since then, analysis of the information provided by Norman and information we are slowly gleaning from a preliminary set of discussions with a possible convert from counter-intelligence, suggests otherwise. It seems that although the creature calling himself Winston was out of favour with Moscow in the years prior to his death, his tactics were finally understood and appreciated over there. In a nutshell, we believe that several Russian groups operating in Britain are copying his methods. Although the training school that produced James and Norman is no more, there may be as many as five other such schools producing misinformation specialists for work in the English-speaking world, with at least half of them concentrating on this country.'

Over the last few weeks we had all been made aware of this belated Russian acceptance of Winston's methods, but it was startling to hear it presented in this way. I looked across at James Cameron and we both winced.

Stephanie, one of the youngish female members of the team, raised her hand to ask a question. 'Gordon, I keep hearing about misinformation techniques but I have a devil of a job understanding how or why they should work. I thought I must be being stupid but over the last few days I've discovered that others have the same problem. Is it possible that someone could give us an actual example that would make everything clearer?'

Gordon was initially irritated by the interruption but then said, 'You have made a good point, Stephanie, it is absolutely necessary that we all understand what we are up against. Norman, you have probably used these techniques most often, could you give a few examples?'

I was a little taken aback by this request and I had to think before I responded. 'When my wife and I first joined Winston's team we found the techniques difficult to understand even though we had been given several examples. Elaine once described the procedure as being similar to employing public relations consultants who then give out negative messages about your company over a long period of time but you never discover what they are really doing.'

I saw immediately that this statement had not added to the general understanding of the subject. In the circumstances I added,

'The best explanation I ever heard was the one James gave me when I first met him. It came after I refused to believe that Winston could have masterminded the welfare state. I suggest James repeat the explanation he gave to me at that time.'

James gave me a dirty look and said, 'Thank you, Norman. If my memory serves me right my explanation at the time was a very simple one because I was trying to penetrate a very small brain.'

He waited for the laughter to fade and then explained: 'It started with the fact that Winston had isolated something like nine or ten Labour politicians who were both senior and gullible enough for his needs. He had already used the misinformation techniques to get them to the stage where they desperately wanted the welfare system to be adopted if it could be afforded. However, at that time most of them would have expected the Treasury to be totally against it on the grounds that it would bring the country to its knees. What I am going to describe relates to the time when the Treasury was about to get involved but the same simple techniques were used in all the early stages of this exercise.

'The problem Winston faced was how to prevent the Treasury from opposing the idea. Well, he started by getting hold of a quantity of internal Treasury memo pads. Then he first arranged for two selected politicians to receive anonymous handwritten notes from an apparent political sympathiser within the Treasury. He guessed correctly that the politicians concerned would not make it public knowledge that they had received leaked information. Instead they must have hoped they would continue to get valuable information from this source as long as they were in power. However, if one of the politicians had decided to make the leak known then an equally effective plan would have come into being. The messages sent to the two politicians were similar and basically argued the same thing—that instead of the welfare system creating economic chaos it would provide an enormous boost to the country. You have to understand that many of the left-wing politicians of the time were besotted with the stories coming out of the Soviet Union announcing extraordinary collective and individual production rates from workers who were happy because they were protected from the cradle to the grave. If you think that these left-wing politicians were unduly naïve, you should know that the British right-wing press carried these stories about amazing Soviet production rates on a regular basis.

'So the intention was to give these Labour politicians the idea that an establishment plot existed to deny the Labour Party the opportunity to stay in power for a long time. Within the next few weeks further anonymous notes were supposedly sent from the Treasury indicating examples where the Treasury had been horrendously wrong with their forecasts in the past. With two of the incorrect forecasts there was a claim that they had been made for political reasons that didn't favour the party in power at the time.

'Then one senior socialist received an anonymous letter from a US citizen with socialist tendencies working in the American Embassy in London—it was Winston, of course. The writer provided a copy of an internal embassy memo, which apparently reported that American economists were forecasting that the creation of the welfare state would result in an enormous boost in productivity. The memo also argued that the exercise would be copied all over Europe and the rest of the world, leaving the USA surrounded by communist countries. The memo apparently urged the strongest possible overt and covert pressure to stop the British taking the welfare route and as the Americans were already openly against it, the story couldn't be ignored.'

James finished by saying, 'There were other letters from members of the public, in other words Winston and his team. They all played a part in the deception. At one point he organised an anonymous letter to be circulated within the Treasury itself but by this time he was probably showing off. In the end the Treasury accepted the inevitability of the welfare state without putting up much of a fight. By this time of course the senior Treasury officials all believed that some of their staff actually believed that the welfare state would bring economic joy.'

As he finished it was noticeable that several members of his audience were smiling in wonder at what they had heard.

Seeing this, James put his hand up and said, 'Please don't smile at the story—the result made you and your families far poorer than was necessary and the effect will linger for a long time.'

Gordon was anxious to get on with his story. 'I started this session with some very worrying news. To have accepted Winston's ideas so completely must mean that the Russians understood the effect of these techniques on the British far sooner than we did. The logical conclusion is that the Russians were quicker on the uptake simply because they knew of Winston's activities long before we did. After all, until James dropped into our lap we had never heard of Winston and we think that the official intelligence bodies may still be unaware that he existed in a very specific role that made his operation so different from the usual espionage activities.

'From our combined studies over the last year or so it's apparent that conventional espionage carried out against our country by the Russians and others has had very little effect on our well-being. Against that, Winston's misinformation tactics have had the most devastating effect on the country and this remains true even if only a fraction of his claims are justified. Winston's tactics now appear to be totally appreciated and understood by the powers that be in Moscow. If we were at war we could expect our government to spend a great deal of time condemning our opponents and manipulating our own media by praising every aspect of our own actions, whether or not these actions were military or economic—but we're not at war and we cannot expect help from our politicians.

'Without doubt the misinformation practices that have caused us so much damage since 1945 will now be increased to a level that will make our efforts to stop them almost meaningless. The inevitable conclusion is, therefore, if we cannot stop our enemies from training misinformation specialists, should we concentrate in future on forcing our own government to take the simple step of indulging in positive pro-British messages?'

There was general agreement at this stage that Gordon had reached the logical conclusion. Almost inevitably in such circumstances some of the comments made indicated that the speaker had always favoured 'the talk to the government approach'. Gordon was about to continue but James interrupted him:

'I'm sorry to break in, but over the last few minutes I've heard several people express a view that we should have been directing our efforts at the British government before now. I also noticed that it was the newer and less experienced people who made these comments. They should know that we have always struggled to find a safe way to expose what is going on and we have never found one. Think about it and you'll realise that just walking into a police station or contacting a national newspaper with the information we have is fraught with danger.'

It was clear that some of the group were not convinced by his argument. There was a short silence and then Stephanie said, 'I think we may be seeing evil and danger where it does not exist. I completely agree that a succession of British governments has done nothing to protect the country and the people. But I don't see them as the enemy—I'd be prepared to risk it.'

I expected Gordon to intervene at this point but he was obviously waiting for further comments. I decided to add my own:

'I appreciate Stephanie's statement that she'd be prepared to take a risk and without doubt we will all need to take risks in the future. However, I for one could never see a safe way of approaching the authorities, even though I could prove some of my claims. If I had approached them six months ago I would only have been risking my own neck—now I would have to be very careful to avoid risking all your necks.'

After waiting a moment or two for my words to take effect, Gordon said, 'I would now like to tell you what I've been doing for the last two weeks. After our last meeting I farmed all the necessary work out between you and decided to spend my time thinking. It was already becoming apparent to me that we would have to change tactics and like James and Norman I am firmly of the opinion that the risk involved to our group will increase dramatically if we do. Faced with and being responsible for this situation I needed expert advice. I couldn't risk getting this advice from a living person, so I had to resort to seeking help from the real expert on the subject who just happens to be dead. Those of you who were present when we confronted Norman for the first time will remember that before the boozy party started we shared out Winston's loose-leaf manuscript. The first words I read in Winston's hand related to the surprise he felt at the help he'd received from the British government and the institutions. If I had read the set of documents from the beginning I may not have thought there was anything unusual about his observations on this subject, but in the event it stuck in my mind. I began to think that Winston thought that there was more to this government assistance than simple incompetence. Hopefully James and Norman will now understand why I have pestered them continually in recent days for information on what, why, where and when Winston raised the subject of unexpected government help. Let's stop now for a break of fifteen minutes, but before we reconvene I would suggest that you consider the fact that Winston was an incredibly gifted man and for something like twenty years he probably analysed the actions of the British government in more detail than anyone else.'

During the break James whispered to me, 'I'm not sure what the punch-line is going to be but Gordon has obviously acquired Winston's knack of timing a comfort break in order to get his audience to concentrate on a key statement.'

Before continuing with his presentation, Gordon produced a large chart, which was headed 'Winston's thoughts on the security provided to the British people'.

Our leader looked at the chart and then said, 'I appreciate that may seem an odd title, but believe it or not, Winston's notes frequently refer to this subject and he repeats one statement three times. It goes like this—"The first duty of a politician must be to protect the citizens of the country and the best way to do that is to protect the country." James and Norman have both told me that he frequently used these words when he was relaxing or had been drinking heavily but apart from saying that he wasn't referring to military defences he didn't always explain himself further. If you didn't know the damage Winston had done to this country and why, you could almost believe he was a British patriot from reading these passages. I believe the answer to this apparent dilemma is that the man was constantly trying to understand why what he believed to be the basic level of protection necessary wasn't provided to our citizens. Thankfully, however, he did put some of these thoughts into words and I would like to go through them briefly.'

Then after pointing to a heading on his chart, he continued: 'He frequently asks himself why identity cards have not been re-introduced, arguing that we all carry driving licences, car insurance forms and a variety of credit cards. In his opinion, there can be no valid reason for not introducing identity cards now because only criminals, illegal immigrants and terrorists would suffer from their introduction.'

From the discussion that followed it was apparent that all the Eyeglass members agreed with the statement made by Winston.

Gordon allowed the discussion to develop for a few minutes and then continued his presentation.

'Winston points out that opinion polls regularly show that ninety per cent plus of the British people want murderers to be hanged and other dangerous people kept in prison for a long time. Individual politicians have from time to time expressed similar views but never do anything about it. In fact the time spent in prison for murder and serious crimes is reducing year by year. In this very important matter the politicians totally ignore the wishes of the population and argue that there is no correlation between the deterrent of the death penalty and the number of murders committed. Winston argues that those that make such claims are either lying or stupid. In the immediate post-war years an average of forty murders a year were committed in Britain and a good proportion of the population had lived through a violent war and had been trained to kill. Then they abolish the death penalty and now the number of murders each year can be counted in the many hundreds. He goes on to say that there is obviously a very close correlation between the level of crime in a community and the severity of the penalties for being found guilty of committing such crimes. Since 1945 the crime rate has increased at an enormous rate in the UK. But during this time almost all new legislation has been aimed at protecting the rights of the criminals. Now we have a situation where members of the underworld can be caught in the act of carrying out serious crimes, then quite properly be found guilty and sentenced, only for them to be released on a technicality contained in legislation introduced since 1945. When the guilty get off on technicalities, the effect on police morale and therefore future effectiveness is devastating, but the lawyers get more and bigger trials and therefore even bigger fees. Winston concludes that if the legal profession is not involved in some conspiracy then we must be being governed by the biggest collection of lunatics ever to obtain power anywhere and if that is correct their next step will be to close the asylums and release their friends.'

Hands were being raised as Gordon paused at this point. He listened to the questions and answered them all in one statement.

'I agree with you all—these comments are made by citizens of this country every day of the week and very few of them really believe that it's all part of a government conspiracy. I also accept that the statements I have read out were not part of one simple statement by Winston, but they all appear at some point in his notes. To me that indicates that the man was constantly being surprised by the actions of the British government.'

With that he continued by pointing at the next heading and reading from Winston's notes.

'The British people are regularly told that this country has to import a significant proportion of the food and other raw materials consumed and as a consequence we have to export or die. No British government has ever taken protective action, but in the USA they have what they call the "Buy America Act", by which no public sector organisation can buy goods from abroad that are produced in the USA. The Americans do not have to export or die but nevertheless they protect their own manufacturers as far as they can. The rest of the world knows the situation but accepts it.

'The Japanese have exported their goods all over the world in recent times but have carefully controlled imports by imposing quotas on virtually everything. When the oil crisis hit the world in November 1973, the Japanese banned all non-essential imports—again the rest of the world just accepted it, but these situations are never given publicity in this country. There are some basic internationally accepted rules for what used to be called free trade. All Britain's competitors appear to bend these rules on a regular basis and all are aided and abetted in their actions by their national governments. This country, of course, plays it by the book and as a result its citizens suffer.

'As I understand it, Winston played a significant part in the widespread immigration that this country experienced after 1945. Therefore it's very surprising to read a handwritten paragraph in his notes, stating "Immigrants have traditionally been welcome in this country, but in the past these immigrants were coming here because they preferred the British culture." Why, against the wishes of the British people, have the politicians wholeheartedly accepted the introduction of competing cultures and the terrorists that some of them harbour? Other western countries have accepted immigrants but have managed to limit the numbers to ease assimilation and have avoided wholesale acceptance of other cultures. In this country there are now umpteen different cultures facing each other in almost all the major cities and towns.'

After pausing for a moment or two, Gordon then addressed his audience, pointed to the headings on the chart and then added his punch-lines.

'All these comments are contained in the draft manuscript of one of this country's most damaging enemies. Comments that in many ways are opposed to the main theme he was trying to get across. He was in fact struggling to find an answer to why these situations were occurring and now I think I know the conclusion he was rapidly reaching and why he may have been preparing to wind down his operation even before becoming seriously ill. I think he believed that a secret society had formed in Britain prior to the outbreak of World War II. Furthermore he was rapidly coming to the conclusion that this secret society was controlling government actions and that it shared his own aims—to destroy Britain economically. But strangely he seems to have been far more afraid of this group than he was of either British Intelligence or Moscow.'

Arthur intervened at this point: 'I think it's possible that this fear was due to some extent because he attributed the early Eyeglass executions to this group.'

Most of those present took a great deal of pleasure from this statement.

Gordon decided to bring the discussion to a close: 'I accept that Winston may have got it wrong and that our government is just incompetent. But I know that to varying degrees all of you now believe that there has to be more to it than that. Whichever way you look at the situation I now believe that we have to change tactics, but there is considerable danger in challenging the government head on. I would suggest an adjournment until tomorrow but in the meantime I would ask you all to consider the possibility of splitting our organisation into two parts. If this is agreed to, I imagine one section would concentrate on putting pressure on the government as we have been discussing and the other would carry on as before by chasing, and where necessary eliminating foreign agents. For safety reasons I would suggest that only the leader of Eyeglass should have regular contact with both parts of the organisation.'

From the moment when Gordon told his audience that he believed that Winston was convinced that an anti-British group was at the centre of British politics I experienced a brain seizure of some description. The attack was similar in some ways to those that occurred on the Ostend to Dover ferry and at Tintagel. I didn't feel ill or elated as I had done on previous occasions but I felt my brain was being split into various distinct sections. One of these sections continued to follow Gordon's briefing word for word. Another tried to understand why I had completely forgotten that Winston himself had told me of his suspicions regarding a secret society and a third section sought out reasons for the many other occasions when my brain had let me down in this way. In a strange way these various sections of my brain ran along independent routes for a few seconds before coming together again.

I was suddenly aware that Gordon was addressing me:

'Norman, do you feel ill or does the look of despair on your face indicate your disbelief at what I have been saying?'

I shook my head and said, 'There is something I need to say, but give me a moment to recover.'

I was aware that my situation was causing some concern and I heard Arthur say, 'Recover from what?'

It took me a little time to collect my thoughts before I was ready to respond: 'I think some of you at least are aware that I was subjected to brain-washing techniques when I was a child. The only effect that I know that this has had on me is that sometimes I've forgotten things that I ought to have remembered. Far from experiencing disbelief at Gordon's conclusions I suddenly remembered that in a moment of weakness, Winston himself confirmed all these conclusions virtually word for word.'

My colleagues were all staring at me and eventually Arthur asked the question that was apparently in all their minds: 'How could you completely forget something like that?'

I gave them all the answer that had formulated in my mind just seconds earlier: 'I now not only remember him telling me but I also recall him telling me to forget it. I also suddenly remember a number of other things he told me to forget going back to an incident in London shortly after I entered the country.'

James Cameron's voice broke the silence: 'Unlike you, Norman, I did receive an education in understanding brain-washing techniques while at the training school, but after the problem with Stephen they probably decided that with Elaine and yourself on the course they ought not to risk it. It's a bit like hypnotism, they use a combination of words to trigger some action and the combination of words can be given by mistake.'

I took comfort from these words and said, 'Thank you, James, I feel better for knowing that. Presumably you and I could experiment to isolate the relevant words and then do something to counteract the effect.'

James stared at me for a while, looking doubtful. 'Norman, reading Winston's manuscript made me realise that I and all my class at the training school had also been subjected to brain-washing techniques. You will remember Winston's view that people born away from the sea will always be subject to seasickness. Well, that was clearly a ruse they came up with because they couldn't be sure that sea travel would not start to undo the techniques they had used. It was logical to assume that the problem with young Stephen was caused because he'd been involved in a traumatic shipwreck, but they couldn't be certain.'

Then James addressed Gordon: 'Can you see any problem with my telling everyone here about my conclusions?'

Gordon shook his head and James continued: 'Norman, rightly or wrongly, I think you and I are permanently flawed. I think that there is always going to be a risk that the trigger will be accidentally pulled and we'll forget something important. For that reason I've suggested to Gordon that we should both work as individuals within the team. In other words we shouldn't be given any authority—do you agree?'

I didn't have to think about it for very long:

'Yes, I agree with that completely. When you mentioned just now that you had been brain-washed I suddenly remembered reading in Duschinsky's notes that you had also been given the treatment. Yet I didn't take it in at the time and I haven't thought of it again until now.'

As I looked up I saw a lot of heads shaking.

Of necessity, Eyeglass is a democratic organisation and that evening as we relaxed it wasn't noticeable that some of our group thought that Gordon was being a little over-cautious in his summing up of the dangers we faced in simply trying to influence the British government. On the other hand, the existence of another anti-British organisation working from inside the country was accepted by all concerned.

CHAPTER TWENTY

After several days of intensive discussions, Gordon eventually managed to get a majority agreement to split the Eyeglass operation down the middle. Once this was agreed he asked all seventeen of us to put ourselves up for election, not only for which section we wanted to be part of in the future but also for the leadership of the combined operation. Gordon had been in complete control of Eyeglass only for the few months since Megan died but he'd been shouldering most of the burden of work for many months prior to that because of her illness. He was clearly feeling the strain now and saw the opportunity to let someone else take over.

When the election results were counted, however, Gordon was an almost unanimous choice to retain the leadership. I think he was both surprised and a little disappointed with this result but he accepted the responsibility and the vote did give him the full authority that he had perhaps previously lacked. The vote put me, very firmly, in the traditional business of dealing with the foreign agents. Members had not only been asked to vote for which section individuals should go to, they were also asked to give a reason for their choice. The reasons in my case included my experience in dealing with foreign agents and the problem of a man with no background and real proof of his origins taking on what could be a high-profile role. When Gordon saw the references to high-profile roles, he berated the individuals who made them and argued they were in danger of forgetting the risks involved in facing up to the government.

Within forty-eight hours the two groups of eight were going their separate ways in the knowledge it was possible that they may never meet anyone from the other group again. Although Gordon was the only direct link between the two groups, a complicated system of 'last resort' contact was laid down to re-establish ties if anything should happen to the key players. Arthur was put in charge of the new activity and James Cameron joined him in order to give both groups some direct experience of misinformation techniques. Saying goodbye to James again seemed a little unreal. We were both a little self-conscious when shaking hands for the last time and I was somewhat taken aback when James finally said,

'Perhaps next time we meet it'll be in hell.'

My group was put under the control of an ex-civil servant of late middle-age called Margaret. In recent times I had discovered that Margaret had been one of Megan's first disciples and she had the reputation of being very Megan-like in that she saw things clearly and was decisive. She convinced me of her qualities in these management skills during her first session in charge. There was some discussion that a young man working in a specialised engineering company could be a misinformation specialist.

Margaret asked for the evidence against this person to be quickly summarised in front of her. When she was satisfied that the evidence was strong enough she said, 'Right, let's grab him.'

After quickly telling two of the younger men to come up with a plan to kidnap the man 'within twenty-four hours', she doled out jobs for the rest of us and gave us all similar deadlines.

Gordon had originally departed with the other group, which was rapidly becoming known as 'the soft touch' to the rest of us. We were surprised when he returned within three days and I was even more surprised when he asked Margaret and me to join him for an after-dinner drink. Our leader was looking a little sheepish as we sat by the bar in our hotel and Margaret pressed him to explain what was troubling him.

His response was to look directly at me and say, 'It's proving very expensive moving people about and we need to do the job properly. It would be nice, Norman, if you could release some of the money you promised us—say three or four thousand. I hate asking for it but we do need it now.'

I was surprised at this statement because I had arranged the various accounts so that the Eyeglass management could draw the original £5,000,000 as and when they wanted it and I thought I had explained this in detail. My colleagues were very relieved when I confirmed that they could draw the whole £5,000,000 in one lump sum or take it in stages if they were concerned about the Revenue taking an unwelcome interest in such a large sum. Margaret then suddenly announced she was tired and was going to bed but before she left she couldn't resist a little jibe:

'No wonder Her Majesty's Treasury is always in a mess—it's run by men.'

As she left us I suggested to Gordon that Margaret was a real asset to the organisation, to which he replied, 'Yes, I'm looking forward to the day when she takes full control.' As an afterthought he added, 'I really am getting too old for all this.'

He then began to thank me again for transferring money to the organisation and apologised for not understanding the system I had set up. He smiled and said, 'After her last remark I intend to ask Margaret to devise a plan for dealing with the money—then we'll see just how good the female of the species is when high finance is involved.'

I was feeling tired by this time and prepared to take my leave of him.

'Gordon, I can't keep up with you youngsters, I must go to bed.'

'Norman, before you go I'd like to make a further point. I have been trying to think of some way that the Eyeglass operation could do something to help you in return for your donation. I suggest that as soon as pressure of work allows it we should attempt to discover how you and your wife came to be living in an orphanage in the Ukraine.'

Before I could respond he said, 'I have vague memories of a

ship carrying British children to Canada in the early years of the war being sunk by a U-boat in the Atlantic Ocean.'

For some reason that I couldn't explain this news wasn't a complete surprise to me but no new memories were released and I ranted and raved for several minutes about the brain-washing techniques I had endured. Gordon was sympathetic but added, 'Don't get your hopes up too much because the chance of a Russian ship being in the Atlantic at that time can't be very high.'

I agreed with him but added, 'If I had known that a ship carrying children had been sunk I would have probably taken the risk and followed it up earlier. I suppose I could still do it myself in my spare time.'

'Norman, I have already taken some action to begin the work and it'd be much safer for us to do it because people being questioned would always want to know who was asking the questions and why.'

I reluctantly accepted the logic of his argument, but this offer of assistance by Gordon created a problem for me because I had already agreed to Andrew carrying out an investigation into his family origins provided he delayed it until 1985.

After thinking about the problem for a moment or two, I decided I could trust Gordon with the two secrets that I had held back from him until now. To begin the confession, I told him how I had discovered that my son was still alive and that I had managed to re-establish contact with him.

When I had finished he grinned, 'So that's why you asked all those strange questions when we were interrogating you.'

'Gordon, I realise that you may feel I am not totally committed, but I don't want Andrew involved in any way with Eyeglass and I have already agreed to him carrying out his own investigation into his family background providing he does not attempt it before 1985.'

Gordon smiled: 'Most of your colleagues in Eyeglass including myself have taken steps to avoid our families being involved. As far as the investigation we are offering is concerned, I suggest you tell your son that you've found someone to do the search in a way that avoids undue risk to either of you. If we don't find the answer by 1985 he can begin his own investigation, and even then we may be able to provide valuable information for him on areas where we have drawn a blank.'

I happily agreed to his suggestion and then told him that my second secret was that I had been following Winston's example by writing my memoirs.

He smiled at me and said, 'Not another one! Where have you got up to?'

I had to think before I could answer his question but then truthfully reported, 'I'm almost up to the part where half a dozen thugs forced their way into my house.'

After threatening to pour his drink over my head, he said, 'Megan kept a diary but when she discovered how ill she was, she asked Margaret to write it up for eventual publication. Just prior to Megan's death Margaret and I agreed with her that for safety reasons no attempt should be made to get it published until the dawn of the twenty-first century.'

I readily agreed that any possible publication of my own scribbling should be subjected to the same time frame.

Having eased my conscience by informing Gordon of my remaining secrets I ought to have been able to look forward to a good night's sleep. However, as I relaxed on my bed that evening I kept thinking about the story Gordon had told me of the wartime sinking of a ship containing British children. When I eventually got to sleep the inevitable happened and my once-recurring nightmare returned. Previously, in my dream, I had been desperate to see the face of the person who had pushed me on to a dinghy. Now for some reason I was dreading it. In all the previous dream sequences my saviour was always behind me in the water and I assumed that if I had seen a face it would have been that of my father or mother. Now I entered the sequence fractionally earlier than before and I saw that the face of the person swimming towards me was that of a teenage girl or woman in her very early twenties. The rest of the sequence was as before and I seemed to feel the same sharp pain in my side as I was lifted on to the dinghy.

I woke up screaming and sobbing and soon became aware of someone knocking on the door of my hotel room. It was my colleague Colin, who wanted to know what the hell was going on. I had to admit I had been having a nightmare—a statement that didn't impress Colin at all. After he left I tried to come to terms with the dream. The young woman could have been my mother or she could have been just another passenger on the ship. Even more likely, of course, the whole thing was just some trick of my mind.

I tried to concentrate on the face I had seen in the hope it would provide a link towards remembering my past but I wasn't successful. I had difficulty in getting back to sleep again that night. My thoughts raced between my inability to overcome the brainwashing I had been subjected to and the fact that if Gordon was right and most of the children on the doomed vessel were travelling without their parents, then mine might still be alive.

As always happens after an almost completely sleepless night, I dozed off when I should have been waking up, and as a result Gordon had left when I surfaced for work. In the circumstances it was some time before I could urge him to begin the search for my family's origins. Later that day I was disturbed to hear Colin telling another colleague about my nightmare and offering the opinion that I was probably mentally disturbed. In the circumstances I decided not to react to this comment. After two further nights seriously interrupted by the same nightmare I informed Margaret that I needed a break for a few weeks and I collected my things and drove down to Cornwall.

I felt better while at home and I busied myself cleaning, exercising and updating the manuscript. A week into my break I decided to spend a few days with Andrew. His life was progressing well even though the most beautiful girl in the world had disappeared from view. I explained to him that a source I couldn't divulge had agreed to begin an almost immediate investigation into our family history. He was happy about this and I could see he was relieved that at the very least someone else would do part of the legwork in the investigation.

My agreement with Margaret was that I would phone in and

make contact or leave a message every three days I was away. The day after I returned to my home having met Andrew I made a telephone call but found that the line I was calling had been disconnected. In the hope that a temporary fault was responsible I repeated my attempt to get through on several occasions over the next few days, but the line wasn't obtainable. I was getting very worried at this turn of events but eventually got a coded message from Margaret which simply said 'coaching inn—Newport Pagnell'. I took it that something was wrong and I had to go to a coaching inn or something called The Coaching Inn in the town.

When I got to Newport Pagnell I found that it contained one clearly defined old coaching inn called The Swan Revived. I parked my car in the hotel car park and enquired about rooms for the weeks ahead, but didn't commit myself to anything. Then I spent some time in the bar without recognising anyone. I wandered back to my car with the intention of looking for another inn in the locality that might contain someone familiar to me.

But as I started my car a vehicle pulled alongside me driven by Sebastian, one of the Eyeglass members who had joined the soft-touch section of the organisation. With him in the car was Colin, who was gesturing that he intended to transfer to my car. Sebastian drove off at speed and as Colin got in my car I asked, 'What the hell is going on?'

'Just concentrate on driving, you'll hear the story in full very shortly.'

Within minutes we pulled into the drive of a large detached house in its own grounds. Seconds later I was greeted by Gordon— a very sad and worried-looking Gordon.

During the next few minutes I heard that the group we had unfortunately called the soft touch had been dealt a very serious blow. Having accepted Gordon's warning Arthur had split his team into two groups of four. The intention was that the operation should originally be seen to contain just four people, Arthur, Graham, James and Stephanie. This group had targeted two cabinet ministers and two other prominent politicians. These politicians were approached on the basis that the Eyeglass group had evidence of serious wrongdoing that could be countered only by positive government publicity. Their intention was to make it clear to the politicians that they didn't want to involve the media in any way. By this statement they hoped that they would be seen and listened to.

Within four days of first approaching these politicians Arthur and Graham had been killed when a lorry driven by a drunken driver crushed the car they were driving. The accident had happened at three a.m. on a country road. Gordon continued my briefing:

'We have no idea why they were on that road in the early hours of the morning and the lorry driver involved claims he didn't remember drinking or driving the lorry that night.'

I started to say something but Gordon intervened: 'You haven't heard it all. Two nights later Stephanie was raped and murdered while walking in the Yorkshire Dales. The very same night James was burnt to death in his own car outside a church. The police apparently believe he was trying to burn the church down at the time because they found partly burned Satanist documents close to the car and others pinned to the church door. As the deaths of our friends took place in varying parts of the country and involved people who were not obviously associated with each other, the police have so far not connected the incidents.'

The four remaining members of Arthur's group were all present while Gordon was recounting the story and they were adamant that Stephanie was planning to remain in London the evening in question and were equally certain that James went to bed several hours before he was killed. When I had recovered enough from the shock of hearing about the deaths of these friends and colleagues, I became aware that I was in a room with a dozen very frightened individuals.

The tension wasn't helped when Colin suddenly said, 'Imagine the planning and the organisation necessary to carry out four murders in such a short time. Not only that but then to make two of the deaths appear accidental, give one of them a sexual motive and make the other look like a crime that back-fired.'

It seemed to me that I had to do something to change the mood and so I tried to put forward an alternative interpretation on what had happened.

'I agree that all four were murdered, no other conclusion would make sense, but I think it's possible that whoever did it was acting in a state of panic and got lucky.'

Almost everyone in the room tried to speak at once to ask for my reasons for making such a statement and the general tone of the questions wasn't very flattering. Having intervened to counteract the prevailing mood of depression, I wasn't initially that well prepared to make a detailed explanation. However, when I thought about it further, I realised that there must be a great deal of truth in the statement I had made. Therefore, I continued with some enthusiasm:

'Our approach must have been seen as a short-term threat, otherwise they would have studied our group of four more closely to try to establish who else might be involved. The fact that they acted so quickly suggests to me that they believed it was just a team of four.'

Colin interrupted: 'Unless of course they were relying on the rest of us fleeing and being too scared to open our mouths in future.'

All eyes were still on me so I tried a different angle.

'Let's start again by putting ourselves in their position. They know of four of our members but can't be sure how many more are in the background. If they decided it would be too risky to delay the executions, then Colin's point is valid. In such circumstances they would need to kill all four people quickly and do it in such an efficient way that other potential enemies would be impressed and terrified by their efficiency. As all four of our people had given their names and addresses to the politicians it would be a relatively simple task to call Arthur and suggest a late-night meeting in some remote spot. If you hijacked a big enough vehicle you could be certain of killing the occupants of the car by crashing into them and then all you have to do is to drug the usual driver and frame him. At that point you find you have killed two of your enemies and have two to go. Suppose you managed to inject drugs into the last two as they're entering their respective homes, then it's a very simple task to take your victims to the site you've chosen for the murders. Given the nature of the last two murders the police are not going to be surprised even if they do find evidence that a drug was administered prior to death.'

I had been thinking and talking at the same time during my attempt to improve the collective mood and was preparing to stop at this point when a further thought entered my head.

'On the other hand, the bodies would certainly be examined for evidence of drugs and if a couple of days later a group claimed that four of their friends had been murdered because they were trying to influence senior politicians, the drug evidence would be very important. In the circumstances we could expect several national newspapers to follow the story up—come to think of it, if we now just provided the newspapers with the names of our colleagues and what they'd been doing, that would surely be enough to get them on the case. Given these circumstances I'm sure that whoever killed our friends believed they had got all the members of our team. Therefore, they're probably sitting back thinking they have solved their problem and are actually passing the initiative back to us.'

In all probability most of my colleagues realised that I had started talking just to improve the general morale and that various other interpretations of the murderers' reasoning and actions were possible. Nevertheless, the notion that the initiative was now back in our court was taken up with enthusiasm and fear was largely replaced by the determination to fight back. At the earliest opportunity Gordon asked six of the team to evaluate what our options were in future attempts to influence the government. He was keen that we should approach a new set of politicians and try to do it privately and avoid going through government offices. He also asked them to consider seriously whether or not we could risk involving the national press. The possibility of involving the media was on the face of it very attractive but carried with it many problems. Previously all thoughts of utilising the media had become less attractive the more it was considered. Nevertheless, we all recognised that our changing circumstances justified a further rethink of the situation.

Both Gordon and Margaret thanked me for improving the general morale of the team.

Gordon said, 'It was only when you were speaking that I realised your experience in political executions is probably second to none.'

I think he was joking, but Margaret brought me further down to earth by adding, 'I thought you were tying yourself in a knot big enough to hang yourself when you were talking but somehow you slipped through the noose.'

Later that evening Margaret and Colin approached me and asked me to study a film they had taken of a drug-influenced interrogation they had carried out on the young man suspected of being a misinformation specialist. They wanted to know if my past experience would enable me to see things they might have missed. Before showing the film they told me they had tried to recruit the young man but when they realised this was unlikely they had been forced to create yet another fatal accident. I had no problem with the action they had taken because there was no alternative. Nevertheless, as I watched the film I started to feel desperately sorry for the man. Like both Elaine and me he was very likely fired by the desire to bring peace and justice to the world, and like Elaine, Mary Maher, James and others was a victim rather than a villain. For that reason I didn't pay enough attention to detail when the film was first shown, and partly because of that and because something didn't feel right I asked Colin to run it through again.

Halfway through the second showing I heard the man make a reference to the company he worked for and my mind was suddenly swamped, first by fear and then the certain knowledge of where my future lay. Eventually, I became aware that the film had stopped and that both Margaret and Colin were asking if I was feeling ill. I didn't want to create further alarm and despondency and so I made some excuse that the film had brought back unpleasant memories. However, at the first opportunity to speak to Margaret on her own, I asked her to find some excuse to arrange an urgent private meeting with Gordon.

Margaret arranged the meeting by making sure everyone else was very busy and working to tight deadlines. As soon as we were alone together I reminded them of the time I had spent at Risley, the headquarters of the body responsible for nuclear energy in the UK.

'The young man in the film was working for a company that makes a significant number of the control systems used in British nuclear establishments.'

Margaret immediately intervened: 'Norman, I think I can relieve your anxiety—we have checked that out and I have been assured that producing faulty control equipment is unlikely to cause a problem in a nuclear plant.'

I nodded and agreed with her: 'Yes, the assumption has always been that equipment will be tested stringently before it is put *in situ*. In addition, I was always led to believe that any control piece that is faulty can only be a small part of the checks and balances in place and therefore the chance of a system being sabotaged during manufacture and then causing a disaster is remote. But that's not what I want to talk about. The young man I saw in the film was almost challenging you to believe he might be trying to induce manufacturing faults. As a misinformation specialist he would in other situations be satisfied to cause production problems, but if he did so in the company he was with all he could do was lose them the contract and that would be counter-productive from his point of view. On the other hand he could take advantage of the many contacts he is likely to enjoy with the maintenance and operations specialists in the various nuclear plants, and then misinformation techniques would really come into their own.'

At that moment Gordon tapped me on the shoulder and said, 'If you have horrible news in store for us and it involves misinformation techniques in nuclear plants, could I ask that you delay your explanation until I've got myself a large drink?'

He went away to get a bottle and came back saying, 'I really don't think I can take too much more bad news at the moment.'

Both he and Margaret were very surprised when I replied, 'As it happens I think that on balance the implications are positive rather than negative.'

I tried to explain my reasoning: 'If I had been in that young man's position, I would really enjoy making contacts with the relevant maintenance people and over time I would try to be as enthusiastic as possible in dealing with them. I would ask if they had any ideas for improving the safety systems. By asking that, you would find out those who thought there was a need for further safety systems and those who thought there were already too many in place. However, you would also be certain to hear of near misses that had so far gone unreported. I might wait until a real incident was reported and then anonymously give the press other tit-bits of information I had picked up from my contacts. In each case though I would change the details slightly. Not enough to enable the Risley people to reject the story completely but enough to convince my informant that the information wasn't leaked by me. I have to admit that when I was watching the film earlier on I thought they might be trying to create a nuclear meltdown. Now I think it's more likely they're just trying to increase the number of reported incidents, because in a democracy, where most things are picked up by the press, that's all you need to do to spread gloom and despondency and an atmosphere of failure. On the other hand, create a nuclear meltdown and you might find that the country you're trying to destroy develops a Dunkirk mentality.'

Margaret and Gordon spent a moment or two thinking and chatting about my claim and finally Gordon remarked, 'Well, okay Norman, I think we both buy the notion that they're not looking to create a meltdown and we should be able to counter the effect of other people taking that fellow's place in future. Nevertheless, I don't understand why that should make the discovery of their plans for our nuclear industry positive rather than negative from our perspective.'

'I will explain but would you mind if I take a moment or two to collect my thoughts?'

They agreed to this and left me alone to mull over the thoughts and ideas that had come to me while watching the film. Thoughts that were responsible for the most severe headache I had endured in recent times. In asking for this time alone the self-preservation elements in my make-up were screaming that I should back away from the enormous and frightening task I was contemplating taking on. But it wasn't long before I had to accept that I didn't really have an alternative. My life had taken many twists and turns, but in a way the pattern was laid down when my parents or guardians had tried to get me to safety by shipping me to Canada in the early part of the war. I had seen an opportunity to fight back against my country's enemies and I was probably uniquely qualified to carry out the task. Against that, the alternative benefits I could bring to Eyeglass were questionable because of the brain-washing dilemma, and I really did owe my country something.

I called for my colleagues to rejoin me and began my explanation. 'We're all agreed that we could significantly reduce the effect of misinformation techniques aimed at this country if we could get the government on our side, but sadly we're not even close to doing that. The alternative is to stop the problem at its source in the Soviet Union. To date, we have taken it for granted that the only way to achieve that would be to bring about the collapse of communism. It is also generally believed that the only way we could bring about the collapse of communism would be by all-out war, which nobody in their right mind would advocate. The reason why no other alternative end to communism is in sight is that the Russian leaders have a blueprint for remaining in power. When the peasants revolted, Stalin had millions of them exterminated, and when he thought there was a danger of dissent in the army he had all the generals and senior officers killed. Stalin's replacements have followed his lead, so we've always assumed that change from within was impossible because they would simply execute the ring-leaders of any potential revolt. But supposing their enemy was dangerous incompetence in nuclear establishments? What would they do—execute all the operations and maintenance staff and ensure a series of meltdowns? I think we have found the Soviet Union's Achilles' heel. I believe that misinformation in the Russian nuclear plants and military establishments would be relatively simple to carry out and would devastate the men in Moscow.

'Think about it. That could be the real weakness of their political system. The terror of a serious nuclear accident would probably bind the people of a democracy together but it would surely destroy the Soviet system, because they have only one way to deal with problems and that is to eliminate any potential challengers.

'Suppose following an accident or the increasing threat of an accident, the scientists called for Western help. What would happen? If the Kremlin rejected the call they might not initially eliminate the scientists or remove them from control. But if the situation didn't improve they would either have to back down and ask for Western help or brave it out. With either option their instincts would be to take action against the scientists either because they needed someone to blame if they were forced to get outside help or to stop them talking if they didn't—then the situation would get worse. Overall I would rate our chance of creating chaos in the various Russian nuclear establishments by using misinformation tactics to be at least fifty-fifty. If we achieved this chaos then the overthrow of communism would follow soon after.'

Margaret and Gordon were looking at me with strange expressions on their faces.

Margaret was the first to react: 'I can see the logic in your argument and perhaps we should try to pass the idea anonymously to the military. But even if they were enthusiastic it would take them years to put everything in place and to train the people to carry it out.'

I felt my throat getting increasingly dry: 'I know quite a lot about the nuclear industry, I'm already trained and one person might be enough. All I would require in addition would be a couple of weeks spent with maintenance specialists in British nuclear establishments, a couple of weeks on a Russian refresher course and safe passage into Russia.'

After a long silence, Gordon licked his lips several times and then said, 'We could arrange that.'

Three months later, on 1st January 1983, I was ready to begin my journey to the Soviet Union. All that was left for me to do was to say a final goodbye to Gordon. A simple task but it proved easier said than done because like most members of the Eyeglass team he had been forced to keep moving his home base for security reasons. Eventually, I was directed to a small farm cottage that he'd only recently rented several miles north of the English and Scottish border, near Jedburgh. At first I thought I must have missed him or got the wrong address because there was no answer to my knock on the door. However, when I ventured around the back of the house I saw him in the garden standing almost motionless and staring at the horizon. The temperature was only just above freezing-point and I was surprised that he wasn't wearing any outdoor clothes. When he heard me approaching he was at first apprehensive, but quickly regained his composure.

'Norman, are you trying to frighten me to death?'

'No, but if you don't wrap up warm you'll freeze to death anyway.'

After bemoaning the fact that he appeared to have lost his once highly trained sense of personal security he took me inside. In front of a warm fire and with a quality malt whisky in my hand I was feeling quite comfortable, but I noticed he still seemed to be deep in thought.

'Penny for your thoughts, Gordon.'

He looked relieved to hear my question.

'Funny you should ask that. Ever since I heard that you'd be calling on me today I've been mulling over the rights and wrongs of telling you about some information we've recently come upon.'

'Why should that be a problem for you?'

'It's a problem because it puts new light on who is responsible for these attacks on our people and in my mind, at least, it raises doubts as to whether we're justified in sending you on what is clearly a suicidal venture.'

For a second or two I began to feel like a condemned man whose sentence of death is commuted at the last minute, but the euphoria wasn't to last.

Gordon bit his lip and continued: 'It's this unseen enemy we have been calling the Secret Society. Without doubt a number of leading figures in British politics are involved but it's equally certain it's being directed from outside the country.'

I studied his face. 'Presumably you're going to tell me that it's being directed by Moscow?'

'No, the Russian threat clearly remains but I think we face an even greater threat from a more traditional source—western Europe. And this time it appears to be centred on Brussels, which you'll have to admit really does raise a lot of interesting questions.'

In answer to my further questions on the subject he said, 'We can't be sure of anything at the moment, but it does look like some latter-day Napoleon, or Hitler even, has used the existence of the EEC to dig under our defences and has begun a misinformation campaign to destroy us.'

From further discussions we concluded that we really did have two separate enemies and both would have to be dealt with. In the circumstances I had no other option but to continue my journey to the Soviet Union.

As I was preparing to leave he said, 'I'm sorry you have such a long outward journey lined up and that I've added to it by your having to come up here.'

'Don't worry, I really don't see it being a problem. It's a long drive down to Dover but it's somehow fitting that I should depart from the place where I entered the country as an enemy nearly thirty years ago. Gordon, as I keep saying, I have tied up all my loose ends and I wish you, your team and my country well.'

He held on to my hand for a long time and with tears in his eyes said, 'God bless you, Norman—I hope you can succeed without bringing about a heavy loss of life.'

I assured him I would try.

POSTSCRIPT

Burlington Hotel
Folkestone
Kent
England

5th January 1983

Dear Andrew,

At my final meeting with the people looking at our
family origins I discovered they have made some
progress but it's slow going. Nothing is likely to be
available for you for some time, but just in case I'm
wrong will you look in *The Times* on each of the
four days I mentioned each month and look for a
message relating to the code I gave you. Once it
appears, I suggest you telephone from a phone box in
London to get further details. The people helping
are my friends but for your personal safety please do
not agree to any meeting with them or provide them
with your name or whereabouts. As you know, I have
always believed it would be dangerous for you to
make contact with these rather special friends of
mine. After a meeting I had a couple of days ago I
am now convinced that the risk to you from such a
meeting has multiplied by at least a factor of two.

I have also made arrangements with a reliable friend to store the manuscript that I have recently completed. I have asked him to ensure that on or after Monday 6th January 2003 the document is to be submitted to a suitable publishing house. Bearing in mind the subject matter I anticipate that some publishers will be wary of getting involved or that they are then legally prevented from doing so. For that reason I have made sufficient funds available for him to contact as many publishers as he needs to in the UK and then, if it should be necessary, the USA.

I am aware that you would have expected to read the manuscript before then but I promise you my ongoing aim in all of this is to protect you. If and when you do get to read it you'll immediately see that all the names are false—this again is done for security reasons. On the other hand, as you'll recognise from your own involvement in the story, I have tended to be accurate with regard to the places where the incidents took place. I don't believe this constitutes any form of security risk and in any case I found it necessary to avoid undue confusion when putting pen to paper.

A twenty-year delay in publication may seem excessive but I believe it's necessary to protect you, my friends, our beloved homeland and myself in case I'm exposed during my final assignment or I succeed too well.

I have not told you this before, but when I finally tracked you down in Norwich I was consumed with the thought that I must somehow tell your mother that I had found you. Then I realised that she had been leading me to you all the time. Try to think kindly of us both.

Dad